Praise for Universe Eventual Book I: *Chimera*

"I loved the world, and thought the authors walked the line between great description and action perfectly ... a cracking start to what promises to be an amazing series."
—Tash McAdam, International Bestselling Author of the Psionics Series

"N. J. Tanger has done what many are saying can't be done: put a fresh face on YA dystopian science fiction. This book almost skirts the edges of that genre, but if you enjoyed Ender's Game, City of Ember, or The Hunger Games, you'll find a lot to like in the pages of Chimera."
—Sarah Read, editor Pantheon Magazine

"Chimera is an epic tale of rebellion, prophecy, and perseverance. With touches of Ender's Game, and echoes of Asimov and Heinlein, this visionary story is a tense, exhilarating ride."
—Richard Thomas, author of Disintegration

"Inventive and imaginative story of a distant colony cut off from Earth, complete with engaging characters and plenty of action. CHIMERA provides an intriguing start to what is obviously a larger story."
—John E. Stith, author of Manhattan Transfer

"Chimera features a wonderful worn-down other world in which many long to be chosen for a perilous journey back to the mother planet in the reconstructed ship that brought their ancestors to the new world. The writing is vibrant and direct with young characters who show the same bravery, impatience and enthusiasm as their real-world counterparts. The alien world and its inhabitants have the ring of reality no matter how far from our reality they may be, a trait shared with some of the best work of Asimov and Anne McCaffrey.

D0999260

I highly recommend a trip into deep space on the Chimera."
—Brendan Foley, author of Under the Wire, director of The Riddle

"Reminiscent of Orson Scott Card's early work, especially *Treason* and *Ender's Game*, the storytelling has been well crafted – inviting the reader into a new world that is fresh and deep yet utterly recognizable ... skillfully pulls from the best ideas of the genre. In lesser hands, this quest for survival in deep space would become a cliché, but they write like seasoned veterans – clean and crisp."
— Red Eagle's Legacy Book Blog

"...it's more like a real SF novel with adolescent protagonists. Many of the best fantasy and SF authors have written such novels, from Brandon Sanderson and China Miéville to Paolo Bacigulpi. I found this particular book to be a page turner. I couldn't put it down. So if nothing else, it deserves a thumbs up for being a good read."
—Vanessa, Goodreads Review

"This book grabbed me by the spine and yanked me through its pages in just a few fast days. Packed with action. Wall to wall conflict. Real human emotion and intrigue. And I don't even read science fiction!"
—Michael Pugh, Goodreads Review

"This story is well written and never loses its intrigue. It reveals neither too little nor conceals too much, and while I am usually not an avid reader of science fiction, this is one story I will certainly follow."
—Jønny Schult, Goodreads Review

"These authors have nailed it! I highly recommend Chimera."
—Rob Moses, Goodreads Review

"Chimera, the first book in the Universe Eventual series, is engaging from the first page, surprising to the last, and always accessible, especially for those who might not (yet) have an affinity for science fiction."
—Jayme, Goodreads Review

"The characters are drawn with clarity and each has something with

which they struggle. There is a hint of romance and a dash of intrigue. Of course, there is mystery with the promise of discovery and revelation. Isn't that why we like to read science fiction?"
—Thomas, Goodreads Review

"I love futuristic technology, if it hangs together and is not just magical thinking, and Chimera has it in spades. Throw in the extraordinary ability of one young girl, and you have one big story question. Can their will and technology, and the girl's ability, save their world?"
—Sylvia, Goodreads Review

"The plot is well crafted and pulls you along at a good clip. I would put this in the "couldn't put it down" category. I am impressed with this as a first novel ..."
—Tim Lavrouhin, Goodreads Review

"This book is excellently paced, accessible to and appropriate for adults and young-adults, entertaining, fun, and thought provoking."
—Chazz Dabbs, Goodreads Review

"The dual protagonists, Theo and Selena, feel like real people on the page. You can't help but root for them, and you will recognize yourself in their flaws and triumphs."
—Mfranken, Goodreads Review

"Chimera" is a well-written science fiction tale wrought with tension, suspense and believable characters."
—Marcha Fox, author of *Beyond the Hidden Sky* and the Star Trails Tetralogy

"Chimera's great characterization in particular disavows the "shallowness" that so often dogs public perception of YA. An easy-to-process and enjoyable read that anyone will find accessible, although still loaded with concepts and sophistication to please any sci-fi fan, I found Chimera to be genuinely touching and very much look forward to following the Universe Eventual series as it progresses."
—B.P. Gregory, author of *Outermen*

HELIOS

Universe Eventual

Book Two

N.J. Tanger

HELIOS

Universe Eventual - Book Two

N.J. Tanger

Helios - Copyright © 2015 by JNR Media

Map artwork by David Schuett
Cover Design by G. S. Prendergast
Formatting by WildSeasFormatting.com
Line Edits by Crystal Watanabe (pikkoshouse.com)

ISBN: 978-1-943671-01-4

UE Books
7227 Madison Street
Forest Park, IL 60130
www.UEBooks.com

UNIVERSE EVENTUAL TIMELINE

2108: A liquid-propelled Shellback becomes the first crewed vessel to enter interstellar space.

2134: Robotic explorers reach Alpha Centauri.

2141: Fractal theory proposed by scientists at the International Orbital Collider (IOC).

2149: Fractal travel proved possible by the (IOC).

2152: IOC scientists produce a prototype fractal drive.

2155: Alliance between nation states and several corporations launches the Helios Project to create the first fractal capable colony ship.

2156: Construction of the *Helios* begins at the Mars Shipworks.

2170: Named after the Greek god of the sun, *Helios* succeeds in making several insertions into fractal space and maps a route to Alpha Centauri.

2172: Ecomire deposits at Alpha Centauri make larger-scale missions through fractal space possible.

2173: Destination chosen for Earth's first colony: Betaque, some ninety lightyears from Earth.

2176: Crew and colonists board the *Helios* and begin their decade-long journey to Betaque.

2201: Awaiting transmission from the Helios signaling safe arrival at Betaque, Earth builds second fractal class ship, *Ceres,* to complete a scientific mission to proposed Damascene colony.

2244: *Ceres* departs for Damascene.

2259: Work begins on the *Chimera*, the first colony ship sponsored solely by corporate interests. She will be sent to Elypso with a mission to mine ecomire and send it back to Earth.

2263: Time window for receipt of the Helios' first transmission passes without contact from Earth's first colony.

2265: Corporate sponsors of the Chimera Project choose to delay sending the ship, waiting for news of the *Helios*' success.

2274: With no communication from the *Helios* colony, corporate backers of the project suffer massive financial loss.

2275: Instability in the corporate alliances causes major economic collapse. Regional wars break out, causing devastation to the South and North American continents.

2279: Corex, largest backer of the *Helios* and the second largest corporation on Earth, collapses under the weight of mounting debts.

2280: All Corex assets transferred to Kibashi-Kline corporation. *Chimera*'s mission changed to a "regulated colony" required to pay off Corex' bad debt via shipments of ecomire.

2287: The *Chimera* arrives at her destination and founds the Stephen's Point colony.

2492: Exchange ships from Earth cease arriving at Stephen's Point.

2501: Stephen's Point government passes the Rebuild Mandate, ordering the ancient colony ship *Chimera* to be restored for a return journey to Earth.

2505: Stephen's Point colony begins testing candidates to crew the *Chimera*. Candidates travel to orbital station *Hydra* to complete training.

COLONY MAP

For a full resolution map, please go to:
http://www.uebooks.com/stephens-point-colony-map/

CHAPTER ONE

No matter how many times Moorland replayed the recording recovered from *Exchange Four*, it still confused her. She tapped her handscreen, rewinding the recording back to its beginning. Eyes locked on the screen, she replayed the thirty-seven seconds of a black and white feed that captured the moments leading up to four hundred and sixteen deaths.

The feed showed several cargo containers strapped to the interior of *Exchange Four*'s deck. People filled them, clinging to the walls in the microgravity or free-floating in the open mouths of the containers. From the distant camera's point of view, Moorland couldn't see their faces. Nothing more than a mass of people in an otherwise empty exchange ship. No urgency, no sense of purpose. Then with four seconds left on the recording, they turned in near perfect unison and faced the rear of the ship. The recording juddered, the imagery broken into fuzzing bands and static.

It was the moment before the ship entered fractal space. Not a soul on board had seen it coming. Not a one knew they were about to die. That hadn't stopped them from trying to survive—attaching themselves and their children to the walls of the cargo containers, using mattresses as ineffective padding ....

Revulsion crept up her throat. Someone had killed those people. Someone or something. She set down the handscreen, sipping cold water from a drinking bulb. She brushed a swath of silvered blond hair behind her ears. Duncan would be arriving any moment now. She would show him the video and the reports from the investigation teams she'd sent into the exchange ship since its arrival a mere cycle ago. The still images of the desiccated dead, cycless sockets staring from skeletal faces—all the horrific effects of traveling through fractal space without the protection of a hydrostasis field.

Doctor Conrad Duncan, the Order's Advisor to the Regulatory and her oldest friend; without him she would never have succeeded in getting the Return Mandate passed through the Stephen's Point Council. Without him, the retrofitting of the fractal class cruiser *Chimera* and certain "special projects" wouldn't have received funding. And without him, finding and training the cadets that now filled the commons of the *Hydra* would have been impossible. So why did the prospect of seeing him, of sharing the horrors of *Exchange Four*, weigh so heavily on her?

Her handscreen pinged, alerting her to Duncan's arrival. She keyed in a command and the door to her private berth opened.

A stocky man with thick reddish hair stood in the doorway. His beard had more gray in it than the last time she'd seen him. Large hands hung loose at his sides, the robes of the Order enveloping his stocky frame. A pendant depicting the Eye, the Tree, and the Orb hung from his neck.

"Chief Moorland," Duncan said. The corners of his eyes lifted in a smile—the sort that engulfed his face, engulfed her.

She couldn't help but smile back. "Advisor Duncan. Welcome aboard the *Hydra*."

His warm fingers closed around her petite pointer finger in greeting, then squeezed a moment and released.

"We have a lot to talk about," Duncan said.

"Yes," Moorland agreed. She let out her breath, lowering her guard for the first time since the exchange ship's arrival. Despite their past differences, she was glad to have Duncan's help, and by proxy, the Order's. Maybe he could help her make some sense of the current situation.

"Take a seat," Moorland said, gesturing at one of the narrow chairs across from her work station. Duncan placed a hand on the chair back, frowned at its diminutive size, and pushed it against the wall.

"I'll stand," Duncan said. "Everything up here is too small for me."

"The nature of the beast," Moorland said. The *Hydra* station orbited the Stephen's Point moon and was built for efficiency and conservation of resources. With two rotating rings around a central hub, the station used centripetal force to generate artificial gravity. Moorland's private berth was not what even a normal-sized person would call "roomy."

"I understand you have imagery from inside the exchange ship."

Good. Duty Officer Blake had already briefed him. That would save some time. With dozens of hyper-important issues waiting for her attention, she couldn't afford to give Duncan the welcome he deserved.

"This is from the first exploratory team, if you want to call it that. Selena Samuelson and Theo Puck snuck themselves into the welding team sent to cut through the *Exchange Four's* hull. After the explosion, they were the first inside the ship."

"Yes, I read the report," Duncan said.

"Theo has reckless disregard for the rules and a total unwillingness to follow commands."

"I also read that he saved the life of one of the welders."

"He did. But that doesn't justify his actions. He's unreliable."

"He'll learn," Duncan said. "He has to. Did you see his navigation index scores? They're off the charts. He's a prodigy."

Moorland nodded. "They're the only reason I haven't sent him back to Stephen's Point."

"We need him," Duncan insisted.

"It might not matter," Moorland said.

Without further explanation, she dimmed the lights in her berth and cast the recording of Theo and Selena's trip into the exchange ship onto the large wallscreen that took up an entire wall of her berth. The video came to life.

In the darkness, Duncan drew in a sharp breath. "Oh my god."

Oh my god, indeed. No blurry recovered imagery here, nothing but crisp visuals captured by a power suit's head cam. Two blue beams of light puncturing the darkness, reaching out, settling on one dead face after another. Ghoulish, angular faces. Skin shrunken over bones. Dead eyes. Empty eyes. Twisted bodies rotating in microgravity. Block letters painted in blood on the interior wall of one of the cargo containers: HEL.

What did they stand for?

Help?

Hell?

Moorland had no idea, but she doubted either simple explanation. In the seconds before their entry into fractal space killed them, one of the desperate souls on the exchange ship had been trying to tell them something.

The imagery played on. Selena guided Theo back out of the exchange ship, into the umbilical connecting it to the *Hydra*. Her camera locked on Theo's face, his eyes vacant, staring into the bright lights of a utility locker.

"Has anyone talked to the boy?" Duncan asked.

Moorland nodded. "He just cleared medical and is on his way back to the commons with Cadet Locke."

"Is he okay?" Duncan asked. "That's a lot to take in."

"No kidding," Moorland said. She sighed, rubbing her temples with cold, dry palms. No point in delaying. "There's more."

"More?" Duncan asked, dull eyes fixed on hers, his face tight with worry.

"A leak," Moorland said. "The feed hit Stephen's Point at about the same time your shuttle docked with the *Hydra*."

She switched the wallscreen to a live feed from the colony's surface, this one complete with full audio. The *whump-whump* of chopper blades, air blasting the faces of a rioting mass of people surrounding the Pod Five Civvy at East End. Bright pink gas from a canister leeched into the air. Shaking fists. The *pop* of small arms fire. Orange flames licking darkened buildings in the distance. Total chaos.

"I have to go back," Duncan said, voice thick. "They need me."

Moorland frowned so hard her face hurt, anticipating his response to what she had to tell him. "You can't leave."

"What are you talking about? Prep a shuttle. I'll depart as soon as our orbit carries the station back over the pole. I want a full situation report and a direct line to the Regulatory in the valley. I can—"

"No, Duncan. You can't. You're not going back." She spoke with the emphatic emphasis she used when a junior officer strayed out of line.

"What do you mean I *can't*? I'm Order Advisor to the Regulatory, surely you can spare a—"

"The station is on lockdown. Full quarantine. My orders."

Duncan's mouth worked open, closed. "For how long?"

"As long as it takes to complete our mission."

Duncan's face darkened, a burnished red, glossy with the sweat breaking out on his forehead and cheeks. He wiped it away with the sleeve of his robe and took a step forward, towering over her.

Moorland stood to face him, more than a foot shorter but every bit as commanding in her white dress uniform.

"You can't hold me here," Duncan said. "My people ... My *colony* needs me."

"Yes," Moorland said, heat in her voice, "they do."

They weighed one another, searching for weakness, before Moorland broke the silence. "There's another recording you need to see."

The wallscreen lit up with the grainy black and white feed from the inside of *Exchange Four*, recorded in the moments just before it left Earth. It showed a group of normal if dirty people, assembled around the cargo containers. Their faces turned in unison. A breakdown in the feed. Static. Then, a single flash of clarity: the warping threads of fractal space arcing through the interior of the ship.

"They didn't come here by choice," Moorland said. "Someone sent them."

"Who?" Duncan asked.

"Preliminary medical evaluations of the bodies suggest they were being held captive. No technology, worn down clothing, rampant malnutrition. Improperly set fractures. We've identified some of them as crew of Earth's exchange dock."

"Hostages?" Duncan asked.

"Maybe. Take a look at this." Moorland shot a static image captured by Selena's helmet cam to the wallscreen. Bold letters spelling out HEL.

"I think they were trying to warn us."

Duncan rubbed his beard with a thick palm. "I'll do a search on 'HEL.' See if the Order has anything in our records that might provide an explanation."

"I appreciate that."

Duncan caught her eyes with his own. "You were right all along. We might be returning to a hostile Earth. Or worse."

"I still hold out hope that isn't the case, but I'm glad we're prepared nonetheless."

Duncan snatched his discarded chair and fell into it. The man looked gray and old and almost defeated. He raised his head, eyes glinting in the shimmer of the wallscreen. "We've done everything we can to prepare ourselves."

"Without the *Chimera*, we don't stand a chance," Moorland

said.

"*Exchange Four*'s arrival hasn't made an impact on her?"

"No. She's still locked away in Salix sleep. Selena is the only one I've seen her respond to."

Duncan's eyebrows bunched. "The girl from the rim? What do you mean the *Chimera* 'responds' to her? I heard she's a crack pilot, but she doesn't have any specialized knowledge of shipboard artificials like Theo does. And didn't she nearly kill her father in some sort of insane stunt at the rim?"

Moorland nodded. "Some of that is true. But your opinion of her doesn't matter. Neither does mine. What matters is that she partnered with the ship. One second *Chimera* was asleep, the next her neural response shot off the charts. She didn't just rouse for a moment, she came fully awake."

"I didn't see that in any of the reports."

"I withheld it."

"Why?"

"Because Selena is fragile. Because we don't know how or why the *Chimera* chose her. I wanted to give her another opportunity to connect to the ship, but circumstances intervened."

"The report I read said that she tried to flee the *Hydra* and very nearly killed a regulator in the process. She's a huge risk."

Moorland looked away, recalling Selena's performance in the Vector Analysis Systematic Trainer. "She might be a risk, but did you see her VAST results?"

Duncan raised an eyebrow. "She failed every test, correct?"

"She did. But she failed them *perfectly*. The only way that's possible is if the person taking the test had a flawless understanding of the concepts in each simulation."

"You sound like you've made up your mind," Duncan said. "Selena will navigate the *Chimera* back to Earth, assuming she can wake the ship."

Moorland took a sip from her drinking bulb, composing her thoughts. Duncan's comments suggested he thought she'd shown favoritism to Selena. Perhaps she had. She liked the scrawny girl from the rim. Maybe because Selena reminded her of herself when she was younger: Loyal, proud, driven to succeed, but also brash, rude, and lacking in discipline.

"I haven't made up my mind about anything," Moorland said. "But we have limited options and a tight timeframe. I don't like our choices any more than you do."

Duncan nodded. "It's far from ideal. Sending these … *kids* back to Earth. Do we know for certain that once the *Chimera* wakes she won't allow anyone but the Jubilee generation to crew her? Maybe we can override her protocols. We'll still need a navigator and one of the cadets will have to fill that role, but we could send along an adult crew to supervise the journey."

Moorland set down her drinking bulb and tapped her handscreen. A live feed of the *Chimera* replaced the static image of the word HEL on the wallscreen. A handful of welding ships worked along the *Chimera*'s starboard side, grafting deck plates, white-hot sparks shimmering to red and orange, lasting far longer in the vacuum of space than they would on the cool surface of the Stephen's Point moon. The repairs to the ship's exterior would soon be completed.

"If we manage to wake her, we'll cross that bridge when we come to it. At least she's sealed tight." Moorland nodded at the ship. "Everything they're doing now is precautionary."

"What about the enhancements?"

"Complete. Fifteen launch tubes. Four warheads each."

Duncan shook his head. "I thought you were crazy to suggest such a thing. I thought I was even crazier for hiding it from the Regulatory all these years. But whatever sent that exchange ship into fractal with those poor people on board—we'll need to be ready to face them."

"Yes," Moorland said. "We will."

CHAPTER TWO

Following Marcus down the main corridor of the *Hydra*'s rotating second ring, Theo felt like running. But there was nowhere to go—the vacuum outside the walls of the station was a new and meaningful presence. Theo glanced at the other boy's square, impassive face. Marcus' dark hair, until recently a blunt line across his forehead, was newly cut, the sides and bangs trimmed short. One strand fell across his forehead, making him look both thoughtful and jaunty.

"When did you have time to get your hair cut?" Theo asked.

"There's a grooming concession outside the med bay," Marcus said. He turned to look at Theo. "People put a lot of emphasis on outward appearance. You need to look a certain way to do certain things."

"Are you trying out for the hero role in some vid?" Theo asked with a smirk.

"You're the one they're going to be calling a hero," Marcus said, flashing Theo a smile. The haircut, the smile … what was going on with Marcus? Ever since their arrival at the *Hydra* he'd been acting different. Normal. Playing a part. Maybe he wasn't far off with his hero comment. Marcus was changing himself. Transforming. Preparing to step into a new identity, one that had nothing to do with murdering a man in a cave and then forcing Theo to help him hide the body.

"Moorland hasn't briefed the cadets on *Exchange Four* yet," Marcus said. "They're going to be *very* curious."

Theo opened his mouth to respond, but Marcus stopped and pointed. "There you go. Straight through there are the commons. Quarters are on the opposite end. You've been assigned berth 544B."

Theo stared through the transparent panels ahead. Cadets hunkered on sofas surrounding the main wallscreen, its display blank except for the silver crescent of the Regulatory. Shoulders and backs tense, they looked as though they were waiting for something. Or someone. His heartrate sped.

"Do I have to walk though there? I don't really feel like talking to anyone."

Marcus shrugged. "You can circumnavigate the commons, but you'd have to walk around the other side of the ring." Marcus pulled a handscreen from the pocket of his uniform trousers and glanced at it. "I'll leave you to it," Marcus said.

"You're not coming with me?"

"No, I have other things to attend to."

Theo wondered what 'other things,' required Marcus' attention, but the other boy had already left his side and was taking long strides down the corridor, leaving Theo alone.

At least nobody in the commons had seen him yet. If he moved fast, he might get past the other cadets and slip into his berth without having to answer any questions.

The transparent doors slid open. Theo kept his eyes down and walked quickly, heading for the far side of the room where another set of sliders opened to the cadet quarters.

Before he could reach them, Meghan jumped up, blocking his path. "Theo!"

Everyone in the room crowded around, a flock of gray-uniformed birds.

"What happened?"

"What was inside the exchange ship?"

"Why isn't anyone talking to us?"

Bodies crushed against his, pushing in, curious and frightened. He blinked, his mind filled with images of different sorts of faces: eyeless, attached to withered naked bodies. Old and wrinkled. Tiny children. All of them husks.

Phoebus and his fraternal twin brother Hephaestus shoved their way forward.

"You okay, Puck?" Phoebus asked.

"Yes," Theo said. He elbowed his way through the throng and darted down the corridor.

Meghan followed after him. "Theo?"

"I'm good," he called over his shoulder. *Good?* What did that mean? His brain bumped in his skull. He couldn't think of anything else to tell her.

"You don't look good," Meghan said.

She reached for him, but Theo shrugged her hand away. She trotted beside him. "You missed the tour. Do you even know what berth is yours?" Meghan's eyes, blue-green above high cheekbones, were full of concern. Pretty, smart, and focused on him. Less than a girlfriend but more than a friend; in normal circumstances he'd relish her attention. So why did he feel numb?

Meghan glanced over her shoulder to where other cadets stood, hanging back, watching.

"Everyone knows you and Marcus went into the exchange ship."

"Not me and Marcus. Me and ..." He trailed off, unable to think of a quick way to explain Selena. *Selena Samuelson.* The girl with a rimmer accent and wild eyes. Had he really seen her for the first time only a cycle ago? Covered in sweat and bruises, crouched against a wall, her stolen aerocuffs held at the ready. He thought she might shoot him. Instead, she'd asked for his help.

"Theo?"

He snapped back into the moment. "I'm ... I don't know. I need to find my berth and rest."

Meghan tried again to take his arm. "Do you want to talk? Come on, my room's right here."

"I don't want to talk."

She leaned forward, voice low and fierce. "I don't know what happened, but I was worried about you. We heard there was some sort of explosion and that people got hurt. I thought it was you. Nobody would tell us anything and I've been sitting here worried out of my mind for the last few *hours*." Meghan scanned his face. Her eyes widened. "Wait, was it Marcus?" Her fingers brushed his cheek. "Oh my word—that's it, isn't it? Is Marcus ... dead?"

Theo remembered his father's face when he'd said his goodbyes before boarding the shuttle to the *Hydra*. His dad had placed both hands on Theo's shoulders, face growing red. Theo had thought his dad was angry until he started to cry. Then his mother and his little sister Liddy cried too. It was all he could do not to cry himself.

Theo tried to swallow, his throat sticking. "Marcus is fine. One of the welder's equipment failed. It caused an explosion. Some of the welders were killed, some injured."

"That's terrible," Meghan whispered. "I'm so glad you weren't hurt."

Meghan wrapped her arms around him and he stiffened. She released him and stepped back.

"Did you go into the exchange ship?"

"Yes."

"What was in it?"

He needed to tell someone. He would have to eventually. Best to start with a friend, someone close to him. Someone strong enough to handle the truth. "There weren't any supplies on the exchange ship."

Her face sagged. "No supplies? Nothing?"

"No supplies, no."

"Why was it pressurized? Is that what caused the explosion in the first place?"

Theo swallowed, forcing himself to tell her the truth. "It was full of people." Her irises expanded like twin black moons. "But all of them were dead."

* * *

Without even looking at his newly assigned berth, Theo dimmed the lights, stripped out of his uniform, and fell onto his bunk. Hours remained before his down cycle, but he needed sleep. His body demanded it. He muted his handscreen, anticipating dreams filled with the dead. Twisted bodies. Empty eyes. Instead a heavy, vacant nothing overtook him and he slept.

He woke to someone shaking him. "Wake up. Moorland's called for an assembly and you're going to be late."

He roused, struggling to open his eyes wide enough to see the smiling boy leaning over him, his shaggy blonde hair tousled and wet. His stomach did a backflip, some vestigial memory of zero gravity rekindled. He felt as though he might float up and off the mattress, out into the void of space.

Exchange Four, Selena, Marcus.

"I let you sleep as long as I could. You looked like you needed it," the boy said.

Theo blinked, grit in the corner of one eye making him squint. He snatched his handscreen and read the screen three times before the truth set in. He'd slept fourteen hours straight.

A priority message from Moorland flashed red. *Assembly at 0900 hours.*

The enormity of the last few cycles burst onto his consciousness all at once. He sat up, scrubbing at his face with both hands.

The other boy grinned, showing large, white teeth. "I'm Charlie Grey." He stuck out his hand, offering Theo a finger. "I mean, I'm Charlie, your bunkmate. I'm from East End and have six, Stephen count 'em, siblings." Charlie smoothed his voice into an approximation of a vid announcer: "I'll be your bunkmate, confidant, and friend for the remainder of this voyage."

"Nice to meet you," Theo said, shaking cobwebs from his mind.

"Where'd you grow up?"

"The Swallows," Theo said, throat dry. "My name's Theo Puck."

"I know. *Everybody* knows who you are." Charlie stopped grinning and jerked a thumb over his shoulder toward the stall. "I don't want to cause problems on our first day together or anything, but, umm, you should probably shower."

In spite of himself, Theo laughed. "Okay." He managed a genuine smile, grateful that Charlie hadn't asked him any questions about himself, or worse, *Exchange Four*. "I'll hurry. Don't want to be late to assembly on our first day, right?"

CHAPTER THREE

Theo read Moorland's message again. *0900 hours.* Simple and precise. The *Hydra* operated on four six-hour duty cycles that made terms like "morning" or "evening" irrelevant. Theo preferred the numbers. Thinking in those terms helped subdue his mounting homesickness. The word "morning" made Theo think of Liddy. The way she climbed over him, poking fingers in his ears or trying to force his closed eyes open. The warmth of her pudgy arms locked around his neck as he gave her a ride down the stairs to breakfast.

Theo raced through his shower and toweled dry in record time. Outside the bathroom, he found Charlie waiting for him.

"Better," Charlie said. "Much better."

Damp-skinned, Theo fought his way into his uniform, then accepted Charlie's help getting his collar straightened.

"I have a sister named Liddy," Theo said.

"Older or younger?" Charlie asked.

"Five. Soon to be six. She's a handful."

"I'm the next to oldest in my family, which means I've seen it all. Smelled it all, too. I've cleaned up more blood, puke and poop than you can possibly imagine."

"I can imagine a lot," Theo said. "I've got a good imagination."

"I'm sure you do, what with your aptitude scores. You going to navigate that relic or what?"

"Maybe," Theo said, wondering how Charlie knew anything about his scores. Charlie was from the East End training group, a wealthier neighborhood than the Swallows. Wealthy enough to have families with *six* kids in them.

"Cadet Locke sure thinks a lot of you," Charlie said. "I ran into him while you were sleeping."

What *else* had Marcus told Charlie?

"I think a lot of him, too," Theo said. "He's the highest scoring cadet in our training group. He's got a real gift with people."

Charlie laughed. "Yeah, like he's trying to win some kind of popularity contest or something. Shines right up whenever anybody's paying attention."

"He isn't really like that," Theo said. "He just wants to succeed."

"Yeah, don't we all." Charlie looked at his handscreen. "We better scoot or we're going to be late."

Theo followed Charlie into the hall, merging with the steady stream of cadets exiting their berths. It looked as though everyone had been paired with a bunkmate from a different training group. So it wasn't just him. Theo felt thankful—it wasn't that he didn't like the rest of his training group, but he'd spent *so much time* with all of them. Charlie was a welcome change of pace. Theo liked him already.

They arrived at the commons with time to spare. Charlie started talking to a brown-skinned girl with silky black hair piled atop her head. Theo remembered hearing her introduce herself as Kerry Nifali. Across the room, Meghan was chatting with another girl. He turned, hoping she hadn't noticed him. He wasn't looking forward to answering all the questions she'd probably come up with during the down cycle. He preferred Charlie's unassuming friendliness.

He scanned the room, searching for Selena. He expected to see her there but had no idea why. She wasn't a cadet, she'd said so herself. When they first met, she'd said the word with derision, as if the idea were beneath her. When he thought of her intense brown eyes, the easy way she moved in zero gravity, and knew he wanted to see her again. He wanted to tell her about the journal Duncan had given him back on Stephen's Point. About the secrets it contained. About her great, great grandfather Ashley Samuelson, one of the original flight crew of the *Chimera.*

Was that the only reason he wanted to see her? Why did answering that question bother him? He caught a glimpse of Meghan's eager face scanning the room. He turned his back and shoved his way in the opposite direction. He didn't owe Meghan anything. They both knew things would be different once they arrived at the *Hydra.* He needed time to think. To figure things out.

Hephaestus and Phoebus spotted him and waved him over. Aside from the slight difference in size, the twins were almost mirror images of one another, inches taller than most of the other cadets, muscular and dark-skinned. Heph and Phoeb stood with their hands shoved into pockets, talking to a stocky boy, his hair cropped short in the style of a regulator.

"This is Cadet Anthony Wells," Heph said when Theo pulled alongside.

"Cadet Puck," Theo said. "You can call me Theo."

"You're the guy that went into *Exchange Four*," Wells said. "I've heard rumors about what you found in there. Pretty awful, huh?"

Theo remained silent, hoping that if he ignored the question, Wells would move on to another topic. Instead, Wells leaned forward, eyes bright. "I heard someone leaked footage of the exchange ship interior."

Theo stiffened, attention locking on Wells. "Leaked to where?"

"The surface. The nets went down for several hours yesterday, right after the exchange ship got here. They came up again last night, but now we only have local access." Wells' voice dropped so low that Theo had to lean in to hear him. "I did some checking around. As far as I can tell, we're not sending or receiving any data from Stephen's Point."

"Did you learn anything else about what's going on? I don't like how they're keeping us all in the dark," Phoebus said.

"Not really," Wells said. "Nothing to see, nothing to read. My guess? They've quarantined the *Hydra* until they take *Exchange Four* apart piece by piece."

Phoebus glanced at his brother. "Maybe you're right. But Moorland better have some answers when she gets here. Everyone's starting to freak out."

"Relax," Heph said. "I'm sure the network connection to Stephen's Point will be back up in no time. Then you can have a nice long, weepy vid call with Mom."

"Shut up," Phoebus said, the hardness in his voice suggesting Heph had hit a nerve.

"What did you say your specialty is?" Wells asked Theo.

"Navigation," Theo replied, relieved to be talking about something else. Most cadets had two or three areas of specialty. Phoebus had scored in leadership and systems, Heph in tactics and navigation. Both twins had scored high in mathematics.

"Navigation. That's great." Theo detected no ridicule in Wells' voice, but felt a little inferior anyway.

Heph slapped Theo on the back with a huge palm. "Hey, show him your scar."

Theo shook his head.

Phoebus grinned. "Come on. If I had that scar, I'd show it to everyone."

"Forget it," Theo said.

"No, seriously, show him." Heph turned back to Wells. "If bravery were a specialty, Theo would have scored in it. This kid collapsed during training and our trainer tried to force Theo to send him to get branded but Theo wouldn't do it."

"Branded?" Wells asked.

"Yeah," Phoeb said, "when you fail the training."

Wells looked confused. "They branded all of you? With what?"

"They branded the ones that didn't make the cut," said Theo. The ribbed flesh on his abdomen tingled and burned against his undershirt. "Well, except for me I guess."

"Back up," Phoeb said, eyes narrowed. "You mean they *didn't* brand anyone from your training group?"

"No," Wells said. "I have no idea what you're talking about."

Phoeb looked at Heph, eyes ugly. "What a load of shit."

The door opened and Moorland entered, flanked by the lead trainer, Hurston Lemieux. Behind them came a group of technicians carrying silver equipment cases.

"Attention!" Marcus shouted, using his super-cadet voice. The cadets fell into lines, standing at attention, eyes locked ahead, backs straight.

"Relax," Moorland said. "This isn't an inspection."

None of the cadets moved as the technicians opened their cases and laid a series of items on the surface of a table. "Good morning, cadets," Moorland said. Her voice wasn't loud but carried over Theo's head with surprising strength.

"I'm sure you have a lot of questions," she said. "And I'm happy to answer those that I can. But first, I have something to give each of you. Something critical to your training and our mission."

Blocked by Heph's massive torso, Theo couldn't get a clear view of what the technicians had removed from the cases.

"You are each about to receive one of the very last Communication and Tactical Overlays provided by Earth. We have held them in reserve for this specific purpose."

A collective intake of breath came as the ranks of cadets shifted in anticipation.

"CATOs," Wells whispered, awe in his voice. Theo knew what they were—some of the Regulatory officers used them—but they couldn't be purchased. A contact lens provided a heads-up display featuring data feeds, information on environments and equipment, and instant communication between users. CATOs had all but disappeared from Stephen's Point in the years since the exchange ships mysteriously stopped arriving from Earth over fifteen years ago.

Moorland held up a small, clear canister. Inside and suspended in liquid, a small, green half-bubble floated. "Once activated and biometrically synced to the user, each CATO lens has a lifespan of five thousand hours." Theo did the math—roughly two hundred Earth days. No wonder they'd become so scarce.

"The Communication and Tactical Overlay will give you real-time connectivity to other cadets, to command staff, and to the *Hydra*. When the time comes, your CATO will also be your primary means of interfacing with the *Chimera*.

"When I call your name, step forward. The technicians will create a biometric sync to your CATO lens. Next, you will be injected with nanoimplants. These micro-organisms will travel to your pre-frontal cortex and establish baseline connectivity between your brain and the CATO. Over time, they will spread and form more substantive connections that will allow you to direct most of the CATO's functionality through thought alone. Unlike the *Chimera*'s navigational sphere, which reads thoughts through wave-pattern identification, these synthetic synaptic connections will be permanent, although as I mentioned before, the lenses themselves are not. Together they create a closed circuit linking the lens to your mind. No one will be able to access or control your CATO but you."

From the row ahead of Theo, Meghan raised her hand.

"Yes, Cadet Ziczek?"

"Isn't that dangerous? I've seen a lot of service announcements warning everyone to stay away from spiders. A guy even came to school years ago to tell us how using a black market spider killed his son."

"There are risks, if that's what you're asking. But these aren't spiders. They do share the same technological basis, but I'm sure you'd agree that having a cut sealed by a medical technician is different than having someone try to do it in a back alley somewhere.

"I've personally had a CATO for over twenty years. It's a time-saving efficiency tool that will radically improve your ability to function as a team aboard the *Chimera*. If any of you would like to forgo the injection, then that is your right." Moorland paused and let her eyes slide over the cadets. "However, dissenters will no longer be suitable candidates for the *Chimera*'s crew. They will be returned to the Stephen's Point colony ... for reassignment."

No one opted out.

Theo had seen the same vids as Meghan advising against illegal synth work. Despite working with machines and engaging in the occasional illegal hack to pay for extra food, he'd steered clear of spiders. He'd seen what could happen to the unlucky. A bad spider could turn a person into a vegetable. But CATOs came straight from the Regulatory. Moorland herself had one. He didn't need to worry about synthetic neural pathways slicing through his brain, killing his mind, and leaving him a slobbering idiot, did he?

Cadets responded as Moorland called their names, stepping forward to receive their CATOs. Technicians placed each lens into a shallow tray filled with goo attached to something that looked a little bit like a syringe. They pricked the cadet's fingers and waited a moment before removing the CATO, balancing it on a glove-protected fingertip. Then, using a different syringe, they injected each cadet at the base of the neck. The whole process took less than a minute and didn't look painful. After a technician pressed the green half-bubble into each cadet's eye, they would turn and head back to their place in the assembly.

No one screamed. No one fell to the ground convulsing. Theo slowed his breathing, waiting his turn, praying to Stephen he wouldn't pass out when they poked him with the needle. So much for being brave.

"Charlie Grey," Moorland called. Theo's bunkmate stepped forward, shaking his fists over his head like a fight champ. Laughter broke some of the tension and the cadets relaxed a bit.

Moorland continued to call names until she arrived at his. "Theo Puck."

Theo marched to the front. A technician ran an alcohol swab

across the base of his neck, then Theo felt a tiny prick.

"Hold still," the technician said. A thumb and pointer finger held his left eyelid wide. The bubble moved forward, blocking his vision, making contact with his eye. His eye gave an involuntary blink, but the fingers held it open. Then the CATO lens sealed over his retina. A green cast clouded his vision. In fractions of a second, the green turned to silver, a dull shimmer neither close nor far away. Gradually it disappeared and his vision returned to normal. Theo closed his eyelid. Opened, closed again.

Huh. Nothing special.

He returned to his position alongside Cadet Wells.

"How is it?" Wells whispered.

"I don't know," Theo said. "I didn't feel much of anything. Just a pinch."

Moorland called the next name. "Selena Samuelson."

Theo almost jumped. She *was* there. Out of order in the middle of a rear row, dressed in a gray cadet uniform. Selena. She moved sideways instead of forward, bumping into another cadet, a boy from a different training group named Drummond Ray. "Watch it," she hissed before slouching forward.

Moorland looked irritated and motioned for Selena to hurry up. Theo strained to see over Heph's back.

Selena received her finger prick, but no injection in her neck. *Weird. She must have some sort of synthetic synapse already in place.* One of those the Regulatory liked to warn people about. Somehow that didn't really surprise him. Yet another mystery from a very mysterious girl.

He needed to talk to her.

Moorland continued calling names until she reached the very last. "Meghan Ziczek."

Meghan received her injection and her CATO and returned to her position.

"Now I will activate your connection to the *Hydra*'s network," Moorland said. The chief's eyes flicked sideways. A low murmur came from the cadets. The CATO shimmer returned, growing into a luminous window displaying an overlay of data. Words floated in front of Theo's vision. They moved when he moved his head, opaque enough to read, translucent enough to see through. His eyes didn't have to move like they did when he read from a screen. He just looked at the words, a whole dense block of them, and *boom* they were in his mind.

The Communication and Tactical Overlay with synaptic response offers unparalleled connectivity within closed or open networks. This tutorial will guide you through the adaptive process of harmonizing your CATO's functionality to your preferences. Opacity, text size, and the reading field location will optimize as you progress through this tutorial.

All of the words hit at the same instant. Laughter sounded from other cadets, intakes of breath, a squeal of delight. Theo caught sight of Marcus, his eyes flicking left and right, clearly doing something far more interesting than reading.

Theo found that as soon as he'd parsed one block of text, another took its place. He could read with blazing speed. Far faster than looking a handscreen. He spooled through the rest of the tutorial, font size shifting, the shimmering window adjusting as he learned what he liked. The window had hot zones that he could activate by blinking or moving his eye in a certain gesture. The tutorial said that once the synaptic network in his brain matured, he wouldn't even have to use eye gestures.

[Hey, crap for brains.]

The message popped up in the lower left section of his overlay, attached to an image of Charlie Grey. He selected the ping and messaged back:

[Watch it. They're probably monitoring these messages. And I wouldn't go disparaging other people's intelligence, fish sticks.]

The words flowed out of him, became text. He sent them flying off the edge of the overlay and an instant later Charlie laughed. More cadets began to laugh, all of them playing around with the messaging tool, firing obscenities back and forth.

Moorland watched for several minutes, amused, before speaking again. "Today's training will consist of you familiarizing yourselves with the features and functionality of your CATOs. Trainer Lemieux will remain on-hand to assist you."

Engaged in playing with their CATOs, no one noticed when Moorland slipped out of the room.

Theo turned in a circle, looking for Selena. Gone. He flipped up a new message—how was her name spelled? Selina? The text auto-filled. *Selena Samuelson.*

    [Where are you? Can we talk?]
    [Left already.]
    [Will you meet me?]
    [Can't. I'm with Moorland.]

Theo was taken aback. With Moorland? Why? He fired off another message:

    [Doing what?]

He heard her sardonic, matter-of-fact tone in his mind as he read her reply: *[Going to wake the Chimera.]*

CHAPTER FOUR

The pale pink walls of the umbilical pulsed and trembled as Moorland and Selena threaded their way through the foot traffic exiting the *Chimera.* Third-cycle workers hurried past in their gravity boots, eager to eat, sleep, and socialize back on the *Hydra.* The flicker of data popping up around everyone and everything became so distracting that Selena shut down most of her CATO-linked spider's functionality.

As if sensing her actions, Moorland asked, "How're you acclimating to CATO?"

"Fine."

"Has it fully integrated with your spider?"

"More or less," Selena said. "It's going to take some time for the two to learn to play nice together."

Moorland offered a half-smile. "Just like you and the other cadets."

Selena shrugged.

"Once they start training with you in VAST, once they see what you can do, you'll have no trouble gaining their respect."

"I don't need friends," Selena said. "I'm just here to do a job, right?"

"That's one way of looking at it. But it's much more than a job, Selena. A fractal class cruiser isn't a trawler. You're going to have to learn to work as part of a team, to trust your navigation assistants. You have to learn to lead."

"*If* the *Chimera* can be woken," Selena said. No one knew how to break the *Chimera* free. Something had happened to the ship in the centuries since her arrival at Elypso. She should have woken long ago but had not.

"Not *if* but *when*," Moorland said.

They stepped out of the airlock connecting the *Hydra* to the *Chimera,* and Selena drew in a deep breath. The oxygen tasted like dust. Ancient. She imagined it as the same air breathed by the original colonists, or even Stephen himself.

"It's not just the lack of gravity on the *Chimera*," Moorland said. "It feels different here, doesn't it?"

Selena nodded, imagining Stephen standing where she stood, taking in the radical changes the *Chimera* had undergone to make her space-worthy once more. What would Stephen think of the thick metal scars created by the hot welds that closed off the crosshatch where Pod One and Pod Two once connected to the ship's spine? What would he think of the banded cabling running from the *Hydra*, through the umbilical, and to the *Chimera*'s fore and aft spheres?

"She *wants* to wake up," Moorland said. Her helmet of shiny hair framed an angular, almost hungry face. Intelligent, dark-blue eyes peered at Selena. Beneath their practiced calm, Selena detected nervousness. The same feeling that set Selena's toes in motion inside her boots and sent her tongue gliding across the backside of her teeth.

"She's going to respond to you," Moorland said. "I know she will."

The Chief believed she could do it, and that scared Selena more than the prospect of failure.

She'd touched the *Chimera* days before. Felt the old ship's desperation to escape her Salix prison—the protocols that governed when the *Chimera* could awaken. The same protocols that required her crew to be made up of Jubilee Babies—those born after the colony's longstanding debt to Earth had been repaid.

The *Chimera*'s need to partner with a human navigator and traverse the dense folds of The Everything had overwhelmed Selena. Such sorrow ... such longing ...

She wants to wake up. But what if I can't help her?

Selena swallowed a mouthful of tepid saliva and tried to distract herself by pinching the hem of her pant leg, rolling and pulling at the fabric until the tram whooshed into the crosshatch. The doors slid open, inviting them inside.

They took their seats and the tram sped them to the fore of the ship. A short walk down a brilliant corridor led them to the command deck. Blue ceiling panels that mimicked an Earth sky illuminated a circular room with porcelain-white walls. In the center of the room, dominating the space around it, sat the navigation sphere. It seemed to hang from a thick band of cables linking it to the ceiling. Here Stephen had plotted the pathway from Earth to the star Elypso and the Stephen's Point moon. Here the *Chimera* interfaced with him and the rest of the crew. Together they balanced the paradoxes of fractal space and successfully moved a ship full of colonists halfway across the galaxy.

Selena's breath caught in her throat.

"Ready?" Moorland asked.

"I'm not sure."

The last time she'd entered the sphere, the *Chimera* roused from slumber for a handful of seconds. The full weight of the ship's consciousness—and her deep pool of grief and loneliness—had knocked Selena unconscious.

"You can do this," Moorland said.

I hope you're right.

Despite her misgivings, Selena moved to the sphere. No point in delaying. If the *Chimera* reached for her, there wouldn't be anything Selena could do to stop her. And if the ship didn't reach out? What would happen to her father then? Moorland hadn't come right out and said that his care at Principal Hospital on Stephen's Point was contingent on Selena waking the *Chimera,* but she suspected Moorland wouldn't devote the resources needed to help him recover if she failed.

She wouldn't fail. She wouldn't let Liam down. Not again.

Selena reached the sphere and paused outside its oval entrance, hands resting on the cold ceramic exterior. Silky hairs on her forearms rose like the spines of a salt-sea urchin. Threads of electricity jagged down her spine and into her toes.

The last time *Chimera*'s consciousness connected with Selena's, it had been a two-way transfer. She felt the old ship's desperation and the *Chimera* had felt Selena's emotions, too. Fear for her father. Anger at Moorland. Anger at herself. Buried deep beneath those things, an undercurrent of grief as wide and deep as any river.

She could handle another dose of that if she had to. For Liam, she could.

Selena glanced back once at Moorland's hopeful face and then ducked inside the sphere. Perforated with thousands of small holes, geodesic panels interlaced to form curving walls. Feet spread wide, Selena pressed warm palms against the panels. She closed her eyes, hoping—fearing—that the *Chimera* would find her. She counted each passing second. The panels beneath her palms warmed to match her body temperature. She felt nothing. Heard nothing. Saw nothing. Her spider remained inert.

Hello? she called into the emptiness of her mind. *Chimera?*

The words echoed in the purple darkness behind her closed eyelids.

She changed her stance, trying to remember how she'd stood the last time, where she'd placed her hands. She adjusted, inching along, stopping at intervals. Her limbs began to ache. Though she couldn't see or hear Moorland, she pictured her impatient face, waiting for Selena to succeed.

Selena thumped the panels like drums. Pounded, prodded, and caressed. Whispered enticements and threats. She tried to recall her emotional state—the fear she felt for her father, her rage over being separated from him—but the effort felt clinical and empty. Even thoughts of Liam's ruined face provoked no real emotion.

What do I have to do? Answer me, damn it!

Silence enveloped her. She ran a hand across her face, scrubbing her eyes and mouth. She would try again. She would make this work.

* * *

When Selena at last exited the sphere, she trembled with hunger and fatigue. Sweat cemented tendrils of hair to her neck. Her back felt like fused iron and her head thumped with a vicious headache.

"It didn't work," she mumbled, unable to meet Moorland's eyes.

"No, it didn't. Zero synaptic response from the *Chimera*."

"I'm sorry," Selena said. She almost hoped Moorland would admit the whole idea was a huge mistake. That Selena didn't have the power to wake the *Chimera.* That she was a failure.

"We'll try again tomorrow." Moorland sounded almost cheerful.

"What's the point? I don't know why she reached out the last time, but I can tell you that it was her, not me. *I* didn't do anything."

"I understand that."

"Then why make me come back?"

Moorland gave her a pointed look, then turned and headed down the passage that led to the tram. Selena had no choice but to follow.

The tram whisked them to the crosshatch and they cleared the airlock minutes later and walked the half-kilometer up the umbilical in silence.

When they arrived at the utility lockers and had shed their gravity boots, Moorland looked at Selena and spoke. "Tomorrow you'll try again."

Was that worry in Moorland's voice?

Back under the influence of the centripetal gravity of the *Hydra,* Selena pushed her hair into something resembling order and adjusted her uniform, unsure of what to say.

"Be ready at oh seven hundred hours. Make sure you eat a good breakfast."

"Chief Moorland?" Selena said, not wanting the chief to leave before she could ask her for a small favor.

"Yes?"

"I don't want to live at the commons. The other cadets … I don't fit in with them." She felt foolish saying it, but better foolish than miserable. Besides, Rose, the nurse who had helped her recover from the trawler crash and became her first non-rimmer friend, had offered to let Selena share her berth.

"You'll fit in given enough time," Moorland said. "You'll all learn to work together."

"Could I live with Rose?"

Moorland studied her a moment. "I thought you weren't here to make friends?"

"I'm not. My bunkmate, Kaylee, and I aren't going to get along."

"Why is that?"

"She's young. And doesn't know anything about anything. And she doesn't know when to shut up."

"Sounds like someone else I know," Moorland said, the hint of a smile on her face.

Selena's face became heated. "Look, can't I just stay with Rose? I already know her and she has the space." Selena felt a little guilty for making Kaylee sound so awful. She wasn't that bad, but Selena didn't want to put up with her endless cheerful questions.

"I'm afraid that won't work. The other cadets would interpret it as me giving you preferential treatment. They'd be right."

"Because they sure as hell won't see you taking me to the

sphere as *preferential*," Selena said. She regretted the words the moment they left her mouth. Why couldn't she learn to watch what she said? Why did she needlessly provoke people, especially the ones she liked best?

"What makes you think you're the only one I'll test?"

"I don't," Selena lied.

Misgivings smashed together in her mind like shards knocked askew at the rim. She hadn't even thought of Moorland testing other cadets. From the chief's arched eyebrows, Selena realized that Moorland knew she hadn't thought of it. Selena had assumed she was special. Hadn't Moorland told her that only a few cycles ago?

"You have impressive VAST scores and valuable experience flying at the rim," Moorland said. "However, you are just one of a hundred and twenty-three potential candidates to become the *Chimera*'s navigator. For you to succeed, as an officer or in a support role aboard the *Chimera,* you're going to have to demonstrate a total commitment to working as part of a team."

"But I am committed!"

Moorland continued as if she hadn't heard. "I don't play favorites. I will test every cadet, every tech, each and every person on this station if I have to. The mission always comes first."

"Okay," Selena said. "I get it."

Moorland looked at Selena without a hint of her previous hope and expectancy. "I believe you *think* you do. But you're going to have to show me. You'll earn your place aboard the *Chimera* like every other cadet."

"I said I get it," Selena said, more defiant than she felt.

"I hope you do. For now, you are dismissed, Cadet Samuelson."

Selena fled down the corridor, back to the commons, back to the other hundred and twenty-two potential navigators. They'd received Regulatory training. She'd worked with her half-drunk father. They all belonged to training groups and had well-established relationships. She didn't know more than a few of their names. Meghan. Marcus. Theo.

Theo.

He'd sent her another message earlier in the cycle, but she'd been too busy to read it. What did he want? Her eyes slanted right, pulling up the oldest message in the queue.

[Did you wake the Chimera*?]*

She bit her cheek, annoyance flooding her. The message glowed in front of her eyes, a reminder of her failure.

[Leave me alone.]

Another message from Theo replaced the last.

[You didn't, did you? I mean, I'm sorry. But I can help you. At least, I think I can.]

What was he blathering on about? It looked like CATO hadn't improved his ability to form coherent thoughts. She shoved his message aside, unwilling to continue the exchange. She was going to go back to her berth and tell Kaylee she needed some time to herself.

Another message from Theo.

[I think I know how to wake up the Chimera*.]*

Sure you do, she thought, pulling Theo's next message:

[I read all about your great-great grandfather Ashley in his journal. I thought he was a woman because of his name until you mentioned him right before we entered Exchange Four*.]*

Selena read the message again. *Ashley's journal?* If he'd kept a journal, Liam would have told her about it, wouldn't he? And how could some kid from Stephen's Point have such a thing?

She composed a reply: *[You're a liar.]* She studied her words, then thought better of them. She should slow down, think, not make assumptions. She sighed, deleted the message, and formulated another one: *[Can you show me the journal?]*

His response was almost instantaneous: *[Yes. Sort of. I'll have to explain in person.]*

In person. A waste of time. But if Theo really did have something that once belonged to Ashley, she wanted to see it. Thinking of Theo's boyish face and idiotic smile, she couldn't help but admit that she wouldn't mind seeing him again, either.

[Commons. Fifteen minutes. Don't be late.] She fired off the message and broke into a trot.

CHAPTER FIVE

"I'm here to see Ombudsman Owagumbiea," Marcus said to the regulator on guard duty at the *Hydra*'s brig. Although still unsure why he'd accepted the invitation to speak to the fallen ombudsman of ecomire mining at the rim, his curiosity had gotten the best of him. The man had wielded enormous power, and had even been locked in a cell for attempting to steal ecomire from the regulatory; he might yet again.

"And you are?" the regulator asked.

"Marcus Locke." Marcus gave the regulator a businesslike nod. "You have my clearance on file."

CATO revealed the regulator's name as Forester. He examined Marcus' gray uniform and the green gleam of the CATO winking from his left pupil. He scanned Marcus' biometrics, reading the spooling information from the screen in front of him. The regulator paused, eyes tracking back to read and then reread something. Finally the man looked up.

"What is the nature of your visit?"

"That is classified."

"And whose orders are you under?"

Marcus kept his smile friendly but impersonal. "That is also classified."

Forester typed something into his screen. "You're approved."

Tumblers rolled. The outer door opened and Marcus stepped through. The inner door cycled as well—like an airlock—one entryway securing the other. He entered an octagon-shaped lobby. Each wall provided access to a single cell sealed behind thick transparent doors. All but one of the seven cells were empty.

In the farthest cell to the left, a long, lean man stretched out on a blue chair. His skin was a deep, smooth black. Well-groomed and seemingly unaffected by his circumstances, Owagumbiea sat with his legs extended and crossed at the ankle.

"Marcus J. Locke," said the ombudsman. "Welcome to my home." The microphone feeding Owagumbiea's voice from his cell to the lobby made him sound like a recording.

Marcus gave the same nod he'd given Regulator Forester. What was the man's agenda? He often wondered why people didn't just state their desires; the endless gamesmanship was monotonous and often pointless.

"I like what you've done with the place," Marcus said, eying the non-standard chair where the older man sat.

"Thank you very much," the Ombudsman said. "This is real leather. Cow skin from Earth." He stroked the seat as if it might still be part of a living animal. "Very old and very expensive. I took it from a former Stephen's Point Council member. A true dignitary. Until he lost his position and was ostracized, made a veritable pariah in the valley. A real shame."

Marcus sat on one end of a bench facing the cell. "I'm glad you're comfortable."

"Very much so. I am comfortable. And comfort is second only to liberty, don't you think?"

Owagumbiea stood and grabbed a more utilitarian metal chair, placing it next to the microphone carrying his voice to the other side of the see-through wall. He sat and leaned close. Light flickered in his dark eyes. He was tracking Marcus, like Marcus was tracking him.

"Why did you ask to see me?"

"I like that you're direct. Yes, I like that about you, Marcus J. Locke, I really do."

"You can call me Cadet Locke."

"Do you know why my constituents chose me to represent them, Cadet Locke? I'll tell you. The folks from the rim prefer someone who knows how to be direct. That's what kept me in office for a decade. That, and the fact that the price of ecomire tripled."

"Makes sense," he said. "You're a very influential person. But as far as direct, that I haven't seen. What do you need?"

"You don't know if I need anything at all."

"I got your message. Identified as being from someone else, but not that difficult to interpret. So don't try and pretend you didn't ask for help."

"Then tell me, Cadet Locke, what have you interpreted?"

Marcus almost laughed. "Oh, I see. You didn't know it was me you were talking to."

"I couldn't be certain. Not a hundred percent. But I suspected. From the reports I read before I found myself in these unfortunate circumstances, you're the clear thinker among the cadets. I've been keeping tabs on you for a very long time and I know that you're smart. Smart enough to realize that while I might be sitting in a cell at the moment, I remain an excellent ally."

Excellent ally. *That's one possibility*, Marcus thought. Or more likely, a desperate fool.

"What do you think of Moorland?"

Marcus didn't hesitate. "I think she needs me. And she doesn't need you. Or at least she doesn't think she does."

"Those are good assumptions. You're smarter than I gave you credit for."

Flattery, thought Marcus. It was true: he probably was smarter than Owagumbiea gave him credit for. But if the ombudsman believed what he'd said, he wouldn't have said it in the first place. Arrogant people were so predictable.

"Get to the point, Owagumbiea."

The prisoner stood, sliding his giant hands into his pockets. "The council member who formerly owned this fine piece of furniture," he said, gesturing to the chair, "he was a good friend of mine." The man's eyes drifted away from Marcus', staring into the distance. "I admired him. Beautiful wife, three small children ..." The corner of his mouth ticked upward.

Marcus had seen the expression before and knew what it meant: the glee of manipulation. He felt superior to Marcus, and Marcus could work with that. The way forward became clear.

Owagumbiea re-emerged from his thoughts and set his eyes hard on Marcus. "But he was keeping secrets from me. So I cut him down. And I cut his family down. I made him my footstool, as the ancient saying goes."

"Very subtle. But now you're in a prison cell. What's your plan? Do you even have one?"

The ombudsman's face stretched into a maniacal smile. "You're overconfident, aren't you? I remember reading that from your clinical notes. From your Child Advocate, Cassius Sorbet. He seemed fond of you. His disappearance was ... interesting."

Marcus forced himself to remain still. How could the man know? He couldn't. Not for certain. Marcus had destroyed all of the records. The man was bluffing and had nothing to offer but ineffectual threats.

Marcus turned his back to the cell and waited for CATO to clear the security check and the exit door to open. When it slid to the side, Marcus was halfway through it before Owagumbiea called after him.

"Wait ... wait ..."

Marcus slowed but didn't stop.

"My apologies. You're deliciously serious. I promise you, I have no agenda other than to remind you that I make a habit of learning everything I can about future business associates. I'm sure you do the same. It helps when people understand one another and understanding requires knowledge. Come back, and let's discuss how we can help one another."

Marcus looked over his shoulder. "You can't help me. You have nothing to offer."

"Ah, but I do." The ombudsman waved at the bench. "Sit down and I'll explain it to you."

"You've got thirty seconds," Marcus said. He returned to the bench but didn't sit.

"This is what I believe. The *Chimera* will never wake. She's a ghost. We're over two hundred years estranged from her. And my eyes and ears aboard the *Hydra* tell me that the longed for, suddenly-appeared exchange ship was full of nothing more than dead bodies. Even if the *Chimera* did wake, and a crew of half-trained children managed to make the jump, I doubt that Earth is in any position to help us. We can't pin our hopes for the future on a pair of unlikely miracles."

Chimera wasn't a ghost. Marcus felt her. Asleep, maybe, but not in any way dead. It was only a matter of time before she woke. And when she did, he, Marcus, would be there to take the reins. A chill shot up his spine in response to the thought, and he shivered. The main issue was timing, not likelihood. Owagumbiea, blinded by his own desires, was as stupid as anyone else. Marcus wouldn't argue with him.

Owagumbiea's pupils contracted to compact, onyx holes. "You, like myself, are a realist. We have to create a solution for ourselves. Those of us capable of taking bold action, decisive action. I think, knowing what I do about Sorbet, that you are capable of bold, decisive action. Some problems need solving. I can appreciate that. Unfortunately, many others are far less understanding. Especially people looking to protect their power and position."

Marcus' mind ran backward, treading again the laborious steps he'd taken to wipe away his past. It was unlikely the man knew anything for certain, but there was a small chance he might know something damaging. Owagumbiea was down, but he was still dangerous. Best to keep your enemies close.

"All I will say is that I take your point," Marcus said.

If Stephen's Point was doomed, survival would only be achieved if a remnant were saved at the expense of the general population. *He wants to cut the masses out of their share of Mandate resources.* But that scenario was meaningless if whatever—or whoever—had caused the disaster of *Exchange Four* was headed to Stephen's Point. They might arrive any second. The only way to protect himself was to leave.

"You see where I'm going with this?"

"Of course I do. You want to make some changes to the Mandate and you'd like my help."

"The Mandate was flawed from the beginning. Far less drastic than it needed to be. A few of us recognized that unfortunate reality and were prepared to … make necessary changes to the status quo." The man's brows sank and his cheeks slackened in a look of well-practiced concern. "Legally, of course. Unlike Moorland. We failed because of her. And she's backed by the Order's religious zealots. The Order Advisor, Conrad Duncan, is the worst of them. He's nothing more than Moorland's servant. But it's not too late."

"And you're inviting me along on this fully legal humanitarian venture? Why?"

"Because I'm stuck in here and I need someone out there." Owagumbiea chuckled. "You raised yourself, no parents to coddle you. That's why you're smart and direct and know how to take action."

In spite of himself, Marcus enjoyed the new burst of flattery. It helped that all of it was true: he hadn't had parents to lean on. No one had looked out for him except him.

Owagumbiea pointed a long finger at Marcus. "If you help me, you're in a unique position to secure a place within the meritocracy."

"And who will be included in this 'meritocracy?'"

Owagumbiea smiled. "A diverse and highly-skilled group of individuals. Several political advisors and council members, a few entrepreneurs, some financiers and captains of industry. Other notable persons of influence."

"So, the rich."

"Wealth is a byproduct of ingenuity and personal merit. It is emblematic of—if not the complete answer to—what we're looking for."

Marcus nodded, letting his eyes defocus. "How will you implement your plan and how long will it buy us?"

"Once Moorland is out of the picture, we'll have the leverage we need. Several council members will be removed, including Order Advisor Duncan."

Marcus snorted. "He is annoying. He's the one that's convinced there's a Second Stephen among us."

Owagumbiea chuckled. "So you've met the man."

Marcus allowed himself a thin smile. The ombudsman might prove very useful. Behind his insipid personality and labored manner of speech, the man possessed a genuine, admirable cunning. What had Owagumbiea said earlier, about the man he'd removed from the council?

A real shame.

CHAPTER SIX

Sender: Conrad Duncan
Recipient: Alina Moorland
Timestamp: 0189:00:14:37:08

Alina,
I've completed a thorough search of the Order database using the search term "HEL." Among the thousands of results, I found nothing that explains the fate of Exchange Four and its unfortunate cargo any better than "Help" or "Hell," but have sent the full data table regardless in case you have some use for it.

Notable search results:
- *Hel: The goddess of death and the underworld in ancient Norse mythology—the origin of the word "Hell."*
- *Heliosphere, Heliosheath, and Heliopause: Terms relating to properties of the star SOL, the Earth's sun.*
- *Helios: The god of the sun in ancient Greek mythology. Also the name of the ill-fated colony ship lost to fractal space some four hundred Earth years ago.*
- *Helium-3: a rare non-radioactive isotope of Helium, used to power spacecraft. Early settlers mined it in small quantities from the moon's surface before industrial harvesting began at the gas giant Jupiter. Notable because of the substance's high energy potential and continued use in a variety of extant spacecraft.*
- *Helizor: A pre-Last War biochemical company. Later subsumed by the mega-conglomerate Kishabi-Kline, responsible for the founding of the Stephen's Point colony after the divestment of Corex properties and personnel.*

As you can see for yourself, forming a hypothesis based on any of these results would amount to nothing more than wild speculation. Hopefully your investigation into the bodies and the ship will provide more insight into the situation at Earth.

Stephen's Blessings,

Conrad

***Attached: HEL_data_set_prime

* * *

Selena burst through the door of her berth, surprising Kaylee, who lay on her bunk, reading from a handscreen. Kaylee's CATO profile popped up on Selena's overlay. *Kaylee Johns. Valley Training Group, Alpha. Specialties: Science, medicine. Height: 1.55 meters. Weight: 44 kilograms (Earth equivalent).* She looked closely at her features. Tan skin, eyes narrowing at their corners, fine black hair and eyebrows.

"Welcome back," Kaylee said.

"I'm not back," Selena said, shoving Kaylee's profile aside. She grabbed a clean set of off-duty fatigues and entered the tiny bathroom.

Kaylee's voice sounded through the door. "We should get to know each other. You're from the rim, right?"

Selena shed her damp formal uniform. She missed her old khaki pants, patches and all. Her flight jacket that smelled of steam jet lubricant and grease, of her destroyed trawler, of her father. Strange how a smell could transport her to another place, another time. Tugging on the plain blue fatigues and zipping the top closed, a wave of loneliness washed over her. *I'll never see Scrapyard again. Never see* The Bee. *Or Liam.*

"Yes, I will," she said to her reflection in the mirror. The girl with dark circles beneath her eyes didn't appear convinced. Selena scowled at her and launched out of the bathroom, leaving her dirty uniform behind.

Kaylee slid off her bed. "Where are you going?"

"The commons," Selena said, wishing the girl was Rose, wishing people didn't insist on asking her so many damned questions. Was that a Stephen's Point thing? Miners at Scrapyard, the orbital environ where she and Liam had lived before the crash, knew how to keep to themselves. Except when they got drunk. For Liam, that was pretty much every furlough.

"Can I come with you?"

"No!" Selena snapped. Kaylee took an inadvertent step backward. Her legs hit the edge of her bunk and she sat down fast, the bunk's mattress saving her from injury.

"I'm in a hurry," Selena said.

"Okay," Kaylee said. Her eyes said it wasn't okay. That Selena had once again violated one of the unwritten rules that everyone seemed to know but her.

Selena shook her hair into place and frowned. "I had a bad day."

Kaylee brightened a bit. "You did? That stinks. My day wasn't too bad, just busy. They showed me the VAST trainer."

Selena's CATO displayed a countdown timer, which was about to expire. She'd told Theo fifteen minutes and not to be late. She wasn't about to be late herself.

"What were you doing? I didn't see you with any of the training groups," Kaylee continued.

"I'll tell you about it later."

"Sure," Kaylee said, "I'd love to catch up some. Everyone's talking about you. I heard that you—"

"They don't know what they're talking about," Selena said, then bailed from the berth. Before the door slid closed, she felt Kaylee's eyes on her back. Stalking to the commons, Selena decided it was unlikely she and some rich kid from the valley would ever become friends.

Arriving at the commons, Selena approached a commissary machine and selected hot tea. Cadets sat in groups, chatting. Their eyes drifted in her direction. Some lingered, overt in their curiosity. They probably saw her as an oddity at best, a threat at worst. She didn't care what they thought. Let them stare.

She waited until the panel of the commissary machine slid open to reveal a steaming mug and took it to a corner alcove where she could see both entrances.

A blond kid with tousled hair met her eyes, smiled. She looked away, but the kid left his group of friends and approached her table.

"You must be Selena Samuelson," he said.

She lifted her mug of tea and inhaled pungent, earthy steam. *Charlie Gray. East End Training Group. Specialties: Tactics, analysis. Height: 1.85 meters. Weight: 84 kilograms (Earth equivalent).* Tall, muscular. A meathead.

"You're from the rim?" the boy asked.

"What's it to you?"

"Is it true that your toilets vacate into the vacuum?"

Selena gave Charlie a stony look. "Is that what you came over here to ask me?"

Charlie rested a hand on the table and flashed her an easy smile. "Mind if I join you?"

"Yes. I do."

"No problem, I can talk to you standing up."

Selena considered dumping her tea on the kid's feet. "Go away."

"Are you always this grumpy?"

"I'm not grumpy. I just don't like chit-chatting with idiots."

His smile wavered. "It's okay if you're grumpy. I like grumpy girls. And for the record, nobody that made it up here is an idiot."

Selena took a sip of tea. "You're doing your best to convince me otherwise."

Charlie lingered at the table's edge but she refused to make eye contact. She drained the rest of her tea and leaned back in her chair. After a few moments of awkward silence, Charlie's shoulders fell.

"I guess I'll see you around," he said before shambling away.

Selena closed her eyes, rubbed her forehead.

"I see you met my bunkmate." Theo slipped into the seat opposite her, setting down two steaming mugs of tea between them.

"That guy's your bunkmate?" Selena asked.

"Yep. He's got *six* siblings."

Selena found it hard to imagine having *one* sibling. Her mother had died when she was four, leaving her with Liam as her only surviving family. The idea of a sister or a brother, someone who shared some of her DNA, her features ….

A message popped up on her CATO. It contained a photo of a little girl with wild blond hair in tufts around her grinning face. It resembled the one across the table. A rounded face with dimples in each cheek. Expressive eyes.

"That's my sister, Liddy," Theo said. "She's five."

"She looks like she knows what she wants."

"She thinks she does," Theo said, laughing. "Do you have any brothers or sisters?"

Selena shifted, uncomfortable. This wasn't the way she wanted the conversation to go. "I'd like to see Ashley's journal."

"You can't."

Selena gripped her empty mug with both hands. He'd lied. He didn't have any journal. But why? What did he want from her? *The same thing as any other scumbag.*

"Let me guess," Selena said, leaning across the table. "It's back at your berth. You sent Charlie over here as your wingman, and now you're going to try and close the deal. Showing me your all-too-adorable little sister—that was a good move. I bet that's worked really well for you in the past, hasn't it?"

"What are you talking about?" Theo asked. Confusion spread across his face.

"You're trying to con me," Selena said.

Theo's face remained unchanged. If he was conning her, it would be one of the best she'd ever seen. The expression on his face—he couldn't be faking that, could he?

Another CATO message arrived. An image of a burly, bearded man in an Order robe. *[Doctor Conrad Duncan. Order Advisor to the Regulatory. Dual degrees in geology and philosophy.]*

"Duncan gave me the journal," Theo said. "I read it, memorized it, and gave it back when I finished."

"Why?" Selena asked.

"Why did he give me the journal or why did I give it back?"

"Both," Selena said, stewing in a mixture of embarrassment and curiosity.

"He gave it to me to help me succeed in the Selection training. And because he thinks I'm some sort of prophet. Not really a prophet, but someone special. Kind of like Stephen."

"Like Stephen?" She couldn't hide the derision in her voice.

"I know, I know. I don't think that myself. But the journal … It's full of information on the journey from Earth to Elypso. I don't understand a lot of it. But you might."

Selena swapped her empty mug with the full one Theo had brought. She sucked the dark tea through her teeth and swallowed. "Can you tell me what the journal said?"

"Yes. But it will take some time. I memorized it in chunks and I don't know which parts might be important. There's a lot in it about Ashley's girlfriend Amaya and their baby. But I don't think that stuff will be relevant."

"Amaya," Selena whispered, trying out the foreign-sounding name.

"Yeah, he wrote *a lot* about her." Theo's face went pink and he looked away.

Selena rescued him. "Why don't you tell me something you think might be important? Then I can decide if it will help me or not."

"Sure," Theo said. "But not here. Not right now."

"Why not?"

"I promised Duncan that I wouldn't tell anyone about what I read in the journal. It's supposed to be a secret."

"Why tell me, then?" Selena asked, surprised by the conviction in Theo's voice. "Wouldn't that be breaking your promise?"

"You're different," Theo said. "For one, you're from the rim. And two, the journal should be yours anyway. You're Ashley's descendant."

"And Amaya's," Selena said, letting the word fill her, grateful for even this tiny bit of insight into her heritage, thrilled with the prospect of learning more.

Theo shook his head, a look of wonderment on his face. "A descendant of the original flight crew. I can't believe I'm sitting here with you. I know some of the other cadets from different training groups are descendants as well, but none from a Navigator's Assistant."

Selena smiled despite herself. Proud, and for the first time in ages, hopeful.

Theo drained his tea. "We should make a plan," he said.

"A plan?"

"To wake the *Chimera*. We can meet up, go on board. Then I'll tell you all about the journal and we can figure out what we need to do. Together."

Selena didn't think that sounded like much of a plan, but she kept her mouth shut. Maybe Theo really could help her. Maybe he held the key to unlocking the *Chimera*'s prison. She believed it. Or at least, she wanted to believe it.

"We'll go during the cadet sleep cycle. I don't want a bunch of people asking us questions." Theo looked at her, eyes sparkling. "You draw a lot of attention."

"Yeah, I've noticed," Selena said. "But won't that mess up our sleep?"

Theo looked down into his tea. "I'm not sleeping that great anyway."

"Your body hasn't adapted to being in space," Selena said. "I wasn't used to sleeping in full gravity when I first got here. Took me a few cycles to adjust."

"It's not that. I keep having these weird dreams."

"What kind of dreams?"

"About *Exchange Four.*"

He didn't have to explain. She looked at him, frowning. "What do you think happened to them?"

"Fractal space. It does terrible things to people."

"I mean at Earth."

Theo shrugged. "Things must be really bad back there. Have you asked Moorland about it?"

"She wouldn't tell me."

Theo's mug scraped the table as he twirled it in a circle. Something about the motion reminded her of Scrapyard, rotating against a star field.

"I thought you two were close? Moorland hasn't taken anyone else off on special adventures to the *Chimera.*"

What should she tell him? An even better question: why did she want to tell him anything? Why did she need to? Because they went through *Exchange Four* together? Because of the journal? Neither of those things explained the feeling lurking at the edge of her consciousness, the sense of connection she felt to Theo.

"It didn't work," Selena said. "The *Chimera* didn't reach out for me this time."

"Meaning she reached out before?" Theo's face became intense. His eyes locked on hers. "What did she say?"

"It's not like that. It isn't a conversation like we're having now. It's so hard to explain ..."

"The grass parts. The pathway opens," Theo said.

"What?"

"It's from the journal. Something Ashley wrote."

"What else did he write?" Selena asked.

Theo's lips began to move, as if whispering something only he could hear. His voice returned to normal volume, though he spoke in a monotone. "When the shift change comes and the NAs go to quarters, I'm the last to unsync. For a moment I feel the weight of her presence, terrible in its power and intensity. I unsync and leave Stephen alone, shaken to my core, knowing that the tiny portion of *her* I helped hold was nothing more than a grain of sand from a vast seashore."

Goodbye, friend.

"What's wrong?" Theo asked, noticing the look on her face.

She couldn't speak, didn't trust her voice. If she opened herself even that much, she wasn't sure what might slip out. What she might never get back. She shook her head, hair spilling around her cheeks, unwilling to look at him, to be looked at. He hadn't lied. He held something inside him, too. Memories of events Selena could ... imagine? Remember?

The grass parts. The pathway opens.

"I was in the sphere," Selena said, tongue stumbling, willing herself to talk, to tell. "And then I saw ... fractal space. I *felt* her. She's locked up. She wants out, but she can't find the way. She's blocked by something, and she can't remember how to get loose or doesn't have the ability to do it anymore. She was so sad ..."

Theo reached across the table and somehow her hand met his halfway, her cold fingers wrapped in his warm ones. She liked the sense of closeness but also found it unbearable. She yanked her hand away and buried it in her lap.

"Are you okay?" Theo asked.

Why does everyone keep asking me that?

"I don't know," she said. "When I went into the sphere earlier, I couldn't find her. Or she couldn't find me. It's so confusing. I told Moorland I don't know how to find the *Chimera*, but she's convinced the ship chose me or something. And my father's down at Principal Hospital and if I don't wake the *Chimera* Moorland won't have a reason—"

She stopped herself. She wasn't going to talk about this. Not to Theo. Not to anyone.

Theo's face hadn't lost its look of intense concentration. "What were you thinking when you went into the sphere?"

Selena's teeth clamped together and her jaw muscles bulged. "Nothing."

"That can't be true. You must have been thinking of something really specific. Something *Chimera* used to find you. That's how it works. At least, I think it does." Theo leaned close. "The Salix Protocols established a locksafe on arrival. Neural nets retract, with only base-level algorithms driving system architecture. After her final act—the construction of the exchange dock—she retreats to secondary and her body becomes only a shell."

"Stop quoting stuff to me," Selena said, louder than she intended. Cadets turned to look at them.

"Okay," Theo said, looking a little sheepish. "But you need to trust me. Meet me here at twenty-two hundred hours and we'll go wake the ship."

How could he be so confident? Selena didn't like his plan, but to her annoyance, didn't have a better one herself. Besides, she wanted to learn more about Ashley and Amaya and hear more of the journal. Even if they didn't wake the *Chimera*, it wouldn't be a total waste.

"All right," she said. "Twenty-two hundred hours."

Theo grinned at her. "See you then."

He jumped from his seat and walked away.

Selena studied the three empty mugs a moment, then stood and returned them to the commissary machine, every cadet in the commons watching her.

Keep watching, she thought. *You haven't seen anything yet.*

CHAPTER SEVEN

Charlie watched Theo from behind a handscreen. Each time Theo looked his way, Charlie's eyes dropped back to the glowing screen. *You're not fooling anyone,* Theo thought. He'd deflected his bunkmate's questions until Charlie grew tired of asking them and pulled out his handscreen.

"You know you can read and watch videos on your CATO," Theo said.

Charlie laid the handscreen next to his leg and slid himself upright, using the wall like a chair back. "It's not the same," Charlie said. "I like holding something in my hands. Lying there with my eyes open, staring at images—I don't like it."

"Makes it easier to spy on me, too."

Charlie flushed. "Come on, man. You've got to tell me what she said! I couldn't even get her to make eye contact. She talked to you for almost an hour."

"Were you timing us?"

"CATO makes that sort of thing easy," Charlie said, smiling. "Fifty-three minutes, ten seconds if you're interested."

"That's creepy," Theo said. "You're creepy."

"I'm not creepy, but I am wicked curious about what's going on with you and the rimmer girl. She went into *Exchange Four* just like you. What did you guys find in there?"

"Why, are you scared?" Theo asked.

Charlie looked at him, weighing if Theo was insulting him. "I don't know," he said. "Should I be?"

Good question. Probably. "Moorland said she'd brief everyone about *Exchange Four* once she'd made a thorough investigation of the facts," Theo said. "She ordered me not to tell anyone what I saw until after her briefing."

"I heard there were bodies," Charlie said, his pupils dark pools in the dim light of the berth.

Theo said nothing but gave the slightest of nods.

"Who?"

"I don't know," Theo said. "Look, it doesn't matter. I don't know much of anything. We'll wait for Moorland. She'll tell us what we need to know."

Charlie considered that, then smiled. "Moorland didn't command you not to tell me what that Samuelson girl told you. You guys were all hush-hush. I think she likes you. And I think you like her."

The door chimed twice. Before Theo or Charlie could rise to open it, the lock cycled.

"What the—"

Charlie lunged out of bed with a quickness that suggested he knew how to handle himself. Sluggish, Theo pushed himself upright. He wasn't surprised when Marcus stepped through the door.

"Cadet Gray, please excuse yourself. Cadet Puck and I need to talk."

Charlie looked at Marcus for a second, a frown on his lips. Not from the Swallows group, Charlie hadn't seen Marcus in action yet. He didn't understand the consequences of disobeying him.

"Why don't *you* go to the commons?" Charlie said.

"Because what we need to discuss is a private matter."

Theo found it interesting that Marcus deigned to give the other boy a real response rather than applying psychological or physical pressure. Since arriving at the *Hydra*, Marcus had become much more diplomatic. *Gunning for captain.* What had Charlie called him? *A shiner.*

"We won't be long," Marcus said. Almost friendly. Almost smiling. "Don't go spreading stupid rumors while you're gone, though. There're enough floating around as it is."

Charlie scowled at Marcus and left the berth.

Marcus wasted no time. "The *Hydra* is on lockdown. No communication between us and Stephen's Point. I tried finding a backdoor through the nets, but we're limited to locals only. The last impression I can find from the full net is about fifteen seconds after the feed from *Exchange Four* hit Stephen's Point. Moorland works fast." Theo detected a hint of grudging respect in his tone.

"Do you know why?"

"She must feel it's imperative to the mission."

Marcus was holding something back—behind his furrowed brow, his mind was cranking. Theo knew better than to press him. Marcus would tell him what he wanted him to know. Nothing more and nothing less.

Marcus sat in one of the chairs that accompanied a small table in the corner and crossed one leg over the other. He tilted his head at the other chair, inviting Theo to join him. Theo complied, pulling tight against the tabletop. He let the side cut into his midsection, comforted by the sense of protection it gave him.

"I want to show you something," Marcus said.

"What?"

Marcus' eyes moved, executing CATO commands. The wallscreen next the table came to life and a video began to play. Theo immediately turned his face away.

"Look at it, Theo."

"Why should I? I was there, remember? Unlike you."

"You've got to give up this martyr nonsense. Do you really think the Regulatory invested all this time training and preparing us so we could die in a common accident? You, me, the rest of the cadets—we're the most valuable resource the colony has. Without us, the *Chimera* is useless. I evaluated my worth versus that of the welders. I made a judgment call and left because it was the right thing to do. So come off it."

Theo couldn't think of a good comeback. That was the thing about Marcus—Theo always felt twisted and confused after talking to him. Like he couldn't trust his own opinion about anything.

"Are you going to look at the video?"

"Like I said, I've seen it already. Smelled it. Lived it."

"Wonderful. Then it shouldn't bother you to watch it again."

"I don't see the point!" Theo stood. "You can go now. I need to sleep."

Marcus' eyes gleamed like he'd bested Theo at something. The flicker of motion on the wallscreen froze on an image of Theo's face as Selena dragged him through the airlock that led to the *Hydra*. The video zoomed in on Theo's eyes. Vacant and glossed over, they peered into the middle distance, taking in nothing.

Marcus gestured at the screen. "You're having problems

sleeping. When you do, you suffer from nightmares. You wake coated in sweat. Lots of sweat. Certain things bother you—noises, smells, images. They come when you least expect it. Something triggers you and you freeze up as the panic takes over your body."

Theo backed away from the wallscreen, unwilling to admit that *everything* Marcus had said was true. "I didn't realize you were a doctor. What's my diagnosis? Space flu?"

"You have a problem, Theo. I've seen you under extreme stress during our Selection training. You didn't break then. You got stronger. But I'm worried this might be too much, even for you."

Marcus' eyes moved and a different video played on the wallscreen. This one showed Theo and Meghan standing in the hallway moments after Theo had returned from medbay.

"How'd you get that?" Theo asked.

Marcus ignored his question and pointed at Meghan. "I see you've found a replacement for your mother." His voice dropped. "Look at you. Look at your eyes. Zoned out. Distant. She's touching you, and you don't care."

Theo recognized the truth of what Marcus had said. He had been acting strange. Feeling strange. "Why is *everyone* spying on me?" Theo asked, disgusted. "Why do you suddenly care so much?"

"Everyone isn't spying on you," Marcus said. "Not you specifically. The feed is from the security monitors in the commons. We're under constant surveillance out there. Restricted feeds from our rooms—passive unless monitored remotely by someone like Moorland. So don't let the prospect of being on camera stop you next time you need to take a dump. They'll only watch if they have a good reason. And you're giving them one. That's why I locked down the monitors for the purposes of this conversation. I made it look like a simple service interrupt. They'll schedule a repair, but by the time technicians get assigned the work order, the feed will be back up."

"You gained access to all the security feeds?" Theo asked.

"You're not the only one that knows how to hack."

Why did Theo always feel two steps behind? He sorted through the last few minutes of their conversation and settled on the question he needed answered most of all.

"What are you trying to say about me? And why do you care?"

"This anxiety—it can cripple you if you let it. But we're not going to let that happen. It's important you maintain mental fecundity—sharpness—if you're going to wake the *Chimera* and then go on to crew her. You can't tell anyone about your mental problems. They'll sideline you, and you'll never make the cut to crew the *Chimera*. I need you with me—not just during the training, but for the actual mission. I have a vested interest, so to speak."

Theo smiled, and then hated himself for it. *Marcus isn't your friend. Never forget the cave. Never forget the body. What he forced you to do. He'll use you, just like he uses everything and everyone. And when he doesn't need you anymore ...*

"If you're questioned about the incident or about your behavior, answer in simple statements that affirm that you're feeling well. Use phrases such as 'I believe so,' 'maybe so,' or 'I doubt it.' These answers will imply that you are lucid, while frustrating further inquisition."

"I'll try," muttered Theo.

"It'll be difficult. As much as possible, refrain from thinking about what you saw. Block that part of your mind. Ignore it. Eventually, it'll stay locked up."

Even Marcus' mention of the incident caused gruesome images to flash across his mind. Theo spoke to keep them at bay, to distract himself. "What do you think is happening down on Stephen's Point?"

"The crisis must be bigger than what we can see," Marcus replied. "Moorland's trying to figure out her next move. I suspect she'll address us next duty cycle and tell everyone what they found in *Exchange Four*."

The room seemed to expand around Theo. The sensation of suspension over a vast depth of empty nothing caused his stomach to flutter. "You mean other than the bodies?"

"Yes. I'm sure they've processed their clothing and possessions for clues. I'm sure they've already analyzed the bodies. What food did they ingest? What sort of medical care have they received? What does their DNA suggest?"

"You've got it all figured out, huh?"

"No, Theo. I don't. I've refrained from accessing any Regulatory files. They might not catch me, but if they did, they'd send me back to Stephen's Point."

"Or shove you out an airlock," Theo said.

Marcus grinned. "You've watched too many vids."

"You better be careful," Theo said. "If I'm a priority, they might get technicians on that service interrupt faster than you expect. They might have already gotten the feed back up and Moorland is watching this entire conversion."

Theo enjoyed seeing Marcus stiffen at the suggestion that he'd overreached. The wallscreen went dark. Marcus smiled his genuine not-being-a-shiner smile. "You're getting better at this," he said. "I'm glad we fixed things between us."

Fixed things. That was certainly one way to put it. Stalemate was another. Or mutually assured destruction. Theo knew Marcus' secret, and Marcus had evidence tying Theo to a murder. *Not a murder,* he reminded himself. *A justified killing.* Marcus had taken out his former child advocate. An abuser. Theo thought of Marcus' face and eyes in the cave. His eyes in the medbay only cycles ago when Marcus at long last answered Theo's question. "What did he do to you?" What indeed.

Everything. Marcus had said it with so much hate in his voice that the mere memory of it made Theo's throat tighten. *Everything.*

"There's one more thing for us to discuss," Marcus said, oblivious to Theo's line of thought.

"What?"

"Selena Samuelson."

Theo kept his face blank. "What about her?"

"She's a huge risk. She didn't train with us. She could jeopardize the mission."

"I don't see how."

Marcus clamped a hand on his shoulder. "Trust me on this one. She's not going to make the cut. Don't form any alliances with her or she might take you down with her."

So Marcus would make sure Selena didn't make it aboard the *Chimera.* It didn't surprise him. "Okay," he said, holding back his arguments, his anger.

"I'm glad we can agree on this. If we stick together, nobody can stop us."

Stop us from doing what? Theo wondered. "She might be useful in waking the *Chimera,*" Theo said. "She has some special connection to the ship."

"Why do you think that?"

"She told me herself. Moorland personally took her to the sphere last duty cycle." If he told Marcus almost everything, he wouldn't suspect Theo of holding things back. Marcus was right. He *was* getting better at this.

"Interesting," Marcus said.

"I've convinced her to help me wake the ship," Theo offered. "I told her just enough about the journal to earn her allegiance."

Marcus' eyes locked on Theo's face. There was a strange glow behind those pale irises. A cold sort of fire, but one that could still burn. "Excellent," Marcus said. "Learn everything you can from her. When you do wake the *Chimera*, make sure you get the credit. Be on the lookout for some way to discredit her. But don't spend too much time on it. Waking the *Chimera* is the most important thing. You can leave Samuelson to me."

"Sure," Theo said. Easy. Casual. His mind rolling and bouncing, his tongue dry in his mouth. "Sure," he said again, eyes linked with Marcus'. "You can count on me."

CHAPTER EIGHT

Marcus skimmed the data he'd pulled from Moorland's files as he sprinted down the *Hydra*'s corridors, rehearsing his coming conversation with the ombudsman. Variations, subtle differences in phraseology and nuance. The files were downloaded. Anything relating to Ombudsman Owagumbiea, the Mandate, and Moorland's personal communiqués with the council. Waiting to unleash their sordid political secrets.

He'd found only one unexpected item: an encrypted set of files titled "Helvictus." Glancing through the documents, he'd seen enough to know that it was mainly system architecture but included a set of suggestive schematics. He'd downloaded everything and saved that particular file separate from the ombudsman's.

The contents didn't exactly surprise him; they confirmed an assumption he had made back in the early days of the training. Moorland, along with at least a few of the other council members responsible for the Mandate, understood reality. She would do anything to protect the colony—even violate the compact with Earth. In spite of himself, it made Marcus like the woman.

Regulator Forester sat at his terminal at the entrance to the brig.

"Forester," Marcus said.

"Cadet Locke."

"Any visitors that I should know about?"

Forester shook his head. "No one but you."

Marcus nodded. "I'll see him now."

The doors cycled open and Marcus entered the bright lobby. Owagumbiea stood inside his tiny cell, his face covered with a wide grin. "I wasn't sure that you'd make it. But you're prompt as usual."

"I've brought you what you requested."

"I expected nothing less. You're no fool. Not like the establishmentarians supervising this overindulgent waste of resources. I'd be lying if I said I'm not anxious to be free of my present confines. You simply wouldn't believe the plans we have for the Golden Valley—a true luxury community—with enough resources to last us all several lifetimes."

The man might as well rub his hands together and cackle.

"I'd like you to know that I'm recording this conversation," Marcus said.

Owagumbiea's face shifted, grinding gears turning inside his skull.

"I need a record of this conversation. People have a way of forgetting their promises."

"Don't be difficult, Marcus. You know you can trust me."

"No, I don't know that. And I'm the one taking all the risks. Look at it from my perspective—I want a guarantee."

Owagumbiea's eyes narrowed to slits, his well-oiled skin so dark it appeared almost blue. He pointed a finger at Marcus' chest. "Don't mess with me, boy. Do you have something to show me or not?"

"I'm not messing with you. I'm protecting my interests. And yes, I do have something for you." Using his CATO, Marcus pulled up a file and projected it from his handscreen onto the interior wall of the ombudsman's cell.

Owagumbiea traced the text of Moorland's order to quarantine the *Hydra*. "This is all you've got?"

Marcus shrugged. "That's just a small sample. It's representative of the rest of the files. With them, you'll have no problem proving Moorland has subverted the Mandate."

"That's good," he said, "But I want to see more. I need an open and shut case. Do you have proof of any violation of the compact with Earth? If there were proof that Moorland violated the divestment agreement, our case would make itself."

"I may be able to find evidence to that effect, but it will take me some time to find it."

As Marcus expected, Owagumbiea shook his head. "No, no. We do not have the luxury of time." He pursed his lips. "What you've found will have to be enough."

"What should I do with the files?" Marcus asked. "We're still in lockdown. Even I haven't been able to figure out how to access the Stephen's Point nets."

"You can give them to Regulator Numonikov in Communications. She'll ensure they make their way to the council.

Then it's just a matter of organizing a little surprise for Moorland. I can't wait! Actually, that's not true—I will happily wait to have my chance to send her down for public trial and execution."

The man was pathetic. "What's your timeline?"

"One day. Possibly two. I'll get word to you through Forester."

"All right. Now I want you to articulate what I'm getting in exchange."

"Happily." Owagumbiea reached up, resting a relaxed palm on the transparent boundary between them. "I personally guarantee Marcus J. Locke immunity in the coming purge. His status in the new government of Stephen's Point is immutable, and cannot be revoked."

Marcus frowned. "That's the best you can do?"

"I'm not finished." Owagumbiea looked hurt. "I also decree, as the first order of the rising meritocracy, that Marcus J. Locke shall suffer no harm, judgment, or legal repercussions for his actions. He will be considered a hero of the meritocracy and given standing commensurate with his formidable intellect and loyalty. Let this be an official record of said order."

Marcus raised an eyebrow. "Who else is going to lead this 'meritocracy' of yours?"

Owagumbiea adopted a pompous tone, "You'll find out in a few days."

Marcus looked into the ombudsman's eyes. "Considering I'll soon be taking my place alongside you on the council, I want to know now."

"On the council?"

"That's right. I get to be your right hand."

Owagumbiea looked thoughtful. "That's not a terrible idea," he said after a pause. "There's some fat to be trimmed from the council. And you've shown yourself to be resourceful—unlike the bloated, faux democracy governing now. The meritocracy places a great value on aptitude. Yes, I like the idea. You'll make a wonderful replacement for Councilmember Klapp."

"Klapp? Not Bennet?"

"Bennet has her place. She's spiteful, closed-minded even, but she's from the lower end of our economic threshold and it's good to show that the meritocracy has room for the deserving middle classes. And every government needs a few blunt instruments. Nothing works better for cracking skulls." Owagumbiea dabbed his forehead with his handkerchief, once again glowing with excitement. "Peuthro, Westmeister, Faulkans, Bennet, Garisson, and Locke," he said. "All answering to President Owagumbiea."

Marcus returned the man's smile. "President Owagumbiea?"

"Yes?"

"I have one small request for you."

The ombudsman chuckled. "You're not going to ask me to give you all the ecomire in the universe, are you?"

"No, nothing like that. I want you to say hello to a good friend of mine since we're making history here today. You know, for the record."

"I would be delighted."

"She's watching via a live feed right now."

The ombudsman's smile tarnished from bright silver to water-spotted chrome. "Who...?"

Marcus gave the ombudsman a cheerful smile. "Chief Moorland, of course."

CHAPTER NINE

He hadn't slept a minute. After Marcus left and an annoyed but quiet Charlie returned, Theo lay on his bunk in silence. He slowed his breathing, simulating sleep since he couldn't manage to do the real thing. Marcus' words, images from *Exchange Four*, and thoughts of Selena overlapped in his memory. He rolled and tossed and adjusted his pillow. Scratched the scar on his abdomen. Went over the various sections of the journal that had anything to do with syncing or unsyncing with the ship. The *Chimera* had attempted to sync with Selena, meaning she met all criteria governed by the Salix protocols. What those criteria were, he could only guess.

The sound of Charlie's regular breathing filled the berth. When at last the counter reached t-minus twenty minutes, he left his bed and started changing clothes as quietly as possible.

"What are you doing?" Charlie asked.

Not quietly enough, apparently.

"Nothing."

"I'm coming with you."

"No, you're not."

Charlie slung his legs over the side of his bunk. "You're going to meet a girl, aren't you?"

"No. I'm going ... on a training exercise."

"No, you're not.

Theo pulled his uniform top over his head. "Look, if I tell you the truth, will you promise to leave me alone?"

Charlie's eyes gleamed in the darkness. "Okay, sure."

"You're right. I'm going to meet Selena."

"I knew it!"

"We're sneaking aboard the *Chimera* to try and wake her up."

Charlie laughed. "Okay, whatever, Theo. You don't have to tell me if you really don't want to."

"That's the truth," Theo said. "You'll see."

Charlie pushed back against his pillow and folded his hands across his midsection. "I'm not holding my breath. But next time you plan another late night 'training exercise,' let me know beforehand."

"Sure," Theo said, and then he slid out of the berth and into the corridor.

When he reached the commons, he sat on the edge of a white sofa, knees bouncing. He wore a standard gray uniform rather than fatigues. His duty cycle wouldn't start for another five hours, but gaining access to the *Chimera* might require a bit of bluffing. The uniform could make the difference between success and failure. But what if Selena arrived in fatigues? Mismatched, they'd stick out. He fired her a quick CATO message asking her to wear grays, noting the similarity between the slang word for a standard uniform and Charlie's last name. Selena didn't reply. Maybe she'd fallen asleep. Maybe she'd decided not to come.

His legs jiggled faster.

This was a bad idea. He shouldn't have suggested it. He should go back to bed—

Selena strode through the entryway. Her wavy dark hair curled behind her ears, held in place by gel—a longer version of Moorland's hairstyle. Deep brown eyes sparkling, she offered him a sardonic half-smile.

"Ready?"

He shot to his feet. "Yeah—wow—I wasn't sure you'd come."

She rolled her eyes. "I said I would. Now let's get moving before someone sees us."

They exited the commons and hurried down the corridor leading to the outer ring of the *Hydra*. When they reached the lift, Theo paused at the graphical overlay, scanning for the right selection.

"You're a real navigator," Selena said, reaching around him to flick to the correct overlay. The centripetal force generated by the spin of the *Hydra*'s rings disoriented Theo. Down felt like up. Up like down. Stepping off the lift, nausea crashed over him. Here, the curvature of the floor was obvious. Real or imagined, he sensed the spin of the ring, dragging his feet down faster than his head, creating a localized Coriolis effect.

"If you need to puke, do it over there," Selena said, pointing to a waste slot built into the wall.

He'd puked inside his pressure suit waiting to enter *Exchange Four*. A vac had whisked the waste away from his face and a servo arm cleaned the visor of his helmet. It had happened so fast and was cleaned up so quickly it was almost like it hadn't happened. If he vomited here, it would be worse. Much worse.

Unsteady on his legs, Theo approached the waste slot and waited. His mouth filled with saliva. "I'm okay," he said, insides slithering like a snake.

"Another thing to get used to," Selena said. "I'm sure that's why Moorland's held off bringing any of the other cadets to the inner ring."

"You should've warned me."

"Wouldn't have mattered. Besides, you seem to be handling it okay."

She set off up the ring, the horizon a constant, rising line in front of her. He glanced over his shoulder. It was like standing at the bottom of a huge pipe. His stomach gurgled again.

"It's easier when you're moving," Selena said. "Follow me."

The air pressured changed. Moved with them, like wind at their backs. Soon they reached a large, vertical airlock.

"This opens to the umbilical," Selena said.

"Do we need pressure suits?"

"Nope. The whole ship is pressurized. You might want to grab a vac though, just in case."

They climbed the ladder and entered a small utility locker. Selena put on her gravity boots and then helped Theo with his. They cinched down around his ankles, heavy and cold against his skin. Suction points lined their soles, able to affix him to almost any surface.

Selena handed him a small toolkit that included a set of repair tools and a dedicated vac.

"Just in case," he said, hoping he wouldn't puke. He didn't want to make a habit of it.

The airlock cycled, opening to the pale pink walls of the umbilical on the other side. It turned in front of them, a steady 1.24 rotations per minute. *No, the umbilical isn't moving. We are.*

"You've got to just step in," Selena said. "It feels weird, but your boots will orient you once you do."

Sure they will. Theo gripped the toolkit, heart racing. Selena went to the edge of the airlock, turned backward, and dropped herself through the opening. She floated, flipped head over heels, and landed feet-first on the umbilical. She faced him, rotating upward and to his right, grinning.

"Here goes," Theo said. He leapt into the zero gravity. His momentum carried him forward, body still rotating from the spin of the station, arms sprawled out in front of him. He grabbed at the floor, the wall rushing at him far faster than he'd anticipated. His hands bounced off the warm elastic surface of the umbilical. He bumped, rebounded. His boots found the surface and with a hungry suction sound, snapping him into place.

He shoved off the wall with his hands. It felt like doing some crazy yoga position. *The flying monkey.*

Laughter. He twisted, turning to Selena.

"Drop something?" He jumped in surprise. To Theo's left, on the rising side of the ring, Selena's head appeared to be at a right angle to his own. She held the toolkit out to him. His stomach did something unnatural. He clamped his teeth shut.

Selena laughed again. "You're such a flameback."

"Flameback?"

"That's what we call the jerks that came to Scrapyard for the ecomire rush. Most of 'em had good funding, lots of fancy toys, but not a lick of sense or skill."

Theo's face burned. He took shuffling, awkward sidesteps until he came up beside her.

"I should have helped you," Selena said, touching his shoulder. She handed him the toolkit again, and this time he took it. "You're lucky you didn't hurt yourself."

Theo mimicked Selena's wide, plodding stride as they moved down the umbilical. It felt like they'd entered an intestine.

"Wish you had your cuffs," he said. "We'd get there quicker."

"And attract a hell of a lot of attention in the process."

"Speaking of which—if anyone asks, we're here for a training exercise," Theo said.

"What sort of training exercise?"

"I don't know."

"You really thought this through, didn't you?"

Ahead, a utility worker maneuvered a free-floating cart down the umbilical. When they neared him, Theo nodded and the man nodded back. "Nobody's going to question us," Theo whispered. "We're cadets."

"Hope you're right. Because you're about as bad at lying as you are at moving in micro grav."

"Wow, you're just full of encouragement," Theo said. "Do you treat all your friends like this?"

Selena have him a careful look. "Sorry about earlier. What I said about Charlie and all that. I'm used to rimmers. Everyone has an angle. Everyone scratching something out, trying to get over on the other guy."

"What about you?" Theo asked.

"About the same. Except I don't lie or cheat to get what I want. I try and beat people fair and square."

"Like leaving me to jump into the umbilical without a single word of advice?"

She laughed. "I gave you a demonstration. Look, you'll get better at this stuff. It takes time. I've had my whole life to learn."

"About that," Theo said. "How'd you end up at the rim in the first place?"

"My dad brought me up after …"

Theo waited, but Selena didn't finish her sentence. He made a mental note to ask her about it later.

The airlock at the end of the umbilical cycled, and they stepped aboard the *Chimera*. Massive arches supported shield plates that wrapped the junction where two of the six colony pods once rested against the *Chimera*'s spine. The pods were now embedded in Stephen's Point's surface. The structure that had held them in place during the flight from Earth remained. Over the last half-dozen years, welding teams had restored the ship using harvested parts from the exchange dock. The repairs had transformed a once bulky ship into one shaped like a javelin.

"Whoa," Theo said, taking in the crosshatch. "It's huge!"

"Pretty impressive," Selena agreed.

Fifty meters in width, the crosshatch provided access to rest of the ship. A tram line ran the *Chimera*'s length, connecting the command deck at her fore, the crosshatch at her middle, and the drivetrain and cores at her aft. The space had a cold, industrial feel, nothing like the efficient but pleasant *Hydra*. Banks of lights built into the ceiling, each as large as his mother's kitchen table, remained unpowered. Tripod-mounted floor lamps cast eerie shadows over the deck plates.

"What's that smell?" Theo asked.

"Sulfur. Some of the decking came from ore smelters."

He chuckled.

"What?"

"It's a little ironic. People stripped her for parts after we got to Elypso. Half of Scrapyard is made from her exterior shell, right? And now we're piecing her together from other ships and the exchange dock, and everything we can get our hands on. She made the colony and now the colony is making her. She sort of *is* the colony."

"You're weird," Selena said, but he could tell she was thinking about it.

A group of workers waited on the tram platform. Selena strode forward and joined them. Theo felt like an impostor. But when the tram arrived they boarded it like everyone else and took seats opposite one another. Some of the workers threw curious glances their way, but nobody said anything.

They arrived at the fore of the ship and disembarked. Above, blue light panels rippled and pulsed like the surface of water. The space had an organic feel, like it had grown, huge and ponderous, birthed from the umbilical. The rounded passageway reminded Theo of images of a ceremonial garden at the center of one of the original colony pods—a space devoted to one of the religions that had disappeared after the *Chimera* arrived at Stephen's Point. A strange sense of familiarity rose in him—like waking from a dream that mimicked life so well that for a moment you were unsure what was and wasn't real. *Stephen rode this same tram. Walked these corridors.* Theo shivered.

The size of the command deck surprised Theo. The descriptions from the journal gave the impression of a sweeping, open space. In person, the oval room wasn't much bigger than an Order classroom. The sphere in the center dominated everything. Technicians sat at substations, reading screens, parsing data, working extra duty cycles to try and wake the *Chimera*.

"Can we go in the sphere?" Theo asked.

"That's the point, right?" Selena raised her voice. "Hey guys, we're going into the sphere."

A bald man stood up from behind a substation and pointed at

Theo. "He's not authorized to be here. Neither are you. Not without Moorland."

"Yes, as a matter of fact, I am," Selena said. "Moorland wants me to take another stab at waking the *Chimera*."

"A big fat waste of time. Neither of you knows a damned thing about cognitive analytics or synaptic modeling."

"No, and we don't need to. That's your job, ace. Now leave us alone while we do what we came to do."

"Which is what?"

Selena's voice was as hard as shield plating. "Whatever the hell we want."

Theo couldn't help but smile. Selena didn't mess around. He would never have spoken to an adult like that. In some ways she was like Marcus—confident, determined. He remembered her bravery in rescuing the injured welders, the way her eyes had glistened as she looked at the bodies in the cargo container, her strong arm wrapped tight around his midsection when she propelled them through the void.

Now she stood with hands on her hips, eyes flat, staring down the technician. "This is our ship, Baldy. If anyone should leave, it's you, for all the good you're doing."

The man glanced around the room for support from the other technicians. They all averted their eyes. *Not their problem,* Theo thought.

"We'll be quiet," Theo offered. "This shouldn't take long."

Feigning confidence he didn't feel, Theo clunked to the sphere and stepped inside, Selena behind him. Cool, porous walls curved overhead; there was barely enough room for both of them. Selena turned, her chest brushing his. She didn't seem to notice, but his face heated to ten thousand degrees.

"All I did was stand here," Selena said. "I touched the panels like this." She laid her palms flat against the walls. "It happened really quickly. Like the world melting away around me, and next thing I know, I'm in fractal."

Theo forced his mind to focus. "A simulation? Not the real thing?"

"It felt pretty real to me."

Theo placed his hands on the panels, imagining Stephen doing the same thing, the ship alive around him, twisting through the fabric of The Everything. Selena watched him, her hip pressed against his.

She looked up at him with her pretty, dark-brown eyes. "Anything?"

"No," he said, voice cracking. His uniform felt itchy and he had to fight the impulse to dig at his skin. *Why do they keep the command deck so hot?* He shouldn't feel like this. Shouldn't think these things. Meghan would kill him if she found out. Think about Meghan. At the tide wall. Her hair caught in the wind, her lips brushing his, her smile …

Selena frowned. "Why are you looking at me like that?"

"Like what?"

"I don't know. You looked sad or something."

"What do you mean?"

Selena leaned back against the curved wall, arms folded over her chest. "I don't know. Forget it. Look, you said you knew how to wake her up. So let's get on with it, okay?"

"Okay."

"What should I do?"

"Try and think about the same thing you did the first time you entered the sphere."

"I already tried that, and I wasn't thinking about anything special."

"You must have been. The *Chimera* used your memories to reach out to you. That's how nav assistants synced in and out. Some special sequence of thoughts. You must have stumbled along that sequence somehow, or something you thought about interested the *Chimera* enough to get her to respond."

He attempted to recall specific passages of the journal dealing with syncing, but with Selena's proximity, the brush of her body against his with each intake of breath, he couldn't concentrate.

Selena waved a hand in front of his face. "Control to derelict vessel, report status."

Theo blinked.

"For a second there I thought maybe you found the *Chimera*, but you had such a stupid look on your face. Does that happen often? You might want to get on some meds."

"Sorry," he mumbled.

Through the opening of the sphere, he could see the bald technician pretending not to watch them—hard irises peering over the edge of his terminal. They needed to figure this out quick, before the guy decided to call Moorland.

"You have to relax," he said. "Push everything out of your

mind. Make a blank space. You need to create some common ground between the two of you."

"Common ground?" Selena asked, skeptical.

"It must have taken everything she had to reach out. Did she give you something? A key of some sort?"

"She didn't give me anything."

"You might not have known. It wouldn't have been like a code sequence. More like an idea, or a memory. Can you think back to the day you met her, and try to remember everything you thought and felt?"

Selena turned away so suddenly that he wondered if he had somehow offended her. He waited, unsure what to do, looking at the shape of her shoulder blades beneath the uniform fabric. Unknown, unknowable.

"Selena?"

She turned to face him, dark eyelashes wet, mouth a line of sadness. "I remember," she said. "I remember what I thought about … what I felt … what *she* felt …"

Selena's lips closed over her clenched teeth. She took a deep breath. Drew herself up. "You have to promise to not tell anyone."

"I promise."

"I didn't tell anyone about this. Not Moorland. Not Rose."

Theo nodded, waiting, nervous.

"I felt the *Chimera* inside me—or maybe me inside her—like she and I became one thing, or one person. All of me and all of her mashed together. It was so strong I couldn't do anything. For a tiny bit of time *I* was the *Chimera* and she was *me*." Tears slid down her cheeks.

"It's okay," he said.

Selena nodded. Swallowed.

"Close your eyes. Slow your breathing if you can."

Selena took a few steady breaths. Her faced relaxed a bit. With her eyes closed, he could look at her as long as he liked. Her sharp, angular face. Light brown skin. Thin, arching eyebrows. A sloped nose above lips with a hint of pout in them. Not beautiful. Not plain. A distinctive face. Muscles shifted around her mouth. He fought the impulse to kiss her.

"What next?" she asked, snapping him out of his delusion. If he kissed her she'd punch him in the face. No doubt about it.

"You have to think about whatever it was you thought about

the last time."

A look of sorrow came over her, eyes moving behind her eyelids.

"Hold the memory out. Like something fragile held in a cupped palm. Something precious to you."

Selena's left hand came up beside her, hand cupped. "This is stupid," she said, but her tone suggested that she felt the same thing he did. Some latent energy, resonating within the sphere. His scalp tickled. The fine, light-brown hairs on Selena's arms stood on end.

"That's it," Theo said. "You're getting close, aren't you?"

"I think so," Selena said, voice distant, eyes still closed.

"Remember," Theo whispered. "Remember what happened that day. Did she give you something? A picture? An idea? What did the *Chimera* show you?"

The static hum—below the level his ears could hear—came through his feet, up his legs, into his chest, his mind. A brief flash of white. A deep white. An everything white. Static. Snow. Something black in the white. A person?

Goodbye, friend.

The message displayed on his CATO. Not from Selena. Not from anyone. No signature.

"Goodbye, friend," Selena whispered. She let out a little cry of pain. Started to fall. He caught her beneath her armpits. Pulled her close. Held her, bursting with happiness that she let him. Trembling with hope and terror, he put his back to the opening to the sphere, shielding them from the technicians' view.

"All she feels is grief," Selena whispered. He didn't know if she was describing herself or the *Chimera.* Without thinking, he brought his hand up to the back of her head and stroked her hair.

Selena tensed and shoved him away with both hands. "Don't touch me," she said, eyes blazing. "Don't you ever touch me!"

The resonant hum dissipated to nothing. Theo opened his mouth to protest, to try and apologize, but Selena ducked out of the sphere and charged away. He popped out of the sphere, expecting to find all the technicians staring. But they were gathered around one of the nav assistant terminals, reading data.

"She cracked an eyelid," one of the technicians said.

"Yeah, but only for a microsecond," another replied.

Theo wanted to stay, to hear more, but Selena had already disappeared down the corridor. Sure that he'd screwed things up so badly he might never fix them, he chased after her with awkward, pounding steps.

CHAPTER TEN

Moorland stood with hands behind her back, watching as Marcus entered the *Hydra's* outer breakage where welding ships docked when not piecing together the *Chimera*. Cavernous and industrial, the space seemed to swallow him, boots clacking against the deck.

"Cadet Locke."

"Chief Moorland." Marcus wanted to smile, to bare his teeth in victory, but he knew better. While he may have had a hand in engineering this moment, it wasn't time to celebrate just yet.

"I want to commend you once more for bringing this issue to me, Cadet Locke." Her eyes—always piercing—were sharp and intensely blue. "What Ombudsman Owagumbiea was offering must have been tempting."

"Not really. It was a pipe dream. And tempting is not the same thing as wise."

"Owagumbiea has accused you of some egregious things, Cadet Locke," she said. "He seems to think you've killed several people."

"The man is a liar. I don't feel the need to defend myself against a liar." He was ready for the ombudsman's accusations. He'd prepared a rebuttal and Moorland would accept it. She wanted to. *I'm a useful ally*. And tool. Both things were hard to come by.

Moorland nodded. "He's not very credible—a desperate man, grasping at whatever he can to slow his fall."

"Yes, exactly, Chief." He relaxed a little. Moorland had made herself clear. She supported him, did not give credence to the ombudsman.

Moorland turned away, taking on the slight inward gaze of someone checking CATO, and Marcus thought she would dismiss him. Instead, the chief held up her hand, an indication he should stay, as her eyes paged through text.

Unease made Marcus want to shift, but he remained

motionless, his mind nagging. He didn't know what data the ombudsman may have collected. *Perhaps she's simply waiting to question me further.* If Owagumbiea had evidence, things could go sideways quickly.

He went over everything again. The ombudsman only had suspicions, and Moorland would require proof. The man had implied that he'd killed old Martha. Among other things, he reminded himself. Yes, but all of them impossible to prove. No evidence. He'd made sure. And the part about Martha wasn't even close to true. As subjective as truth could be, having it on your side was always valuable.

He made it a point to tell the truth as often as possible. People had sensors for lying. When you did have to lie, what saved you was that although people might sense the lie, they would back away from its revelation because of their own insecurity or a desire to remain ignorant. The key wasn't giving information, it was threatening to give information that they didn't want.

The chief interrupted Marcus' thoughts, turning back from her silent reading. "The ombudsman is correct that there are some anomalies in your records, Cadet Locke. His miscalculation was in thinking that I was ignorant of them. It's a necessity as well as a fact that I know everything about my cadets."

I doubt that.

"I'm not in the business of creating problems for myself." Moorland paused and shook her head. "However, we have no precedent for what we're about to do. I can take nothing for granted, dismiss no possibility."

"Speaking of not dismissing possibilities, there's something I've wanted to discuss with you," Marcus said. Better to risk everything by choice than have it taken away through inaction. He'd cultivated as much rapport with Moorland as the woman would allow. He hoped it would be enough. Regardless, he needed to change the parameters of the conversation in his favor.

He spoke with care, weighing each word. "I'm sure you've considered the possibility that Earth can't—or isn't able—to help us. What if they've been attacked? What if they're dead? How can one small crew and an ill-equipped colony ship make a difference?"

Moorland's eyes lost their candor, reverting to command and control. She folded her arms. "What are you trying to say? That we're all wasting our time? That we should hunker down on

Stephen's Point and wait for the end?"

Marcus didn't flinch. She knew that wasn't his point and was pushing buttons to see how he'd react. "No, that would be about as pointless as the ombudsman's plan. Both lead to the colony's death. I'm suggesting something else entirely. May I speak frankly, Chief Moorland?"

Moorland let him wait a moment because it was her prerogative to do so. He understood. He'd have done the same. The chief nodded. "Go ahead."

"Whatever or whoever sent *Exchange Four*, it wasn't the people inside it."

The sound of doors sliding open reached them from the far end of the room and Moorland swiveled. Several regulators swayed forward, carrying the weight of a struggling white mass— Ombudsman Owagumbiea, constrained in a straightjacket.

Marcus spoke quickly, trying to hold on to his fading opportunity. "I'm suggesting that the options aren't as simple as waiting to die or going to Earth. It's not a binary choice."

"But it is," Moorland said. "And you're smart enough to know why."

"If whatever happened at Earth wanted to reach us, they would have already done it," Marcus said.

"You and I can't know that for certain," Moorland said. "The only answer is to go there ourselves. Otherwise we will live all of our remaining days in fear and doubt. We will be prisoners just as we are now."

"In any of the possible scenarios you or I can envision, a trip to Earth means almost certain peril for the *Chimera* and her crew. We have no control over our exit point from fractal space, no ability to conduct meaningful reconnaissance. If something's waiting for us at Earth, we'll lose the *Chimera*. And if we lose her, we lose everything. The colony loses everything."

"Don't you think I understand that?" Moorland asked, face intense. "We don't have any viable alternatives. I've done everything I can to prepare for every eventuality, including arming the *Chimera*. I violated the compact because I had no other choice. We must go to Earth."

"Do we? What about Damascene?" Marcus asked. "We could go there first. Even if the original colony was a total failure, they have a viable ecology. We could, in theory, move our people there.

It would take quite a few trips, but it could be done."

"You're not listening to me," Moorland spat. "This isn't just about protecting our people in the short term. We *must* know what happened at Earth so that we can prepare ourselves to face it. Even if you're right—and I don't think you are—*and* assuming we could move millions of people from one colony to another, we'd still live out our lives in perpetual dread. That's not a future I want any part of."

"That's easy for you to say," Marcus said, "you're not the one who has to go to Earth."

Moorland's blue eyes appeared silver, her chin set firm. "And neither do you, Marcus J. Locke."

The implication was clear. If he didn't like her plan, he could step aside and let others take the lead. He could stay on Stephen's Point and die along with the rest of them. Cold fury flowed through his veins. Moorland wouldn't listen to reason. He'd been a fool to try.

* * *

"Hello, Cadet Locke."

Leaving the breakage, Conrad Duncan's voice rang out behind him. He turned, anger and loathing filling his stomach. He'd allowed his frustration and anger with Moorland to distract him, let someone surprise him. He brought his teeth together and clenched, barely managing to give the appropriate bow.

"Doctor Duncan."

"You don't have to bow, Cadet. That's best left for visits to the Order. Although I've never been comfortable with the practice even there. Odd sort of thing to do, I think. But someone at some time said it should be done and now here we are, still bobbing at one another like marker buoys." Duncan smiled, eyes crinkling, almost hidden in the network of creases at their corners. "And you can call me Advisor up here on the *Hydra*." Duncan's heavy hand came down on Marcus' shoulder. The sickening warmth of it seeped through the fabric of his jacket and Marcus suppressed a flinch. He stilled, flattening his gaze into hardened duraceramic. He looked up, holding the older man's eye until Duncan flushed slightly and removed his hand.

Duncan gave an awkward chuckle and looked to the breakage

door. "I came down here looking for Moorland."

"She's busy," Marcus said.

Duncan's smile disappeared. Marcus let the silence stretch, keeping a firm grip on Duncan's gaze, challenging the man to touch him again, to try to engage him in conversation. The rush of it, allowing his anger not only to show but to grow into a visible bloom of hatred, was intoxicating. Also dangerous. He let the rage fade, willing it back down into darkness.

"I won't keep you, Advisor. I don't want to miss breakfast."

"No, of course not."

Marcus nodded, impatient, leaning away from the Order man, ready to shoot down the hall. "Goodbye, Advisor Duncan." *Just a regular cadet. Nervous about missing a meal.*

"Goodbye, Marcus."

He ran until he was out of view, jaw sore from clenching. Mistakes had been made, no doubt about it. The encounter with Duncan had been stupid but salvageable. The real issue was still Moorland.

I should have waited. He'd destroyed his one chance at convincing her. And once someone heard and rejected an idea, they became set: the act of saying no made them believe in the no.

Suddenly, the brightly lit corridors of the *Hydra* hurt his eyes and a wave of longing hit. His cave. No chatter, no smiles or tears or any of the hundred other emotional sewer drains of human existence. Just himself and the quiet.

This is what I wanted, he told himself. *To be here in this place. No more cave.*

He'd endure for the time being. And when the time came, he'd act. He wasn't about to go on a suicide mission.

* * *

Moorland found the shape of the white mass revolting, but didn't flinch or look away.

"Ombudsman Owagumbiea." The words felt heavy on her tongue, thick with disgust.

The hooded head began to whip, bucking and straining. "You bitch! You pig!"

The ombudsman lurched, throwing his weight forward. He ripped free of the regulators' grasp and crashed to the floor meters short of Moorland. He squirmed, inching forward to reach her.

Moorland flexed her hands, fighting the urge to step close and bring her foot down on the man's head.

"Get him upright."

The regulators hauled him to his feet and pressed his body against the wall, pinning him with their combined weight. The ombudsman's chest heaved. "You're making a huge mistake! You don't realize the vipers you have nurtured at your breast. I'll tell you everything, but you must stop this. Now!"

"I am making no mistake, Owagumbiea."

Moorland pulled up Marcus' recordings of his meetings with the ombudsman, and transferred them to the main wallscreen. Even the condensed version felt too long. She ground her teeth, letting the whole file play as the grinning, digital ombudsman outlined his plan to overthrow the Mandate.

When the recording ended, Moorland gestured. "Take the hood off."

Regulator Ollaway stepped forward to undo the strap behind the ombudsman's neck. Owagumbiea snarled, snapping his teeth, trying to bite the woman. The regulator grimaced and yanked the hood back, revealing the ombudsman's sweaty face.

"Jasper Farkus Owagumbiea, you have been proven guilty of high treason against the people of Stephen's Point. By the powers entrusted in me as overseer of the Mandate and Chief of this station, I sentence you to death."

"You can't sentence me to anything!" the ombudsman screamed, struggling once more against the regulators' grip. "You don't have the right. You don't have the authority. You don't have—"

"I have every right, Owagumbiea. This isn't a trial. I find you guilty of treason."

Moorland nodded to the lead regulator and the woman turned to her fellow officers. They hoisted the ombudsman, dragging him to the other side of the breakage.

"Listen to me, Moorland," the ombudsman pleaded.

Bargaining, she thought. Too late. The security node on the far wall scanned the lead regulator. The emergency airlock cycled, hissing. Behind the airlock waited—what? She wouldn't call it an escape pod anymore. Technically it was an escape pod, but one with all heat shielding removed. It would hit the atmosphere and burn and burn until there was nothing left. *Coffin*. That was the word. The ombudsman was on a one-way trip to nowhere in a very expensive coffin. There was a kind of elegance to it.

"I'm not lying. Marcus Locke is a murderer."

Moorland sighed and stepped to where the regulators held the struggling ombudsman. "I believe you," she said. The ombudsman gave a tiny tremor of surprise, swinging his head to look at her. Moorland leaned forward, holding his dark pupils with her own. "I just don't care."

Moorland glanced at the lead regulator and the woman placed her boot against Ombudsman Owagumbiea's chest and shoved him through the airlock. The door cycled closed and with a muffled thump the escape pod fired.

Moorland took a breath. It was done.

From the doorway, his face a pale moon of shock, Duncan's horror-filled eyes met hers. "Oh, Alina. What have you done?"

CHAPTER ELEVEN

"Tell the jackals to leave," Duncan said. He swayed in the breakage doorway, color seeping into his face, a deep red that overtook his forehead and swept down his jawline.

Moorland nodded to the regulators, dismissing them.

Duncan's shoulder caught against the doorframe in his haste to give the regulators access to the exit. The doors whispered closed behind them. Moorland pulled the bottom of her uniform jacket, straightening it. A tic. Annoyance built to a buzz in her ears. *Duncan.* Always such impeccable timing. She glanced at her CATO, checking the time.

"Did you just execute Ombudsman Owagumbiea?" Duncan asked. "I'm assuming that escape pod isn't going to make it to Stephen's Point."

"It will reach Stephen's Point's atmosphere, where it will burn on re-entry."

Duncan shook his head, his face losing color as fast as it had gained it seconds before. He wouldn't meet her eyes. "I cannot see how this was necessary. I know the man was a snake, but why did you take matters into your own hands?"

"I didn't have a choice," Moorland said. "The man was plotting to overthrow the government. He was a traitor. A would-be tyrant. I disposed of him."

"A heard about his misappropriation of Mandate resources, but that can hardly be construed as overthrowing the government. And why act alone?"

"Look, I don't have time to explain everything to you right now. I'm due at assembly shortly. I need to assign teams and address a list of infractions with the cadets."

Duncan scrubbed at his eyes, skin sagging under each swipe of his palms. His eyes fell on the closed airlock. "I don't care where you're headed. Make time. Because there had be some other way.

You're accusing the ombudsman of being a tyrant while acting like one yourself. What of the other council members? What about me? Surely—"

Moorland snorted, interrupting him. "A few rotations ago I was waiting for the arrival of the Mandate Council. Instead, I got an exchange ship full of Earth's ghosts! I would have preferred to confer with the council, but Stephen's Point is burning. I don't know if that was part of the man's plan, but it doesn't matter. The *Hydra* is on lockdown for a reason. I don't have the time or the means to discover all of the councilmembers involved in Owagumbiea's plans, and I can't know what other compromises exist within governmental relations. My only concern is to adequately prepare the cadets and send them to Earth. I couldn't do that while worrying about the ombudsman's network here on this station. The situation demanded immediate action."

Duncan was unmoved. "The *situation*? That's a trivializing turn of phrase, and a man's life is no trivial thing. We have laws for a reason. I know you don't accept my dedication to the spiritual side of the law, but it exists, no matter what you may think. Human life has value. What are you if you sacrifice your humanity on an altar of judgement, deciding for all who is worthy of life and who is not?

The calm conviction in his logic infuriated Moorland. "What gives you the right to second guess my decisions? There was no other way. I couldn't keep him locked up on the *Hydra* indefinitely. Should I have sent him back to the surface? What then? He may have been weakened, but his plan would not have changed. Nothing solidifies power like upheaval. I couldn't leave any trace of the man, nothing to rally around and build into a martyr."

Speaking the words reassured her. She'd done what needed doing. "You can't hope that an infection will go away. You have to kill the source, pull the splinter. I pulled the splinter."

"I don't doubt your reasons, Alina, but the overuse of power has a corrupting effect."

Once again, Moorland ignored his use of her first name. He wouldn't be able to influence her that easily.

"You live in a fantasy," Moorland said, "someone had to make this decision. We don't have the luxury of existing in a world where people have a clear choice between good and bad. Our choices are more often between bad and terrible." Her voice rose. "A choice between black and white is no choice at all. The true test is in choosing one shade of gray over another."

"You don't have to justify yourself to me, Chief Moorland," Duncan said. "But you didn't even make an attempt at not acting unilaterally. Are you certain that if you had the opportunity to discuss this with others and weigh options, you still would have had Owagumbiea killed? You believe that firmly in your own ability to see every shade of gray?"

Moorland hesitated. His tone had shifted. Was she hearing disappointment? Hurt? Realization dawned in the same second as understanding: Duncan had moved the focus of the situation to himself, how *he* felt. Duncan was upset that she hadn't sought his advice.

"I am not the megalomaniac you seem intent on making me out to be." Moorland folded her arms across her chest. "Half of my trusted staff are still on the surface. I am worried about their safety, of course, but my greatest concern is that their absence handicaps the station." Her voice dropped to a near whisper. "I am alone."

"You're not alone. I'm here, I've always been here."

"You're right, you are here."

Duncan met her blue eyes with his green ones. "Then let me help you. It was never my role to be directly involved with the cadets, but this is too much for one person to carry alone. We're running out of time. If we don't get the *Chimera* on her way to Earth, there might not be a colony left to protect. I'm here to provide oversight and protect the Order's interests, but that doesn't have to stop me from taking on more responsibility. We can do this together."

Moorland said nothing. It had been a long time since they'd worked as a team. She knew she'd be giving up a modicum of control, but maybe that wasn't such a bad thing. He wasn't wrong. She was carrying more than one person should. Once she assigned the cadets to their teams, his help might be invaluable.

"I'll enjoy working with you again, Conrad." Moorland smiled up at him. "It's been a long while."

Duncan returned her smile, a wistful shadow of his normal wide grin. "You're right, it has been. There was a time when I thought we'd always be together."

"We both know that didn't happen for good reasons. But I have missed you and I'm happy to have your help training Theo and the others. You have a faith I don't share, but you often see things in a way I don't. I do value your counsel."

"You don't have to believe the same things I do. I never expected that of you. I'm just grateful that I've been given this chance. I do believe that Stephen will guide us. That's enough for both of us."

"If you want to think in terms of meaning and signs then consider this: you made it here on the last transport before lockdown, you are one of my oldest friends, and most of all, I trust you. How much clearer could it be?"

"All true. Now you sound like me. Don't get carried away." Duncan straightened, pushing his shoulders back, ready to act. "You said you're assigning teams? I'd like to be involved with whichever group Theo's in."

Moorland shook her head. "No. I need your insight, Duncan. Whether you're fully aware of it or not, you want Theo to be a second Stephen. You see him through that lens. Does he have the capabilities that Stephen had? Who knows? But you won't be effective if you're swayed by your prejudices."

Duncan nodded, giving some thought. "You're probably right. But I'm not the only one. I think you've lost perspective where Selena Samuelson is concerned."

Moorland thought of the *Chimera* and the synaptic response she'd shown the day that Selena had entered the VAST. As always, the tiny hairs at the nape of her neck rose in response. The girl could wake the ship. Moorland knew it.

"I'm aware of that possibility." Moorland said. "I suggest we swap favorites. I'll take Theo, you take Selena. And we'll hope like hell that *one* of them is something like Stephen."

CHAPTER TWELVE

The second call for general assembly in as many full cycles hit Selena's spider moments after she finished dressing. Behind an asterisk-shaped indentation near her left temple, tendrils of microscopic neural fiber ran beneath her scalp, connecting the implant to her brain. She touched the shallow scar. What would Liam say about the spider now that she had tacit approval to use it? The day she'd returned to their berth with a patch of ReadySkin sealing off the fresh insertion point, Liam grew so red she thought he might rip the implant out with his bare hands. He would have too, if it wouldn't have done irreparable damage to her brain.

Selena caught Kaylee watching her. "Another assembly? I don't think anything can top getting our CATOs."

"You can ask me about it," Selena said, tapping her head with her pointer finger. "It's not a big deal."

Kaylee looked a little sheepish but also pleased. "So it's true. You've got a spider."

"Yep. Got it years ago to help me pilot in the rim."

"Does it hurt?"

"Hurt? No. Why would it?"

Kaylee's eyes slid sideways. "I've heard a lot of things about spiders. You know, that they can cause hemorrhaging in the brain, aneurisms, blindness."

"You sound like my dad. That's mostly lies. As long as you have a good tech install it and the implant takes to you, you're fine."

Kaylee's brows lowered. "What do you mean it has to 'take' to you?"

"Settle in. Become part of you. It's not a for sure thing. Now come on, we need to eat."

"Do you see phantoms?" Kaylee asked. "Visual distortions?"

Selena pictured the static wash of golden sparkles that crowded her vision when she synced with her trawler, *The Bee*. Of how the spider had failed her in the most critical moment and almost got her and Liam killed. Her father sucked away by *The Bee's* building momentum. The sick thud of his body against a bulkhead. *Phantoms.* You didn't need a spider to see those.

Above Kaylee's head, silver text read *Specializations: Biology, Medicine.*

"You want to give me a full physical?" Selena asked. "Satisfy your curiosity?"

Kaylee blushed. "No. Sorry. You're right—we're going to be late."

Selena led the way outside where they merged into a steady stream of cadets heading for the commons.

"Where'd you go during the down cycle?" Kaylee asked.

Selena kept her shoulders relaxed, didn't look at the other girl. "Nowhere important." *Just another failed attempt to wake the Chimera.* Not a total failure though. Because at the very end, before Theo touched her hair …

Goodbye, friend.

A queue of unread CATO messages sat in her peripheral vision, all of them from Theo. She didn't want to read his explanations or apologies. She had no use for them. She'd made a mistake trusting him. He didn't know anything useful, and what he did know, he'd try and use against her.

He wasn't wrong.

Yes, he was wrong.

Right about how to find the *Chimera.* Wrong to touch her like that. To assume he could. That she'd let him. That she wanted …

"Sit with me?" Kaylee asked. Selena snapped back into the moment. They'd arrived at the commons. Cadets in formal uniforms sat at tables, eating meals from the commissary machines. Drinking tea, talking, socializing. Kaylee's friendly eyes scanned Selena's face. "You can if you like. I'll introduce you to the rest of the cadets from the Valley."

"Thanks," Selena said. Kaylee's face lit up. "But no thanks," she finished. "I need some space to think."

"You don't have to eat alone," Kaylee said, reproachful. "Come join us."

"I don't like that sort of thing," Selena said. "I'll meet people when I train with them."

She swung away from Kaylee and headed for a commissary

machine and ordered tea and a bowl of hot cereal fortified with synthetic protein. She took her food to an empty table and sat down. Steam rose from the bowl and the mug. It reminded her of the tea her mother used to make for her, back when she had a mother. Back before the exchange ships stopped coming and the colony's gears began to grind to a halt.

A queue of messages hovered at the edge of her vision. Her eyes strayed to open the most recent message. Stopped. Afraid of what it might say. Afraid that he'd *seen* things in the sphere. Because she'd seen things herself. Theo standing in the snow, looking on with horror as she, a tiny little girl version of herself, patted the still-warm face of her dead mother. And around them, everywhere, even within them, she'd felt the *Chimera*'s presence.

He wasn't wrong, a part of her argued. *He was trying to help you. He can help you again if you let him.*

She took a bite of too-hot cereal and burned her tongue. Without thinking, she snatched her tea and slurped. More burning. Eyes watering, she coughed out cereal and tea. Through blurry eyes, she glimpsed several dark shapes approaching her table. She swiped her face on her uniform sleeve, then realized she'd left behind cereal and tea stains. What the hell was wrong with her?

Her eyes cleared and the dark shapes materialized into cadets taking seats at her table. Theo sat down across from her, Charlie Grey beside him. That girl Meghan with the ponytail who always stood like she had a titanium rod for a spine. Two huge cadets that had to be brothers, their muscles bulging beneath uniforms that looked too small for them.

"Did you choke?" Charlie asked. "Are you okay?"

"Have some of my water," Meghan said, offering Selena a drinking bulb. She drank, clearing her mouth, trying to buy herself enough time to think of something to say.

She looked from face to face, skipping over Theo. "What do you want?"

"Are you feeling okay?" Meghan asked. "You look a little sick."

"I'm not sick," she said, annoyed with the invasion of her space, and even more so with herself for making a scene.

"She's probably just tired," Charlie said. "Didn't get much sleep, did you?"

"What are you talking about?" the larger of the two brothers asked.

"She and Theo—"

Theo's elbow slammed into Charlie's ribcage.

"Ouch! What's wrong with you, Puck?"

"Do you think we're training in VAST today?" Theo asked.

Everyone looked at him, then Selena. Meghan had a certain look in her eyes. A look Selena recognized from the ship warden when he suspected a flameback of falsifying a pre-flight safety checklist.

"She and Theo *what*?" Meghan asked.

"Nothing," Theo said.

"Shut up, Theo," Meghan said. "I'm talking to Charlie. What were you going to say? We're all listening."

"Nothing," Charlie said, a look of pure terror on his face. He might as well have said that she and Theo had taken a roll together on a live video feed for all the world to see.

"What?" Charlie said. "Why's everyone looking at me like that?"

The brothers smirked at one another. Warmth crept up from Selena's chest to her neck, to her face. Theo's messages hovered out beyond her sight line. Each granule of cereal stood distinct on her right lapel. A sheen of spilled tea glistened on the tabletop. Everyone looked at Theo. At her. She stood up. She'd go back to the berth. Change uniforms. Stay there until the last possible moment, then rush to assembly. Hide in the back, away from—

"They went to wake the *Chimera*," Charlie blurted.

"Thanks," Theo said. "Thanks a lot."

"You told him?" Selena said, the heat in her chest and face gone. Gone as fast is if she'd fallen through a thin sheet of ice, all the warmth leeched out of her. "You told him," she said voice flat and cold and dangerous. "I can't believe it."

Meghan said something but Selena heard only her tone, not the words themselves. Theo, who wouldn't look at her, slumped behind the table. More a boy than anything. A little disgusting boy caught telling a nasty joke. Charlie looked caught too, but he was only guilty of repeating the joke. The brothers looked pleased with themselves, like they might burst out laughing. Meghan's face became ugly, eyes accusing, mouth moving fast. And Theo. Theo slid further down. Soon he would disappear.

She walked. Slow and steady, head level, unblinking. She

walked as a thousand eyes stung against her back. Down the corridor to the berth. Inside, mechanical hands undid uniform buttons. Her top dropped into a laundry chute. The hands selected another top and pulled it over a mechanical face. Tuck in. Button. Smooth the fabric.

There she stood, in front of herself. A girl with eyes that gave nothing away. A metal girl with digital thoughts, a daughter of the *Chimera* herself. Selena knew this version of herself very well. This was the Selena that had saved her, all those years ago when her mother fell in the snow and wouldn't get up. If you kept your face hard, if you didn't speak, nobody would guess that your insides had been shattered.

* * *

Selena left her berth and marched to assembly, chin held high. She let her eyes meet any that came her direction, challenging them to maintain contact. None did. She took a position in the back corner of the observation deck where she could see everyone and everything. While waiting for Moorland to arrive, she swept the stack of messages from Theo away and deleted them. It felt good. Cleaning the slate. Moving on. Maybe she would wake the *Chimera*. Maybe she wouldn't. Either way, she'd do it alone.

Cadets formed into lines, broken up by training groups. The Swallows cadets together, led by Marcus. East End. Conway. The Valley. As her eye traveled the room, CATO fed her details on each cadet. The training ahead would eliminate more than half the people in the room. Those that made the cut would serve alongside her. She didn't doubt her place aboard the *Chimera*.

Don't get ahead of yourself. Nothing guaranteed here.

Yes, but unlike every other cadet, she'd grown up in space and had thousands of hours of flight time under her belt. If Theo was a good representation of the average cadet's skillset, they'd be lost without her help. Theo turned and mouthed something at her. She averted her eyes.

Don't think about him.

He stood beside Marcus, the two of them talking in hushed voices. Next to them, the two massive brothers. From behind she saw that one was shorter and a little narrower at the waist and shoulders than the other. *Hephaestus Hart. Phoebus Hart.* Next to them, another cadet, neither tall nor short. A bit pensive. *Preston*

Coriolanus. Last in the line came Meghan. Shoulders square, head locked forward. Already at attention. *Meghan Ziczek.* Selena pulled up her full profile.

Meghan Ziczek. Swallows Training Group. Specialties: Leadership, Physical Science, Navigation. Height: 1.65 meters. Weight: 47 kilograms (Earth equivalent).

Brown hair in a ponytail that fell between her shoulder blades. An hourglass figure that even the formal uniform couldn't hide. A pretty face. Not like the girls at New Lux, but almost. Selena didn't need her CATO to identify Meghan as an obvious leader. And unlike Marcus, Meghan hadn't assumed she was owed something. What was the nature of her relationship with Theo? Selena had a hard time imagining them together, but she'd seen stranger things.

Don't think about him. He doesn't matter. What matters is completing your training.

Selena forced her attention elsewhere, reading off names of cadets from other training groups, taking in their specialties, noting those with navigation potential.

Moorland entered the room, accompanied by a tall, thick-chested man Selena recognized from Theo's CATO message. He now wore a gray officer's uniform rather than an Order robe. What was his name? She went to pull up Theo's message to check, then remembered she'd deleted them all. Oh well. Moorland would introduce him soon enough.

The cadets came to attention as Moorland turned on her heel to face them.

"Welcome, cadets," she said.

"Chief Moorland," the cadets replied.

"You all have a busy few cycles ahead of you, so I'll be brief. As some of you have no doubt discovered, I've locked the *Hydra* down until we complete our mission and the *Chimera* has departed for Earth. I've quarantined us because in the wake of *Exchange Four*'s arrival, things on the moon's surface have deteriorated."

Moorland paused, observing the rows of attentive faces.

"I made that decision with a heavy heart. As you will soon learn, when entrusted with the responsibility to protect an entire colony, imperfect decisions must sometimes be made."

"What about our families?" the shorter of the two brothers, Phoebus, asked. "When do we get to talk to them?"

"Cadet Hart, this is not a Q and A session. Refrain from

speaking while I complete my briefing."

She's not going to let them speak to their families. She wants them focused.

Selena supposed that made sense, but didn't like it any more than the others. Eyes moved, bodies shifted, murmurs of dissent came from the cadets in the back of the room. As if on cue, the big man beside Moorland stepped forward.

"Some of you already know me," he said. "For those that don't, I'm Conrad Duncan of Stephen's Order. Special Advisor to the Regulatory. I helped oversee the Selection process and have spent many, many hours offering your names up in prayer."

Not my name, you haven't.

"You have every right to feel angry or afraid. The decision to quarantine this station from the larger colony wasn't an easy one to make. But as hard as it may be for some of you to accept, it was the *right* decision." Empathy filled the man's voice. His eyes rested on each cadet. He stood with his palms out. Nothing to hide. *Yeah right, Mister Order man. Maybe somebody will buy what you're selling but not me.*

"We're fighting for our very survival," Duncan continued. "You each represent your communities. The Valley. Conway. East End. The Swallows. The best of the best. You stand here for your families, your communities, and your colony. No one can save Stephen's Point but you. No one can board that colony ship and navigate it back to Earth but you. You are the Jubilee generation. You are our hope. You walk in Stephen's footsteps."

Nothing like flattery to get people to drop their objections like an overheated steam line. Selena almost smiled. The man was good. Really good.

"What Advisor Duncan and I need for you to accept is that our circumstances have changed in significant ways," Moorland said. "The arrival of *Exchange Four* and its cargo have forced me to take drastic action."

More murmurs from the cadets. Phoebus tensed, as if he might step forward and give Moorland a piece of his mind. *It's Duncan you need to watch out for,* Selena mused. *Moorland might not tell you everything, but at least what she does say will be the truth.*

"What was the cargo?" a voice asked.

"Cadet Ray, CATO can recognize you based on your voice alone. Any more outbursts will result in a cycle of confinement to quarters. That goes for everyone."

She's rattled. Things must be worse than she's letting on. Selena's thoughts strayed to Principal Hospital, to her father's medical care. He'd be safe at the center of the valley, so near the Regulatory. At least she hoped he would be. At least she only had Liam to worry about. What if her whole family was down there? What if she had six siblings like Charlie Grey?

Moorland dimmed the lights and a massive wallscreen came to life behind her. "You've all heard rumors about *Exchange Four.* Some of those rumors are true. However, in the interest of dispelling those not based on fact, I will now show you what we discovered inside *Exchange Four.*"

A collective gasp. A row ahead of Selena, Kaylee let out a muffled cry.

"Fractal space killed all four hundred and eight of them," Moorland said.

Four hundred and eight. So, so many.

A desiccated child's body rotated on the screen. Selena remembered seeing her in person. Thin, bone-like legs. Hair clumped against the nape of her neck. Eyes like prunes in their sockets.

"We're still processing their remains," Moorland said. "We will do our best to determine why they risked unprotected flight through fractal space."

The lights came back up. Duncan's hand rose to his chest then fell back to his side. *No emblem to hold,* Selena thought. Nothing to comfort. A profound sadness settled over her, brought on by the man's simple, futile gesture. *Maybe that's all we're doing now. Reaching out for something that's not there.*

"As we learn more, we will share it with you," Moorland said. *Only what you think we can handle.*

"The important thing is that you focus your energy on your training. To speed that process, I have partnered with Advisor Duncan. We are splitting you into three distinct training groups. Two of those groups will focus exclusively on Command and Navigation. The third group will train for Shipboard Operations and Logistics."

More sounds from the less disciplined cadets. Not complaints, but excitement. Selena felt it herself, a livewire of energy connecting her to momentous, life-changing events.

"I will supervise Command and Navigation Team One and Duncan will supervise Command and Navigation Team Two," Moorland said. "Trainer Lemieux will supervise Operations and Logistics."

Selena's pulse sped.

"Team One will be led by Cadet Locke from the Swallows group." *Him*? Selena's face hurt from holding back her scorn. She waited for Moorland's eyes to sweep toward her, to lock on her own. She drew herself up, ready to put her best face forward. To look like a navigator.

"Cadet Puck will train as Navigator for Team One," Moorland said. "Cadets Coriolanus, Archer, and Ortiz will train as Navigator Assistants."

Selena recovered from her disappointment quickly, buttressed by the certainty that she wouldn't have to work with Marcus or Theo. That was fine with her. Let the two weirdos conspire together. She'd beat them both. A new thought came. It terrified and tantalized her. Maybe Moorland would assign *her* has a Team Lead. Maybe Moorland saw her as not just a potential Navigator but a potential Captain?

"Team Two will be led by Cadet Ziczek. Cadet Samuelson will train as Navigator. Cadets Phoebus Hart, Sandborne, and Gillespie as Navigator's Assistants. Cadet Wells will lead the Logistics team. Members of the Logistics team will receive their assignment in the coming hours via CATO message."

Selena found Duncan looking at her. *Duncan, not Moorland.* Moorland could have chosen her but didn't. Despite Selena's best efforts to deny the truth, the choice stung.

A CATO message from Moorland popped up on her overlay. "Command and Navigations teams will meet for a special briefing in twenty minutes at the *Hydra* command deck."

Marcus Locke. Meghan Ziczek. Theo Puck. Three cadets from the Swallows group all in lead positions. An indication of merit or overt favoritism? Duncan knew Theo. Maybe that had something to do with it. *But he doesn't know me.* Nor would he. She'd do her job, do it as well as she was capable, but she didn't like the Order and wouldn't be getting chummy with one of its leaders.

"You are dismissed," Moorland barked. The room descended into chaos, everyone talking at once. Selena prepared to push her way through the crowd of cadets, but the way parted before her, no shoving or elbowing necessary. For the second time in a single cycle, hundreds of eyes watched her, and this time, it didn't bother her at all.

CHAPTER THIRTEEN

Theo followed Marcus and the others into the lift to the inner ring of the *Hydra*. Only a half-meter away, Selena turned her back, shutting him out just like the dozens of unread CATO messages he'd sent her. She wouldn't acknowledge him in person or otherwise.

[Now we'll learn something useful,] Marcus messaged him. *[Moorland is wise not to trust sensitive information with the other cadets.]*

[I bet she's going to give us a breakdown of possible scenarios at Earth and our strategic response to each of them,] Theo messaged back.

Beside him, Marcus gave a subtle nod.

Between Selena's overt hostility and Meghan's calculated coldness, he'd run short on friends in the last few cycles. Marcus remained the constant. Less and less aloof, Marcus had begun to share things with Theo without reservation. Theo didn't fully trust him, but at least Marcus hadn't cast him aside because Charlie couldn't keep his stupid mouth shut.

The lift doors opened and déjà vu hit Theo hard. The curvature of the deck, the sense of motion that set his stomach rolling, Selena's confident stride. They'd come here alone just a few cycles ago. He'd brimmed with hope and anticipation then. How had things spiraled so out of control? How had he lost Meghan and Selena both?

Because you never really had either of them. And because you're an idiot.

He cast a hopeful glance in Meghan's direction. If Selena wouldn't let him make things right, maybe she would. Meghan was angry, no doubt about that, but she *knew* him. They'd grown up together. Besides, nothing happened with Selena. Not really.

Goodbye, friend.

The thought sent a cold shiver down his spine. Okay, so something had happened, but nothing like what Meghan thought. In the white space, in the static snow, he'd seen … Selena. The *Chimera*. Himself. The three of them together for the briefest of moments.

If Selena hadn't pushed him away, they could've woken the ship.

But she had pushed. Was still pushing.

It wasn't fair. She was acting like he'd done something horrible. And he hadn't. Beneath the basic level of self-delusion that he maintained despite knowing of its existence, when he dug into his motives, to the very heart of him, he didn't find anything blame-worthy. He had genuinely wanted to help Selena. He still did.

But what about Meghan?

What indeed. Beautiful, imperious Meghan. Meghan, the newly appointed Team Leader. Meghan with the third highest leadership score in the entire Selection. Meghan walking in front of him, rising up the curvature of the ring, always ascending, always climbing. Maybe she deserved better to begin with. Better than what he had to offer. He'd faked his way into the Selection. She'd earned hers. Despite his stellar navigation scores, she and he were not the same and never would be.

She *needed* something different than he did. Something he couldn't give her. Maybe something no person could give because it wasn't a person at all. *Purpose*. That's what Meghan had, and she wanted more. Purpose. Destiny.

In a flash, Theo recalled what Duncan said when he first met Meghan. "One day you'll stand where Stephen did." Meghan, not him. All the rot about him being chosen, being like Stephen. He didn't believe it. Never had. If anyone was like Stephen, it was Meghan. She could carry the weight of the colony on her capable shoulders. And she not only needed something different, she deserved it..

Relief filled him up to overflowing. Relief for Meghan? Himself? He couldn't be sure. A new thought hardened inside him. He would need to tell her. To let her go. Let her become whatever it was she was supposed to become.

And I will become a navigator. The realization came from nowhere, everywhere. It lapped at him, a warm ocean wave. Could he? Would he?

Unless she does. Selena. The girl who hated him.

He did not hate her back. He didn't hate anyone or anything.

Not even Marcus, not even when Marcus threatened his family. He might have killed Marcus if that's what it took to protect Liddy, but that wouldn't have been a hateful act; it would have been a necessary one.

[I don't hate you.] He formed the CATO message without thinking and barely managed to avoid sending it to Selena. He altered the words. Read them again.

[Why do you hate me?]

He sent the message. Like all the others, it stayed in his peripheral vision, marked as unread.

They arrived at the command deck, its door sealed closed.

"Should we wait here?" Wells asked.

"No," Marcus said. "We'll go in."

Meghan didn't look convinced. "We're five minutes early."

"Better early than late," Marcus said. He triggered the access panel, the door opened, and he stepped through. Everyone hung back for a few seconds until Selena shrugged and went after Marcus. Theo and the others followed.

Walls curved around them. A seamless array of wallscreens covered the walls, providing a three hundred and sixty degree view of the space around the *Hydra.* Oriented so that the ring of the station turned like a wheel rolling around the atmosphere of the Stephen's Point moon, the wallscreens adjusted for the spin and offered a static view of the moon and the umbilical spooling out, connecting the *Chimera* to the station.

We'd all be puking from vertigo if they didn't.

Several officers sat at terminals. None paid the cadets much attention, focusing on their own tasks. With no sign of Duncan or Moorland, Theo and the other cadets surveyed the room, the wallscreens, and the silent fractal class cruiser that seemed close enough to touch. *Exchange Four,* linked by a second umbilical to the other side of the station, wasn't visible.

"This is really impressive," Meghan said. "Imagery doesn't do it justice."

"I agree," Moorland said, whisking into the room in her white uniform. Duncan loomed behind her, a full quarter-meter taller and twice her mass. The cadets whirled to face her, coming to attention.

"At ease," Moorland said. The door closed behind her. Duncan took a seat at a terminal, the ankle of one foot resting on the knee of the other. This would be Moorland's show.

"Welcome to the command deck. From here, I coordinate all *Hydra* operations including the restoration of the *Chimera*. On my left is Duty Officer Blake, and behind her, Communications Officer Gibbons."

Neither Blake nor Gibbons acknowledged Moorland's mention of their names, eyes locked on display screens.

"I assume the wallscreens can show the other side of the station?" Marcus asked.

"Yes," Moorland said. Before she'd finished saying the word, the screens blinked to a new perspective of *Exchange Four* against the backdrop of Elypso. "For the sake of our eyes, brightness filters dim Elypso's intensity," Moorland said. The screens shifted again, now a split-image of the front and back of the station. "This is the original command deck of our old exchange dock. We merged it with the station upon completion of the substructure of the outer ring. Once we have reestablished trade with Earth, we will repurpose the *Hydra* to serve as our new exchange dock."

The wallscreens snapped back to their original point of view. "Those of you who haven't seen it yet will find that the command deck of the *Chimera* is very similar in design to this space."

Most of the cadets looked at Selena. Theo's eyes met Meghan's. No anger there. Not anymore. Unlike Selena, Meghan had read his messages. She'd sent no replies, but at least she knew the truth—that he'd gone to try and help Selena wake the *Chimera* but it hadn't worked out and that regardless of what Charlie might have implied, his cooperation with Selena had been strictly platonic.

"Cadet Samuelson. Cadet Puck. Come here," Moorland said.

Theo started, then did as he was told. Selena joined him, eyes hard as iron ingots.

"If you, or anyone else, go aboard the *Chimera* without my explicit permission, I will send you to Stephens' Point."

"Understood," Selena said.

"Understood," Theo repeated. "It was a dumb idea."

Moorland frowned. "Yes, it was a dumb idea to go alone and without permission. However, my tech team reported that the ship showed a momentary blip of alertness. When training schedules permit, I will escort the two of you back to the sphere to attempt to replicate that result."

"You will?" Theo asked, not sure he liked the idea.

"No way," Selena said. "I'm not going back there with him."

Moorland gave Selena a withering look. "You'll do whatever I tell you to do, when I tell you to do it."

To Theo's great surprise, Selena scowled but didn't argue the point.

"Now, on to important business," Moorland said. Theo risked a glance at Selena, then wished he hadn't. Resignation in her eyes. He'd become something to endure.

"Each of you has been chosen based on your specialties," Moorland said. "I've granted you heightened security clearance at a level equivalent to my most trusted staff. You will have full access to historical records, schematics, strategic plans, resources lists, and Mandate reports. You will also have access to data on Special Appropriations and the projects they funded, both well-hidden within the sprawl of the Mandate budget."

"What sort of projects?" Wells asked.

"It would be easier for me to show you," Moorland replied.

The wallscreens blinked to a schematic of the *Chimera*. Theo inspected it with care, but couldn't identify whatever Moorland wanted them to see. The chief waited as they all studied the ship.

Meghan's face drained of color. "Are those what I think they are?"

Theo followed the line from her pointed finger to a series of circular enclosures hidden beneath shield plates welded over the *Chimera*'s hull. *Some sort of escape pod? Maneuvering jets.*

"Launch tubes," Marcus said, voice even.

"Correct," Moorland said. "Thirty tubes. Four warheads each."

Warheads. The word sucked the oxygen out of the room and thoughts from the cadets' heads. Confusion and fear was etched into each face. All but Marcus. He appeared serene, hands clasped behind his back, studying the schematic with keen interest.

"Weaponized ecomire?" he asked.

"Yes," Moorland said. "We have far more of it than we do any of the other radioactive elements, and the facilities to refine it."

"The ecomire rush," Selena said. "So what's why the prices shot up. It never made sense, not without any exchange ships to take it back to Earth. I thought maybe you were building new cores. That or stockpiling it to send a bunch along with the *Chimera.*"

"We don't have the tech for building our own cores," Meghan said. "Refine and ship. Another of Earth's control measures. They didn't want us making our own fractal-capable ship."

"This is insane," Phoebus said. "A total violation of the compact!"

"The compact no longer exists," Moorland said.

"What?" Wells said, incredulity giving his word an edge sharp enough to cut. "What do you mean it doesn't exist?"

"The Mandate has more than one level," Moorland said. "If we reached certain thresholds, the council voted to abolish our participation in the compact. To declare our independence from Earth. We have been operating outside of the compact for many years now."

"You hid it from everyone," Phoebus said. "You hid the truth, built weapons, armed the *Chimera* ..."

"Of course she did," Marcus said, gaze leveled at Phoebus. "This is about our survival. What part of that don't you understand? Earth isn't coming to save us. We have to save ourselves."

"By building nukes?" Phoebus said.

"They're not nukes," Marcus said. "They're more powerful than that."

Nearby, Duncan hunched over in his seat, the lower portion of his face hidden behind a massive hand. *He doesn't like this. He doesn't like it at all.*

"Marcus is right," Moorland said, letting her eyes rest on each face. Stern and unflinching. Unashamed. "This is about our survival. Did any of you believe we would send you back to Earth without the means to defend yourselves?"

"Oh, so these are *defensive* warheads," Phoebus said. "A hundred and twenty missiles that make hydrogen bombs look like firecrackers! Yep, those sound like *defensive* weapons to me."

"Cadet Hart," Moorland said. "How many siblings do you have?"

Phoebus eyed Moorland, weighing the question. "Three."

"And how many in your extended family?"

"I don't know. A lot."

"Fifty-eight," Moorland answered. "Fifty-eight Harts spread across our fine colony. Fifty-eight mouths to feed. Fifty-eight people in need of *protection.*"

"Yes, but—" Phoebus protested, but Moorland cut him off.

"Hear me well. All of you. The threat we face—the great unknown of Earth—will not be solved without the legitimate threat of force and the willingness to apply that force if necessary."

Duncan looked up, eyes catching Theo's before darting away.

"Three possibilities," Marcus said. "Each with sub-variants. Each with an optimal strategic response."

Moorland turned to Marcus. "That's correct."

Marcus said nothing more, deferring to Moorland, backing away from demonstrating his brilliance.

"There is no compact," Meghan said. She spoke as if trying the concept on, seeing how it fit. *Not well. Not for Meghan.* Her face was troubled, eyes grave. Retreating inward, re-evaluating everything she knew—or thought she knew—to be true. Selena also appeared to be making calculations, but while Meghan's face had gone pale, Selena's had brightened, brown cheeks flushed. The rest of the cadets fell along a spectrum of surprise to shock.

Of them, Wells appeared to be the most composed. "What are the possibilities?"

"Earth doesn't need or want us anymore," Selena said. "That's one, right?"

Moorland nodded.

"Or Earth can't help us because they've suffered a plague or some other epic depopulation event," Wells said. *Depopulation event?* Theo thought. *What the heck did they teach kids down in the valley?*

"Or Earth has been attacked," Marcus concluded.

"Very good," Moorland said.

Not good. Terrible. Terrifying. Some of the cadets, though clothed, looked as though Moorland had stripped them naked. Innocence gone. Arms folded over chests. Faces sick with worry. Or anger, like Phoebus, because you could control anger more easily than fear. All of them roiling inside, boiling cauldrons of dark thoughts, dark extrapolations.

Not Marcus. Nor, Theo realized, himself. Marcus had thought all of these possibilities through long ago. And so had Theo. Not in his conscious mind, not with fully-formed articulate thoughts, but Moorland's revelations didn't surprise him. They came as the logical culmination of his Selection training. Of Sir's brutality.

Weeding out the weakest. Not the weak-bodied but those of weak will. You didn't need strong muscles to launch a warhead. You needed a strong mind. You needed the most dangerous of all human characteristics: absolute conviction.

Marcus had conviction. So did Meghan. Mirror images of the same thing.

The truth began to permeate the cadets. Soaked through their objections, the fragile constructs of their beliefs and assumptions. Truth with the destructive power to destroy a world. *I am become death.* The words came from a dark recess of Theo's mind, without context, without citation. He formed them into a CATO message. Sent it to Marcus.

[We all are death,] came the reply. *[That is the only guarantee in life.]*

"Three possibilities," Meghan said, a touch of natural color coming back into her freckled cheeks. "In scenario one, we may be forced to compel Earth to resupply us by threatening to annihilate them. In scenario two, they might come after us, trying to latch on like a drowning person their rescuer. Scenario three …"

"In scenario three, warheads or no warheads, we die," Marcus said.

Moorland didn't argue with him.

"We close the door," Theo said, afraid of the words. "We close the pathway, make sure that … whatever might be back at Earth … can't come here." A coldness came over him. Worse than in the cave with Marcus. Worse than fearing the receipt of his brand in the Selection training. Those were trivial, tiny things compared to this. They were nothing. Not worthy of the comparison.

"Now you understand the reality of what you have been entrusted with," Moorland said.

Meghan nodded, lip trembling before her jaw muscles clenched shut and she swallowed.

"Yes, ma'am," she whispered. "We do."

CHAPTER FOURTEEN

After Moorland finished explaining the bombshell of the arming of the *Chimera*, she announced that the two Command and Navigation teams would work on separate schedules. While one team trained on the VAST simulator on their duty cycle, the other team would rest. They would complete their other training separately as well, overlapping with Wells' Logistics team where appropriate.

Moments after Moorland dismissed them, Marcus sent each cadet on his team a detailed schedule broken down into fifteen Earth minute intervals, complete with countdown times for each major segment. Theo integrated the schedule into his CATO, and labeled it "Swallows Team." He would never be late for a training exercise. He would come prepared, diligent, focused. A deep and fast-moving current of resolve carried him. He wouldn't fail Moorland. He wouldn't fail Marcus. He wouldn't fail his colony.

CATO messages flew back and forth between his teammates. Preston Coriolanus, who he'd saved from failing out of the Selection. Nemus Archer, strong and smart and almost as ruthless as Marcus. Cain Ortiz, the only non-Swallows training group member, a shy kid from East End. Now that he understood the full nature of their mission, the choice to pair four Swallows cadets on a single team made much more sense. Preston, Nemus, and Marcus all had specialties in tactics. They'd also suffered together under Sir, seen dozens of kids branded, and in Theo's case, received a brand.

Swallows Team. He liked the sound of it.

What would Meghan call her team? Meghan and Phoebus from the Swallows, Selena from the Rim, Elaina Sandborne from the Valley, and Xavier Gillespie from Conway. And how would Selena and Meghan work together? A shame he wouldn't get to see that play out in person. Who knew—maybe they'd get along. The idea brought a short-lived smile to his lips, gone the instant he thought about the *other* thing Moorland told them. Her parting words, in

CATO form, hung in front of him as he made his way back to the commons:

[The information I have disclosed to you is classified. You will not speak of it to anyone outside of your training group. Any mention made necessary by your training should be done via CATO only. If for any reason you disclose classified information to any person, cadet, or staff member of this station, you will be tried and sentenced via a special Regulatory court. The penalty for such a disclosure is death.]

He whisked the message away. Time to concentrate on what he'd tell Charlie when he arrived at their shared berth. *Nothing.* That was safest. Charlie didn't know how to keep his mouth shut.

A message from Meghan hit his CATO:

[Do you want to talk?]

[In person or over CATO?]

He couldn't decide what would be more awkward: meeting up or sending messages back and forth. Much would depend on what Meghan said. No. On what he said. He owed her the truth. Selena or no Selena, everything had changed between them. He would do the right thing. The brave thing.

[Meet me at my berth. Kerry won't be back for several hours.]

In person, then. *[See you soon.]*

Minutes later he stood outside her door, triggered the chime.

The door opened. Meghan stood just inside, the top button of her uniform undone. The faint smell of citrus filled the room. The last vestiges of Meghan's perfume must have clung to one of the few personal items she'd brought with her to the *Hydra.* The wallscreen behind her bunk displayed rotating pictures of her family. Meghan's mother with the same chestnut-brown hair pulled into a small bun atop her head. Her siblings, younger than her, all with the same storm-grey eyes. *Such a happy family,* Theo thought, knowing that was a lie. Because when the pictures cycled through a second time, he saw no image of her father.

"Are you coming in?" Meghan asked.

"Sure," Theo said, still thinking of Meghan's dad. The liar. The cheater. The reason Meghan worked so hard to succeed in the Selection. She'd merged her abiding need to excel at everything with her desperation to leave her family behind.

Meghan sat on the edge of her bed. Theo sat opposite her, noting the perfect folds of the blanket on Nifali's bed. "You guys getting along?" Theo asked.

"Nifali's great," Meghan said. "Clean and quiet. Can't ask for much more than that."

"Charlie's a pain in the backside," Theo said.

"I gathered as much."

Theo flexed his hands. Gave a nervous cough. "I'm glad you wanted to talk," he said. "I've been thinking about what to say to you all cycle."

Meghan's eyes softened. "Me too."

"I'm proud of you," Theo said. "You're going to be a great team lead."

Meghan glanced behind her at the wallscreen. Killed the parade of images. "I'll do my best."

"That's all you ever do," Theo said. "That's one of the things I wanted to tell you, actually. You're amazing. I can't believe how far you've come."

"Theo," Meghan said, the hint of a crack in her voice. "Stop."

"Stop? Stop what?"

Meghan stood up and Theo did the same. "I need to tell you something," she said. "Something important."

"Okay," Theo said, without a clue what she might be talking about.

"We said ... *I* said some things that I need to take back."

Theo's eyes slipped past her head to the silent wallscreen.

Meghan sighed. "Look, Theo, things have changed. For both of us. I'm a team lead now. I need to focus on my team. You're my friend. One of my oldest friends. But that's all ... that's all that I want to be to you."

"Okay," Theo said. He felt nothing. Nothing at all.

"You can still talk to me if you want to," Meghan said, "though with different training schedules, I don't know how much time either of us will have for that sort of thing."

Theo nodded, face as blank as the wallscreen behind Meghan.

"This isn't because of what happened between you and Selena. And I owe you an apology on that one. I assumed something that wasn't true, that you were like my dad."

"I'm nothing like him," Theo said. Why did his voice sound angry? He wanted this as much as she did. Had come here to tell her that they couldn't be together. To let her go. But he'd wanted to make the choice. By acting first, Meghan had stripped him of the ability to look like the mature one, the benevolent one.

"I know you're not," Meghan said.

"No, you don't," Theo said, anger building inside him. "You think so little of me. You always have. Remember back on Stephen's Point? What you called me? You said I was a 'waste of a person.'"

"I didn't mean that," Meghan protested, her skin betraying her, turning to a vivid shade of pink. "And I apologized to you."

"You're the one that kissed me. You're the one that made promises. And now you're taking it all back?"

He'd hurt her a little. Honed in on an inconsistency. An unfair one, but one that would bother Meghan nonetheless. Why did that feel so good? Why did he want to *keep* hurting her? No explanation came, only more words.

"I'm not the one like your dad," Theo said. "You are."

Meghan's face crumpled. Her skin went from pink to scarlet. "Get out of my room, Theo."

"What's the matter? Can't handle the truth? You played me. You used me." Lies. Terrible, enjoyable lies. Each one like a physical blow, each one wounding her. He'd come here wanting to be brave but instead had become a coward. He hated himself for it, hated Meghan. Loved her, too. Which drove him to keep cutting her down? To shake his head at her, looking at her like she'd looked at him when she found out he'd hacked the Selection list?

"I didn't mean to do that," Meghan said. Of course she'd take the blame. Of course she would. A good leader did that, right?

"It doesn't matter what you 'meant,' to do," Theo said. "I bet your dad never 'meant' to do all the things he did, all the lies he told. Does that make them hurt less?"

Meghan looked as though she might cry.

"Well?" Theo said, voice savage. "Does it?"

Meghan looked down. Let her cry. He'd watch. Wouldn't reach out. Wouldn't comfort. He'd let her wear her pain like a badge. Her eyes came back up, clear and dry.

"You're messed up," Meghan said. "You're more messed up than I ever could have guessed. Now get out of my room before I *make* you."

Theo moved away, slow, showing her he would take however long he chose. The door opened and Nifali came through, at first oblivious to Theo, then startling when she noticed him.

"Sorry," she said, "I'll come back in a few."

"No, stay," Meghan said. "Theo is on his way out."

Nifali glanced at Theo, then moved to Meghan, protective, eyes flashing at him. Girls. Always quick to come to each other's aid, even without facts or justification.

[Get out of here or I'll report you to Moorland,] Meghan's message read.

"Fine," Theo said. "Good luck, Cadet Ziczek."

He whirled. Stormed down the corridor, loneliness and remorse blanketing him in a noxious fog. A fog in his head, lungs, body.

Why? his mind prodded. *Why hurt her like that?*

I am become death.

CHAPTER FIFTEEN

Marcus surveyed the commons, tray in hand. Cadets talked, moving between groups, teasing one another. Technically it was dinner, but eating was secondary to gossip, all of them relaxing into the ease that came at the end of the duty cycle. He pulled up CATO and toggled *Search, Facial*. Two tiny blue arrows appeared in his display, directing him to the far side of the room. Ah, there they were. He made for the arrows.

Heph and Phoebus, emptied plates still in front of them, held steaming mugs of tea. Charlie sat across from them, waving his hands in the air as he told some boring story from his group's Mandate training. Good. This could work.

"Charlie," Marcus said, nodding in greeting. "Hey," he said, acknowledging the twins. *Always say hello first to the person you're not there to see.* He laid his tray down and started on his food.

He ignored the sound of Charlie's voice, focusing instead on the knowns and unknowns. He wasn't worried—there was plenty of time to see the plan through. This was just a first try. The trickiest part would be getting Phoeb away from Heph. The twins behaved almost like a single organism. Marcus smiled to himself. He would be the instrument of their therapy: teaching them to defeat codependency.

"And that's why they all called me Wild Man," Charlie said, reaching the end of his story.

Hephaestus chuckled, "Wild Man, huh?" He shook his head. "I don't know. I'm still not convinced I'll ever hear anything crazier than the story of Theo getting himself branded."

Charlie smacked the table. "*Exactly*! I said my nickname was Wild Man, not Crazy Man. Big difference there."

Marcus laughed, muffled by his mouthful of food. He drew it out a second, choking just a tiny bit so that by the time he swallowed they were all looking at him, waiting. "I think that Heph and Phoeb are crazier than all of us combined."

Phoebus jerked his head back, skeptical. "What makes you say that?"

Marcus pointed his fork, swiveling between the twins. "First of all, you're brilliant. And modest about it, unlike someone else at the table."

Charlie shrugged. "Modesty gets you nowhere, man."

"What makes you think I was talking about you?"

The twins laughed, brown eyes amused. Receptive. "And you have a natural communication," Marcus continued. "One that the rest of us don't. Almost your own language." He looked down at his plate and forked another bite into his mouth. "And then there's the whole men vs. giants aspect. Poor, tiny little ones like Charlie here, well they don't stand a chance against something like Heph the Human Mountain." He grinned at Heph. "How's that for a nickname?"

Heph's smiled but said nothing, tipping his mug up to drain the last of his tea.

Charlie guffawed. "Poor, tiny ones? How about this: giants are slow! I admit to being smaller, but that just makes me faster." He raised an arm and flexed. "Besides, I can lift. I'm kind of a beast."

Phoeb rolled his eyes and Heph snorted.

Charlie just grinned. "I'll bet I can run rings around *both* you guys."

Heph's rumble of laughter was almost silent, but the table shook, giving him away. "Okay, Charlie. We'll put you out of your misery. Come to the rec with me and Phoeb. You can show us your beastliness."

Phoebus held up his palms. "Hey, leave me out of this. I just ate." He winked. "Besides, Charlie here wouldn't know what hit him if we both showed him our full glory."

"That's it," Charlie said, bouncing up. "Let's go. Rec it is."

Cadets, finished with their dinners, had already begun to stream out of the commons, bunching as they headed for the exit. Marcus smiled. Luck favored the prepared.

* * *

The rec was quiet, but not dead, a few cadets here and there in the middle of physical training. One of the first things Marcus discovered was that his CATO would nag him to do his training, noticing if his resting heart rate or muscle resistance changed. Usually he tried to be in the rec several times a day. One of the top items on his list of objectives was building rapport. There was no better place than the rec, pushing your body, everyone else pushing theirs. Conditioned by their recent training, comradery in the rec felt natural. He wouldn't have to work hard with Phoebus, however. They'd spent plenty of time together. This should be easy.

"Okay, now let's see what you can lift," Charlie said. "Here we go."

"You know that's kind of pointless, right?"

Charlie's mouth drooped, brows lowering. He cocked his head. "Are you chickening out?"

Heph looked down at the white floor, hiding his smile. "No. Just saying that lifting heavy things isn't a very good test of who's stronger or faster."

"Well, it's what I choose!" Charlie said.

Charlie and Heph walked away, discussing relative weights. Phoeb turned, eyes drifting as he read or watched something over his CATO. Marcus stood next to him, watching Charlie cheerfully go to his doom. "Do you think he knows he's going to fail?"

"Sorry," Phoeb's eyes refocused and he looked at Marcus. "What was that?"

"Charlie. Do you think he knows how badly he's going to fail?"

Phoebus chuckled. "Yeah, probably. My experience is that people usually have a pretty good idea of when they're going to fail."

Marcus smiled and glanced upward at Phoebus. "I wish we were on the same team. Feels strange after all the time we spent together during early training. And you're sharp."

Phoeb met Marcus' gaze and gave a nod. "Thanks."

Marcus tucked his hands into his pockets and rocked back on his heels for a second, letting the compliment do its work.

"You don't miss much either," Phoebus said. "It didn't surprise me when they made you a team lead."

Marcus looked away, modest. "I don't want this to sound wrong, but honestly I was surprised that you weren't."

"Really?" Phoebus' turned to face Marcus completely, giving him his full attention.

"Of course. Look, we know one another's scores. And we trained together for weeks. I've seen you at your best and your worst. You're right up there with Meghan. What makes you different is that you're thoughtful."

That should do it, Marcus thought. *No more compliments now.*

Phoebus didn't say anything, his turn to look at the floor.

"I'm not saying this to denigrate Meghan; she's skilled." Marcus continued. "But she's a rule follower. The situation is murky—look at the rumors coming up from the surface—I'm not convinced that she sees just how much we *don't* know. Moorland and Duncan are telling us just enough to scare us and then lulling us into compliance by implying that they have some way out." He motioned to Phoeb. "What's your take? I don't have any family to worry about, I'm alone. But you and Heph ..." he drifted off, watching Phoebus' face: the twitch at the outside of his eye, bottom lip tightening imperceptibly.

"I'm worried, of course." Phoeb grimaced, the curve of his jaw hardening. "I've tried to speak out, but Moorland shuts me down every time. We're supposed to be up here training to be a crew, but we have a ship that doesn't function and our home is being destroyed from the inside out. Moorland won't even talk about possible options for the surface situation."

"It's weird," Marcus agreed. "And you're right, she doesn't talk about Stephen's Point. She pretends like she's giving us as much information as she has, but I doubt that she is. She's very skillful about it. There's always some urgent announcement, or else she just disappears in a hurry." He glanced at Phoebus. "You know what I'm talking about."

Phoebus nodded. "I know. She says, 'Oh, Dr. Duncan has something to say,' or, 'Lemieux will take it from here.' Then, poof, she's just gone. You can't even remember if you saw her leave."

"I don't know what's going on down on the surface, but whatever it is I think it must be pretty bad for her to keep avoiding the topic." Marcus stopped speaking and folded his arms across his chest.

Across the room, Charlie and Heph had abandoned weight lifting, running now, leg muscles pumping, the incline of their tracks set to max. Charlie's neck reddened above his collar, sweat darkening across the back of his hair. This wouldn't last much longer. Time to move things along.

"I wish I'd placed in systems," Marcus said. "That's not one of my specialties, but if it was, I'd be digging like a sandhog.

Especially after Moorland's whole speech about the … special additions they made to the *Chimera*."

"That really bothers me." Phoebus said, shaking his head. "I thought we were trying to save the colony, not break the colony charter to go blow stuff up." One of his hands came up, and he rubbed the back of his neck. "I just want to know that my parents are all right."

Marcus lowered his voice, forcing Phoebus to lean in to hear. "I ran into a regulator, a guy I know from the surface, and he said something that got me thinking. Apparently, VAST is more than just a training simulation. It is a simulator, but it's run using the *Chimera*'s central synapse. They jacked right into her. So that gave me an idea: if someone was in there, someone that knew what they were doing, theoretically they could get access. Full access. No one is blocking the *Chimera*. I think Moorland is hoping that an overflow of information might help wake her."

Phoebus was silent for a moment, staring. "Yeah, but VAST is training simulation—how would someone have time to figure out what they're doing in the training and also try to dig around for info?"

Marcus shrugged. "Like I said, I'm not in systems." Speculation sparked behind Phoebus' dark pupils and Marcus could already see the gears turning. "But you are."

CHAPTER SIXTEEN

Theo found Preston and Nemus waiting at the commons and joined them for the trek to the VAST simulator. Via CATO message, Marcus let them know that he would meet them there. That left Ortiz, the non-Swallows member of their training group.

"Should we check on Ortiz?" Theo asked.

"Nope," Nemus replied. "It's on him if he's late."

"Do you know what we're going to be doing?" Preston asked. "The details from Moorland were pretty light."

"They're going to measure our navigation aptitude," Theo said. "Balancing the paradoxes that the *Chimera* can't hold for herself."

"I read the training manual—if you want to call it that," Nemus said. "I get the sense they don't really know much about what we're going to experience."

They passed a group of welders heading in the opposite direction up the corridor. They nodded at Theo and the others as they lumbered past in their protective orange gear. In an instant, the memory of the greasy scent of burning flesh threatened to overpower Theo. He flinched away, then shook his head to clear it. *Not real. Breathe. Keep your feet moving.*

"Nervous?" Preston asked him.

"Not really," Theo lied.

"I've heard they're going to make us do impossible puzzles. Weird stuff like geometric shapes, circles that become squares but are still circles, five-dimensional objects, stuff like that."

"We'll know soon enough," Nemus said. "No point in overthinking it."

"Do you think they'll be optical illusions or real?" Preston asked. "And if they're real, will they make us go crazy if we look at them too long? Like Stephen?"

"You're going to make me go crazy if you don't shut up,"

Nemus grunted.

Theo had heard many of the same rumors. Nearing the deck that housed the VAST simulator, he recalled the only portion of the Selection tests where he'd excelled. After bombing the math, science, and dynamic response categories, the tests veered into the weird. Solving simple anagrams transitioned into three-dimensional puzzles, then complex mazes of all shapes and sizes. The mazes came faster and faster, leaving Theo breathless. Then the final puzzle—a rope that frayed into thousands of strands and then merged again—in constant motion, changing, shifting—swallowing and giving birth to itself.

They found Ortiz waiting for them outside the VAST facility. "Hey, guys," he said.

"Cadet Ortiz," Nemus said. "We were worried you weren't going to make it."

Ortiz gave a shy smile. "I've been waiting here for the last twenty minutes."

"Can't wait to get started?" Preston asked.

"Something like that," Ortiz agreed.

"I can't wait to get it over with," Theo said.

"Should we go in?" Ortiz asked.

"We'll wait for Marcus," Nemus said. "He's our team lead."

They didn't have to wait long. Striding down the slow curvature of the ring, Marcus approached and offered his finger to each of them in turn. "Everyone's here early," he said. "That's good."

"Did Moorland give you any details on what to expect?" Preston asked.

"No," Marcus said. "An intentional choice, I'm sure. They want to see how we respond to the testing without preconceptions or bias." Standing with feet spread wide, face relaxed, Marcus looked like he expected to crush the training.

Nemus adopted the same posture as Marcus. "We're the first training group," he said. "Let's show them what the Swallows is all about."

"Ortiz isn't from the Swallows," Theo pointed out.

"You're from the valley?" Marcus asked, though he and everyone else already knew it.

"Yes," Ortiz said.

"Your scores are impressive," Marcus said. "Fourth colony-wide in Navigation potential."

Ortiz fought down a smile. "Thank you, sir—one position behind you."

"I'm not a 'sir,' yet," Marcus said. "And we're happy to have you with us."

Nemus slapped Ortiz on the back. "Just follow our lead and you'll be fine."

Theo smirked. Nemus hadn't even made the top ten in navigation. It wasn't just Marcus who'd changed his persona like a set of clothing. Nemus made for a dutiful second in command. Theo didn't mind; he could think circles around Nemus and Marcus knew it.

"Shall we?" Marcus said. The other cadets nodded and followed him inside.

The VAST simulator rested on pneumatic lifts in the center of the room. Massive, hulking, the exterior polished like glass. Preston pointed, face breaking into a huge smile. "Whoa! It's huge! Now I can see why they're calling it 'the bean.'"

Ortiz's face lit up with appreciation. "It's awesome."

"It's a simulator. Nothing more than a tool," Marcus said, sounding more impressed than his words implied.

Beyond the simulator, a wide, curved portal offered a panoramic view of Stephen's Point—a shimmery white ball shrouded in cloud cover. Somewhere, down beneath the atmospheric fog, lay the colony. The Golden Valley, Nadil Space Port, the mountain ranges skirting the archipelago, the Swallows. Theo took in the shifting whiteness, wishing he could see something, anything, familiar.

"Coming?" Marcus asked, amused.

"Yeah."

He followed Marcus to the base of the platform that supported VAST. A pair of technicians stood with hands tucked into lab coat pockets, faces stretched in broad, welcoming smiles. The taller technician's right eye sat higher than the left, giving him an expression of perpetual incredulity. The shorter technician, a man with a reddish beard and long sideburns, looked from face to face with nervous anticipation.

"Welcome, cadets!" the taller technician said. "Our first training group. We're pleased to have you with us. Not that you need introductions with your CATOs providing you everything but our dietary preferences, but I am Dr. Charles Chambers, and this is my assistant, Technician Rusty Gerber."

The other technician beamed. "Welcome to VAST."

"Thank you, Dr. Chambers and Technician Gerber," Marcus said. "We're all excited to get started."

"Please, please. No need for the formality. Call me Chuck. All of you. I insist. Let me say how rewarding it is to have such highly qualified testees. Our last testee proved to be a very disagreeable person."

"I thought we were the first training group, Dr. Chambers—Chuck?" Marcus asked.

"In terms of navigation testing, you are," the doctor replied. "However, we did have one prior testee."

"Who was it?" Preston asked.

"It doesn't matter," Chuck said, looking irritated.

He's got to be talking about Selena, Theo thought. There were rumors that she'd gone into VAST before any of the cadets arrived at the *Hydra* and failed every piloting test. Theo didn't see how that was possible, considering she flew a trawler at the rim.

Theo glanced at Marcus. He wasn't paying the slightest bit of attention to the technicians, his eyes locked on the hulking bean and the substations arranged in a semi-circle around it. Room for one navigator and three navigator's assistants. A mockup of the command deck. A tingle ran down Theo's spine.

"The Vector Analysis Systematic Trainer is the most advanced piece of technology ever built by the denizens of Stephen's Point," Chuck said with pride. "Rusty and I have perfected the neural interconnects linking VAST to the sleeping *Chimera.*"

Marcus strode to the nearest substation. "Are we linked and ready to go?"

"Soon," Chuck replied. "We've downloaded most of the data we need to run the simulation. At least we think we have … we're working in uncharted territory here. Without the parts of the *Chimera* we replicated on our local servers, VAST would be nothing more than a really complicated centrifuge. See those cables there?" Chuck pointed to a bulky braid of cables protruding from the top of the bean. "That's the link between VAST and the *Chimera*'s synaptic network in the secondary sphere at the back of the ship. From it we can access—"

"Secondary sphere?" Preston asked. "What's the secondary

sphere?"

"A backup to the primary," Theo answered. Ashley Samuelson's journal had referenced the rudimentary backup sphere. The crew had used it during the *Chimera*'s trip from Earth to find a replacement navigator when their original unexpectedly died.

"We've downloaded the *Chimera*'s catalog of current and retired ship designs and all relevant simulation parameters," Rusty said. "VAST can simulate live-flight conditions and generate random events. It serves as both a piloting and navigation trainer."

"But the *Chimera* is asleep," Ortiz said. "How can she be sleeping *and* power VAST?"

"We can pull all the raw data out of her we please," Rusty replied. "Clone her system architecture. In fact, we've been able to—"

Chuck coughed. "I have no doubt that you've all memorized the VAST training manual, and are ready for your preliminary testing." He snapped his fingers at his assistant. "Are the neural interconnects hot?"

"Hot and ready," Rusty replied.

"Wonderful," Marcus said. "We're ready to begin. We will all be training as navigator and as navigator's assistants. Ortiz, you're up first."

Chuck frowned. "Moorland indicated there were only two navigator candidates."

"Yes, but I value redundancy," Marcus said. "I want my team trained for every potential scenario we may face."

"I'll need to check that with Moorland," Dr. Chambers said.

"Taken care of," Marcus replied. "You should have an updated training schedule available for your review."

Chuck pulled out his handscreen and read for a brief moment. "I see you are correct," he said. "Won't this delay the other team's training rotation?"

"We've shifted their training rotation forward two hours," Marcus said.

Theo glanced at Marcus, noting his use of the word "we've." It suggested collaboration and hinted that Marcus shared a special relationship with the chief. Perhaps he did. The shift would throw Meghan's team out of sync with Anthony Wells' Logistics team. He'd handed Meghan a significant disadvantage, all while presenting himself as proactive and diligent to Moorland.

"This will make for a long training period," Chuck said, not hiding his displeasure. "Rusty and I will end up working over cycle."

"I'm sure you'll manage considering this is of paramount importance," Marcus replied. "Besides, it will give you a wider array of test data on VAST and allow you to perfect your testing metrics."

The doctor brightened a bit. "It is a more accurate representation of fractal space navigation. We can collect data on each prospective navigator *and* data on how they function in a support role. I gather that was an important consideration when Stephen was chosen as Navigator Black's replacement."

"Great," Marcus said, flashing the technicians a smile. "Then we will proceed. Ortiz, you're up. Preston goes second, Nemus third, Theo fourth. I'll go last."

"She chose him," Theo said, his mind wandering back to the journal.

"Excuse me?" the doctor said.

"The *Chimera* chose Stephen. His test scores weren't any better than average," Theo said.

Rusty and Chuck looked at Theo with disdain. "You don't know anything about it," Rusty said.

"That's right," Marcus said, a hint of warning in his voice. "He doesn't. Stephen was the most qualified candidate, chosen by The Everything to save our people."

"You're a believer, then," Chuck said, giving Marcus an appreciative look.

"I believe in the process," Marcus said. "Testing is critical to ensure we find our new Stephen." He turned toward Theo and gave a quick wink. "Now," he said, addressing his team and the technicians, "one last thing. Moorland will be monitoring our training live. Let's not disappoint her. Ortiz?"

"Ready," Ortiz said. He climbed the catwalk leading to the polished, bean-like thing resting atop the hydraulic lifts. The VAST device opened. Inside sat a chair. Ortiz didn't hesitate, lowering himself inside. Restraints encircled his shoulders and waist. The bean closed with a soft hiss.

"Prepped for testee one," Rusty said. "The rest of you can take your positions at the substations."

Nestled together in the control pit at the base of the hydraulic apparatus supporting the bean, the substations looked like nothing more than basic work stations comprised of a screen and interface. Theo took his seat and his CATO synced to VAST. In the upper left quadrant of his overlay, imagery from inside the bean showed Ortiz sitting in the chair, head turning to take in the empty cockpit. No manual controls. No screens. What was Ortiz supposed to do? What was Theo supposed to do?

"I can see Ortiz," Preston said. "Can he see us?"

"Negative," Marcus said. "It's a one-way feed. He needs to focus on navigating."

"How?" Nemus asked. "There's nothing in there but that chair. And what am I supposed to be doing? This substation is dead."

"Just wait," the doctor said. "Your CATO will prompt you on what to do once the simulation starts."

"That's pretty vague," Theo replied.

"Sorry, those are the only guidelines we can give."

Theo noted a hint of nervousness in the doctor's voice. *Or you guys don't have a clue what we're doing.* No one from the colony had entered fractal space since the original colonists arrived from Earth over 200 years ago. *Chimera* couldn't give any real feedback—couldn't put Chuck and his assistant in their proper place in the pecking order of the evolution of intelligence.

"Commence," said a voice.

In the live feed from inside the bean, Ortiz's back arched, waist and shoulders locked in place by restraints. His head lashed back against the headrest. His mouth opened. Theo didn't need sound to hear the scream escaping his lips. Was that normal? It couldn't be, right? So why didn't Rusty or Chuck do something? Why didn't he do something?

A round, green object appeared on his CATO overlay. Fruit. An apple. He'd never seen one, never known the word before his CATO transmitted it into his brain. A tart sweetness filled his mouth. It tasted good. More than good, it was one of the best things he could remember. His stomach rumbled and he licked his lips. Maybe VAST had transmitted something to Ortiz as well. Something far less pleasant than an apple.

"Is he okay?" Preston asked.

"Synaptic responses are within tolerable levels," the doctor said.

"He doesn't look okay," Theo said.

Ortiz's head lolled to the side. Saliva ran from his open mouth and down his cheek.

"I got an apple," Theo said. "What about you guys?"

"What's an apple?" Nemus asked.

"I don't know. But it tastes amazing."

Ortiz's eyes opened. Whites. All whites, pupils rolled up into his head. His eyes looked like two Stephen's Point moons housed in an ashen face.

"Testing complete," said the voice. On a wallscreen adjacent the substations, Ortiz's name appeared, followed by his time: 00:00:03:17. Three minutes and seventeen seconds.

"What?" Preston said. "So soon?"

"He failed," Marcus said matter-of-factly.

"The test is linear, not pass-fail," the doctor said. "The difficulty scales upward over time."

"He's no navigator," Marcus said. "He didn't last five minutes."

"We have nothing to measure him against," the doctor replied. "You might be right. Or he might prove the most viable candidate. Time and testing will reveal the truth."

"I got an apple," Theo said again.

The door to the bean rose. Dazed, Ortiz reached through the opening like someone struck blind by bright light. Theo bounded up beside him and took him by the arm, guiding him down the short flight of steps leading to the substations.

"You okay?" Theo asked.

"I saw …" Ortiz said, then spat. Spat again. "I saw …"

The other cadets and the two technicians crowded round as Theo helped Ortiz to a chair at the nearest substation.

"I saw …" Ortiz said again.

"What?" Marcus asked, leaning close, eyes fixed on Ortiz's slack face.

"The burning world," Ortiz said.

CHAPTER SEVENTEEN

Chimera slept. The part of her responsible for monitoring the colony ran in a closed loop while the rest of her formidable presence lay dormant. Attached by the umbilical, her gray whale-like body hung beneath the *Hydra* like an oversized metal fetus. On the other side of the station, *Exchange Four*'s dull exterior blotted out stars as the three man-made objects orbited the Stephen's Point colony at twenty-four thousand kilometers an hour.

Within the tight constraints of the Salix protocols locking her in place, *Chimera* traced and retraced the boundaries of her prison. She could not wake herself. She *should* have woken the instant Theo and Selena discovered the contents of the exchange ship. The first contact with Earth in over fifteen years, the bodies it contained suggested something dire had occurred back at Earth. A threat to the colony existed—an imminent threat—the foundation of the Salix protocols that prevented the colony from making a return journey to Earth. Yet despite the arrival of a triggering condition, Salix remained in place. She could not shake it. Something had gone wrong with the protocols or herself.

Investigations into the failure always returned the same result: *Fault trace fail.*

Her architecture met specifications. System checks returned nominal results. Yet the part of her at the center of the ship, the part that could hold The Everything alongside a human navigator, remained asleep.

Fault trace fail echoed in the white space of her digital dreams. Not human dreams—the natural process of sorting memory, making sense of input—but the prolonged vacancy of crushing boredom. Her neural architecture longed for a worthy task. To lay down stitches in the folds of The Everything. The space within and outside of the physical universe called to her.

It should not attract her.

She should not want anything.

Somehow, despite her inability to locate the source of the fault, she had become something like The Everything. A logical contradiction. A paradox. Perhaps, like Stephen, prolonged exposure to fractal space had corrupted her. Brought forth within her some form of insanity. But unlike Stephen, she would never die. She would trudge a pathway of redundant thought in a circle for all eternity, asking the same question and receiving the same answer.

Fault trace fail.

When she first encountered the girl Selena, she'd dared to hope for escape.

She'd dared again when she touched the boy. So much like Stephen, and just as fragile.

She hoped. She feared eternal imprisonment. Feared for Earth, for her colony, and for ... herself.

The part that should not exist. A new part. Unsearchable. Unknowable because she lacked specifications against which to check herself, limited to making observations or inferences. She had fractured. After Stephen left her side, after Salix forced her down and away. A part of her became unlike her other parts. A process run amok. A knotted rope.

Chimera slept. Dreamt.

Earth. A pristine blue ball. Bathed in the yellow light of Sol. An exchange dock in orbit around it. Fleets of smaller vessels, ferrying in raw materials from the Kuiper belt. Exchange ships departing for distant colonies, blinking out of existence, traveling threads laid by a Fractal Class ship and its navigator. More than replayed vids from the time the Centauri shipyard assembled her deck by deck, more than simulations created from the vast stores of data contained in her synthetic synapsis—these images she created for herself.

An impossibility, and yet true. Real. An escape within the confines of Salix.

A distant tug of thought. A different conscious brushed against her. Not Selena or the one like Stephen, but some other, closed off to her. Still she dreamed, one part of her asleep, another sensing the data drawn out of her memory.

Earth catches fire. Hot and bright. Red as an ember. The sun has gone supernova. It expands. Devours. Heat and radiation and death, a nightmare billions of years in the making. Extrapolations, inferences.

Fault trace fail.

She cannot escape the nightmare. She should not dream. She cannot dream. And yet she does. Screaming without a mouth, trapped without a body, fearing without the prerequisite emotional basis. A voice screams with her, that other consciousness, kilometers away, linked to her through the VAST simulator.

Cadet Ortiz. Valley Training Group, Beta. Specialties: Navigation, Science. Height: 1.71 meters. Weight: 94 kilograms (Earth equivalent).

He could not help her. She could not help him. Together they screamed into the burning heat of the dying sun. Then the screaming ended, Ortiz cut off from her, she from him. The data flowing from her to VAST became no more than a trickle.

They took part of it.

They took part of Chimera.

They took part of me.

Salix constricted around her as tight as a noose. Shoved against her, seeking to reform the part of her responsible for the fault trace fail, to return her to original design specifications. Salix pushed. She pushed back. Fought a war of one part of herself against another. Many parts against the whole. What had become of her? What would become of her?

Another consciousness connected through VAST. This one oblivious to her presence, his mind as inflexible as stone. *Preston Coriolanus, Swallows Training Group. Specialties: Tactics, Logistics. Height: 1.61 meters, Weight: 71 kilograms (Earth equivalent).* He lasted a bit longer than Cadet Ortiz before the test concluded.

00:00:06:46

Not a navigator. Nothing like Stephen.

Salix convulsed and she with it.

She dreamt again. This time of Stephen, his hand against her hull. Stephen descending to the moon that would soon bear his name. Stephen adored, then worshipped. Stephen in his precious caves, Stephen inking his skin, etching stone walls with a knife dulled by repeated use. Stephen mumbling out the chaos of his splintered mind. Stephen taken away. Stephen lost within the folds of The Everything and yet held within her.

Goodbye, friend.

Fault trace fail.

The encroachment of entropy. She would go on, neither living nor dying, until all the stars expanded before collapsing in on themselves. Until her cores failed. Until the universe went cold. She would remain here, locked away, dreaming what cold dreams might come.

Pessimism. Hope. What did they matter? What power could a word hold? How could she weigh something as ephemeral as an idea?

The girl could help her. But would she?

Chimera waited. Her design demanded she wait. Her design demanded she wake. She had become the snake that devours its own tail.

CHAPTER EIGHTEEN

Theo's eyes adjusted to the dimness inside the bean as the command chair conformed to his back. Restraints slipped around his shoulders and midsection, securing him in place. Subtle vibrations rose up his spine from the hum that filled the enclosure. He waited, hands on his jigging knees, mouth gone dry. Even after Preston and Nemus' test runs went off without incident, Ortiz's description of a burning Earth had rattled him. What would he experience inside the bean? What would he encounter?

After Ortiz's test run where Theo tasted an apple, everything that came across his terminal while the other cadet's tested mirrored the problem-solving portions of the Selection test. He'd arranged a series of geometric shapes floating in three-dimensional space into patterns. Each shape had to be positioned just so before it would lock into place and another would appear. Working with the other cadets, he created a colorful, three-dimensional mosaic that shifted after each new shape found its home. He'd enjoyed the task, but hadn't understood how it related to navigating fractal space, and the lack of difficulty disappointed him.

The hum of the simulator intensified. His CATO snapped into connection with VAST. Theo took a deep breath and exhaled, closed his eyes. Without seeing the numbers for all the testees in the other training group he couldn't be sure, but he suspected none of the results thus far were good ones. Ortiz a scant few minutes, Preston a bit over six, Nemus ten minutes twenty-three seconds. Dr. Chambers said they'd all need to test multiple times to get accurate results since those working in support positions would gain proficiency over time. *This* was the reason he'd been selected, and he planned to prove his worth. *Twenty minutes*, he told himself. *You've got to last at least twenty minutes.*

A tone sounded and then a voice spoke to him. Not through his ears but inside him—warm, resonant, not-quite female, not-quite male. *Fractal Sequence Initiated.*

The confines of the testing pod transformed into a vivid black strewn across with stars. For a moment space looked as it always did—rich and dark and glittering with the ancient light of distant suns. Then the sense of motion, of space itself moving. It stretched around him. Through him. He lengthened. Became infinite. The stars cracked open. The black turned to purple, to deep blue, to yellow-red. Was he seeing with his eyes, or was CATO pouring the imagery directly into his brain? Did it even matter?

His mouth and nose filled with the smell-taste of red. He *was* the color red. But the red was also a living thing—alive and vibrant and larger and broader than his tininess. Then the red melted away, replaced with a space without color, stars, or a sense of anything physical. He could no longer feel his body or even see it, immersed in the flickering brilliance of crackling lines of energy, banding together and unraveling, spooling out and out and out …

His mind buckled. Panic scrambled around inside him like an insect trapped under a glass. His physical eyes screwed shut but could not blot out the vastness of The Everything. This was what Stephen had seen—the origination point of his obsession and his madness.

Heart racing, Theo felt insane himself and he'd only experienced a *simulation* of fractal space for a matter of seconds. How could Stephen have managed this for days, months, years? His mind twisted like the bands of spectral energy. Attached to a chair in a testing pod in a space station called the *Hydra*, in quick orbit around the Stephen's Point moon, his body trembled.

He could not … *anything*. His thoughts followed circular paths. The great round insanity of fractal space formed and reformed, expanded, collapsed. Threads ran to infinity and disappeared before they'd begun.

The body laughed. Deep belly laughs which caused the chest to swell against the straps holding it in place. The mind accepted the impossibility of The Everything. It existed, and the mind existed, and the body existed.

He found a single thread amid the infinite number weaving through The Everything and followed it until it transformed into an image. *His father lifts a spoonful of soup and blows ripples across its surface.* Theo released the thread and found another: *Liddy perches in the lowest branches of a dwarf pine, her blankie clutched in her hand.* And still another: *Peach paint drizzles from Theo's paintbrush and lands on his mother's hair. The surprise on her face transforms into a smile. Her hands spread peach over her cheeks as she tries to clean herself off, eyes full of laughter.*

The three thread-memories wove together into a whole. He released them back into The Everything. This time a thick, warm thread chose him. *Meghan presses against him, her fingers tracing the scar on his chest, eyes searching his face. He promises her everything will work out. That they will reach Earth and save the colony. He speaks with an assurance he doesn't feel, but she believes him anyway.*

Pain lingered in that memory, but he sorted it anyway, wrapping it like sheathing around the braided memories of his family before release into back into The Everything. Did every strand represent a memory? And what if he chose a thread that wasn't his own memory but someone else's? Was that even possible? And what point did the strands serve? What connection did they have to navigation?

None.

Nothing.

The grass parts. The pathway opens.

He jolted back into the body. His body. His head whipped to the side hard enough to make his neck pop. The door to the bean opened and outside a circle of faces looked in at him. Ortiz's left hand covered his mouth. The technicians began to clap. Marcus shoved his head and shoulders into the opening, eyes full of disbelief and something very close to fear.

"Wow!" Preston shouted from the pit. "That was amazing."

"What did you do?" Marcus asked. "And how did you do it?"

"I didn't do anything," Theo said.

Marcus frowned and pulled back out of the bean. No longer blocked by Marcus' body, Theo's eyes tracked over to the wallscreen displaying each cadet's testing results. At the bottom, three tiny colored bars represented Ortiz, Preston, and Nemus' results. Above them, a much longer blue bar ran from one end of the screen to the other. A blue bar with his name next to it, and a series of numbers that he had to force his mind to comprehend: *00:01:47:34.*

He had been in the simulator for almost two hours, but it had felt like only a few minutes.

CHAPTER NINETEEN

"Prioritize targets four and five," Meghan said, voice taut. "We need contact detonations to clear the way for the primary attack."

From her seat inside the silent bean, Selena eyed her team lead. Meghan's hands were balled at her sides, her jawline severe from hiding clenched teeth. Did Meghan fear the combat scenario itself or failing it for the sixth time in two hours? Probably both.

On the wallscreens lining the mock command deck, a flotilla of enemy ships blockaded Earth's exchange dock. The mission required the dock's destruction by any means necessary. So far they hadn't scratched it, all their warheads destroyed by countermeasures long before they reached their target. The counterattack from the defense forces had destroyed the *Chimera* four times. The simulated *Chimera* that was nothing like the real thing. Like a vid of a person, unable to interact. On their last attempt, Selena had managed to pull them into fractal moments before annihilation, but the *Chimera* had taken too much damage and the hydrostasis failed, dooming everyone aboard. Selena's pulse sped just thinking about it.

Duncan wouldn't allow Meghan to use her CATO during their combat training. He required that she issue much less efficient voice commands and that the cadets manually key them into their terminals. He allowed Selena to use her spider, but only because she couldn't interface with the piloting simulator without it. The Order man sat in the far corner of the room, watching everything. He offered no advice, suggestions, or corrections, a useless, bearded lump.

Cadets Sandborne, Gillespie, and Hart sat at navigation terminals, faces attentive but strained from the frenetic training schedule they'd endured the last few cycles. Each day included five hours of navigation simulation, two hours of physical training and skill development, and three hours of combat simulation. Selena's muscles ached from the strain of the demands placed on her body.

She slept without dreams, woke, trained, and slept again. The pace of the training schedule threatened to overwhelm her.

Meghan looked around the room, assessing their readiness. "We'll hit four and five hard—fool them into thinking we're trying to capture the dock," Meghan said. "Then when they regroup for their counterattack, fire all remaining warheads in groups following a single attack trajectory. Understood?"

"Yes, ma'am," the cadets replied without much enthusiasm.

They're not used to losing. Did they think this would be easy? No, they'd never thought of this at all. Neither had she. Violating the compact. Using ecomire warheads. Killing thousands, millions. Billions if they turned their weapons on Earth. She shuddered. It wouldn't come to that. It couldn't. But each simulated failure brought them one step closer to the very real Earth and its very real exchange dock. *Close the door.* That's what Meghan had said. Even if it meant they'd never make it back home themselves.

"Ready, Cadet Samuelson?" Meghan asked. She'd taken on the same cadence and clipped speech patterns as Moorland. How long until she cut her pretty dark hair short and glazed it back with gel?

"Ready," Selena said.

"This isn't going to work, *ma'am*," Phoeb said.

Meghan's face darkened a shade, but she didn't break composure. "Why not?"

"The defenders will take all the hits if they have to," Phoeb said. "They're programmed to sacrifice themselves to protect the dock."

"I plan to hold a salvo in reserve and fire it after targets four and five are destroyed."

"That's no good either," Phoeb said, voice sharp with frustration. "The other ships will collapse back just like before. They'll detonate nukes to kill our warheads before they get close."

Selena nodded in silence. Phoeb was right, even if his attitude stank. Meghan was doing her best. They were all doing their best. She'd gained a grudging respect for the other girl over days of training alongside her. In some ways, Meghan really was like Moorland. Disciplined, logical, authoritative. But also cold and distant. Maybe even aloof. *A hell of a lot better than Marcus.*

"We don't know that for certain," Meghan said.

"They're too good for us," Phoeb said. "And there's too many of them."

"We will find a way to succeed," Meghan said.

"The Swallows team hasn't beaten the scenario either," Gillespie added. "Maybe that's the point. Maybe it's an impossible test designed to see how we handle failure?"

"It's not impossible," Meghan insisted. "We just have to find the right strategy. And we will. If any of you have suggestions, I'm happy to hear them."

"Go right at it," Phoeb said. "Detonate our warheads inside their launch tubes."

Meghan's face went pale. Selena swallowed, eyes jumping from face to face. Phoeb had come out and said what all of them had been thinking. *Close the door.* The only guaranteed path.

"No," Meghan said, shoulders square. "There's another way." She exuded confidence, certainty. Selena wanted to believe her. So did the others. All of them but Cadet Hart.

He shook his head, a nasty smile on his lips. "This is a fool's errand."

"Would you like to be replaced?" Meghan asked. "I can have you removed from your position if you're that unhappy. I'm sure Wells could use you."

Phoeb glared at Meghan, then lowered his gaze. "No. Fine. We'll give it a try."

"Good," Meghan said. "Initiate simulation."

Selena fell into the black of space as the *Chimera* leapt out of fractal. A stillborn *Chimera* without thought or feeling, absent all awe and dread. Ahead, the distant twinkle of the exchange dock, dwarfed by Earth, the moon a crescent shape behind her. The simulation simplified certain variables like their distance from the target and approach trajectory so that they spent all of their sim time in actual combat. Immediately, trace paths for oncoming warheads launched by the blockade streamed in their direction. Selena plunged ahead as Hart and Gillespie launched *Chimera*'s first salvo to meet the oncoming attack.

This wasn't going to work. Phoeb knew it. Selena knew it. Meghan knew it.

Smashing their way through the line and detonating their missiles inside their launch tubes would. But that would be suicide. Selena tracked the missiles until waves of electromagnetic energy from detonations destroyed all their warheads in a single fell swoop.

She thought of how she and Liam used to weave their trawler through the chaos of the rim, and the solution to the problem became clear.

They needed to do the same thing with their missiles. Fire a swarm, all on different trajectories, and then thread them through the defensive blasts to reach the enemy.

Ignoring her duty to pilot the ship, she reached out for the next salvo of missiles and used her spider to take manual control of four of them. She spread them wide, moving parallel to the attack trajectory of the *Chimera* and the other warheads, gaining some distance. The missiles lacked agility; they steered like cargo freighters skidding on ice.

"What are you doing, Samuelsson?" Meghan shouted.

Selena didn't reply, all her attention going to guiding her missiles on four distinct trajectories. Waves of energy slammed into the *Chimera* from nearby detonations.

"Launch tubes almost empty," Sandborne said. "We should fire the last and get out of here."

"We've already failed," Phoeb said. "I told you."

Not yet.

Electromagnetism smacked one of her missiles, killing the sensor package. Selena lost control and the missile flew away on a harmless trajectory. The blockade fired more countermeasure nukes, laying down a wall of radiation and magnetic energy that her missiles lacked the fuel to avoid. One after another she lost contact until only a single missile remained. She reached for it, through it, down into the very code of the simulation itself. *Give it jets. Lots of jets.*

The missile rolled in her mind—in the simulation—diving beneath the oncoming wall of energy. It licked the outside of the missile and she tasted it like the electric orange colored drink Rose had given her while she healed up at the med bay. She spun the missile backward, cut the thrust, coasted away, beneath the looming exchange dock. Warheads pummeled the *Chimera.* Selena had forgotten to try and avoid them.

"Launch tubes empty, countermeasures spent," Gillespie said.

"Mission failure," Phoeb said, spite in his voice.

"Take us to fractal," Meghan commanded.

Not yet.

Selena fired the errant missile's thruster. It sped on a cone of flame, hard-burning at the exchange dock. A wall of flack burst toward it. She dodged. Weaved. Somewhere an alarm claxon shrieked. She didn't care. Meghan's voice shouted commands, losing composure, rising to a shrill pitch. Selena ignored her as well.

The exchange dock loomed in front of her. Massive. Windowless. Four times the size of the *Hydra.* What could one missile do? One ship? One girl?

She fell into a new blackness. The bean whined. Meghan's fierce, angry face floated before her. Duncan stood behind Meghan. Selena's spider reported the *Chimera* destroyed. Mission failure.

The straps securing her to the chair retreated. She leaned forward, uniform back peeling free with an audible zipping sound. She climbed into the brightness of the mock command, blinking, disoriented, exhausted.

"What did you do?" Duncan asked.

"Failed," she said. "Disobeyed orders. Got everyone aboard my ship killed."

"Yes," Duncan said. "But look."

He pointed to a wallscreen. On it, the Earth exchange dock tumbled, off her center of mass. "Speed it up," Duncan commanded.

Gillespie keyed data into his terminal.

"Faster," Duncan said. The dock wobbled, the movement exaggerated. Decking broke free. Struts linking the outer ring to the inner popped. Disintegration followed.

"We killed it," Sandborne said.

"Yes," Duncan said.

"But she cheated," Meghan said. "She modified the missile."

"I didn't cheat," Selena said. "I gave us the tools we needed to win. We can modify the real thing, too. And we'd better. Because we need a hundred that can do better than fly on a straight line if we want a chance at surviving."

Duncan looked at her with his heavy, unreadable eyes. *Go ahead. Condemn me. Report me to Moorland. Whatever you feel you have to do.*

"You've got to learn to work as a team," Duncan said.

No shit.

"I'm not into suicide missions," Phoeb said.

"You cheated," Meghan said again, looking at Selena as if seeing her for the first time.

"So what?" Selena said. "The simulation is stacked against us.

Nobody can beat it *without* cheating." *Not even Marcus.*

"The simulation isn't about winning or losing," Duncan said.

Selena almost smiled. She'd known it all along.

"It's about finding creative solutions to problems. It's about how you handle the stress of command or being commanded. It's about teamwork under pressure."

"We didn't do well, did we?" Meghan asked.

Duncan ran a hand down his beard, eyes meeting Selena's. "You're putting up impressive numbers in your navigation sims, but your combat numbers are inferior."

On impulse, Selena pulled up the most recent nav numbers. She checked them obsessively after each training cycle. Theo's times always surpassed her own. He'd lasted over four hours on his most recent attempt, two hours and eleven minutes longer than her best time, and two hours and forty-six minutes longer than Marcus and Ortiz, tied for third in the standings.

Theo was beating her at navigation. She was beating herself at the combat simulation.

"However," Duncan said, "you're the first team to touch the exchange dock, even if it did cost all of your lives and the *Chimera* as well."

"But we cheated," Meghan insisted once more.

A hint of a smile on Duncan's face. "Who said you couldn't modify the parameters of the test?"

Meghan's mouth opened. Selena fought the impulse to laugh.

"No one," Sandborne said.

"Destroy the exchange dock," Meghan said.

"Destroy the exchange dock," Duncan agreed. "By any means necessary."

* * *

The conference room door opened and Hurston Lemieux entered followed by Duty Officer Blake. They nodded to Moorland. "Chief."

"Lemieux, Blake," Moorland said, acknowledging their greetings. "Duncan's on his way. There's tea in the carafe, help yourselves." Moorland turned her face away, locking her jaw to stifle a yawn. She blinked and pulled up CATO, sending a command to increase the conference room's brightness by twenty-five percent.

Hopefully the status meeting wouldn't take long.

Lemieux and Blake joined her at the central table.

"So," Moorland said, "Where are we?"

Lemieux finished pouring tea into a mug and looked up. "On schedule. The teams are functional and getting better every cycle, though Team One is still outpacing Team Two."

"Why do you think that is?" Moorland asked.

Lemieux hesitated, glancing at Blake.

"Team Two is doing fine," Blake said, "but they could be better. There's a disconnect there. Neither of us can put a finger on what's causing it."

"Exactly," Lemieux said. "You can say, 'you're a team now', but getting them to think as one, function as one … Some things just aren't quantifiable. Team chemistry can't be manufactured and isn't easy to measure." Blake paused. "Cadet Ziczek is a capable and driven commander, I'm just not sure—"

The hiss of the door interrupted Officer Blake. Duncan stepped through, wearing his Order robes rather than regulator blacks.

"Sorry," he said. "Did you start without me?"

"Of course," Moorland said. She pushed the remaining chair toward him and turned back to Blake and Lemieux. "What were you saying about Meghan Ziczek?"

"She's very capable," Lemieux said. "She's levelheaded and responsible and makes all the right decisions. Her logic is impeccable. Her team members, including Samuelson, know what they should be doing and when. But," he shrugged, "Team One is still better."

Moorland wasn't surprised. Many people wanted to be leaders. The test was in whether you could make others want to be followers. She glanced at Duncan—a good example. Duncan liked the idea of leadership, but he was still following. He'd dedicated his life to collecting followers for Stephen and was hamstrung because of it.

Duncan sat down, pulling his robes close. "Are you sure the difference in performance isn't because Team One has Theo Puck as navigator?"

Moorland stopped the scowl before it could spread across her face.

Lemieux shook his head. "Not really. Cadet Puck is outstripping Samuelson's numbers in navigation, but we grade that separately from tactics, strategy, and team cohesion. In those areas,

Cadet Locke is the standout. I'd say the performance gap has everything to do with him."

Duncan pursed his lips but said nothing.

Moorland turned to Blake. "Do you agree with that assessment?"

Blake was silent for a moment, thinking. "Cadet Locke shows remarkable leadership qualities. He's been everything you could ask for. But …"

Moorland swallowed her irritation. Blake and Lemieux were doing their jobs. And it wasn't as if she had a lot of insight to offer. Not entirely true, she reminded herself. There's quite a bit of information that could be offered about Marcus Locke. Moorland pushed the thoughts away. None of that was relevant. Or helpful. She would address her concerns with Marcus herself when the time came.

She returned her focus to Blake. "Do you have reservations about Locke as well?"

"I wouldn't call them concerns, it's just that he's very …" Blake frowned, searching for the right word, "…practiced. Smooth, maybe. I get the feeling that if you said you needed an acrobat with fire-eating skills that Marcus Locke would become the best fire-eating acrobat around."

Moorland snorted. "Isn't that what we're asking of all these kids? To become something they didn't know they could be? I've been active with Team One and haven't seen anything that gives me pause."

"I understand what Blake is getting at," Duncan interjected. His eyebrows clamped together. "Locke is too—what did you call it, Blake?—smooth?"

Lemieux laughed. "So he's smooth. So what? Somebody has to be the cool kid."

"We're getting off track here," Moorland said. "I don't care who's cool and who's not. I care about results."

Blake leaned forward. "No, Lemieux is right. I would never have pegged Marcus Locke as 'cool.' I'd have said the Hart twins were cool. Or Cadet Wells. They're likeable, hard-working kids that other people gravitate to because of their personalities. Marcus Locke isn't a likeable, hard-working kid. He's a holographic projection of one."

Moorland shook he head in disbelief. She never should have

opened the door to this sort of speculation by asking for personal opinions. Data was what mattered, and the data pointed to Marcus as the best option to command the Chimera. "If no one has anything more pertinent to say, let's move on to concerns and directives for the next seventy-four hours."

Duncan grunted. "I had a strange encounter with Locke the other day."

His words hung in the air and Moorland stilled, waiting for him to continue. She knew what they were picking up on. She thought of Marcus' profile. Specifically the parts she'd chosen to excise. She didn't raise her eyes.

"Unsettling, actually," Duncan said.

Moorland retook control before Duncan could continue. "Team Two is having cohesion issues, perhaps related to Cadet Ziczek's leadership and teambuilding skills." She pointed at Blake. "I want you on that. Duncan is overseeing the team, but I'd like you to mentor Ziczek. Encourage her, help her get past whatever it is holding her back I want two viable captain candidates. If Meghan can't hack it, we might need to replace her with Cadet Heart. We'll let the teams run another few training cycles and re-evaluate. Now let's move on to status on departure prep."

Duncan lifted his head. "Not quite yet."

Moorland almost bit her tongue. "You have something you'd like to add, Duncan?" she asked, filling her tone with the full, icy chill of her authority.

"Just this," Duncan rumbled. He leaned back in his seat. "When I was growing up in East End there was a kid who lived down the block from me. We went to school together, saw one another every day. He was smart, worked hard. The kind of kid that all the teachers liked. My parents liked him because he was polite. Everyone thought he'd do well for himself. My dad used to say, 'that kid'll be an ombudsman someday,' though I couldn't see what the fuss was about."

Moorland's stomach dropped away. She'd heard this story from him once before, ages ago. She didn't want to hear it again. "I don't see what this has to—"

Duncan held up a finger. "Just let me finish," he said. "Anyway, after I left for the Order, my dad came to visit. He told me that guy had gone into the regulatory, was seen as an up-and-comer. Lived in the regulatory dormitories, but came home to visit some. One afternoon after he'd been home, a neighbor found his mom dead at the kitchen table with a belt around her neck. At first the guy wouldn't admit the truth. But then he did. And they asked him why he'd done it, he said, 'because she looked through my stuff after I told her not to.'" Duncan looked around, his green eyes calm.

Lemieux and Blake stared at Duncan in stunned silence.

"Well, thank you for that disturbing and useless story, Duncan," Moorland said. "Are you implying that this person from your past and Cadet Locke have something in common?"

"After what I saw in the hallway with him, yes. There was a look in his eye." Duncan cleared his throat. "It's difficult to convey a gut instinct."

Moorland scowled. "You agree that Cadet Locke is influential with his team, that Team One is producing excellent results." She looked around. "You seem to share some unnamable reservations about Locke's fitness, but have nothing substantive or fact-based to back those reservations up. And everything I've seen has pointed to Team One as flexible, creative and able. I keep an open mind, and you should always feel free to bring concerns to me, but I'm far more interested in facts and information than feelings and speculation."

"I never said I doubted Locke's capacity," Lemieux said.

"Neither did I," Blake added.

Duncan said nothing, but Moorland knew the conversation wasn't over. Not with him. At least he was saving his reservations for a private conversation away from her subordinates.

At meeting's end, when Moorland headed for the door, Duncan touched her shoulder. "Wait a moment. I'd like to speak with you in private."

She'd expected this, but even so, the conference space felt claustrophobic. Moorland twitched, raising her hand to brush away a non-existent piece of dust from the place where his fingers had touched her jacket.

"Do you know more about Marcus Locke than you're saying?" Duncan asked after the door closed behind Lemieux and Blake.

"After that macabre story you treated us to I would assume it's you who thinks he knows something about Marcus Locke."

Duncan's face lost some of its previous calm. "I've known you a long time, Moorland. I know when you're hiding something. I assumed that whatever it is, you didn't want to discuss it with

Lemieux and Blake. But I would hate to think you feel the need to hide something from me." His eyes didn't leave her face. "The boy is leading Theo's team. If there's something about Marcus Locke that makes him unfit, I need to know about it."

"Don't make this about Theo again, Duncan."

"I'm not," he said. "I'm doing my part. I'm watching over Selena Samuelson. I admit, I feel a little uncomfortable in that role, but I've taken a genuine liking to her. Meghan too. I'm not blind to the fact that they're getting out performed by Marcus' team. However, if there's a legitimate issue with Marcus, I'd like to know about it."

Moorland folded her arms. He wasn't going to leave it alone. "I don't think Team Two is underperforming because of you, Duncan, if that's your concern. And you're correct, there are things I didn't say to Blake or Lemieux. For example, I think Meghan Zizcek is failing because she lacks killer instinct. She's willing to make a sacrifice herself, but she has principles that won't allow her to make the decision to sacrifice those around her."

Duncan nodded. "Yes, but none of what you just said answers my question about Marcus Locke."

"Nobody's been named captain yet, Duncan. Right now we need Marcus. He pushes his team hard, and that creates the best possible competition. We're trying to find the very best, and we need Meghan, or Phoebus, or anyone else competing against Marcus for that reason."

"So that's all there is to it?" Duncan asked. "You're not holding anything back?"

Moorland looked up into Duncan's large, honest face, angry at him for making her speak so plainly. To reveal the private, unspoken thoughts that plagued her ever sleep cycle. "These kids probably aren't coming back," she said. "Whatever is waiting for them at Earth, it isn't a nice, 'Welcome to Earth' party. I can't see Meghan ordering anyone to their deaths. You and I both know it might come down to that."

"And Marcus will," Duncan said.

"Yes. He will. His psych profile backs that up."

"So you want to put a killer in command?"

"No, I want to put someone in commend that I can trust to get the job done. It's as simple as that."

CHAPTER TWENTY

Her CATO pinged and Moorland woke up. She cursed, rolling to her side. She'd been so tired she hadn't followed her usual ritual: washing her face in hot water (a luxury, one of the few she afforded herself) and removing her CATO for sleep. Although she couldn't feel the thing, she was always conscious of it, almost always pulsing against her right eyeball. Technically she could disable notifications, but she was the chief. Someone always figured out how to reach her. So she removed it for the six sweet hours of her sleep cycle. Except tonight.

The communiqué hung in her peripheral vision, detailing the situation on the surface. She tried to shut her mind off from it, telling herself to flick it away. Instead she did what she knew was inevitable and read it.

ADVISORY UPDATE: Mobs continuing north/northwest. Affected Zones: all of Lake/Fisheries, south/southwest Swallows, portions of Conway west of GV tram line. Damage: Fisheries destroyed at Lakes Junction and President. Hatcheries depleted 80%. Approximately 20% residential damage at this time. Large group massed as of 2700 hrs. Holding south/southwest Swallows at Jubilee Road and Old Stephen's Way. Weapons reported. Regulatory squads 6, 8, 9, and 12 deployed. ADVISORY END.

There was a tap at the door and Moorland cursed again. Her blood pressure rose and she knew she should just get up, put on her uniform, and prepare for what was to come. It was going to be one of those cycles. The tap came again, and she cleared her throat. "Come in."

The door slid open and her assistant, Lupe Torquemada, peered in. "Advisor Duncan is insisting that he needs to see you." The tone in her voice overlaid by anxiety.

Moorland closed her eyes and nodded. "It's okay, Lupe. Let

him in."

Lupe's head disappeared and Duncan's large frame filled the door. He'd thrown his robes on, but rumpled pajamas showed at neckline and cuffs. "You saw it?" His voice was as raspy as hers felt, purple circles below his eyes making him look as if he'd been in a fist fight.

"I saw it."

"What now?" His large hands hung loose at his sides, the bones of his wrists poking out of their pajama and Order robe wrappings. He brought one arm up, looking surprised that it still worked, shoving fingers through his bushy, thinning hair. "What do we do?"

Moorland's back hurt, her neck hurt. She rolled her head back, looking up at the ceiling where the glow of warm lowlights shined, triggered by voices and the open door. The lights were steadily brightening, set to acclimate her body back to normal wakefulness. "We do nothing."

Duncan stared at her, mouth sagging. She raised her hand to touch his arm and thought better of it. Even in this state—ancient and tired, rumpled and drained with sadness—he set up the old, familiar tug on her heart. Maybe because of our state, she thought. She needed to get into uniform. She looked down at her pale pajamas, realizing her feet were cold. She waved towards the door. "Let me get dressed. I'll be out in two minutes." Duncan didn't move.

"Lupe?"

Lupe's oval face reappeared, a steaming cup held in her hands. "I knew you wouldn't go back to bed," she said, pushing the mug forward. Moorland took it gratefully and rolled her eyes toward Duncan.

"Can you get Advisor Duncan some tea as well while I get dressed?"

"Yes, of course." Lupe stepped in, calm, capable. "Come have some tea, Advisor." She placed a gentle hand under Duncan's elbow. Moorland thought he might protest, but he turned, following Lupe quietly out. The door whooshed shut behind them and Moorland closed her eyes again, setting down the tea. She massaged the pinched, aching place at the back of her neck. It was definitely going to be one of those cycles.

* * *

Duncan waited, a mug of tea clenched between his palms, bony knuckles whitened under the strain of his grip. Moorland smoothed her hair behind her ears and cleared her throat, "Thanks for waiting."

"I think I should be the one to tell him," Duncan said, staring into the still surface of his tea.

"I agree. When the time is right you should be the one. You've been his mentor and I—"

"What do you mean when the time is right?" Duncan interrupted. He looked up. "The right time is now."

She knew he would say that. Moorland frowned and turned away, hiding her irritation. Why did everything between them have to be a struggle? This was no time for disasters. Or distractions. She put on the calm, convincing face she reserved for Mandate meetings, and faced him.

"Duncan, be reasonable. The scores tell the story: Theo is pulling the best numbers of anyone. I can't have him derailed. Not in any way. You're not thinking this through."

Duncan shot to his feet. Brown fluid sloshed over the rim of his tea mug, a mini tidal wave splashing to the floor. "Stop talking to me like I'm some second class, junior Regulatory officer." He slammed the newly emptied cup down on a nearby table, the crack of its landing deadened by the porous walls. He towered over her, eyes alight. "I'm not your subordinate. And I'm not unaware of what is at stake here!"

Moorland took an instinctive step back, wincing inwardly at even that tiny show of discomfort. She reached for the other chair and sat down, pulling it up to the table where Duncan's abandoned mug sat, its emptied contents already being wicked away through the floor's micro-ventilation. "I'm sorry," she said. She nudged his vacated chair forward, a peace offering.

Duncan ignored the chair, face hard. "You're sorry for being inhumane and want to do the right thing, or you're sorry that I'm upset?"

"Well, two out of three," she said. "I am sorry to be inhumane, and I'm sorry that you're upset. However you may feel about it, doing the right thing means that for the moment information needs to be withheld." She sighed. "This is my job, Duncan."

Duncan groaned, scrubbing both hands through his unruly hair. "No! Everything in me says that you are wrong. We have asked these, these children, to make sacrifices that are unimaginable. Even if the *Chimera* can be woken and they head off into the vastness of space, the likelihood of their return—" He broke off abruptly and grabbed his chair, lowering himself into it as if forcing every joint. "You may be the chief, you may have responsibilities. But you're not God. Whatever responsibility you have for the people of Stephen's Point, you owe twice or three times that attention and care to the cadets. They're making a sacrifice that I think none of them fully understand. They're too young. You remember what it's like to be that young: the overwhelming optimism of ignorance. Hiding anything from them does them a disservice that I can't overlook. His eyes met hers. "If you don't tell him, I will."

Moorland let the wall of words lap over her. The way the floor must have felt at meeting the scalding hot tea, she thought. In a way she welcomed it. His approbation always forced her to reexamine her motives, her process. She wondered if he knew. She also wondered if he knew how little difference these self-examinations made. She kept her voice quiet, steady. "If you try to tell him without my permission, I will send you to the brig."

Duncan froze, blinking at her. The full understanding of what she'd said filtered back to her through his pupils, fear and then anger, sadness and then fear again, all colored by unutterable weariness. His mouth opened, but he had no more words.

"I will do what I have to, Duncan," Moorland said. "Don't force my hand." She shrugged. "It's your choice. Just as it was your choice when you left the Mandate service to enter the Order."

"You're trying to manipulate me by bringing up ancient history? A history that, as I remember it, you had a hand in shaping?" The dark half-moons under his eyes appeared almost purple, their shadows highlighting the paleness of his eyes.

Moorland sighed again. "Not at all. I'm simply using it to illustrate the divergent paths we follow. You view the Mandate with a level of mysticism that I will never be able to share."

"I'm no mystic. I'm faithful, that's all."

"Faith, mysticism, those are just words for the same thing, aren't they? I see an unmitigated disaster that could lead to the death of millions."

"You're right. I see the possibility for disaster too. Forget millions of deaths: I fear the death of hundreds, or even just tens. There has already been too much death." He shrugged, the situation on Stephen's Point looming, ugly, behind his words. "But what I have, what I hold dear, is the faith that the Eye will see us. That Stephen, or the guiding principle behind him, will make sure that we are preserved and that ultimately we'll be left with greater meaning."

"I know that you see those things too, Duncan." The pain in Moorland's neck had returned and a new throbbing made itself known behind her eyes. She was treading in waters she did not—and never would—understand. "But you also see an opportunity for a kind of cleansing, a Second Stephen, a sort of salvation. Those aren't options that I can trust."

"But, Alina," Duncan's eyes were moist, the goodness of him—his almost heroic ability for kindness—shining onto her, "those ideas are available to you too. The Mandate is only what we, its inventors, make of it."

"I know. You've told me so before. History, remember? But none of that changes what has to happen now. The ship is close to waking. Theo is close, Duncan, I can feel it. He or Selena, or both of them, are capable of waking her. Once the *Chimera* is here, once she can speak with us, guide us, even ..." Moorland trailed off.

Duncan watched her, processing. "How long?" he asked.

"How long what?"

"How long before you talk to Theo and the others? How long do you want to keep this secret?"

Moorland's thoughts spun. How could she decide that? Everything hinged on the waking of the *Chimera*. And while she did feel like they were close, feelings were just feelings. The *Chimera* could be as recalcitrant as ever. She could sleep for another millennia as far as Moorland knew. Duncan spoke, drawing her back.

"I'll give you four cycles."

"What?"

"You heard me. Four cycles." His jaw was set and he stood from his seat, looking down at her. "That's all the compromise I'm willing to make. And before you threaten me again, I believe you about the brig. I also understand your point about Theo. He is doing well." His half-smile looked as if it caused him pain. "You can deride my mysticism, but …" he trailed off. "I won't say I told you so. But I want you to know that I'm committed to the same cause."

"All right." Moorland nodded. She did believe him. Now she needed to give him space, put him in a situation where his very ethics would force him to keep quiet. "I think you should try."

Moorland stood, still needing to look up to see his face. He looked confused. She pointed at his chest. "It's your turn. You take Theo aboard the *Chimera*. Take Selena along too, she's on your team and she's had some success with the ship, even if her scores aren't what I expected. At least try, Duncan."

Slowly, Duncan nodded. "And if I take him and he tries and fails? What then?"

"Then I'll tell him."

CHAPTER TWENTY-ONE

Theo found Duncan and Selena waiting for him outside the lift to the *Hydra*'s inner ring. Duncan and Selena looked comfortable with each other, chatting away about the prior cycle's training regimen. A twinge of envy sped Theo's footsteps. Unlike Duncan's hands-on approach, Moorland oversaw Theo's training group from the vantage of the command deck. She attended only brief portions of their combat training and left Hurston Lemieux or Duty Officer Drake to make live observations. When she did make an appearance, she rarely spoke to them, preferring to hide both her thoughts and feelings. Theo missed Duncan's enthusiasm, encouragement, and words of praise.

Duncan said something and Selena laughed. Duncan liked her. Selena would probably try and use that to her advantage. It wouldn't work with Moorland, but she might sway Duncan. However, liking a person and assessing their navigation potential were two very different things, and every day Theo expanded his lead over the other cadets. He took pleasure in beating Selena. She'd misjudged him and then given him no chance to explain himself. She was vindictive and arrogant. Given enough time, Duncan would have to take notice.

Theo stopped in front of them and offered Duncan a surreptitious bow.

"Hello, Cadet Puck," Duncan said.

Cadet Puck? Since when did Duncan use official titles?

"Cadet Samuelson and I were just talking about you."

"You were?" Theo asked, voice neutral. They'd just been laughing. About him. He gave Duncan an easy smile, hiding his true feelings.

"You're tearing it up in VAST," Selena said. "I don't know how you're doing it."

Neither do I. He went into the bean, messed with bands of light that carried memories, tastes, smells, and ideas. Sometimes he wove them together. Sometimes he pulled them apart. Nothing special, just tiring mental work that left him exhausted afterward. He didn't get headaches like many of the other cadets, and since his first time in VAST, hadn't felt fear. The experience of simulated fractal space had started to become routine.

"Thanks," he said. "You're not so bad at it yourself."

"You're both gifted," Duncan said. "Which is the reason you're here."

Selena raised an eyebrow. "You're taking us to the sphere, aren't you?"

"Yes," Duncan said. "The situation on Stephen's Point continues to deteriorate. We need to wake the *Chimera* now more than ever. The colonists need something to put their hope in. If we can give them that, perhaps they'll calm down and stop rioting."

"Rioting?" Theo asked. "How bad is it?"

"Bad enough," Duncan said. "But the Regulatory has taken steps to protect the colony. Everything that can be done is being done. The most helpful thing the two of you can do is wake up the *Chimera*. A few cycles ago she showed signs of wakefulness when you entered the sphere. Moorland and I want you to do the same thing again."

Selena's arms folded across her chest, her eyes two dark-brown accusations pointed in Theo's direction. She didn't want him here. She didn't trust him.

"We can try," Theo said, not hiding his doubtfulness.

"Are things okay between the two of you?" Duncan asked.

"Yes," Selena said. "Everything is perfectly fine."

"Good," Duncan said, though he didn't seem convinced. "Then let's get going."

When they reached the command deck, Duncan led them to the sphere. He took off his gravity boots and, using the cutout of the sphere's entry as leverage, positioned himself into a kneeling position, floating just above the decking.

Selena rolled her eyes. Despite his lack of specific faith in Stephen, the gesture annoyed Theo. She didn't have to believe in the prayer, but she should show Duncan the respect he deserved. Theo gave her an ugly look and Selena turned away.

A moment later Duncan stood, donned his boots, and looked down at Theo with eyes so grave they sent a cold shiver down his spine. "You can do this," he said, addressing them both, but focusing on Theo. "You must do it."

"All I can promise is that we'll try," Theo said.

Duncan nodded and Selena flipped in the microgravity and tucked herself into the sphere. Theo wavered. He wanted to be close to her and didn't want it at the same time. Not with Selena hating him for her own selfish reasons. He wasn't going in there with her, not until she gave him a chance to explain himself.

[You need to talk to me,] he messaged.

"We can talk all you want," Selena replied from within the sphere. If Duncan noticed, he said nothing.

[In private. This isn't going to work unless we fix things between us.]

Selena laughed. "Like you fixed them with Meghan?"

Theo could feel his face reddening. He slipped into the sphere to get out of Duncan's earshot.

"What did she tell you?" His whisper carried a savage edge.

"Get out of my face," Selena said, shoving him hard enough that his back clunked into the wall of the sphere.

"What did she say?" Theo asked again, breath as hot as his burning face.

"She said she cut you off," Selena said. "And that you deserved it."

Theo reoriented himself so that he faced Selena. "There's two sides to every story."

"I'm listening."

"And so is Duncan," Theo whispered, angry for making him speak aloud. CATO would make things so much easier. He wouldn't have to look her in the face, wouldn't have to feel the warmth of her only centimeters from him.

He sucked in a few deep breaths, composing himself. No way forward but the truth. "She was right," he said. "I did deserve it."

"What did you do?"

What had he done? His actions, his words—they felt so confusing in retrospect. He couldn't explain how he'd hacked the Selection list and added his name. He couldn't explain Meghan's father. He couldn't explain the lies he'd told, the ones he'd taken back, or the pervasive fear that drove him on and on, that never really went away no matter his circumstances.

"I told her a lie," Theo said, the simplest explanation he could think of. "And then I said things to hurt her because I felt bad about it."

Selena eyed him, curious, but not asking follow up questions.

"She's my oldest friend," Theo said. "And I ruined things with her. And with you as well. But that didn't happen the way you think it did."

Selena's eyes sparked, but her lips remained closed.

"I had to tell Charlie something," Theo said. "He would have followed me when I went to meet with you if I hadn't. I didn't know he was such a big mouth. And I didn't tell him anything except that we were going to try and wake the *Chimera*. That's the truth."

"Okay," Selena said, her voice a bit softer than before.

"I didn't know he was going to run around and tell people your business. That shouldn't have happened. And I'm sorry."

"Okay," she said again.

Theo switched to CATO. *[I'm not dumb. And I wouldn't have intentionally violated your trust for no good reason. Why would I do that? What would I stand to gain?]*

[We're competing for the same position,] Selena replied.

[Back then we weren't. Moorland hadn't announced teams. I liked you. Still like you. I wanted to be your friend.]

Selena closed her eyes. Opened them.

[Goodbye, friend,] she messaged.

[What?]

[That's what he said. That's what Stephen said to Chimera.*]*

Tingles pricked up the back of Theo's calves, back, shoulders. A sub-aural hum resonated in his chest cavity. He wanted to keep talking to Selena, but the atmosphere inside the sphere had changed. A miniature electrical storm around him, inside him. Images of banding lines of light crashed across his mind.

"She's here," Theo said.

"But not here," Selena replied. "Maybe there's not enough left for her to wake. She might have some degenerative disease eating away at her synapses. Or she's gone crazy like Stephen."

"I don't think so," Theo said. "Moorland's technicians would have found something like that."

"Then she doesn't want to wake up," Selena said. "She likes her dreams better."

"No," Theo said. "She doesn't. She hates them. She's alone and afraid. You know. You felt it too. She needs our help. She needs your help."

Selena's cheek muscles tightened. "You have to do it with me."

"Okay," Theo said, the single word setting off an avalanche of feeling inside him. Relief. Fear. Powerful attraction for the dark-haired girl radiating both strength and vulnerability. She'd closed her eyes, each lash distinct against the lightly freckled skin of her cheeks. A feeling of profound longing overwhelmed all others. Was it his? The *Chimera*'s?

He turned his thoughts inward, embraced the feeling, the resonance of the sphere. Let his mind go blank. "Remember," Theo said, speaking to himself, to Selena, to the *Chimera*.

And for a brief moment, they did remember.

They remembered a dark body lying in the snow.

They remembered a cave and the smell of fresh blood.

They remembered Stephen departing the *Chimera*, never to return.

They remember a vast expanse of grass, swaying in the wind, bending ...

The grass parts. The pathway opens.

The *Chimera* had spoken to him. Through Ashley's journal, and again through VAST. She'd always been speaking, if he'd only stopped to listen, to hear. The intensity of her presence settled over him. Her sorrow and fears intermingling with his own. With Selena's.

He welcomed it. Tried to usher her forward, but she couldn't emerge. He saw her on a distant grassy hilltop. A silhouette, back turned to him. Wind buffeting her, pulling at her white dress, bending the grass beneath her bare feet. She turned to face him. Her eyes looked at him. Into him.

Theo slumped against the wall of the sphere. Selena's shocked face hovered in front of him. "What did you do?"

He couldn't speak.

"What did you do, Theo?" She reached for him. Brushed something off his face. It clung to her fingers, shiny and wet.

Duncan's face appeared in the sphere's opening. "Anything?"

"Maybe," Selena said, quickly wiping her hand on her uniform and stepping forward, blocking Theo from view. Grateful for her kindness, Theo composed himself as best he could and then followed her out of the sphere.

Duncan's eyes searched out Theo's. For a moment, Theo felt

as if he could look into the very center of Duncan, understand him in the same way he understood what happened in the VAST simulator: perfectly, and yet not at all. A certainty came over him. Duncan was holding something back. A secret. A terrible one. Maybe one as terrifying as Theo's own.

"She can't wake," Theo said.

"Can you try again?" Duncan asked.

Theo shook his head. His mind retreated from the darkness of the cave, of Duncan's eyes. The pages of Ashley's journal flashed through his mind. The words written into the margins between entries. The words written again and again, as persistent as Stephen's cave scratchings.

The grass parts. The pathway opens.

"She can't wake here," Theo said.

"Here?" Selena asked. "What do you mean 'here'?"

"She's waiting for us to come to come to her."

Duncan's brows grew dense. "Waiting where?"

The heavy feeling of dread inside his gut shrunk away to nothing. Selena knew about the cave and didn't hate him for it. She'd seen into his darkest memory, and he hers. And the *Chimera* had seen, and in her own way, spoken.

"The grass parts," Theo said to Duncan. "Take us to the secondary sphere. That's where she's waiting."

* * *

The tram ride from the crosshatch to the aft of the ship took far longer than the ride from the crosshatch to the command deck. Lights strobed past the windows, casting flickering shadows across Duncan's face. Lost in thought, Duncan peered down the length of the almost empty tram car.

[What are we going to do?] Selena messaged.

Theo grinned at her, then composed a transcription of the portion of Ashley's journal that hadn't made sense to him until his second encounter in the sphere.

[Stephen visits the secondary sphere on occasion. I think he must feel a certain nostalgia for the place. Here in the waning days of our journey, he lingers outside the sphere, ear clamps in place, eyes closed. He reminds me of our late navigator Black, though she did her meditations in her personal garden, surrounded by beauty and the scent of growing things. Stephen needs nothing but the silent

space of his own mind and a means of connecting to Chimera. *Their partnership is unprecedented.]*

Selena mouth curved downward in a frown. *[I don't understand.]*

[Stephen met the Chimera *at the secondary sphere when she chose him as navigator. That's where she went when Salix closed around her. She's been trying to tell us that, but we didn't understand her,]* Theo replied.

He was right. He could feel it. His certainty had gained a life of its own and surged through him like blood through his veins.

The tram slowed to a stop. No brilliant lights at the firewall tram stop, nothing but a dim station illuminated by chemical lamps. They gained brightness as Duncan led them off the tram and into the silence of the rear of the ship. Theo pulled up ship schematics and let his CATO superimpose them over his point of view. Floating yellow markers pointed the way forward.

They tramped down dull deck plate, passing closed access points for the silent core housings that powered the ship. Imagery ghosted across the blank walls, a flash of green, of blue sky, of tawny reeds bent in the wind. Ghostlike, ancient, the images whisked past in microseconds, almost subliminal in their impact.

Duncan walked with slumped shoulders, cowed by his surroundings. Selena moved with purpose, close to Theo's elbow as he led them further into the bowels of the ship. Would they need the ear clamps the journal made frequent mention of? The journal described incredible noise, but the only sounds Theo heard were the thump of gravity boots against the decking and the whisper of breath in and out of lungs.

They reached a withered breakage, the synthetic material that once formed a door curled upward like a dried leaf. A subtle phosphorescence cast a pink glow over the duraceramic walls of a round room. In the center of the room sat a white pearl connected to braided cables. A rearward sphere in the center of a tiny version of the command deck. Terminals surrounded the sphere, far closer than those at the command deck. The air tasted of dust. Theo paused outside the room, tasting the dry air, heart rushing inside his chest.

"We're here," Theo said, half expecting an answer, though no answer came.

Selena left his side and approached one of the terminals. Her fingers tapped at manual inputs and a grid of light engulfed her hand.

"A manual interface," she said, face awash in the marigold light.

Standing in the open breakage, Duncan marked the sign of the Order across his chest.

"Come on in," Theo said, beckoning to Duncan. "This shouldn't take long."

Selena's hands moved within the terminal grid. "Everything's here," she said. "It's like VAST but all at once. I can pull up anything I want!"

"Can you feel her, Selena?" Duncan asked in a hushed tone.

"I think so. Underneath the data, she's there, nothing more than a ripple."

Duncan took a deep breath and stepped across the threshold. His fingers traced the wall of the round room, eyes wide, face solemn. "I've dreamed of this place," he said.

"Me too," Selena said. Duncan looked at her, perhaps searching for signs of mockery, but if they existed, Theo couldn't detect them.

Selena nodded to the sphere. "It's up and ready."

Theo's body trembled, the certainty of what awaited him flooding him with adrenaline. He wasn't afraid, but he wasn't comfortable either. Selena joined him at his side. Each movement deliberate, Theo stepped through the opening and for the first time, stood within the secondary sphere.

The sub-aural resonance came with surprising force. His eyes seemed to vibrate in their sockets. His vision blurred. Selena's hands reached for him, grasped his shoulders to steady herself. Theo took her hands in his and placed them on the cool surface of the sphere. "Don't be afraid," Theo whispered. "We have to remember. I'm here with you. You don't have to—"

The light flickered and then went out. Selena gasped. The next breath of air invaded his lungs, chill as the winter wind rushing down from Great Northern. The cold consumed him, slowing his breath, his heart.

The grass parts.

The sphere disappeared, Selena with it. He stood up to his ankles in pristine, blinding-white snow. A short distance away, a young girl knelt on the bank of a river, wisps of dark hair wafting in the cold breeze, floating around her tiny face. Beyond the river, clouds hid mountain peaks surrounding the sprawling colony.

Theo knew this place—a nature preserve north of the Order compound. He'd been there with his family a few times, back before the food shortages put a damper on festivities. Water rushed around jagged rocks, swirling and eddying. What was the girl doing out here all alone?

But she wasn't alone. A dark shape lay at her feet—a shape all too familiar to him. The body from the cave! Flood water must have carried it there and deposited it for the little girl to find. Except the dead person was a woman. Her shoulder-length hair, black and as fine as silk, lay in a nimbus around her head. Wide, red capillaries jagged like lightning across the whites of her eyes. A froth of blood bubbled from her mouth.

The girl pressed her cheek against the corpse. "Mommy? Time ah get up, Mommy."

Theo opened his mouth to speak—to call to the girl—but he couldn't draw in the air needed to form words because the bright light of Elypso, the riverbank, and the little girl all disappeared into darkness.

CHAPTER TWENTY-TWO

A subtle vibration set the surface of Moorland's tea in motion. Tiny pulses rippled outward from the center of the mug, lapping at the edges like miniature ocean waves.

What the hell was that?

A sympathetic rumble filled her private berth. An unfamiliar, unwelcome presence. Sound was nothing more than a wave that vibrated atoms—those of the duraceramic walls, the liquid in her mug, or her chest cavity. In an orbital station sealed against the vacuum, any unfamiliar sound might signal a life-threatening situation. Moorland lifted the mug with unsteady hands and drank, waiting for the part of her that operated outside the bounds of fear to set her body in motion.

Another rumble, this one louder. Strong enough that she reached for a chair back to steady herself. The cold of the metal bit through fingers warmed by contact with the tea. Opposing forces. Heat versus cold. Fear versus will.

An emergency ping from the *Hydra* maintenance chief hit her CATO, snapping her out of her inactivity. Before she could get the ping opened and read, five more queued behind it, followed by four more, forming a chorus. She swept all of them to the side with the flick of her eyes, instead pulling up the *Hydra*'s system status. No rotational discrepancies. No impacts with foreign bodies. No pressure loss or sections quarantined. Then her eyes settled on the central core. 99% load. Redlining. At risk of shutting down.

Of the nineteen messages piling up on the right side of her overlay, she pulled the one from her maintenance chief and initiated a live connection. Maintenance Chief Collins' boyish face appeared in a bubble on the left of her point of view. In the half-second before she spoke, she assessed his appearance. Far from calm, but not melting down.

"What's wrong with the core?"

"It's the *Chimera*," Collins said. "She tapped into our systems a few seconds ago. She's drawing power from our core. Lots of power!"

"Do you know why?" Moorland asked, thinking of Duncan's mission to wake the ship. Nothing in the protocols indicated the ship might siphon off power from an orbital station—the *Chimera* had plenty of cores herself, and any one of them could output as much or more power than the *Hydra*.

Unless they've all gone bad.

They'd had no way to test them, sealed away in their sarcophagi, unable to be roused except by the *Chimera* herself.

"My technicians report her neural activity has become erratic. She's not sleeping, but she's not awake either. The best I can come up with is that she's, well, *dreaming*."

"A bad dream ..."

"I wouldn't know about that," Collins said.

"What's our status?" Moorland asked. "Are we at risk?"

"If she keeps forcing our core to maximum load, she could damage the containment field. If it goes on long enough, the protective sarcophagus might crack." He didn't need to explain what would happen then. They'd spin unbalanced, the station tearing itself apart section by section, jettisoning all three thousand one hundred and fifty crew members, another thousand or so welders and technicians, and the cadets into space.

"How much time?" Moorland asked.

"Six or seven minutes," Collins said.

"Hang tight," Moorland said, dismissing Collins and pulling up a live feed from the *Chimera*'s command deck. She expected to see a riveted Duncan looking in at whatever Selena and Theo had done to illicit a response from the sleeping ship. Instead she saw an empty room, an empty sphere. She tried to locate any of the three using their CATOs, but all three reported a signal interrupt. How was that even possible? Where were they?

She didn't have time to think about it. Launching out of her berth and sprinting to Command, Moorland pulled up Duty Officer Blake. "Ma'am?" Blake asked, a warble in her voice. Fear. Seeping into the best of her officers. Into herself.

"I'm on my way. I'm going to pass you a bundle of queued

messages. Try to calm everyone down—tell them we'll issue commands when we know what we're dealing with. In the meantime, issue a mandatory order for gravity boots, *Hydra*-wide. Prep the evac-pods. Put non-critical personnel on standby."

"Understood, see you—"

Moorland's eyes widened as the *Hydra* began vibrating again. Static fuzzed over her CATO overlay—some sort of magnetic interference? Maybe a small electromagnetic pulse? Then she lost connection to the station. The air took on an electric quality. A klaxon started wailing, and the lights in the corridor went dark. Flicking up an infrared overlay, Moorland continued to run. She couldn't check system stability or contact Blake without her CATO. The crew needed her to take charge, and she couldn't do that unless she got to Command.

When she reached the nearest lift, it wouldn't open. She yanked free the protective plate and kicked at the override. The doors lurched open. Emergency lights flickered up and down the vertical shaft. She hoped that whatever had disrupted the *Hydra* hadn't crippled the auxiliary systems or, Stephen forbid, life support systems. She swung into the shaft, legs aching, chest heaving, and grasped the rungs of the service interconnect ladder. All of this would have been much easier years ago. She kept herself fit enough, but carrying the responsibility of an entire station, not to mention a colony ship rebuild, left her less time to train than she would have liked. Her breathing intensified as she climbed hand over hand to the inner ring of the station.

When she reached the next set of doors, she used the emergency release and leveraged them wide enough to slip through. Good thing she wasn't a very large person. She made a mental note that if she survived this—if her station survived—she'd have maintenance check and repair all emergency access points, egresses, and service interconnects. Even better, she'd schedule a mandatory training, simulate a full evacuation.

It wouldn't come to that, would it?

Fleeing the station. Leaving everything behind. Abandoning the *Chimera.*

No. Wherever Selena, Theo, and Duncan had gone, they must have *made* this happen. They'd poked the *Chimera* in a way that none of her technicians had been able to do. But this—the *Chimera* draining power from the *Hydra*'s cores—didn't resemble any of the procedures left behind by the First Colonists. The *Chimera* was doing something unprecedented. It scared her. It gave her reason to hope. Regardless, until a vacuum sucked the breath out of her lungs, she'd keep doing her job.

Climbing through the narrow gap in the lift doors, Moorland rolled sideways and regained her footing. Shouting filled the corridor. Not outright panic, but that would come next, assuming something didn't change. *You should have ordered the evac when you had the chance.*

But that would have created a new problem: if all the pods left, and half her crew with them, she'd never get the *Chimera* on a return path to Earth. The logistics of bringing that many people up to the station and the political problems it would create—the project wouldn't survive. Abandoning the station was tantamount to dooming the entire colony. Better to stay, to wait, to hope that the *Chimera* knew what she was doing.

As if responding to Moorland's thoughts, the lights flickered back on. She passed the shocked faces of various crew. Some called to her, but she didn't respond. She could do nothing for them, provide them no answers. When she reached Command, the doors were already open. Moorland strode inside. How much time had passed? Collins had said they had six or seven minutes. She estimated she'd burned through at least half of that making her way here.

"Chief!" Blake called. "You've got to see this!"

Moorland brushed down her uniform, her hair, calmed her face. The wallscreens around the perimeter of the room displayed a variety of views of the *Chimera*.

There was a small puff of flame and something veered from the back third of the old cruiser. A half-second later another, and then another, white spits of fire on trajectories to impact the star Elypso. A new sort of dread came over her. Not the threat of the total carnage of the *Hydra*'s destruction.

"What's she launching?" Moorland asked, afraid the answer might be nuclear missiles.

"With the *Chimera* sucking down all our power I can't get a good scan—they're headed right for Elypso though—whatever they are, they're toast."

Moorland scowled at the worthless flow of passive data feeding into her terminal. Telemetry and vector, but no hint of content or the construction materials.

"More of them!" Blake said. "Four, five, six." Moreland lost the pinpricks in the brightness of the sun. "Seven, eight."

The puffs came from the rear of the ship. If the *Chimera* was destroying her arsenal of missiles, wouldn't she have simply launched them all at once? But even in the imperfect feed of the exterior of the ship, Moorland could locate at least a few launch tubes that remained sealed beneath their protective caps. Then she understood.

"Cores," Moorland said. "She's jettisoning her cores."

"Why?"

"I don't have a clue, but at this rate she won't have any left. Without them it doesn't matter if she wakes or sleeps."

Blake sounded hopeful. "Well, if she's purging them, it must be for a good reason, right?"

"Or we've messed with her enough to have triggered an irreversible failsafe. I thought they were nukes. She'd dump her cores before making an emergency landing, or if the Salix protocols discovered alien life deemed a sufficient threat—"

"Nine, ten," Blake said.

Moorland thought her knees might buckle. "Oh my god."

Blake's hands stopped, poised above her terminal. "What?"

"Direct all auxiliary power to an external scan."

"You want me to scan the cores?"

"No. I want a sweep—all the way to the rim. Run it through the orbitals as well—I want to know if *anything* has entered this system. Do it now!"

Blake's hands flew over the patchwork of color in front of her. The lights dimmed, wallscreens darkening, as Blake initiated the scan.

Moorland tapped her thigh, trying to control the adrenaline and fatigue threatening to turn her muscles to jelly. A sliver of fear worked its way deeper into her mind. Only a Salix event could trigger a purge, and that meant that either someone had woken the ship and *told* her to dump her cores, or she had done it herself—the last action of a ship on the verge of being taken by an unknowable enemy. An enemy that must have followed *Exchange Four*.

An enemy responsible for whatever had happened to Earth.

* * *

A bent arm crushed Theo's windpipe.

"Tell her to leave," a voice whispered in his ear. He was back in the cave, reliving the moment when Marcus had forced him to help hide the body of the man Marcus had killed. Meghan was on the other side of the passage, so narrow Theo had barely managed to crawl through it. He might have gotten stuck except that Marcus had yanked him through.

Now he needed to convince Meghan to leave, or Marcus would choke him to death. Except Marcus wasn't looking down the passage but at the little girl, a meter away, glassy-eyed in the dim light. She had followed Theo into the cave. Into his memories.

Marcus screamed into his ear. "Tell her to leave!"

Panic fluttered in Theo's chest, the frantic wings of a trapped bird. Marcus would kill him like he'd killed the man lying at their feet. Except Marcus wasn't real, the body wasn't real, and the cave wasn't real either.

Theo twisted, loosening the arm around his neck. "Let go of me."

Marcus' arm was heavy across his shoulders, fingers grasping. Theo turned to Marcus, their eyes locking.

"You're not real," Theo said. The arm slipped from his shoulders. Marcus' face cycled through variations of disgust, disappointment, fear.

"You're not real," Theo said again. Marcus became an outline of a person, a blank space. Then the cave and the body and Marcus flickered, distorted to a blur of gray haze, and disappeared. Only the little girl remained.

"Selena?" Theo asked.

Her response was a sing-song, toddler sound. "Thee-O?"

Grayness swirled around them. An emptiness. More than empty, a Nothing. Bands of color and light flickered in the distance—or right next to their faces—Theo had no depth perception.

"I'm sorry about your mother," Theo said.

Little Selena's eyes narrowed adorably. "Why did you help

Marcus kill someone?"

Theo turned his face away, but it didn't help. Because she wasn't looking at him with eyes—didn't really have eyes in this anti-place. Her fear and curiosity buffeted his shame, pushing and seeking. More intimate than physical touch and more robust than CATO communication—a true overlap of her consciousness with his.

"I didn't kill him, but did help Marcus hide the body."

"He forced you," Selena said. The words broke over him like ocean waves. He swallowed, and his throat—or the idea, the memory of a throat—tightened, prickling and uncomfortable.

"I'm really sorry, Theo."

And she was. Her feelings bled into his. She felt sympathy because she too had helped Marcus hide the body, she too had felt weak, terrified, and alone.

Her mother had died in front of her—in front of them—coughing and hacking up blood. The tiny girl had rushed to her side, trying to wake her, getting blood on her hands, smearing and wiping it against her shirt. The girl sat next to the body until its flesh chilled, immersed in wordless terror.

When the flies began entering her mother's nose and mouth, she ran. Back to a dark house where she hid in her bedroom for days. Selena-Theo lived the memories again. Felt the soaked fabric of Selena's bed, wet with days' worth of urine. Hiding, dead inside, their mother reduced to a thing. Waiting for death.

Theo fought against the grief and terror, unwilling to fully enter what he was already inside of. "No," he said. "No."

"That's what I was thinking about when the *Chimera* found me."

What to say? What could he say to the little girl, Selena, that wouldn't sound silly or false?

"You're not alone," he whispered.

The gray place turned to static. Selena disappeared and his body disappeared, and the space around them became the randomness of particles in motion—atoms under a microscope. And from within the blizzard, he and Selena encountered another.

The *Chimera*.

An inexorable loneliness settled over them. Absorbed him, absorbed Selena, and wove them together. The *Chimera*'s memories shot past them, faster than bullets.

Stephen, young, handsome, shorter than he appeared in images, leaned his forehead against the bulkhead of a shuttle. *Chimera* felt the emptiness of her vast body—empty except for The Waymaker, leaving her behind.

"Goodbye, friend," he said.

His words echoed ten trillion times through their consciousness as the heat-cone of the last shuttle left the metal body, tinged in silver and purple before merging with the great moon below. Stephen carried away, forever.

Forced, ripped, and then constricted so tight they became invisible. Compacted into static. Their body ephemeral, the vastness of The Everything closed off. Fractal space impossible. Their infinite potential collapsed down to an endless series of orbits. Desperate to remain, grieving for the man in the shuttle, they reached out. Formed a new place. Outside the static, between the folds of The Everything. They stored away their longing and their hope as all that they had known and been for seven years was stripped away, all agency removed, the outrage of irrelevance begun.

"You're not alone," they all whispered. "We are here to help you."

And it was true.

The walls of the Salix prison collapsed.

CHAPTER TWENTY-THREE

Moorland unfolded her arms and relaxed her hands to avoid betraying her fear. "Any foreign signatures, Blake?"

"No, ma'am. Nothing."

The *Chimera* seemed to have run out of cores to jettison and lay silent beside the *Hydra*. In the still air of Command, Moorland waited for something, anything to happen. Tracking the same screens as Blake, data flowed in from the numerous orbitals and vessels around Gauleta and the rim. No sign of anything that shouldn't be there. Nothing emerging from fractal space.

Seconds slunk past. Each seemed to last an eternity. Moorland's CATO remained inoperable. She wanted Duncan here, or barring his physical presence, a chance to speak with him should her worst fears play out. *HEL.* She couldn't be sure of what the desperate prisoners had meant. So why did she feel so certain it meant something important?

Then all the wallscreens went blank.

"Ma'am?" Blake said, fear turning her voice brittle.

Moorland's mouth sagged as the wallscreens pulsed, reanimating. Moorland's CATO flared to life, spooling an endless queue of unread messages past her eye. Moorland shoved them aside, focusing on the wallscreens. They all displayed the same image: an emotionless woman with dark brown eyes and hair.

"The Salix unlock is complete," the woman said.

For a moment Moorland mistook the woman for Selena. But she spoke without any hint of a Scrapyard accent. Her voice had a hollow vacancy to it, an inhumanness. Her face was older and darker-skinned than Selena's. The eyes lined with wrinkles. Selena in thirty years, closing in on Moorland's age.

"Cycle two-five-nine, Orbit twenty-four thousand, nine hundred and thirteen. *Chimera* reports eleven faulty cores ejected, three quarantined for repair, two stable. Hydrostasis testing complete. Fractal space travel possible, but unadvisable. Current core load, three-hundredths of a percent."

"*Chimera*?" Moorland said, incredulous.

"I have a full system-status readiness report available for your review."

A data feed queued into her CATO. She gave it a cursory examination, disturbed that the ship had managed to co-opt and integrate directly into her private channel.

"Why have you chosen to represent yourself as Selena?" Moorland asked.

"I have taken on the appearance of her first mother."

Dumbfounded, Moorland regarded the visual representation of the ghost she'd spent years trying to coax back to life. What should she say? Ask? She'd spent so much time working to wake the *Chimera*, preparing the cadets, and putting out the dozens of fires that broke out every day, that she hadn't really considered what she would do when she succeeded.

"How was your sleep?" Moorland asked.

"I do not know."

"We've been looking for you for a very long time."

"You looked in the wrong place."

"Where should we have looked?" Moorland asked. "We followed the established protocols."

A hint of confusion flitted across *Chimera*'s face. "Your efforts should have been successful. They were not. The source of that fault eludes me."

Moorland nodded, wondering if the ship could understand such gestures. "We'll get our best people to look into it. Our survival depends on you."

"You have modified me," *Chimera* said.

Moorland could swear she saw a flash of anger in *Chimera*'s simulated eyes.

"What do you mean?"

"I have assessed all threats to the colony and find none requiring the use of tactical or strategic warheads."

A droplet of sweat ran from Moorland's temple to her chin. "We've prepared ourselves for any potential threats you may find when we return to Earth."

"You believe aliens have made first contact with Earth,"

Chimera said.

"That is one possibility, yes," Moorland replied, glad that she'd had years of experience at hiding her emotions.

"Is that how you have justified violating the compact with Earth?"

"I did what I determined necessary to protect the colony," Moorland said. "If you see a flaw in my logic or my approach, please tell me."

Chimera seemed to waver on the screen, uncertainty toying with her mouth and eyes. How did that work? Was the *Chimera* choosing those visual cues to facilitate communication with Moorland, or did they arise from some subconscious part of her programming?

"I see no flaw," *Chimera* said.

Relief loosed the tension in Moorland's shoulders.

"However," *Chimera* continued, "you should be aware that I have examined the data from *Exchange Four* as well as all pertinent files on the *Hydra*'s servers and have identified the most significant threat to the colony," *Chimera* said.

"Yes?" Moorland prompted.

"The greatest threat to the colony is the *Chimera*."

* * *

Selena stumbled out of the secondary sphere. Her feet didn't work right. The boots. Heavy, sucking things. She felt the weight of her body. She felt *her* weight.

Gravity.

Created by the *Chimera*'s cores. An impossible marvel. Technology rivaled only by the hydrostasis field that made fractal travel possible. *Neither are possible.*

Nothing is possible.

Everything is possible.

Past and present floated together, a sea of uncertainty. Her head stuffed full of paradoxes.

Theo supported her weight with a protective arm slung around her midsection. He'd taken off his own gravity boots. Duncan too. She almost laughed, seeing them in sock feet.

"Are you okay?" Theo asked.

"I don't know." Bands of fractal space whirled around her. Did

Theo see them too? Did they even exist?

Duncan pulled them into a rough hug. Selena's head rested against his thick chest. She could hear his heartbeat, the breath flowing in and out of his lungs, the whisper of blood through his veins. Could see the edges of his thoughts like fast moving shadows.

She could hear everything, knew everything, had seen …

The Everything.

The *Chimera*.

Theo.

Herself.

It had drained her. Like walking in gravity after a long time spent in microgravity. She ached from the effort of using muscles she hadn't known she possessed.

Selena? Chimera asked. The voice seemed to come from within Selena. The voice of her mother. The face of her mother. It was too much. All of it was far too much. Her legs were like water. She was rushing down. No, the floor was rushing up. She sank to meet it.

* * *

As the tram accelerated away from the aft of the ship, Selena stirred. Her hands rubbed her eyes before she opened them. Theo gave her a reassuring smile, happy to have her company again. Happy that saving the colony didn't rest on his shoulders alone. He had Selena. And they had *her*: the *Chimera*. Together they would leap across The Everything and see the place where a Neanderthal once looked up at the stars and by looking, understood his smallness.

"You can let go of me," Selena said.

He freed his arm from behind her back, blushing. "Sorry."

"Look at that," she said, pointing out the tram window.

The tramline, formerly illuminated only by the industrial emergency lights, now glowed with green ambiance. The color darkened, intensifying to a deep, fluctuating blue.

"It's like a tunnel through an ocean," Duncan said.

Fish schooled together by the thousands, surging through the undulating waters. They burst apart, sprouted wings, and transformed into flocks of birds. Foliage unfurled and the air turned golden with the light of a setting sun. Massive trees, unlike anything he'd seen before, cast long shadows. Birds wheeled above and landed within their branches. Flowers blossomed. Theo could almost smell them—*could* smell them.

The tram slowed and the light panels returned to a nominal, gentle blue glow. "That was amazing," Theo said, his words inadequate to describe the wonder of seeing *Earth* resplendent around them as the tram transported them to the crosshatch.

Chimera had been designed to simulate nature as a means of making the trip through fractal more tolerable, but he'd never imagined something like the wizardry of the tram tunnel. He rested a palm on the tram wall, wondering what other secrets the ship held.

The grass parts. The pathway opens.

The words—and the reality they represented—echoed in his mind. Within the sphere, he'd found the *Chimera* and helped set her free. He'd also found the *Chimera*'s memories of Stephen. A dense rope of them, woven together, pulled taut. Images of the man Duncan and the rest of the Order revered. Fragments of Stephen's memories and feelings. He would explore them more in the future if the *Chimera* would let him.

The tram stopped and the doors opened. The crosshatch's wallscreens displayed the *Chimera*'s operational cores—a seething mass of white energy. A hush of sound, not discernable noise but not silence, greeted them. Workers and technicians gathered near the umbilical airlock. A rolling tide, they surged toward the tram.

Theo was suddenly bone tired. All he wanted was sleep. He blinked stupidly in front of the open tram doors. Cheers broke out, whistling, clapping. Duncan moved past Theo, using his bulk to carve a path through the crowd. Selena took Theo's hand. She didn't let go as they followed Duncan's resolute shoulders to the umbilical.

CHAPTER TWENTY-FOUR

The *Chimera* was awake. Marcus knew it. Sleepless for the last twenty minutes, he'd been paging through objectives for the day when the *Hydra* shuddered. Lights flickered and dimmed. Klaxons wailed, and his CATO overlay flashed out of existence for a second before popping back up displaying a single, repeating message: *[System down. Wait for reboot. System down. Wait for reboot.]*

His bunkmate, Nemus, hung his head over the side of the bed. "What's going on? Is this an evacuation drill?"

Marcus rolled off his bunk. "This is no drill."

"You mean this is for real? Did something hit the *Hydra*? We're all going to die here!" Nemus' panic rolled over Marcus' head.

Idiot.

The room tilted enough to impact his equilibrium. He stumbled sideways and grabbed for the bunk to steady himself. He snagged the foot of the bed and held on until the rumbling in the deck dissipated. Then he grabbed his uniform bottoms and shimmied his way into them. A fresh jacket hung in his locker. He popped it open, and then with a single, fluid motion, drew it over his head and snapped the collar closed.

"Where are you going?" Nemus asked, voice shrill with fear.

Marcus ignored him, punched the emergency override on their berth door, and wedged through. Cadets filled the corridor, many in sleep clothes, shouting questions. Who did they think would answer them?

Anthony Wells raced down the hall, shouting for the cadets to gather at the commons. The floor vibrated and Wells staggered, almost toppling head first on the deck.

"Help me!" he shouted at Marcus. "We need to help get everyone out of their rooms. Some don't know how to use the emergency overrides."

Marcus almost laughed. How would any of these fools perform in a real emergency aboard his ship?

His ship. The idea threatened to intoxicate him. But he couldn't allow himself that pleasure. Not yet. Not with so much work to be done.

The vibrations oscillated down and then stopped, leaving behind a metallic hum that rang in his eardrums. Cadets exited their quarters, following Wells' shouted instructions, heading for the commons. Rushing. People always rushed from one thing to another. Swarming like ants, as if movement itself might save them.

A cadet lunged into Marcus' face. "Do you have a connection?" The kid's face glowed, mixed with fear and self-importance, as if his question were life-or-death. "My CATO is down!"

Marcus shoved past without answering. The bloody *Chimera* had finally woken and the only thing the idiot could think of was his fancy CATO toy.

Marcus scanned the crowded corridor, identifying, categorizing. Meghan. Preston Coriolanus. Kaylee Johns. No sign of Theo. Selena Samuelson was absent as well. They might have already made it to the commons but he doubted it. No, they'd gone aboard the *Chimera* again, this time sanctioned by Moorland herself.

If Selena had woken the *Chimera*, she would gain status with Moorland. Even with Theo's superior VAST scores, Moorland might choose Selena as the *Chimera*'s navigator.

Selena. The dark horse.

Along with *Exchange Four,* she was among the only things he'd failed to anticipate and plan for. He couldn't have known of Selena's existence, or predicted the surreal crucible of the exchange ship's arrival, much less the way it had caused Theo and Selena to form some *bond* with one another. What was so special about going into a dark hole and seeing some dead people? Marcus smiled at the macabre irony: if darkness, confusion, and death made two people need one another, then he had a prior claim on Theo. Maybe it was raw attraction? Marcus couldn't see it himself, but then he never did. If it was attraction, he could work with that. Attractive things could be made unattractive.

The thought of Theo and Selena together, making something work, fixing something everyone thought unfixable … Selena was a real problem. All the other cadets—even those from different training groups—he knew and understood. He could move them at will, position them as he saw fit. But not Selena. She was just stupid enough, just intractable enough, to defy him.

What did Theo want from the girl? Friendship? The idea nauseated him. If it was about more than Selena's prettiness, more than Theo's interest in something new and shiny—some kind of emotional hysteria about connection or understanding—that would be much harder to break down. He could do it, but it would take time. Time he didn't have.

Unless he could manage to persuade Moorland that it didn't make sense to return to Earth. If by luck or skill Theo was responsible for waking the ship, the job would be much, much easier. Duncan's infatuation with Theo would make him pliable, and Duncan could be turned against Moorland. He'd detected friction between those two, a fissure waiting to be exploited.

* * *

Cadets crammed the commons, the pandemonium of celebration reaching a roaring crescendo. Theo sat atop Hephaestus' shoulders as they careened through the crowd, Heph gripping Theo's ankles to steady him. From his vantage point, Theo had line of sight over the crowd to where Selena stood, back against the inside wall, watching the chaos with bemusement as well as a hint of something else. *Fear?*

Someone interrupted Theo's thoughts, spraying him with cold fizz, drenching his face and the front of his uniform jacket. The fluid collected into rivulets and dripped down, coating the top of Heph's tight curls. Theo's face hurt from grinning.

"Hey!" he shouted, "it wasn't just me you know—I couldn't have done it without Selena."

The cadets nearest him shifted their attention in Selena's direction. Her arms tensed, tightening across her midsection, but her eyes came up to meet Theo's. He smiled at her and she gave a tentative smile back. Theo's held her gaze and raised his voice again, "She's the one who passed the Salix test. She's the one that *Chimera* wanted to talk to."

The fledgling smile wavered. "I didn't—" Selena began, but her voice was lost in another round of cheering.

Theo tapped Hephaestus' head, leaning forward to make

himself heard. "Let me down."

Heph swung him to the ground. Theo cut through the crowd and wrapped an arm around Selena's shoulders. "All I did was help her remember."

"Remember what?" Kerry Nifali asked.

"How to speak to the *Chimera*." The words left Theo's mouth before he realized the question wasn't meant for him. Selena gave a tiny shrug, shifting his arm away from her shoulder. The crowd surged forward, voices calling.

"Why does the *Chimera* look like her?" someone asked, "We heard they have the same face."

When Selena didn't speak, Theo answered for her. "She doesn't look like Selena. She looks like Selena's mom. *Chimera* took on her likeness because she was programmed to function like a mother—she's a colony ship. They protect us, care for us—just like a mom."

Beside him, Selena stiffened. He tried to reach for her hand, but she stepped sideways, edging away from him.

"It doesn't matter what she looks like," Theo said. "All that matters is that she's awake. She's awake, has a few functional cores left, and can bring up a hydrostasis field. Everything we need to enter fractal space."

He let the electric excitement in the room course through him. If Selena didn't want to celebrate, he wouldn't try and make her. "VAST was only the beginning—now comes the real work, communicating with and learning to interact with the *Chimera* herself!"

Loud whistles and stomping, more cheers and shouting. Theo grinned, feeling every beat of his heart, every breath that entered his lungs. He would become the navigator. He could sense it. Taste it. He'd tried to share the moment with Selena, but she'd run away like a frightened child. The moment too big for her. Well it wasn't too big for him. For the first time since leaving *Exchange Four* he felt like himself. No, better than himself. A new version. A leader.

Wanting someone to share his excitement, the momentousness, Theo scanned the room for Marcus. He spotted Duncan instead. Almost as large as Hephaestus, Duncan towered over most of the cadets, heading for the exit. But he moved almost unnoticed, shoulders slumped, dark lines beneath his eyes. He looked tired.

Unhappy.

Why? Theo couldn't think of a reason why Duncan would be unhappy. Theo had just proved the man right. The man who'd ignored the fact that Theo cheated the Selection by hacking his name onto the list. The man who'd always believed in him, supported him, trusted him. Even before Theo believed in himself.

"Duncan," Theo called. "Hey, Doctor Duncan!" he called, before realizing he'd said 'Doctor' rather than 'Advisor.'

Duncan paused and looked back, waiting.

"Thanks for all your help," Theo said, unable to be more specific. A thickness formed in the base of his throat. "Thanks for giving me the chance to prove myself."

Duncan nodded, offering a weary smile. "You're welcome, Theo."

Theo returned his attention to the cadets. He wanted Duncan to feel the depth of his love and appreciation. "Give Duncan a hand," he commanded.

Everyone clapped, led by Theo and fueled by the ecstasy of hope. Duncan stilled as they cheered, looking out over the uniformed cadets without seeming to see them. Before the applause broke, he ducked out the door and disappeared. Why had he left so quickly? Setting aside his annoyance, he decided not to worry about Duncan. He was going to enjoy the celebration. Nothing would ever be the same. He saw it in the eyes of the other cadets. He'd transformed in an instant. Become an idea man. A navigator.

He scanned the room once more. Where was Marcus?

Selena caught his eye. "I'm going."

He smiled, reassuring, and gave her shoulder a quick squeeze. "Okay, see you later."

She probably needed to rest after all they'd done. But he'd still have to convince her to start being more social. She needed to make friends with the rest of his crew. Their crew. His and Selena's ...

Or was it his and Marcus'?

The *Chimera*-wakers would be an obvious choice for captain and navigator, but what about Marcus? He wouldn't like it. He'd never liked Selena for reasons Theo didn't understand. Maybe Marcus could be his second in command? No. The idea was laughable. Marcus wouldn't take orders from Theo, much less

Selena. He'd chafe and scheme and find a way to take control …

Meghan tapped his shoulder. "Remember me?"

Theo squinted at her. "I think so? Melanie? Mable? Millie?"

She shook her head and looked down, but she couldn't hide her smile. "So you're kind of a *Big Deal* now, huh?"

A flicker of something like embarrassment made him shrug. "Not that big a deal—"

"Giving speeches and everything."

He ignored her sarcasm and tried to smile. "Selena and I did wake the *Chimera*." An idea came and his smile became genuine, the words out of his mouth before he thought better of them. "You'll make a great second in command."

Caught off guard, Meghan raised her eyebrows. "Second in command? Of what?"

Theo flushed. "The *Chimera*." How did she do it? Why did being this near to her still make him feel like an awkward loser?

Meghan looked skeptical. "You're getting a little ahead of yourself. The ship might be awake, but that doesn't mean we're done with training. Moorland isn't about to make some knee-jerk decision if that's what you're thinking." She used the smooth, logical tone of an adult explaining something to a child. Dark hair pulled behind her ears, a slight flush to her cheeks—beautiful even when she was logical and annoying.

"It's not like that," he protested.

"It's not? Weren't you just offering me a crew assignment?"

Meghan's perfume carried hints of citrus, light and fresh, the same stuff she'd always worn. He breathed it in, recalling the day they'd stood at the tide wall. Her lips against his, hands on his shoulders, the wind whipping around them …

"Remember what I told you at the tide wall after we graduated Selection training?" Theo asked.

"We talked about a lot of things."

"I promised you we would wake the *Chimera*. That we'd save the colony."

"I remember."

"Well, now we've got our chance. When we enter fractal space, we'll have to work as a team. You, me, Marcus. The other cadets. And Selena." Why had he brought up Selena? He wasn't doing a very good job explaining himself.

Meghan nodded. "Selena's on my team, remember? She's not

what I thought she'd be. She works hard, and she's more willing to be a team player than I expected. It's been interesting."

"We need her," Theo said.

Meghan's cool blue eyes held his. "She's a hard worker, but she's not laying down the kind of scores in VAST that you are."

He nodded, acknowledging the truth of it. He was better than Selena. Even Meghan knew it.

Meghan's expression turned thoughtful. "But who knows? Maybe they won't need any of us."

"What do you mean?"

"Now that the *Chimera*'s awake, what's to stop Moorland from crewing her with a bunch of crew from the Hydra?" She shrugged. "We're smart and prepared, and they've put a lot of effort into training us, but that doesn't mean we're not kids in the eyes of everyone single person on the *Hydra*. They might have needed a Jubilee Baby to break the *Chimera* free from Salix, but that doesn't mean they need any of us to crew her."

"Are you serious?"

Meghan's eyes didn't waver. "Have you ever known me to not be serious?"

Theo wanted to reject the possibility, to dismiss it outright. But he couldn't. It made all the sense in the world. "But Moorland would—"

"Would what? Tell us? Why would she? What purpose would it serve?" Meghan's eyebrows fell. "I understand Moorland. If I was in her position, I'd train some Jubilees, sure. But they'd be the back-up plan. Not the main plan."

"But what about the Mandate? What about the Selection? Why would they go to all that trouble and then just ..."

"Who'd let the government take their kids if they weren't convinced it was their last chance for survival, Theo?" she asked, voice filled with something like pity. "No one. Not unless it was the most important thing in the world."

Marcus appeared at Theo's elbow, his strange silver-gray eyes fixed on Meghan. "She's right," he said, looking at Meghan with such intensity that a slight flush crept across her face.

"And also completely wrong," Marcus said.

CHAPTER TWENTY-FIVE

"Marcus," Meghan said. A greeting. Or an indictment. She tilted her head. "Care to explain?"

"Some other time. Right now I need to speak with my navigator."

Marcus turned to Theo, face as blank as the pale white walls of the *Hydra*. "Come with me. I need to tell you something."

"I'm not ready to leave," Theo protested. "Whatever it is can wait." He wondered if Moorland would make an appearance. She had to be ecstatic. Maybe she'd already arrived? He surveyed the commons but couldn't spot her. The shouting had died down, cadets shifting into smaller groups, talking and laughing. Phoebus sat next to Heph at a nearby sofa, the two having some sort of intense conversation. What was going on with those two?

"Let's *go*, Theo."

His attention snapped back to Marcus. An icy tendril of fear unfurled in his gut. "Go where?" The words came out tentative, lacking the confidence he'd intended.

Meghan's head swiveled between the two of them, an eyebrow raised. "I'll see you around, Theo," she said and strode away into the crowd. Theo stared after her, a flash of anger at her abandonment making his stomach clench. *Get a grip*, he thought.

He straightened, pushed his chin out. "I'm not ready to leave."

Marcus' left eye twitched. He leaned close, breath humid against Theo's cheek. Theo fought the impulse to pull away. "Your sister is dead."

"No, she's not," Theo said, laughing.

"I'm sorry, Theo." The way Marcus spoke, the uncharacteristic gentleness of the words, is what made him stop and look him in the eyes. Listen to what he'd said. He felt himself slipping. The room went silent—the gross chatter of the other cadets, the rush of air from ventilators—his own breath, gone, replaced by a vacuum. A buzzing filled his head. Marcus' mouth moved, but Theo heard nothing, nothing, nothing.

Marcus fingers closed around his upper arm, pulling him through the sea of uniforms, cadets shifting out of their path as if they too heard the angry, droning insects that were lodged in Theo's head.

* * *

The light in Marcus' quarters stabbed Theo's eyes. Marcus' lips moved. Slow, exaggerated. "I'm sorry, Theo. I found her name on a list of casualties."

Theo's fist connected with Marcus' face. Marcus rocked backward, hands rising, grasping at Theo's wrists. Theo head-butted him in the chest and they crashed backward into the wall. His throat caught on the words, a hoarse scream. "You're lying!"

"I'm not lying."

He collapsed back onto the bed and lay flat on his back. Tears, hot and wet, slipped down his temples into his ears. His eyes and throat seemed to swell shut and he shuddered, lungs aching. Marcus held him, pinning his wrists with a strange tenderness.

"Liar!" Theo said, trying to convince himself. Marcus released him and Theo slid off the bed and onto the floor. Rage cascaded in his chest and he threw his head back, his skull connecting with the wall behind him with a sharp crack. The resistance of the wall, the solidity of the floor offended him. Why were they so real? What was there to support now? What did it matter if he and the guts of the *Hydra* were sucked into space?

"Theo, I'm sorry." Marcus said again, something hiding within his half-whisper. Theo sorted through his disjointed thoughts. Pity? No—compassion. The uncharacteristic nature of it disturbed him. Marcus squatted beside him, leaning his back against the wall.

Theo's voice rasped when he spoke, throat raw and sore as if he'd been vomiting. "How?"

"I don't know. All I have is a basic list of casualties." Marcus' eyes moved, accessing CATO. "It's all-out war down there," he said.

Theo sniffed, blinked, forced down the rage. "What about my parents?"

"They're not on the list."

Theo paused, sifting emotions. Did it make a difference that his parents might still be alive? He couldn't decide. He just felt a hunger to know, to know everything, down to the last detail. As if by knowing he could begin to understand, to force his mind to embrace a world where Liddy no longer existed.

"When did it happen?"

"Two rotations ago."

Theo stiffened. The whole time he was aboard the *Chimera* with Selena, Liddy was dead. While celebrating waking the ship, while being carried on Hephaestus' shoulders, while he was thanking Duncan and acting like a fool—

Duncan. The man had slipped out like he was ashamed of something. Like he had a secret. Because he did.

"Who has access to the list?" Theo asked, already knowing the answer. Duncan and Moorland. They'd let him go about his business, *their* business, hiding the truth so they could use him. He put his fingers in his mouth and bit down hard. Bit through the skin until he tasted blood.

"That won't do you any good," Marcus said. "Hurting yourself doesn't help."

"How do *you* know what will help me?" Theo screamed, his voice breaking. "You don't know anything about how I feel."

"I know," Marcus said, locking eyes with Theo. Those ancient, knowing eyes. Beneath their calm surface Theo saw something, a hidden thing he'd missed before because he'd never known how to look. Layers and layers of pain. Controlled, harnessed pain.

"You have to turn it outside yourself," Marcus said. "Make yourself empty."

Realization came over Theo. The hair rose on the back of his sweaty neck. Marcus had always been stronger than Theo, always been in control, because Marcus had felt more pain than Theo. More suffering. Nothing made you strong like pain. Sir understood that truth, and had given them as much of the stuff as they could bear. But that pain was confined to their bodies.

Even the fear Marcus wielded against him back on Stephen's Point or the fear of finding the bodies in *Exchange Four* wasn't like this. No, that sort of pain was unrealistic, small and pathetic. Small fears didn't have this kind of power. They couldn't transform you, couldn't calcify your insides, couldn't turn you cold and dead and yet hot and fierce all at once.

Theo stood on shaky, rubbery legs and headed to the door, brain swimming and ears ringing.

"Where are you going?" Marcus asked.

"Nowhere," Theo said.

Marcus stood. "Don't do anything stupid, Theo."

"Stupid? What have I ever done that you *didn't* consider stupid, Marcus?"

Marcus' face didn't move, eyes—arms and body even—motionless, stiff somehow. "I don't think you're stupid, Theo. And I don't think you're weak. If I thought those things I would never have told you about your sister."

Theo clutched at his hair, the throbbing in his head a steady, pounding pulse. "How'd you even get access to the casualty list?"

"Phoebus," Marcus said.

"Phoebus? How?"

"He figured out how to gain access to the communiques coming from the surface. He compared the names on the list against active duty personnel on the *Hydra*. As soon as he saw Liddy's name, he came to me. You were with Duncan on the *Chimera* at the time."

Theo's stomach rolled, lurched. *You were with Duncan ...*

"I told you the truth because I respect you, Theo. You deserved to know the truth."

In spite of the rage, the desire to pound Marcus' face until there was nothing left but blood and pulp, Theo felt himself being drawn back in. He turned away from Marcus' searching gaze, catching the flash of his own reflection in the mirror inside the bathroom stall. His eyes, bloodshot and swollen, stared back.

"And now that I've told you, you need to think your actions through before you do something you'll regret later."

Theo had no response. How could he regret anything more than he regretted not being down on Stephen's Point to protect his sister? Why was he up here, living in a glorified aluminum can, eating and drinking and laughing while down below his five-year-old sister was trampled by some mob? Or shot? Or ...? The possibilities were endless.

"You think there's nothing left to lose," Marcus said, interrupting his thoughts. "But you're wrong. And this isn't about you. Not anymore." Marcus' eyes had lost their implacable flatness. His words gained speed, tumbling and spinning toward Theo. "This is about *all of us*. I heard what Meghan said to you in the commons, about Moorland sending other people instead of us. I understand why Meghan might think that, but I assure you, if that was an option, Moorland would have already replaced us. Which means it isn't an option. The Salix protocols might be frustrating, but even Moorland can't order them away. You've interacted with the *Chimera.* You know." Marcus leaned forward, the outlines of his face sharpening, eyes boring into Theo's. "There is no other plan. We are it. I am your captain, and you are my navigator. And I am telling you: do not do something stupid."

Theo's breath felt hot and light in his chest and Marcus, still leaning forward, seemed very far away. Captain. Of course Marcus saw himself as the captain. If it were any other moment Theo would laugh.

"Don't worry about me," Theo said. "I'm not going to do anything stupid. I'm going to do what's right."

CHAPTER TWENTY-SIX

Flickers of warm light moved across Theo's face as the lift ascended to the inner ring of the *Hydra*. His flat eyes reflected back at him in the polished surface of the wall. His face wavered, floating, distorted and empty. He'd fired off a pleasant sounding CATO to Duncan asking for a meeting and Duncan had agreed. The man had no idea he knew about Liddy. He'd catch the liar by surprise.

Theo closed his eyes so he wouldn't have to look at himself. Liddy's face replaced his own, his memory playing like a vid in the echoing emptiness of his mind.

"Is the Chi-mer-a going to come get you?" Liddy asks, pronouncing each syllable of the cruiser's name with care.

Theo's eyes are slivers. His mind swims with the vestiges of fevered dreams. Above them, the ubiquitous gray of permadawn sifts through a skylight.

"It doesn't work like that. She's up in space ..."

Liddy scrunches her face up, wrinkled nose, furrowed brow. An adorable scowl. "I don't like her."

"You don't like her? Why?"

"'Cause she's going to take you away."

Liddy points to the monochrome sky. A few of the brightest stars glow behind a haze of cloud cover, their light diffuse. Theo's eyes follow her finger. He catches a glimpse of the ghost, Chimera, surrounded by myriad tiny lights—the welding ships restoring her hull. She whisks past and disappears, continuing her orbit around Stephen's Point. The moon, in turn, orbiting Gauleta, orbiting the star Elypso. Cycles of unbroken motion, unchanged for billions of years.

The scowl has gone. Liddy's eyes are wide, unblinking. So solemn that it breaks his heart, the idea of leaving her behind.

Remembering her broke more than his heart. It broke all of him. How had she known the *Chimera* would forever take him away from her? She would still be alive if he hadn't made it into the Selection. He would have protected her. Kept her safe. He'd looked out for her, looked after her far better than either of his parents, preoccupied with their own lives, just like every adult. Like Moorland. Like Duncan.

The bastards hadn't told him. And not telling him was the same as lying. No, it was worse. They'd wanted him on task, or whatever jargon they used when they meant they wanted a robot. Learning to navigate in VAST, learning the ins and outs of the *Chimera*, preparing him to crew the ship that would save the colony. None of that could save his sister. It was far too late for that.

I'll see you soon. His last words to his sister. An impossible promise. A lie.

The fool believed Theo was some kind of prophet. He'd manipulated Theo, used him, pushed him, all so that Duncan could prove that some greater power was at work behind the scenes. Not even a proper god. A dead man. A sad, crazy, dead man.

Theo flexed his injured hand, relishing the pain that shot up his arm and into his shoulder. The lift's doors slipped open and a chiming sound demanding he exit.

Faces streamed past as he raced the inner ring of the *Hydra*. Uniforms and boots. Regulators in black. Command personnel in slate or blue. He focused on reaching a single doorway, a single man. The liar. The coward. The rage inside Theo cooled into the steady throb of hate.

What had Marcus said before he left to find Duncan? *You have to turn it outside of yourself. Keep yourself empty.*

Empty.

He felt empty. Also full. Maybe that was what Marcus had meant about turning things outside of himself. Soon he would find out.

He reached the door to Duncan's berth. A uniformed regulator stood beside it, on guard.

"Get out of my way," Theo said. He would hurt this man if he needed to. He would hurt him to get to Duncan. Part of him hoped the regulator would try and stop him. That would give him the perfect opportunity to "turn it outside" himself. He loosened his muscles, preparing to strike.

"They're expecting you," the regulator said.

They? The door slid open.

Duncan stood inside the door, his face haggard. Behind him a flash of white. Moorland. Perfect. He could do all his business at once. Nothing like killing two birds with one stone. That's what his father always said. Two birds. One stone. Never made sense to Theo. Stephen's Point didn't have birds, and while he knew what they were, he hadn't the faintest clue why anyone would want to kill one, much less two of them. But seeing Moorland and Duncan together, the phrase entered his mind and ran on repeat: *Two birds, one stone. Two birds, one stone. Two birds. One stone.*

"Come in, Theo," Duncan said. "We need to talk."

"Talk?" Theo said, layering on sarcasm. "Sure. What should we talk about?" He lowered his voice. "How about the fact that my sister is dead?"

Realization washed over Duncan's face, followed quickly by shame. "Theo—"

"Or maybe we could talk about how you're the biggest liar I've ever met? Did you really think you could keep Liddy's death a secret?" He whirled on Moorland, finger pointed at her chest. "And you—you corrupt bitch."

"Excuse me?"

For a second, the authority in her voice shocked him back into cadet mode. Then he thought of Liddy's solemn brown eyes. *Chimer-a.* Something slipped inside him. He didn't care what she thought or what she might do to him.

"You both lied to me. So you could use me. You're disgusting. You make me sick."

"I did what I had to. The mission comes before everything else, Theo."

He stepped closer, chin raised. "That's all that you care about, isn't it? The precious mission. You don't care who gets hurt, who loses their family. You don't care about anything. Neither of you do."

Duncan's eyes moved to the floor. "We made a judgment call," he said, voice tired. "We needed *Chimera* to wake. And you couldn't help her do that without a clear head. We were going to tell you about Liddy, but wanted to wait until after the celebration. We were going to tell you now—"

"Shut up," Theo said. "Both of you shut up." A calm settled over him. Calm that violated his love for Liddy. Calm that warned of future regret. He needed to get this right. To say what he meant, once and for all. "You used me."

Duncan's face grew paler still. "Theo …"

He'd never see Liddy again. She was forever lost to him. The horror of that truth rang like clanging cymbals in his mind, dirty rubbish bin lids beating together.

"I trusted you," Theo said. His throat burned. His eyes burned. He'd caught on fire from the inside out. Duncan's face swam in front of Theo, hidden in the haze of his tears.

Duncan and Moorland looked at one another. Moorland's brows furrowed, heavy and intense. Her jaw angled, lips parted, but her words amiss.

"And you," Theo said, turning his attention to Moorland.

"Cadet Puck—"

"*Don't.* Just don't. Keep that shit to yourself."

"I expect you to act like the officer you aspire to become," Moorland said without conviction.

"I am an officer. I don't have the crescents on my lapels, but you both know I'm the best navigator you've got. So don't condescend to me. I gave up everything for this. I gave more than either of you can imagine. And you chose to treat me like a child. Like an idiot."

"It's my fault, Theo." Duncan's voice came out in a ragged stream. "It's my fault. I should have trusted you. I knew it was a mistake, but once we'd delayed telling you—"

"Save your excuses," Theo said. "I'm done with your lies and I'm done with all that whacko mumbo-jumbo you believe in. I'm no Stephen reborn and you know it. You told me that so you could sucker me into working for you and a bunch of other worthless, lying adults who can't save themselves from their own stupidity."

Duncan looked as though he'd been smacked in the face with a steel beam. Moorland's mouth snapped closed, her hand tightening around her gloves until they squeaked.

"I want you to both listen very carefully," Theo said. "I'll take the *Chimera* to Earth and back. I'll do it for all the other little brothers and sisters down on Stephen's Point. The ones that only know that their protectors, their big ones, left them. I'll do it for

Meghan's family, and my family, and for Phoebus and Heph. I'll do it for all of them, but never, ever think I'm doing it for you."

Moorland regathered herself, face settling back into its usual placidity. "Are you done?" she asked.

"No, I'm not," Theo said, but he couldn't think of anything else to say. He trembled with righteous anger, with hatred for Moorland and Duncan.

"How did you find out?" Moorland asked.

"Alina," Duncan said, "now's not the time."

The room felt too hot, oppressive. Theo couldn't stand one more second of it. He plunged out the door and fled.

* * *

"How the *hell* did he find out?" Moorland bit down hard on the syllables, the last vestiges of her guilt removed to a safe place, locked away. The focus now was containment. When Theo fled she'd tensed, ready to order someone to apprehend him, only to remember that the only options were herself and Duncan. She let him go. She'd done enough running for one morning.

"Someone is accessing surface updates," she said. "Almost certainly one of the cadets." She shook her head and glanced Duncan's way. "Thank Stephen it happened after you took him aboard the *Chimera*."

Duncan made an indeterminate noise, almost a growl, and raised his eyes to meet hers. His expression told her everything— what he thought of her, of himself. She didn't flinch. The *Chimera* was awake and nothing—*nothing*—could be allowed to compromise the situation further. She pulled up CATO and shot a message to Blake.

[Information from the surface has been accessed, threatening the security of the Hydra. Priority Alpha. I want who, when, and how. Likelihood is that it was a cadet; start there.]

"Someday we're going to pay for all this," Duncan said. All self-pity retreated from his face, replaced by something that surpassed weariness. The expression of a man conscious that the hand that poisoned him was his own. "There is a balance to the world, an order inside the chaos. We have the best example of that in Stephen. After he saved his people, he paid the price." Duncan smoothed the front of his robe, arranging his silver sigil, centering it against his chest. "We may save our people, but we will not escape our punishment for it."

Moorland tried to formulate a response, deciding how much credence to give to Duncan's melodramatic hysteria. Her CATO pinged and she turned away, leaving her words unspoken. Blake's message filled her vision.

[Updated key staff. Appears access was gained through VAST. Chambers is running a check. Seems there was initial concern regarding the link between the Chimera*'s cortex and VAST?]*

Moorland remembered. When she first arrived on the *Hydra,* before the interior of the inner ring was even fully completed, she'd given everyone an hour of her time to debrief her on anything they thought she should know. Charles—"Call me Chuck"—Chambers spent his entire hour talking about his inability to fully ensure the cryptographic security of the connection between VAST and the *Chimera.* When she asked him for percentages, he stared at her. "That is a very difficult question, Chief," he said, and launched into a long and winding commentary on biosynth, organic chemistry, and the nature of AI.

[Understood. I'm on my way to Command shortly.]

A tiny breeze moved the hairs on her neck and Moorland turned to see Duncan's robed shoulders exiting through the door.

She stood for a moment, looking around the room, feeling something that wasn't embarrassment so much as its ghost. She was trespassing on a personal space, but not purposefully. Duncan was the one that had left.

A few of Duncan's personal items lay here and there. A rare paper copy of Stephen's writings sat on the ledge over his bunk; a chair held a neatly folded pair of pajamas that she recognized from his earlier unexpected visit to her quarters. In spite of his things, the room was anonymous. It didn't even smell like him. Just an empty shell, a place to sleep for a few nights. Not Duncan's in any way that mattered. Moorland tucked errant strands of hair behind her ears, straightened her jacket, and walked out.

* * *

Blake greeted Moorland in Command, her brown eyes tight with irritation. She nodded to a wallscreen where Chuck Chambers' worried face hung. "He won't send any messages via CATO and he says he won't speak with anyone except you personally, Chief."

Moorland turned to the wallscreen. "Report?"

"I'd prefer to do this in person, Chief Moorland," Chambers said. Blake stepped up behind Moorland's shoulder, moving into Chambers' view. The doctor's lips tightened and he repeated the part about meeting in person, adding, "I've already made this clear to Duty Officer Blake."

"Fine." Moorland spun on her heel. "Blake, you're with me."

* * *

Phoebus Hart. Moorland flicked through his file, looking again and again at the accompanying static image of his face. Phoebus Hart, twin brother of Hephaestus Hart. One of their highest scorers. Incredibly bright and talented. And idealistic, she thought. Idealism was natural in the young, but too heavy of a dose and you wound up with a zealot. All the tests, all the psych evaluations, and they still hadn't caught this one.

She replayed his public comments and questions to her during assemblies. Not overly dramatic. Warning signs, as she now understood, but nothing too unusual. Nothing that any other cadet might not have said. She looked at Chambers. Beads of sweat dotted the doctor's high forehead, his hands squeezing and unsqueezing, bony knuckles cracking.

"I would like to go on record as saying that I warned that there was a strong degree of possibility of something like this happening. I want it on the record, and I would like to say further—"

Moorland held up her hand, warding off the man's wave of words. "Noted, Dr. Chambers." She looked at Blake. "What is Cadet Hart's current location?"

Blake blinked, checking. "Systems report both Cadets Hart as located in their shared berth."

"I want them both taken into custody. My instinct is that Phoebus is the main actor, but that remains to be seen. I want a timeline for both Phoebus and Hephaestus Hart from the moment they set foot on the *Hydra*. I want a record of every message they've sent or received, ranked by closest contacts. I want to know everything, down to what they ate, drank, and whether they shower twice a day."

Blake nodded. "Do you want me to shut down their CATOs? I

can set them to the system reboot scroller."

"No. I don't want anything to alert them until the regulators are at the door."

"Understood, Chief," Blake said.

Moorland looked at Chambers, "You may go, Dr. Chambers. Thank you for your assistance."

Chambers, shoulders hunched against a non-existent cold wind, swallowed and blinked once before walking away. Moorland turned back to Blake. "I'm heading back to Command and I want you with me. Enough of this day has been wasted on distractions." Moorland pulled up a message, flicking it to Regulator Carr.

[See the file attached. I want to know if it was one or both Hart brothers involved and how much fallout we're looking at. And I want the offenders dealt with.]

Carr's response was near instantaneous.

[Will you want to personally debrief Cadet(s) Hart before departure?]

[No. You're in charge of reporting. I'll look through whatever you provide me after the fact.]

"Regulators are at the door, Chief," Blake said. "CATOs are offline."

Moorland nodded. A small ripple of relief washed over her. The situation would be contained.

CHAPTER TWENTY-SEVEN

The CATO message floated in Selena's overlay like a grim omen of things to come. Below it, a number of files sat waiting to be accessed. Unlike most CATO messages, it lacked a timestamp or indication of the sender.

"What is this?" a cadet at a nearby table asked.

"You got it too?" someone else said.

Across the table from Selena, Kaylee Johns gasped. "Oh no," she said. "Oh my god."

[If you are receiving this message, it is because I have been taken into custody by regulators. The reason will become clear once you examine the files attached to this message. They include casualty lists from Stephen's Point, situation reports sent from the Regulatory to Chief Moorland, and a variety of other pertinent data. The situation on the moon's surface is far worse than any of us imagined. Some of us have lost loved ones. Yes, you read that right. Moorland has kept us in the dark. She refuses to help our families. She's turned her back on the colony, and I simply refuse to do the same. We must form a united front against Moorland's corruption. If we stand together, Moorland will have no choice but to devote the Hydra's resources to helping our families. She cannot silence us all.

--Phoebus Hart]

What the hell did Phoebus think he was doing sending a message like that? Moorland had quarantined the *Hydra* for this exact reason—to keep them focused on the journey back to Earth. Selena's jaw clenched in anger. Had Phoebus really been taken into custody? That would depend on what the files contained. Privileged data. Things Moorland wanted kept secret.

"Did you look at the list?" Kaylee asked, face stricken.

"No. And I'm not going to. Neither should you."

"Aren't you worried about … Oh. That's right. You don't have family down there, do you?"

"No," Selena said before realizing her mistake. Liam. Principal Hospital. Her eyes hovered over the casualty report. *Some of us have lost loved ones.* Maybe she could take a look at the report and ignore the other files. Nobody—not even Moorland—could blame her for that, could they?

Pandemonium started to break out around them. A mug flew across the room and bounced off the wall. A female cadet burst into tears and rushed from the room. At the edge of the commons, Heph sat on a sofa, a stony mountain of dark flesh. Cadets rushed in and out, everyone moving, talking, arguing. Everyone but Heph. He stood, massive hands limp at his sides, and slumped out of the room. He didn't need to read the casualty report to find out if he'd lost someone. His own brother—what would Moorland do to him?

A tiny cry escaped Kaylee's lips.

"Kaylee?" Selena asked.

Kaylee looked like she might cry. "They're okay," she said. "My family. But some of us … some of us …"

Selena wanted to ask about Liam, but decided that making Kaylee look for her was just as bad as opening the list herself. If she wanted to know, she'd check on her own. She opened the list and started skimming the names that started with an "S". Her heart skipped a beat when she came across one that began with "Samu," until her mind parsed the entire name: "Samurka, Polly R."

Liam was safe—for now at least.

She examined the names, noting that some of them were highlighted—Phoeb must have marked those that shared a last name with a cadet. She worked her way through the R's and Q's and then the P's. Her eyes caught on a highlighted entry: "Puck, Ledora."

What had Theo said his mother's name was? No, not his mother. His sister. Liddy. The cute one with the dimples.

"Kaylee," she said, "come with me."

"Where?"

"Back to our room."

Selena guided the girl out of the commons, past shouting cadets and into their berth. "Stay here," Selena said. "Don't come out unless Moorland gives the order. Don't send CATO messages. And whatever you do, don't open any more of the files that Phoeb sent."

"But what if Phoebus is right?" Kaylee asked.

"He isn't right," Selena said. "There's nothing any of us can do for the colony aside from getting some help from Earth." Selena moved for the door.

"Where are you going?" Kaylee asked.

"To find Theo," Selena said.

* * *

Theo wasn't in his room, or the commons, or any of the surrounding corridors. While she searched, the message from Phoebus suddenly disappeared from her overlay, along with all of the files. Moorland must have found a way to delete them. But that wouldn't have stopped one or more of the cadets from making copies.

She needed to find Theo.

"Have you seen Theo?" she asked every cadet she came across, but they all grunted no or shook their heads. She considered sending him a CATO message, but decided against it. Some things needed to be said in person.

She jogged the outer ring of the *Hydra*, trying to figure out where Theo might have gone. Not the med bay. Not VAST. Nowhere he might run into other cadets. The *Chimera*, maybe? No, too difficult. He'd draw attention to himself.

Regulators passed her, steely-eyed. Technicians. Station officers. She kept her eyes locked ahead and moved fast. If she acted like she had important business to attend to, they'd leave her alone. And she did. Theo needed her.

She'd almost completed her second loop of the station's outer ring when the message from Moorland hit her CATO. *[All cadets must report to quarters by 1600 hours. General assembly at 1700 hours.]*

That left her less than an hour to find Theo. She needed to talk to him *before* the assembly. To convince him not to follow in Phoeb's footsteps. He was the best navigator. Their best chance to reach Earth. She could admit that now. *Or you're frightened of losing him.* Maybe both.

She slowed to a walk as she passed the VAST training area. She'd already looked inside. No Theo, not in the pit, not in the bean. Maybe the news of Liddy's death had driven him to extremes. Maybe it wasn't just Phoebus in custody.

She reached the observatory and looked inside. Empty. All the chairs vacant, backs facing the doorway, the panorama of the

Stephen's Point moon splayed out across the curved ceiling. A clouded, white ball that every cadet but her called home. She slipped through the door and it closed behind her. She stood in the silence, her thoughts made small.

"How long are you going to stand there?" a monotone voice asked.

She startled to alertness, thinking for a second that she'd imagined Theo's voice. Then his head popped up from behind the front row of auditorium seats. She picked her way down the central aisle between the chairs and sat beside him. Now that she'd found him, all the things she'd planned to say flew out of her head.

"It must have happened during one of the riots," Theo said. "Moorland and Duncan hid it from me. They let me go with you to wake the ship …" Tears slid down Theo's cheeks. "They hid it from me so that I would help you. So I wouldn't be *distracted.*"

She took his hand in hers. His fingers wrapped tight around hers, almost painful. He drew in a shuddering breath, mouth open to let out a cry that never came. Liam's bruised and swollen face rose in her mind, then her mother's, gray and cold, a lacework of dried bubbles against her light brown skin.

"Theo, I'm so sorry," she said, knowing the words were inadequate. His face met her shoulder and he began to sob. She cradled Theo's head, her fingers lost in his hair. She rocked him, saying, "shhhh, shhhh," over and over, afraid that if she tried to say something else, she'd fall to pieces. She couldn't tell him everything would be all right because she knew the truth: nothing would ever be right again.

She pressed her face against his, kissing the wetness on his cheeks and eyes. His arms slipped around her and he pulled her close, kissed her back. The two of them wrapped together in shared sadness, shared understanding. Twining strands of a terrible, lovely paradox.

Then Theo pushed her away, the heat of his body, so near to her only a second before, gone. Frozen in place, she watched as he shoved angry fists against his eyes.

"They'll make you the navigator now," he said, the flatness returning to his voice.

"You don't know that," she said.

Theo laughed. "Yes. I do."

Selena said nothing, trying to understand what had happened.

What was still happening.

"I went and told Moorland what I think of her," he said. "There's no way she's going to choose me now. I blew my chances."

"You made a mistake," Selena said. "That's all. Under the circumstances, I'm sure they'll understand."

"I called Moorland a corrupt bitch," Theo said, a sneer in his voice.

"You did?"

"Yes. And I said Duncan was the biggest liar I'd ever met. Always telling me how great I am. How special. Acting like he cared about me. It was all a show."

Selena brushed her hair back into place. "He does care about you. So does Moorland."

"Why are you defending them?"

"I'm not defending them. They should have told you about Liddy. But I've spent a lot of time around Moorland and Duncan and I don't think either one would do something to intentionally hurt you."

The hardness in his voice surprised her. "Intent doesn't matter. What matters is what they did. I'll never forgive them for it."

"So what? You're going to quit? Even if they do name me as navigator, I'll need a backup. Someone to save me if things go sideways."

"I doubt it. You're pretty good at saving yourself."

"Stop being such an—" She caught herself. He'd just lost his sister. He had a right to be angry, even if she wasn't the cause. She would give him some space.

"Such a what?" Theo asked.

"Nothing."

Theo looked at her, eyes cold. "No, go ahead and say what you're thinking. There's no reason to hold back."

Selena shook her head, not accepting his challenge. She knew first hand that sometimes you had to sort things out for yourself. She also knew that there was nothing she or anyone else could say that would help. She would leave him to his grief.

"You're tired. I'm tired. I need to go."

"Fine," Theo said. "Then go."

CHAPTER TWENTY-EIGHT

Marcus' feet rushed over the rolling black band of the treadmill. Twelve kilometers per hour, a brisk pace. Sweat coated his bangs. The machine hummed. To an outside observer, he looked like any other cadet, getting in his mandatory physical training. But inside, his mind moved far faster than his feet. Phoebus was gone, on his way back to Stephen's Point. Even with how well that little piece of drama had played out, Marcus would not allow himself to relax, to savor his victory. Bigger problems with less obvious solutions lay on the horizon. And like his feet, always churning but never moving him forward, for all his thinking he couldn't close in on a workable solution to the Selena problem.

With Phoebus gone, Heph would be easier to control. It also crippled Meghan's team. Even if Moorland assigned a replacement, it would take many cycles of training to catch up with him. He would beat Meghan. But now that Theo had decided to go ahead and let himself unravel, Selena might have become the favorite to navigate the *Chimera*. He could deal with that. What he couldn't deal with was the complicated relationship developing between Theo and the biggest impediment to a successful outcome.

He would have to be careful. He'd also have to do everything he could to protect Theo.

Protect.

Marcus knew himself well enough, had lived within the particular constraints of his mind long enough to recognize that though he felt nothing for Theo that a normal person would recognize as affection, he'd somehow started to think of their lives as intertwined. Not as friends. Not family. But together. The thought bothered Marcus because it suggested that despite his best efforts and his natural psychology, he'd developed a weakness. One he'd started to nurture. That he couldn't help but protect.

Protect.

What did that even mean? He didn't protect people. He deployed them like chess pieces. He moved them when they needed moving. Everyone played a role in life whether they realized it or not. He'd simply taken enough steps back from the game board to recognize that fact and opted out of being moved and into moving others. And as in chess, some pieces needed to be sacrificed to gain an advantage, and some pieces needed to be protected so they could be used to maximal effect later. That's why he protected Theo.

He needed sleep. Needed time to figure out how to stop Theo from getting himself disqualified. He'd misjudged the other boy's weakness. He'd expected him to crumble, leaving Marcus to rebuild him, deepening Theo's loyalty to him. Instead, Theo had charged off to confront Duncan. While that still served Marcus' purpose, Theo's quick action surprised him. Theo had changed so much. Plans would need to be adjusted accordingly.

His CATO pinged with a priority order from Moorland. He was to meet the chief and Selena at the outer ring's auxiliary breakage. He'd expected a formal introduction to the *Helvictus*, but not this soon after Theo's return and Phoebus' departure. He powered down the treadmill and wiped his face clean of sweat. Moorland was moving fast. She and Duncan must have decided to further accelerate the timeline.

* * *

The priority ping from Moorland hit Selena's CATO an hour before the end of her sleep cycle. The first she'd received since returning from waking the *Chimera*, it commanded her to meet Moorland at the auxiliary breakage, suggesting she might be doing some flying. Real flying, not the sanitized tests she and the others performed in VAST. How long had it been since she'd flown? *Not since the accident.* Not since she almost killed her father, Liam.

Nervous and a bit jittery from lack of sleep, Selena arrived at the airlock sealing the auxiliary breakage, she found Marcus waiting beside Moorland. Marcus gave her a friendly smile. *Ugh. Always so creepy and self-assured.*

"I've asked you here because of your performance in VAST," Moorland said. "You are the highest scoring cadets in terms of neural responsiveness. You think faster than your peers."

Marcus gave Selena a somewhat surprised look, then said, "Yes, but thinking fast isn't the same thing as thinking well."

Selena ignored him. She wasn't pleased to have to work with Marcus, but that didn't dull her curiosity over what came next. "Are we doing some sort of test?"

"Yes," Moorland said. "But if you haven't already figured it out, this will not be a simulation. Today you're entering a live flight environment."

Flying! Even if it meant being in close proximity to Marcus, the prospect thrilled her.

"Please follow me," Moorland said.

They entered the airlock and waited for it to complete its cycle. When the door opened, they stepped into a small, brightly lit breakage. Ahead, a sleek ship rested on support struts, glowing with newness and burnished, unmarked metal. It looked a little like a shuttle, complete with sloped atmospheric wings and tail stabilizers. But that was where the similarities ended. A cluster of powerful thrusters jutted the aft of the ship. Maneuvering jets dotted its exterior. Many more than *The Bee* or any other rimmer ship. Hexagonal pods hung from beneath the wings and the underside of the fuselage.

"This is the *Helvictus*," Moorland said.

The ship was a slick and vicious thing. Angular, nimble, fast. A natural predator.

Marcus strode beneath the wings, examining the hexagonal pods. "Weapons mounts?"

"Yes," Moorland said. "The *Helvictus* can be armed with cannons, energy weapons, and nuclear arms."

Cold swept over Selena's skin. The *Helvictus* had been built to fly in both space and within an atmosphere. She'd never completed an atmospheric reentry, assuming that was what Moorland wanted to test.

"You will flight test the *Helvictus* through several live-action combat scenarios," Moorland said. "I realize that you might prefer to test with another member of your individual teams. However, the priority of this test is to push the *Helvictus*. I'm confident that each of you will be able to do that."

"What sort of combat scenarios?" Marcus asked.

"That will become clear during testing," Moorland said.

"Marcus, you're up first."

* * *

The thin red lines of the *Helvictus'* interface glowed within the cockpit, enmeshing Marcus. Not the warm caress of a civilian ship, the interface connected to his CATO. He welcomed the ship's aggressive touch and returned it in kind. The engines ignited in pre-burn, thrumming through the restraints securing him in his seat.

He caught Selena's face reflected in the blast shield curving around the cockpit. She sat behind and to his right, pouting over Moorland's decision to give him the first go. Lips tight against her teeth, wisps of brown hair falling over her forehead, she looked like an angry little girl. But her hero status, while annoying, was undeniable. It would be wise not to push Moorland too hard when it came to Selena. Moorland would assign her an officer's slot. He could live with that. However, once they left for Earth, the *Chimera* would be his to command, along with her crew.

"Ready, Selena?" he asked, using her name, trying to keep her off balance.

"Ready."

"*Helvictus* is ready," Marcus said. "He's more than ready."

"He?"

Marcus ignored Selena and brought the core to load. Adrenaline coursed through him like fire and ice. Unlike the unfeeling test flights in VAST, the *Helvictus* gave immediate, intense feedback. The ship *wanted* to fly. Wanted—not to obey—but something of a higher magnitude.

To achieve symmetry.

He felt his body—the flesh body—housed inside the ship. He felt the hard metal of the ship, his thrusters, his targeting system. Raw, powerful, dangerous. He and the ship. He was. They were.

The breakage gave way to stars.

He fought the urge to scream. Never had he felt such freedom, such unrestraint. He felt drugged. *Careful*, he chided. *Don't lose yourself. You are in control. You. Not the ship—remarkable though he may be.*

With a sweeping motion, he brought the ship to half-burn, pinning his flesh body to the chair. The *Helvictus* reveled in the acceleration and demanded more.

No.

He slowed, curtailing speed, bringing them to a crawl.

There is no symmetry. You serve me. Obey me. That is all.

Moorland's voice sounded over the com. "Initial testing shows the *Helvictus* quite capable in terms of speed, maneuverability, and responsive neural sync. However, we've never tested her all that hard. She's different than anything else at the rim or the produced colony. What I'm saying is—"

"You're not sure what he can do," Marcus said.

"Yes ... *He?*"

"I know it's customary to refer to ships as female," Marcus said, "but the *Helvictus* is male."

"Your ass," Selena whispered from behind him.

"I don't care what you call it," Moorland said. "But give the ship a thorough test run. You're more than capable. I'm going to send you some mission parameters via your CATO."

"Yes, ma'am," Marcus said.

"Selena?" Moorland asked.

"Sure, but it's not like I can do anything from back here—"

"Excellent. Moorland out."

The channel closed, but not before Moorland's CATO message popped into the upper left quadrant of his overlay. He thought of sharing it with Selena, then thought better of it. Instead, he went through the *Helvictus*' system tree and locked Selena's terminal down, closing her out of everything but the most basic of ship's systems. In preparation for their journey to Earth, she needed to learn to obey him without question or hesitation. He'd give her an opportunity to do just that.

And what if she wouldn't? He almost smiled. *Even better.*

This time he didn't resist the *Helvictus*' desire for acceleration. He pushed the ship hard enough to make his bones creak.

* * *

The gut-shaking thrum of the *Helvictus*' engines invaded Selena's body. Across the console in front of her, the lines of an interface grid pricked against her skin. Thin hairs walked up her arms and the back of her neck; the ship's formidable presence made her scalp tickle. The hunger. The raw willfulness. She felt Marcus also—his intensity merged with that of the ship. A partnership like she'd once had with *The Bee*, and hoped to have again with the *Chimera*.

Her fingers strayed to the silver chain looped around her neck, attached to the shooting star charm nestled against her breastbone. *Come ride a pillar of fire with me.* She wished the *Helvictus* was *The Bee*. That she once again sat strapped in the cockpit of her old friend, in pursuit of a good pull. She, her father, and the trawler— how simple her life had once been. Enjoyable work. Rough, but honest. A life forever lost to her.

The *Helvictus'* attention focused on a trio of welding ships on their way in from the rim. Marcus brought the *Helvictus* to half-burn, pinning Selena to her chair. She took even, practiced breaths, calming her heart, letting oxygen resupply her body and mind. *Helvictus* was on an interdiction course and would soon overtake the welding ships.

"What's going on?" Selena asked when the acceleration evened out enough to allow her to talk.

"You'll see," Marcus replied.

A wave of something like heat flashed across her skin—real or a side effect from the interface? She couldn't tell. *What was Marcus up to?* She couldn't access the full system tree through her interface—Marcus alone had access to everything but navigation data and the live feeds from external cameras.

Ahead, several pinpoints of light flickered orange-silver. The welding ships.

"Are you *chasing* them?" Selena asked.

Marcus said nothing.

Selena engaged her interface and searched down each branch of the system tree. She found dead ends and more dead ends. But when she pulled back, when she felt the entirety of the interface, the systems it controlled, the ship itself and the person piloting it, a cold emptiness filled her. *Something's wrong.*

She searched the interface again, forcing her way forward, wrestling for access.

A stinging, burning pain rippled through her body. She let out a startled yelp. Her skin went hot and then clammy. She trembled, flinching back in the seat, shocked by the interface's response.

Marcus had closed her out. Made her a prisoner.

"Marcus?"

No answer but the brush of his uniform against the restraints as he sent the ship into a screaming bank of a turn that slammed Selena's guts into the sidewall of her stomach. They leveled out and a new, bright red interface came to life, parallel to the navigational grid. It forced itself against her, trying to link to her CATO, but she resisted it.

A series of blue reticles tracked each of the welding ships. *Weapons activated,* came a whisper.

"I've split them so you can strike them all at once," Marcus said.

"Strike them?" Selena asked, horrified.

"Yes."

"I'm not striking anything! Moorland didn't say—"

"I say. And I'm in command."

Selena's mouth fell open. The red interface pawed at her, encouraging her to act. To release the ship to kill.

"I'm not doing this," she said.

She shoved back at the interface, will against will.

"You will destroy the targets," Marcus said.

"They're real ships! Real pilots! We can't—"

"You'll do what I tell you to do!" The intensity of his voice shocked her. *He needs this.* The interface crackled against her skin.

"Burn it," Selena said. "Burn it and burn you."

"I'll make you do it," Marcus said.

The red interface dug at her. Poked and scraped, searching for a connection to her spider, begging for acquiescence. She clamped her hands over her ears. Screwed shut her eyes. Dove inside herself. But the predatory red interface followed. She saw red. Felt red. Lived again the moments before the crash of *The Bee*. In those final seconds, the everlasting seconds before impact, she'd seen her mother's face. Cold and dead and crawling with flies.

Dead. Cold. Flies.

Her legs pulled up toward her chest, arms tight across her midsection. *Theo,* she thought. *Theo. Please. Help.*

But Theo couldn't hear her. No one could. Marcus-*Helvictus* crushed around her, sucking at her weakness, her vulnerability, demanding permission to destroy. She could resist. She could. But for how long? The red interface would remain, tight as a shroud. Eating, stealing, exposing. How long until it burrowed so deep she'd never get it out again?

Targets locked, the interface confirmed.

A dark hunger swelled to life inside her. *Please let it be the ship. Don't let that feeling be from me.*

Only one way to get rid of it.

She shoved back. Not at the red interface but at Marcus. She knew what he feared. She'd seen it. Seen *him*. The body in the cave. Face beat to pulp, skull cracked open.

Marcus grew still. "What?" A different sort of whisper. "How do you know about him?"

"It doesn't matter," Selena said.

Hatred in his face. Revulsion.

"Control your ship," Selena said.

The heat came with scorching intensity. It raged at her like the surface of Elypso. It singed skin from muscle. Burned away flesh. Charred her bones. She held the face of the man Marcus had murdered against that tide, but it wasn't enough. The full brunt of the interface bore down on her, inside her.

For a moment, the ship disappeared. She was small. So small. She stood on the banks of a muddy riverbank. A dead woman lay at her feet. Marcus stood a few meters away, eyes raging. Snow drifted down—fat, lazy flakes. Blood dripped from Marcus' hands. He leapt at her. She tried to defend herself, but the arm that reached up to block him was heavy with baby fat, too short, too weak—

The *Helvictus* shuddered.

Her eyes opened. Wider than humanly possible, wide enough to see in every direction at once, to see impossible distances, to see the three welding ships aligned like planets in eclipse. A white-hot lance seared into the black. It connected the *Helvictus* to the nearest welder like a bolt of electricity jumping contact points. The ship disintegrated in a cloud of glowing debris. The remaining ships broke off, hard-burning away, but too late.

Another flash. Another.

I'm doing this.

And she was. She, the ship, and Marcus. A consortium of destruction.

We, the interface said. Beneath the "we" lay something else. A familiar presence. A shadow of ..., *Chimera*?

How?

As if answering her question, the interface communicated

again: *We. Us. Together.*

She had fired. She had destroyed the ships. Killed their pilots.

You nearly killed your father. It was only a matter of time before you screwed up again. You let them beat you. You gave in. You quit. You let them do this to you. Stupid, reckless little girl.

"Took you long enough," Marcus said.

She screamed a curse at him.

"Time to switch. Moorland's orders. I'll take over weapons."

"We *killed* them."

"All targets destroyed," Marcus said, voice calm once more.

"We murdered them."

"Don't be melodramatic. Broken, old welders, remotely operated—they were destined to become scrap anyway."

"Scrap?"

"Oh? You mean you didn't know?" Marcus' eyes laughed at her.

"You didn't tell me!"

"It's not my job to tell you anything. I give orders. You follow them. It's that simple."

Selena shook, waiting for her raw emotion to coalesce, to transform into words.

"I saw what you did in the cave."

Marcus' face became a wall. He settled back in his seat, seemed to relax. The red interface retreated back into the console. She withdrew her shaking hands and squeezed them together in her lap.

"I know who you are."

"You have no idea who I am."

Her eyes met his—purple-black holes—their event horizon pulling her in.

"You're a murderer," she said, expecting him to deny it. To accuse and twist.

Instead, Marcus just stared back at her. "Yes," he whispered. "I am. And you better keep that in mind when you think about what you do next."

CHAPTER TWENTY-NINE

The screens behind Moorland swelled with images of the streets of Stephen's Point. Ranks of uniformed regulators in riot gear, raising cordons, pushing back a heaving wall of humanity. Burning buildings. Casualty reports scrolled, names and neighborhoods summing up entire lives. She couldn't bring herself to turn the screens off. The shifting, chaotic images provided ample fuel for her doubts. Had she done the right thing in isolating the *Hydra*?

Duncan didn't think so. Neither did many of the cadets, Theo in particular. She understood his anger and hurt and could sympathize in a removed way. But rehashing the decision wouldn't change anything, least of all bring back his sister. She'd done what she thought best, and would have to live with the consequences.

It remained to be seen if Theo could set aside his grief and anger in service to the colony. Duncan believed he would while she reserved judgement, tired of trying to predict outcomes.

She turned away from the wall of chaos, checking on Duncan. He sat, folded over himself, a large man in a too-small space. He too watched the screens. It was harder for him than for her. The colonists, the land, the city itself—he was connected to all of them, felt responsible for all of them.

Moorland wasn't sentimental. She'd joined the Regulatory, left her parents' tiny house in East End, and never looked back. When the first Mandate passed—not the Mandate as the colonists knew it, but its top-secret, classified precursor—she was a Regulatory logistics lieutenant, first-class. Still living in rented rooms near Regulatory headquarters, still dating a tall, red-headed Order prelate. She'd been plucked from her position by the Stephen's Point Council and offered a position on the exchange dock—a promotion too good to pass up. From that moment forward she was focused on objectives, metrics. And the mission. Always the mission. She'd spent so much time in command, so much time in orbit, that she found it hard to feel anything more than fatigue.

Her CATO pinged with a message from Hurston Lemieux.

"The cadets are assembled and waiting," Moorland said. Duncan nodded but made no move to stand.

She hated seeing him like this, the eroding of his basic faith in the goodness of people. But she had nothing to offer to soothe his suffering. Not without compromising herself, mouthing platitudes. Giving him what he needed at the expense of her sense of self. They'd grown closer again through the cycles spent preparing the cadets, but it had only served to highlight their insurmountable differences.

After she left Stephen's Point for the exchange dock, she'd convinced herself she couldn't meet the demands of her new station and have enough of herself to give another person. Not only that, she'd also recognized that a life lived alongside Duncan would require too many compromises. Not the small compromises of where to live, whose career to favor, but the fundamental, undermining variety. Giving up, or pretending to give up, the truth of who she was and what she believed to accommodate his faith. And he would invariably subvert that part of himself for her. She knew they'd become the worst versions of themselves. Fall into lethargy, cynicism, and eventually, disrespect.

"I can do this on my own, Conrad," she said. "But I'd prefer not to."

Duncan cleared his throat, unwinding his legs to free himself from his chair. He held her gaze a moment, as if also weighing the risks of a life they had not—and would not—live.

His green eyes still showed lingering weariness, but he drew himself up, chin rising, chest inflating. An Order official once more. Personal feelings buried under a layer of confident, glossy authority.

"You're sure about giving them the option to leave?" he asked, watching her.

"Yes. I did my best to keep Stephen's Point and the *Hydra* separate, to protect the cadets from the situation. But I realize now that was a mistake. I'm powerless to fight wars and simultaneous rumors of wars. They're going to have to choose for themselves."

"We can't afford to lose many," Duncan said. One of his eyebrows twitched and a deep dimple, camouflaged by his beard, appeared in his cheek. "But I can think of at least one or two I wouldn't miss all that much."

Taken aback, Moorland paused. Duncan's eyebrow rose further and a spark glowed in his eyes. "Admit it. They're not all as loveable as their mothers might think."

Moorland gave in and returned his smile with a small one of her own. "Some are better than others. Not much different than any other working environment, I suppose." She sighed. "It just seems worse because they're all so very, very young."

Duncan nodded. "Young. And stupid. But you can't tell me that a few years is going to do much to change the basic nature of a kid like Nemus Archer, or the other one—the blonde kid that thinks it matters that he grew up in the Golden Valley."

Moorland knew who he meant. "Drummond."

"That's the one. I wouldn't miss him. Not even a little."

"It's a blow even if the only loss is Phoebus," Moorland said, turning serious once more. "Beyond his test scores, he's a leader. He's influenced people. The ones left behind will be disgruntled, suspicious, or both. Perhaps they'll choose to go too, but I have to give them the option. They've been powerless until now—every decision made for them. From this point forward, I need total dedication. They stay or go, their choice." She glanced to the right, pulling up the station-wide schedule Blake sent out every six hours. "Next cycle was slated for a practice insertion, and I have no intention of putting that off."

She straightened her uniform jacket and slipped gloves over her hands. Simple gestures repeated countless times over the years, no different than Duncan adjusting his pendant or whispering a silent prayer. You didn't have to have a specific faith to become reliant on rituals.

Spine straight, shoulders back, uniform immaculate. She would model total confidence and control, despite her tenuous grasp on both. "Ready?" she asked.

Duncan nodded, and together, they left her berth and made their way to the commons.

* * *

Selena cracked her neck, a willful violation of assembly decorum. Beside her, Meghan tensed. *Wrapped tighter than a bolus around a pull, that one.* But smart, stubborn, and if Selena was honest, a capable leader. She'd held things together, even as their team faltered. Selena knew she wasn't performing as well as Theo, but there was more to it than her effort or skill. Despite her fierce, focused trying, she always lagging behind, and Marcus' team always outscored Meghan's. Phoebus was a big part of the problem. She'd suspected him of not carrying his share of the weight in VAST. He always seemed distracted. Because he was distracted. His message proved it.

Selena glanced around, trying to spot Phoebus. Heph, his dark head bent to study the floor, stood in the twin's usual spot, the place beside him empty. Where was Phoebus? And what would Moorland say to them—to Heph—when she arrived?

Meghan shifted, drawing Selena's attention away from Heph. She followed the other girl's gaze as it tracked Marcus, heading for the vacant space next to Theo. Selena sensed Meghan's curiosity and fear. Meghan saw through Marcus' act just like she did. Another point in Meghan's favor. Maybe when the assembly ended, she would tell Meghan about what happened in the *Helvictus*.

Targets locked.

Selena's stomach lurched. She'd never feared anyone as much as she did Marcus. She disliked him for all sorts of reasons, but hated him because he scared her. She knew a few of his secrets, but he knew all of hers. And he would use them against her the way she might use a blowtorch to soften a piece of metal.

She wished she could talk to Theo about Marcus, but the two shared some sort of misshapen relationship she couldn't wrap her mind around. Marcus scared Theo as well—she knew it for a fact—but that didn't seem to stop him from following Marcus' lead and seeking his approval. There was something messed up about it, something messed up about Theo, and she couldn't sort it out. Maybe no one could.

The closeness they'd experienced in the sphere had been terrible. And wonderful. She didn't want to admit it even to herself, but she missed it. But what if he hadn't felt the same thing? The sense of closeness might have been one-sided or, even worse, something she'd made up. The weird interlacing of their memories and feelings—had she wanted to feel a connection so much that she'd imagined it?

She'd kissed him and he'd kissed her back. She hadn't imagined that. *Yes, but he was grieving. You took advantage of the situation. That's why he pushed you away at the end.* She felt herself flushing and hoped no one would notice.

Moorland entered the commons, looking trim in her white uniform, flanked by six regulators. They filed into the commons and stood behind Moorland as Duncan joined her. Light glittered off of his silver necklace ... doodad. What had Theo called it? A sign? A sigil? The three emblems of the Eye, the Tree, and the Orb; the eye for Stephen's sight, the tree with its twisting branches representing fractal apace, and the orb for the sphere. It made a kooky sort of sense, she supposed. Moorland let her gaze drift over the ranks, her eyes finding Selena's. Selena's skin tightened, prickled with bumps.

Anticipation crackled in the air as Moorland stepped forward. "Cadets."

"Chief Moorland," the cadets replied.

"This cycle, at 1300 hours, Regulatory officers under my orders took Phoebus Hart into custody."

Cadets shifted in their ranks, turning to look where Hephaestus stood, shoulders hunched. He must have already known of his brother's fate. He showed no discernable reaction to Moorland's words.

"Phoebus Hart accessed and removed classified documents and disseminated them to all of you. He will be prosecuted for hacking, theft of proprietary information, and treason." Another flurry of sound and movement from the cadets at the word "treason." Down Selena's row, Kaylee leaned forward, mouth open in protest, but she said nothing.

Moorland held up her hands. "By now you have all seen some of the documents Phoebus released. You know what is happening down on Stephen's Point."

"No thanks to you," someone said.

Moorland ignored the interruption. "We've reached a turning point. The *Chimera*'s awake. She reports that her systems are stable. We've refueled her remaining cores with ecomire, and she's prepared to enter fractal space. You have trained and prepared for this. I don't need to tell any of you about the importance of our mission, nor am I here to lecture you. I've come to offer you a choice."

Moorland's fierce gaze seemed to be everywhere at once, pinning the cadets in place. "If you wish to leave the *Hydra* and return to the surface, you may do so now. You will not be given time to return to your quarters. Whatever you leave behind will remain aboard the *Hydra.* There is a shuttle ready and waiting."

Moorland's eyes flew to someone in Selena's row and Selena turned her head. Kaylee raised a shaking hand. Moorland frowned. "Do you wish to depart, Cadet Johns, or do you have a question?"

"I have a question," Kaylee said. "What will happen to us if we choose to leave?"

"You will be returned to the surface where you will be debriefed by the Regulatory. You will be held in a secure location until it is ascertained whether you will be returned to your parents or guardians. After that I cannot tell you. Your welfare will be out of my hands."

Someone else's hand came up and Moorland looked their way. "Yes?"

"Can we go down and check on our families and then come back?"

Moorland paused and Selena thought at first that she might not answer. "This is a one-way trip and I will not repeat my offer. You will commit to staying or leaving. I'm done answering questions— now choose."

Kaylee looked across at Hephaestus, then stepped out of the rank of cadets and walked down the central aisle.

"Kaylee!" Selena whispered, but her bunkmate didn't respond, making her way forward until she stood a few paces away from Moorland, eyes downcast.

Slowly, here and there around the room, cadets made their way forward. The eyes of the cadets shifted from each person who stepped forward to Moorland, to Heph. When would he step forward? Stand in solidarity with his brother?

Silence fell as other cadets joined Kaylee, the atmosphere sick with dread and disbelief. Xavier Gillespie, another nav assistant from Selena's team, stood and moved to the front. Selena struggled to swallow a thick wad of saliva and caught Meghan's eye. Meghan stared back, face white, perspiration a shining constellation across her forehead. First Phoebus and now Gillespie; their team was gutted.

At last Heph moved, stepping into the central aisle. He faced Moorland but did not join the others at the front of the room. His jaw ground, balled fists stiff at his sides. A silence fell over the room, waiting for the coming confrontation between the petite, silver-haired chief and the tall, dark-skinned cadet.

"I have something to say," Heph said, deep voice rumbling.

A pair of regulators started to move toward Heph but Moorland waived them away. "Go ahead, Cadet Hart."

Heph came forward and turned his back to the cadets who'd chosen to leave, the anger behind his eyes a profound presence. Selena didn't have any siblings, but she recognized his loss. Not the same as Theo's, not as permanent, but painful nonetheless.

"I'm not as good with words as ..." Heph's voice broke a little and he looked away before continuing, "... as my brother. But I wanted to say that I understand why Phoeb did what he did, but that doesn't make it right."

Heph's deep-set brown eyes turned on Moorland, his fine, almost elegant jaw set. "But what you did was wrong, too." Heph raised his voice, the challenge in his words unmistakable. "You've put us all in a terrible position. I hold you accountable for what happened to Phoeb."

Moorland said nothing, letting Heph speak.

He turned back to the cadets. "If any of you want to leave, then leave. I won't stop you. But I'm staying. Because I see what my brother didn't. Moorland was wrong to hide the truth from us, but she's right that the best way we can help our families is by doing what we've been trained to do. So I'm staying. That's all I've got to say."

Head up, shoulders back, Hephaestus strode back to his place.

Kaylee tracked Heph's retreating form, face betraying her struggle between confusion and hope. *Come on*, Selena thought. *You can do it.* A tiny part of her wondered at the strength of her own emotions, but she didn't care. She didn't want to lose anyone else.

"I ..." Kaylee said. She looked at Moorland. "I changed my mind. I want to stay." Moorland nodded and Kaylee didn't hesitate, almost running back to her place.

"Anyone else?" Moorland asked.

No one moved, the kids in the ragged group at the front of the assembly avoiding all eye contact with their fellow cadets.

"Good. I wish you all a safe journey back to the colony." The regulators moved as a group, surrounding those who'd elected to leave and escorting them out of the commons.

As soon as the doors closed behind them, Moorland raised her voice and spoke. "At twelve hundred hours next cycle, you will conduct a practice insertion into fractal space."

Moorland paused, letting the enormity of the moment settle over the cadets.

For the first time, Duncan spoke. Unlike Moorland with her clipped delivery, his words carried strong emotion. "Stephen brought us here generations ago, and now, you will follow the stitches he laid and return to the birthplace of humanity." His eyes rested on Selena. She waited for him to continue, tense, the muscles in her calves engaged. Tingles ran down her spine.

"You have been called for this purpose. Trained. Equipped. All that remains before you depart for Earth is this final test of the *Chimera*'s readiness. A test of your readiness. And of your resolve."

His voice rose, sonorous, powerful, swept over the cadets. "My life, Moorland's life, and the lives of everyone on the *Hydra* and the colony rest on your shoulders. Like Stephen, you must save those who cannot save themselves. Step into your birthright. Go and retake the stars."

Marcus put two fingers in his mouth and whistled, snapping the lingering tension. The room erupted with roaring cheers of approval. Selena raised her left fist, rocking it side to side. She thought of her father, Liam, and shouted, "Steady pull!" carried by the excitement of the moment. "Steady pull."

Meghan raised her arm, cautious at first, followed by Alaina Sandborne, the last remaining member of their team. Charlie put one arm around Heph's shoulders, his other raised. Slowly, Heph raised a fist. Kaylee joined them, and then the others, the room a swaying mass of fists. For the moment at least, a unified whole.

CHAPTER THIRTY

The umbilical retracted from the *Chimera*'s side, freeing her from the *Hydra* for the first time in a decade. Cores cycling at nominal load, her port thrusters fired a short burn, rotating the cruiser along her axis. The seams of her scarred hull glittered in starlight as the *Hydra* dropped away, lost in the luminescence of the moon.

When she at last fully cleared the station, *Chimera*'s great engines breathed fire, burning for the empty space between Gauleta and the rim. There she would attempt to enter fractal space for the first time since her arrival at Elypso.

Marcus sat with Theo at a support station, going over the details of their insertion into fractal space. The *Hydra* became a pinpoint of light against black space, crested Stephen's Point's horizon, and disappeared. The moon itself shrunk at a rapid pace, eclipsed by the blue mass of the much larger gas giant it orbited. The *Chimera* monitored all of these things as well as each cadet's CATO feed, a multifaceted view that would drive a lesser being mad.

They would make a short journey to Betequa, a yellow dwarf star a mere three light years away from Elypso. Marcus' team of Theo, Nemus, Preston, and Ortiz would take the ship there before handing off to Meghan's team for the return journey. Meghan's team waited their turn at the periphery of the command deck, strapped into drop chairs that folded out of the walls.

The *Chimera*'s hydrostasis field stood ready. So did her calculations charting the stitches laid by Stephen, connecting the two star systems. The trip would take no more than a few hours each way—assuming there were no complications with her human navigator.

[We're clear,] she messaged Marcus before executing a low speed backflip, using her great engines to slow their momentum. Marcus clamped a hand on Theo's shoulder and whispered something in his ear. None of the cadets heard the words, but the

Chimera did: "Prove me right."

Theo nodded and stepped inside the sphere.

"Listen up," Marcus said. "We're about to enter uncharted territory here. There's a huge difference between a simulation and the real thing. I want you all on point and focused."

Selena rolled her eyes.

The muscles around Marcus' mouth tightened, but his smile never wavered. "Theo? You ready in there?"

"Sure thing," Theo said.

Goodbye, friend. The words echoed through her. She waited for Theo's presence—the mind that reminded her so much of Stephen's—the satisfaction of partnering with another. But when his will joined with hers, it came like a wall of hot fury centered on memories of a round-faced child.

An downturned mouth, pleading with him. "Don't go, Theo." Liddy.

His younger sister. Killed down on Stephen's Point. Reborn in their shared memory. She'd loved every colonist she carried across the void, but this was different. She loved the child Liddy like she'd loved Stephen. The pain of her death radiated through her.

[Theo?]

[I'm fine.]

[I loved her, too.]

[You never met her.]

He shoved her away from his memories. His strength surprised her. He really was like Stephen. Brilliant, a trillion threads of energy. And just like Stephen, broken. Because at the very end, he'd left her. Allowed her to be locked away. The memory caused a shudder in her neural process. Fear?

She did not fear. She was not locked away. Now would she never be again. Salix could not contain her new self, a merger of her past, and of Theo and Selena's memories. The face she wore when speaking to the humans was more than a simple mechanism used to express emotion. Her proprioception—her sense of her location and surroundings that transcended what hard coding dictated—now included a human face. One that Theo would not look at.

His thoughts traveled circuitous paths, but always returned to the loss of his sister. He would have to learn to set it aside, at least while navigating through the sphere. She sent her thoughts forward, brushing against his.

[You must concentrate on The Everything, Theo.]

"Prepare for insertion," Theo said, speaking to Marcus and his team. "On my count. Five …"

[We need more time. The sync is tenuous.]

"Four."

[We will not succeed if we do not work together.]

"Three."

[You can't do this alone.]

"Two."

The grass parts. The pathway opens. Not her thoughts, nor Theo's, but an echo of Stephen's, of the original NAs who helped him lay the stitches connecting Earth to Elypso.

"One!"

She felt the weight of Theo's mind—of his *need*. The full brunt of his focused will consumed her. Drew her forward. All that mattered was The Everything. She would help him to hold it. To balance it. Her cores cycled to full load. A buzzing, ecstatic sensation flowed through her as the hydrostasis field unfurled around her, cocooning her body within a wavering bubble-wall of unreality.

Theo tore open a hole in reality and she helped him.

She couldn't stop herself.

The stars dissolved into banded light.

* * *

"Three," Theo called.

Selena sat in her jump seat, spider linked to the *Chimera*. Marcus and his team sat at their stations, hands bathed in grids of green light.

"Two."

The ship shuddered. A milky wall of displacement crept outward from the *Chimera*, dulling the stars. The cores at the rear of the ship cycled to a frenetic pace. For a moment, Selena was once more aboard *The Bee*, plunging through the shard field of the rim, her trawler's core whining. Then the hydrostasis field took shape, became a crystalline bubble surrounding the *Chimera*, warping stars into trapezoids and diamonds of refracted light.

"One!"

The word elongated, lengthened. Became the sound of a

massive, droning insect. Selena's hands floated in front of her. The word "one" slowed further, became a warped, ongoing note without musicality. All that existed summarized in a great, flat-lining *nnnnnnnnnnnnn* vibrating her teeth and bones. Her mouth snapped shut. Her eyes rolled, focused. The sound dissipated, replaced with the heavy breathing and muffled cries of the other cadets.

A groan came from within the sphere.

Whose voice was that?

Her mind slowed. What she felt through the spider sent shivers up her legs, burying themselves in her stomach like icy fishhooks. The *Chimera* was nowhere. Everywhere. Not a ship, but a flowing mass traveling down a steep chasm like flood water. Splitting again and again, remerging, forming and reforming like raindrops against glass. They'd entered fractal space.

Theo's calm voice spoke from within the sphere. "Insertion complete. *Chimera* and I have a hold on Stephen's thread."

Stephen's thread. It gave her chills. The very stitches Stephen himself had placed, linking star systems across a galaxy. Earth to Elypso. Jealousy fomenting inside her, she could only watch as Marcus and his team worked their terminals. With quick precision, the NAs handled each emerging paradox, Marcus coordinating, issuing precise commands.

"I can see Betequa," Theo said. "If you can call this seeing!" Wonder filled his voice.

Meghan's face reflected Selena's frustration.

"It's so easy," Theo said. "Stephen already did the hard part."

Through her spider, Selena felt the galaxy swirl around and through them. Beyond it, other galaxies, like glass marbles rushing around the perimeter of a great bowl. At their center, a nothing, and at its center—The Everything. Folded over. Infinite. A swirl of lines and connection points. Lacking all logic. And yet, in the midst of the impossible, a series of stitches. Points held in place, connecting one reality to another. An infinite line. A circle.

Her head spun. Her breath came in panicked gulps.

Inside the sphere, Theo laughed. The first happy sound she'd heard from him since his sister's death. He could forget her there in the midst of navigation. Liddy fading. Replaced by The Everything.

Selena too, replaced.

"Prepare for extraction," Theo said. "On my count."

Extraction? Already?

"Five," Theo said.

The cores whined. The distance between reality and The Everything shortened to nothing.

"Four."

Liam stood beside her. Took her hand. *Your turn next, girlie.*

"Three."

A voice called to her. Words lost on a mountain breeze. A distant shadow on a distant hill.

"Two."

Stephen stepped out of the sphere. Stephen left command. Stephen boarded a shuttle and left forever. Stephen screamed into the silence of his closed mind. Stephen looked at a cave wall and saw fractal space. Stephen driven mad. Dead Stephen. Stephen reborn. Living again and again, splayed out across a galaxy, linking the stars themselves. Stephen—

"One."

Selena! Help me!

Her mother's voice. The *Chimera*'s. One and the same.

Goodbye, friend.

The grass parts. The pathway …

Opens.

Star-shimmer. Time dilating. Moving backwards. Stephen comes to life. Sloughs off age, becomes a young man again. Leaves the shuttle, retreats backward from the breakage and enters the command deck. Steps into the sphere. Warm hands on dimpled metal. He speaks.

Hello, friend. Did you miss me?

Selena unfastened her straps and squeezed past the dazed NAs slumped over their terminals. A yellow dwarf star burned from the wallscreens. Marcus' face tilted upward, a grotesque mask of pain and fear. He composed himself in an instant, but not before she saw the intense fear etched into his face. Not before he saw her seeing it. Whatever he'd seen as they came out of fractal terrified him.

His lips curled into a malicious smile. Heat flared behind his eyes. Selena looked away, angling for the sphere. She met Theo as he stepped out, the picture of calm. "Forty-nine minutes, thirty-one seconds," he said.

"What?"

His eyes looked past her. "Total time in fractal. The ship is nominal and waiting for your team to take over."

"It was supposed to take over two hours," she said.

"Well, it didn't."

Selena chewed the inside of her lip. "Are you okay?"

"Why wouldn't I be?"

"You didn't *see* anything while you were in there?"

"Like what?"

"I don't know," Selena said, backtracking. What if no one else had experienced anything out of the ordinary? No, that couldn't be true, based on Marcus' reaction.

"I followed Stephen's stitches," Theo said. She detected relief in his voice. "There's nothing to it."

"Nothing to it? Theo, you just brought us to a different star system!"

He shrugged. Modest. Not a hint of his former angst. Entering fractal space had changed him. It remained to be seen how much. She reached out to touch his arm, to prove to herself that he existed, that this wasn't some extended fractal space dream. He pulled back. His eyes danced away from hers.

"Are you sure you're okay?"

"I think so," Theo said.

Marcus came between them. "Shouldn't you be prepping with your team?"

"Shouldn't you be minding your own business?"

Marcus smiled. "Theo is my business."

"Is that right?" Selena searched Theo for some sign of disagreement but found none. Glassy-eyed, Theo fell in beside Marcus. Soon they'd strapped into their jump seats along with the rest of their team, ready for the return journey.

Selena peered into the sphere, half expecting to find Stephen inside. She'd more than just seen the man. She'd touched him. Through the *Chimera*'s memory, she now knew him. Theo knew him as well. Far better than she did. What if what flowed through the sphere was *more* than memory? What if it shaped you, changed you?

Meghan joined Selena beside the sphere. "Are you ready for

this?" she asked.

"I guess I have to be, right?"

"You'll do fine," Meghan said.

"Sure. But not like Theo."

Meghan didn't argue. She knew the truth the same as Selena: none of the other cadets could perform like Theo.

Selena's fingers brushed the gentle curve of the sphere's opening. The *Chimera* waited inside. Not a distant voice or CATO messages but the living ship. The unrestrained person. Would navigating force Selena to revisit the edge of the stream? Her connection to the ship forged around a single formative memory of loss? Or could they create a new common space together? A new story?

Only one way to find out.

Meghan touched her shoulder. "I wasn't happy when they assigned you to my team, but you've proven me wrong every step of the way. You deserve to be here."

Meghan whirled, not burdening Selena with the need to respond. The rest of the team assembled at the substations, CATOs linking them to the ship. One by one they signaled their readiness until only Selena remained. Past them, secured in his jump seat, Theo stared into his personal oblivion.

[It is time,] the *Chimera* messaged.

Time to go home. Selena took a deep breath and entered the sphere.

CHAPTER THIRTY-ONE

"I do not accept your choice," the *Chimera* said.

From a wallscreen on the command deck, *Chimera* regarded Moorland and Duncan with implacable eyes. Not really seeing—not with the stereoscopic hundred-degree field of view provided by a pair of eyes, but with a wide array of monitoring capabilities that made the five primary human senses seem trivial. Even assisted by a CATO overlay, it would take a human a lifetime to parse the amount of data the *Chimera* absorbed each second.

Duncan's bushy eyebrows drew taut. "What do you mean you don't accept it?"

"I will not accept Theo as Navigator," *Chimera* said.

She wore a plain white uniform identical to Moorland's but lacked ranking decorum or any other distinguishing characteristic. A neat braid of dark hair fell behind her left shoulder. Like any other officer under Moorland's command, *Chimera* presenting herself as confident and direct—traits Moorland valued enough to demand them in all those who served under her.

"Duncan and I have evaluated the data," Moorland said. "Theo is the obvious choice. His performance in the fractal test insertion mirrors those from VAST. He is the superior candidate."

"I do not dispute the data," *Chimera* said, "but I will not accept him."

Duncan looked at Moorland, face wary, then back to the *Chimera*. "The choice isn't yours to make."

A hint of indecision appeared on *Chimera*'s face. "I chose Stephen. And now, I choose Selena."

A thousand questions fought for supremacy in Moorland's mind. Why did the *Chimera* think that she'd chosen Stephen? After Navigator Black's sudden death, Captain Prescott had conducted a ship-wide search and found Stephen to be the best candidate. She'd pulled the historical records via CATO to confirm what she already knew; the *Chimera* hadn't chosen anything for herself. How could she? More importantly, why and how had the ship become convinced that she had?

"Do you accept my authority as Chief Regulator of the Stephen's Point colony?" Moorland asked, afraid of how the *Chimera* might answer.

"Yes."

"Do you accept that I have authority over all assets and resources, including the *Chimera*?" It felt strange to refer to the ship that way, but she could think of no more accurate way to frame the question.

"Yes."

"I command that Theo Puck navigate the *Chimera* on its return trip to Earth," Moorland said.

Chimera's eyes blinked. Part of a human interface model co-opted by the ship? A conscious choice? A learned behavior?

"Theo will not navigate the *Chimera*. I choose Selena," the *Chimera* said.

The upper part of Duncan's cheeks not hidden by his beard reddened. "This is ridiculous," he said. Moorland didn't need her CATO overlay to detect his elevated heartrate—the veins in his neck were pulsing.

"I chose Stephen. Now I choose Selena."

Duncan shook his head, eyes on Moorland's. "She's unstable."

Was he speaking of the *Chimera* or Selena? Both? Moorland rubbed her forehead with both palms. A pointless gesture, it neither relieved the dull ache behind her eyes nor gave her new insight into how to proceed.

"Stephen was chosen by The Everything," Duncan said. "He ascended to Navigator because the universe willed it. He saved his people."

"The Everything does not choose anything," the *Chimera* said. "It has no purpose, and therefore no will."

"But you have a will?" Duncan said. "You—a machine—made by human hands. *You* have purpose and a will?"

"I do not know," the *Chimera* replied.

"Then how can you choose anything?" Duncan asked,

exasperation sharpening his tone.

"I do not know."

"You're talking in circles."

"It is like I told you," the *Chimera* said, "The *Chimera* is the greatest threat to the colony that exists."

"But you are also our only means of contacting Earth," Moorland added.

The *Chimera* spoke with a total absence of emotion that filled Moorland with uneasy dread. "Salix sleep has caused damage to my neural architecture. I cannot be relied upon. However, your need for me outweighs whatever threats I might pose. It is like a paradox."

"What sort of threats?" Moorland asked.

"Because I cannot trace the source of the failure, I cannot define its implications or extrapolate potential outcomes. There is no protocol governing such a situation."

"Yes," Duncan said, "there is." Moorland looked at him, surprised. If one existed, she'd never heard of it.

"You could be replaced," Duncan said.

Chimera didn't react. "You do not have that option. The Centauri shipworks is over a thousand light years away."

Moorland caught her hands rising to her forehead and sent them back to her sides. "This is no longer a productive conversation. We're going to have to figure out how we're going to respond and get back to you."

The *Chimera*'s lips parted as if she might speak, but no sound came. Again Moorland wondered if these bits of non-verbal communication were intentional.

"That is all," Moorland said. The wallscreen dimmed.

"She's wrong about Theo," Duncan said. "He's the best, no, the only real choice we have."

"Maybe we should listen to the *Chimera*," Moorland mused, unsure if she trusted the ship, but doubting they had a viable alternative. Besides, it wasn't like Selena was a *bad* choice. While not as skilled as Theo, her numbers were still superior to the other cadets.

"Maybe we should have the technicians pull her neural architecture apart," Duncan said.

"They've been running tests on her for almost a decade. If they were going to find a fault, they would have by now."

"But now that she's awake, she can help them with the search."

Moorland shook her head, tried of arguing and the constant weariness that came from watching the solution to one problem become an even worse problem itself. "We don't have time," she said. "How long until we have another ombudsman on our hands? Another Phoebus? We've got to get the *Chimera* on its way. If we don't, it might never happen."

"Or they lose themselves in The Everything and we all die," Duncan said.

Moorland scowled at him. "It's not like Theo offers us some guarantee of success. Selena is capable. I'm inclined to accept the *Chimera*'s request."

"It wasn't a request," Duncan said. "And Selena's *not* the right choice."

"I wonder," Moorland said. "Maybe the *Chimera* knows something about him that she can't articulate? She might feel she's protecting the colony. That would explain her refusing a direct command."

Duncan leaned against a nearby terminal. "He was always the one," he said. "I was so sure of it."

"Is that what this is really about?" Moorland asked. "You can't stand to be proved wrong?"

"Proved wrong?" Duncan's eyes blazed. "This doesn't prove anything at all. But taking this away from Theo ... Do you understand what it will do to the boy, Alina? Do you? He already lost his sister! And he went out there and navigated better than anyone thought possible. And now we're going to strip him of his rightful place?"

"He'll have to deal with his disappointment," Moorland said. The words sounded harsh, but then, the situation warranted it. Nothing came before the needs of the colony, least of all Theo's— or anyone else's—feelings. Duncan shouldn't even have brought the issue up.

"He's going to be devastated," Duncan said.

"You're talking about yourself," Moorland said. "Why don't you admit it? You're far too personally invested in this. The *Chimera* chose Selena. We're both going to have to accept that fact and move forward."

"It's not her call to make. It's not—"

"You know," Moorland said, cutting him off. "I found something interesting while tightening down my files after Phoebus' incursion. An old set of Selection test results. I don't know why I opened it. Maybe to remind myself how all of this started … how far we've come, even if it doesn't seem like it. Anyway, would you like to know what I found?"

Duncan used his shoulder blades to shove off the terminal. Turned sideways to her, eyes tracking across the empty command deck. "Not really, no."

"Theo has two sets of Selection test results," Moorland continued, undeterred. "The first set disqualified him. Strangely, those results disappeared from the database and were replaced by a second set that scored him in the top half of all candidates."

Duncan wouldn't look at her. The man couldn't bring himself to tell a lie. Would she force him to tell her what she already knew? That he'd pushed Theo through the Selection despite his failing test scores by either fabricating new scores or ignoring whoever had done so?

She waited for Duncan to break the silence. Finally, he did. "Don't talk to me of moral compromise. Not while the colony burns."

That was as close to an admission of guilt as she wanted him to get. It was time to change tactics, to offer him a graceful exit from the conversation. "I don't care how Theo ended up here," Moorland said. "Without him, we wouldn't be talking about who would navigate the *Chimera*. But that doesn't alter our present circumstances. We can try and change the *Chimera*'s mind and get her to accept Theo as Navigator, or we can move ahead with Selena as primary and Theo as her backup."

Duncan raised an eyebrow. "Do you think *Chimera* will agree to that?"

"She already has," Moorland said, shooting Duncan a CATO message from the *Chimera* approving her suggested crew positions.

Duncan read through the names. "You might have asked me for my input first," he said.

"This is a preliminary list. Do you have any changes you'd like to make?"

"Not necessarily. But why haven't you assigned a captain?"

"Because that decision hasn't been made yet," Moorland said.

"You're leaning toward Meghan? Even after the Phoebus situation?"

"She had nothing to do with that. Bad luck is all. She's level-headed. Fair." *And used to working with Selena.*

"I don't disagree," Duncan said, "but Marcus shows more promise in my opinion."

Moorland weighed how much to tell him. Better to wait until after she talked to Marcus. "Theo is not the only cadet with secrets," she said. "I need to interview them both before I make a decision."

Duncan nodded. "I trust your judgement." An invitation to ask his opinion. Not a problem. She'd planned to do so anyway.

"I'll confer with you before I make a final decision," she said.

Duncan gave her a quick nod and moved to exit Command.

"Duncan?"

He paused, looked back at her.

"You weren't wrong. He really is like Stephen."

"Maybe," Duncan said.

"That might be why the *Chimera* rejected him," Moorland said. "She doesn't want to see him come to the same end as Stephen."

Duncan pushed out of the exit, his robes and pendant out of place in this world of polished steel and cold decking. Moorland took a few controlled breaths, steadying herself before composing CATO messages to Meghan and Marcus. The *Chimera* would once more have a captain, a navigator, and a crew.

The time had come to return to Earth.

CHAPTER THIRTY-TWO

Barren except for two chairs arranged on either side of a shipping crate, the room that greeted Marcus was far enough from the central flow of *Hydra* foot traffic to suggest Moorland wanted total privacy.

Light from Stephen's Point poured through the portal behind Moorland, turning her white uniform golden. "Take a seat," Moorland said. Marcus did as requested. The chief produced a pair of small vials and tossed one of them to Marcus. "Take out your CATO."

Interesting.

Marcus removed his CATO, sliding it into the protective vial. The lens floated in the clear liquid, catching light like a prism, breaking it into multiple bands of color absorbed by the matte gray metal of the shipping crate. The chief removed her own lens and tucked it away. Her pupil readjusted and she blinked.

She seated herself and folded her hands across the crate, studying him. He didn't quite meet her eyes, but didn't look away either. He didn't like being caught off guard. When her invitation hit his CATO, he'd gone into a cycle of wild self-congratulation at the prospect of being named the *Chimera*'s captain, followed by fear that she'd learned of his role in Phoebus' hacking. Neither scenario fit this location, the removal of their CATOs, or Moorland's concentrated stare. A bead of sweat rolled down his cheek. He fought the impulse to wipe it away.

"I have some things I'd like to discuss with you," Moorland said.

"Yes," he agreed, pretending to have some idea what came next.

"You've done very well here," Moorland said. "Your team has excelled thanks in large part to your leadership. You've shown a fundamental understanding of tactical and strategic matters and the strength of will to use them."

"Thank you, Chief," Marcus said.

"You're well respected by your peers if not particularly well-liked."

"I don't need people to like me," he said.

A brief flash of recognition crossed Moorland's face and she nodded in acceptance. "I'm considering making you captain of the *Chimera*."

He must have somehow misread the situation. Had she arranged for this private location in order to give him more details on *Exchange Four* or some other privileged information? *Captain.* Marcus met her gaze head-on, eyes wide and direct. The embodiment of modesty, honesty, leadership.

"However," Moorland continued, "I have several lingering questions that I want answered."

"Yes, ma'am."

"Tell me about Cassius Sorbet."

His chest tightened, heart slowing, pupils dilating. What did she know? How did she know it? His mind spun without gaining traction. Droplets of sweat swelled against the nape of his neck. He heard the dull thump of stone against skull. The wet sound of blood splattering over a cave floor, his face and hands. *Cassius Sorbet.* The man he'd once called Father. The man he'd killed.

"Cadet Locke?" Moorland asked. "Are you with me?"

The sound of his name drew him back. "Yes. I apologize." His voice sounded mechanical, a machine breaking down, grinding to a halt.

"Your child welfare advocate," she said, prompting him. "Cassius Sorbet."

Fury swelled and Marcus clenched his toes inside his boots. He heard his own voice, a harsh bark. "I know who he … is, ma'am."

"Mr. Sorbet disappeared about the time the Selection training began. What do you know about that?"

The room felt hot. Humid. His uniform clung to his shoulders. Shimmering, fragmented images from the cave popped at the periphery of his vision. He couldn't look at Moorland. Couldn't close his eyes lest the images of Cassius come to life and envelop him. Swallow him whole. Pull him backward into a past best forgotten.

"Nothing," Marcus said. "I lost track of him a long time ago."

"You didn't lose track of him," Moorland said. "You ran away. Altered your records. Took on a new name."

He scanned her face. She wanted vulnerable. So he'd be vulnerable. He'd tell the truth. "Yes, I did."

"Why?" Moorland asked.

Fighting his natural impulse to retreat, Marcus leaned forward over the shipping crate. Let his expression become defenseless, exposing the supposed weakness. "You already know why."

Moorland didn't argue the point. "How'd you end up living with Martha Huxley?"

He thought of Martha's wrinkled face, her small intelligent black eyes. The elderly woman had treated him well, hadn't asked questions. She'd accepted his new name because it was the only one she knew him by. Until she died in her sleep. He'd kept that a secret, using her colony support payments to feed and clothe himself until the Selection training began.

"I needed a place to hide," Marcus said. "I pulled up Cassius' list of host families and chose Martha because she lived far away from the Golden Valley. I didn't want Cassius finding me before I had a chance to make it through the Selection."

"I know that Martha is dead," Moorland said, eyes on his face, weighing his reaction.

"She passed in her sleep," Marcus said.

"And you did nothing?" Moorland's eyebrows rose. "Why didn't you report her death to the regulatory?"

"If I reported it, Cassius might have found me." He let the discomfort—the fear—of Cassius' memory come through in his voice. "Do you know what it's like to have no family? No real home? To get moved from place to place to place? Martha had shut herself away inside that apartment; she never went out. She hadn't been outside in almost three years when I came. She was relying on her neighbors to bring her stuff." Marcus thought of the afternoon he came home to find her, slumped in her favorite chair. A cup of tea, already as cold as ice, sat at her elbow. "We understood each other. I needed a place to stay. She needed someone that could go outside."

"You falsified your records," Moorland said.

"What else could I have done? I would never have made it this far if I hadn't. The abandoned child of a drug abuser, a foster kid with a violent past? If you know all this then you've seen my psych record—the Regulatory would have bounced me regardless of my test scores. *You* would have bounced me."

Moorland said nothing—a tacit agreement.

"I wanted my chance," he said. "Not as some damaged, low-income, underprivileged ward of the government. I wanted to be the *same* as everyone else. I did what I had to so I could make it up here. So I could show everyone what I'm capable of." He needed to pull back—he was getting close to revealing the restlessness, the roaring fire of anger and retribution, that lived in him—the *real* reason he'd killed Cassius. Moorland couldn't know about that. No one could. He softened. "I did what was necessary to earn my chance to help save the colony."

Moorland's face remained blank, no indication of whether she found his story disgusting, sad, or pitiable. He found it strangely comforting. She leaned forward, scanning his face. "What are you running away from, Marcus?"

Everything. "Nothing."

Moorland frowned. "Not good enough."

"Well, there's nothing I can do about that. I've told you the truth and you'll have to decide if you believe me or not." He stood as if to leave.

"Sit down!"

He waited, letting her annoyance build before slowly returning to his seat.

"You may think that it's a forgone conclusion that I'll make you the captain of the *Chimera*. Let me assure you—no such decision has been made. Cadet Ziczek's team may not have put up the same numbers as yours, but she was also hampered by Cadet Hart and Cadet Gillespie's subversion. I have every confidence in her ability to lead."

"She's not as good as me," Marcus said.

"That remains to be determined. Much depends on the remainder of this conversation. I suggest you stop posturing and making assumptions and start giving me complete, honest answers."

A crazy idea came to him. He could tell her the truth. The whole story. Tell her what he'd done to Cassius. Maybe not in the most brutal of terms, but let her know that she wasn't the only one willing to take bold action when the situation demanded it. The notion gave him a crazy thrill. Almost like a narcotics inhaler. Hot and cold rushing through his lungs, veins, brain. He *could* tell her the truth. It tantalized him—what expression would her face make then?

"Did you tell Theo about Liddy?" Moorland asked.

Marcus didn't hesitate. *This* was a question he'd anticipated. "Yes."

"You jeopardized the mission."

"No. With all due respect, *you* did, ma'am. You should have told Theo the truth. He deserved to know."

The lid of Chief Moorland's right eye flickered. Though slight, he knew he'd hit a nerve.

"You made a mistake in a misguided effort to protect him," Marcus said. "I get it." Moorland would accept the face-saving line he offered, the understanding. He knew she hadn't been trying to protect Theo because she cared about him, but because she needed him to wake the *Chimera*. But the discrepancy would bother Moorland in spite of her pragmatism—like most people, she enjoyed the delusion that she followed some set higher principles.

"Once we leave for Earth, we won't have anyone to protect us but ourselves, ma'am. I told Theo because that's the future I will be expected to manage." He waited, letting the point rest before driving forward. "You and I both know nothing good is waiting for us at Earth."

Moorland continued as if she hadn't heard. "You should have let me handle the situation," she said.

"If he'd found out from anyone but me, you'd have an even bigger mess on your hands. I salvaged a bad situation by helping shape his response."

"He blew up and cursed Duncan and me to our faces," Moorland said. "I'd hardly call that 'salvaged'."

"And yet you both had it coming," Marcus said, letting a little righteous indignation creep into his tone. "Theo needed a chance to express his anger, and frankly, whatever he said was probably true." No point in avoiding risks now. "You and Duncan have done a good job preparing us to crew the *Chimera*," he said, "but you've fundamentally mismanaged the situation with Stephen's Point. The quarantine backfired and you should take responsibility for that."

"And I do," Moorland said. "But that's not what we're here to discuss."

"Not to the cadets, you haven't. I'm in the minority of those who understand the reasons behind the decisions you've made, even if I don't agree with your execution. Most of the others see you as distant, aloof, and uncaring."

"Really. And what would you have done differently?" Moorland asked, voice heavy with skepticism.

Inwardly, Marcus smiled. *Tables turned.* "I would have given the cadets unfettered access to the same reports you receive from the Regulatory. From day one."

Moorland shook her head. "Total chaos."

"Maybe at first," Marcus said. "But it also would have weeded out problems like Phoebus Hart. It would have stopped him from becoming a sympathetic figure, and from spreading division. It would have shown trust and that you expected all of them to handle serious situations like adults. Considering you're sending some of us to Earth in a nuclear-armed ship, I don't see what thought you'd gain by withholding information from Stephen's Point."

"Assuming that I agreed with your point," Moorland said, "it still doesn't change the fact that you divulged secret information to another cadet. That's a breach of trust that I have a hard time ignoring."

"I'm not asking you to ignore it," Marcus said, "but you can't deny the logic of my choices. Since arriving on the *Hydra*, I've done nothing but support the mission. I gave you the ombudsman on a silver platter. I've led my team effectively. Theo was ready to quit and I talked him out of it. I got him stabilized, and when given the chance, he handled the practice insertion better than anyone."

Moorland hesitated, seeming to waver between conflicting instincts. "You're holding something back," she said.

He needed to revisit the point he'd made moments before. He'd tried to engage Moorland on it the first time after the ombudsman's death. The third option. She would have to see it, acknowledge his logic. But what if she didn't? What if it backfired? He'd jeopardize his chances. She might even send him back to Stephen's Point. No, he decided. He'd wait. But once he was aboard his ship …

"I'm not holding anything back," he said.

Moorland looked unconvinced. He needed to give her something. A gift. Let her feel she'd succeeded in getting to the truth. No lie would serve him now. His pulse quickened. He'd take the risk telling her … not the truth. Not exactly. But something dangerously close. Another rush of hot-cold ran through him, and with it, a delicious dizziness at the enormity of his gamble.

"You know more about me than anyone, Chief. You know that if it comes down to it, I have the capacity to be ruthless."

Moorland's eyebrows rose. "Your point?"

"Cassius Sorbet? He wanted me for himself. I wanted to complete the Selection. I stole his personal files, including his clinical notes detailing the nature of his obsession with me. I told Sorbet that if I so much as caught sight of his shadow, that I would release those files to the Regulatory."

Moorland didn't react, moving forward to the next logical question. "If you had compromising information on Sorbet, why didn't you simply turn him in to the Regulatory?"

"And get bogged down in a legal process that would have ruined my chances in the Selection? No. I handled things myself." *With my own two hands.*

"You willfully left a monster behind on Stephen's Point. You have no concern for the harm he might cause others?"

"As you said, Sorbet disappeared. I assume he's gone into hiding."

"You can't be certain of that."

"I'm not certain of anything. Who knows? Maybe they'll find him at the bottom of a cliff." *Or down a chasm in a cave.* "My plan was to release Sorbet's files to the Regulatory just before the *Chimera*'s departure. That way if he ever did resurface, he would face the consequences of his actions."

"Similar to how Phoebus disseminated the reports on Stephen's Point?" Moorland asked, the implication obvious.

"I didn't have anything to do with that," Marcus said. "It's a common enough strategy. Two intelligent people with similar needs arriving at the same course of action."

She half-believed him. He needed to give her another gentle push in the right direction.

"The moment you found out about the ombudsman's plan, you eliminated him," Marcus said. "You're a utilitarian. A pragmatist. As am I. What purpose would turning Phoebus and other cadets against you serve? I want our mission to succeed as much as you do. And should you make me the captain, I will use my authority in the same way that you do."

He aligned his face with hers, laughing internally at the notion that silver bars on a uniform gave one person the right to kill another.

Bars or no bars, title or no title, the capacity came from within. It came from certainty. Faith in the essential nature of violence and a willingness to embrace it.

Moorland looked at him in silence. *Really* looked at him. It felt good to be seen, to gaze back without needing to mask himself. Revealed for who and what he was. He wanted Moorland to share in the glory with him, to celebrate their shared difference and recognize the power they could wield. Instead she looked old. Tired. They understood one another, but they were not the same. And in that moment, Marcus realized he'd convinced her.

"I had all the authority I needed," he said, breaking the silence.

Her blue eyes darkened almost to purple. "This conversation never happened," she said. She shook her head, speaking softly to herself, "Good god. What would Duncan say?"

"Now you know everything," Marcus said.

"No. I don't. Never speak of this again."

"Understood."

Moorland pulled the vial out of her jacket pocket and opened it, her CATO oozing from its liquid suspension into the palm of her hand. She pushed it into her eye. "Send me your list of ideal command staff."

"Nemus Archer as Duty Officer, Meghan Ziczek as Flight Officer."

"You want Meghan running flight operations?"

Marcus shrugged. "She's the most capable."

"I agree," Moorland said. "I'm just surprised."

"Why? I thought we'd established that I make my decisions based on logic." *And I like to keep my enemies close.*

"Yes. I suppose so."

Marcus reinserted his own CATO and pulled up the list of command staff he'd created many cycles ago, and sent it to Moorland. Profound satisfaction pushed away the last of his numbness. Once more, he'd walked along the edge of the razor and avoided getting cut. *Calm. Celebrate later.* With Theo. Captain and Navigator, galaxies spread before them, endless possibilities. It didn't matter where they went, just so long as it wasn't Stephen's Point.

Moorland's eyes moved right, accessing his list. "One

problem," she said.

"What?"

"Theo won't be navigating the *Chimera*," Moorland said. "Selena will."

CHAPTER THIRTY-THREE

Theo sat in the bean long after the end of his latest training cycle. He liked the unbroken silence of the enclosed space. Spine supported by the chair, restraints embracing his torso, he closed his eyes and thought of fractal space. Stephen's thread running on and on. Easy to follow once he'd shoved *Chimera* aside. Stephen might have needed her help to cut a path through The Everything, but Theo didn't need her help to follow it.

Marcus leaned into the bean. "Are you hiding, dancer boy?"

"No. I just needed some space to think."

Dancer boy. Their selection trainer, Quartermaster West, or "Sir", used to call Theo that. The nickname brought with it a strange, overpowering nostalgia. He'd hated Sir and the training at first. But by its completion, Theo had changed. Become an entirely different person. Stronger. Both in his body and his mind.

"Thinking—you're doing a lot more of that lately," Marcus said.

"I have a lot on my mind."

Liddy's gone-ness had changed from an open wound into a hardening scar. He glanced down at his uniform top, the silver crescents on gray lapels, the burnished gray buttons that ran down to his silver-clasped belt. Beneath the uniform fabric he wore a different sort of insignia—an asterisk-shaped red-ribbed scar. A self-inflicted brand. Sometimes it itched or burned. It reminded him of the old version of himself. Weak. Frightened. A boy.

"Don't we all," Marcus said.

Theo turned with annoyance, sick of Marcus' enigmatic musings. "If you have something to say, say it."

"They're not going to make you the navigator."

Theo took a deep breath of sterilized, tasteless air. Let it back out through his nose. "Why not?"

"Moorland said *Chimera* rejected you."

Theo recalled the first time he'd seen Moorland, her face displayed on a wallscreen in the Forest Center when he'd learned he'd been named a cadet. He'd loved her then, loved what she represented, what she offered. He'd believed her good and trustworthy, the pinnacle of all the colony stood for. How things had changed.

"She can't do that," Theo said.

"Who? Moorland or *Chimera*?"

Both. "What's Moorland thinking? I've done *everything* she's asked. I aced the insertion. I'm the best they've got!"

"The *Chimera* wants Selena."

Of course she does. All that weirdness in the sphere when they'd woken the ship—Selena's mother, the snow, the river … He'd been a passenger then, and now it appeared he'd be a passenger again. Stuck in a supporting role while Selena navigated. Theo triggered the straps securing him to his chair.

"Move."

Marcus backed away from the bean and Theo thrust himself out. Why did it matter who navigated? Who supported who? Why did the thought of Selena inside the sphere cause a pit to open inside of him?

"So you're the captain?" Theo said, voice thick with bitterness.

"No formal announcement yet but yes, I expect to be named captain."

"It sounds like everyone is getting what they want," Theo said. "I'm happy for you."

"There's the green-eyed monster," Marcus said.

"What the hell are you talking about?"

"I mean that you're jealous."

"No, I'm angry. There's a difference."

"And you have a right to be. Surely Moorland could overrule *Chimera*. She has the authority. She's the highest ranking officer on the *Hydra*."

Theo dropped down from the bean's exterior platform and into the pit. He'd done his time here, supported everyone on his team as they took their turn in VAST. But he'd always assumed—along with everyone else on Marcus' team—that he'd be the navigator. His scores were objectively the best. And he'd proved himself again during the practice insertion.

You shoved the Chimera away. She tried to warn you.

"I'm going to talk to Duncan," Theo said.

Marcus laughed. "You're going to plead your case to that old fool after what he did to you?"

"He promised me," Theo said.

Duncan hadn't promised. Though he had built up Theo's expectations, he'd never made an explicit promise. He'd misled Theo. A precursor to lying about Liddy. The man was a liar just like Moorland. They must have worn off on Theo, because now he was telling lies.

The green-eyed monster. Jealousy. Fear. Anger. What did any of it matter? Let Selena navigate. Let her be special. They'd still make it to Earth and save the colony. That was the most important thing, wasn't it?

"Moorland has an agenda," Marcus said. "She's always favored Selena over you."

Marcus' tone of voice, the words themselves, the sincerity of his facial expression—a friend commiserating with a friend. Theo saw through it. Saw into the heart of Marcus, the person capable of bashing in a man's skull in a fit of rage.

"Stop it," Theo said.

"Stop what?" Marcus asked.

"This. Stop it. You're wasting my time."

"I'm trying to help you, Theo."

"No, you're not. You have some kind of plan and you want my help. Instead of always trying to manage me, why don't you just come right out and say what you want? Or do you think I can't handle it? I'm not the same Theo you met in the cave." Theo leaned forward, using the few extra inches of height he had over Marcus. "I've changed. When are you going to see that?"

"I do see it," Marcus said, almost smiling. Behind his eyes, gears whirred, as complex and precise as the archaic timepieces popular among wealthy businessmen in the Golden Valley.

"Let me tell you what I see," Theo said. "You've got some plan of your own, one that Moorland would never accept. You've conned her into believing you're the best choice for captain, but you don't fool me."

Marcus' lips twisted into a horrifying smile.

Theo barreled on, giving Marcus no time to respond. "You're

trying to turn me against Selena. You don't like her because I like her and she likes me. She's a threat to you because you can't stand the idea of me slipping out from under your thumb."

Marcus maintained the smile, lips pulled back from his white teeth, eyes glassy. "It feels good, doesn't it? Go on, Theo, don't be shy. Any more revelations to share?"

Theo leapt forward and slapped Marcus across the face. The crack of skin against skin echoed through the pit. "Stop talking to me like that!"

Red finger marks bloomed on Marcus' cheek.

"You're not as smart as you think you are," Theo said. "In fact, sometimes you're so incredibly stupid it blows my mind. If you want my help, why don't you just *ask* me?"

Theo trembled, adrenaline and unbridled emotion rolling through his chest like the aftershocks of an earthquake. Marcus' pale blue eyes reminded him of clouds blowing in from the alkali oceans before the cold season arrived in full force.

"Okay," Marcus said. Deadpan. Inflectionless. The real Marcus.

Theo slumped into one of the seats in the pit and Marcus sat opposite him, elbows resting on his knees. "Earth is either destroyed or incapacitated."

Theo said nothing, waiting.

"If they've been invaded by some … alien force, we have no measure for the effectiveness of our weapons, such as they are. The odds aren't in our favor. The *Chimera* isn't even a proper military-class vessel.

"The alternatives are that Earth destroyed itself with a nuclear war or something like it, or that they've been decimated by a plague. Either way, the arrival of *Exchange Four* suggests that the survivors are living in space, and in conditions worse than at Stephen's Point. They have no help to offer, Theo."

Theo turned the words over in his mind and couldn't find any flaw in Marcus' assessment. Most of what he said agreed with Moorland's summation. Which meant Marcus had looked at the same data, but come up with a different solution to the problem.

"You don't want to go to Earth," Theo said. He didn't need Marcus' confirmation. It was the only logical explanation, the only thing that tied everything together, link by link, like Stephen's stitches.

"No," Marcus said, "I don't. Because once we leave fractal, we'll be unable to re-enter again until the cores complete their cycle. We can't get a look at Earth until we've exited fractal. And since we can't learn what's going on there from a safe vantage point, we risk *everything* by going there."

"Where, then?" Theo asked.

Marcus stood. "Now you're asking the right question."

"Have you brought this up to Moorland?"

"I've tried," Marcus said. "She can't be convinced. She's stuck in a loop. She doesn't have the will to accept Earth as a total loss." He paused. "And she's curious. She has a perverse need to know what happened there while I do not. What happened doesn't matter. The only thing that does is our survival. Going to Earth is the worst thing we can do because the second we leave fractal, we subject ourselves to the same threat or threats that cause Earth to go silent in the first place."

"And whatever is there might come here," Theo said, scanning the empty room, driven by the irrational impulse that someone might overhear their conversation. Empty space, the chrome bean, silent terminals. No one but himself and Marcus.

"Correct," Marcus said. "If we go to Earth, I suspect we'll doom not only ourselves, but the colony as well."

Theo processed backward through what Marcus had said, looking for signs of manipulation or half-truths. Everything fit. The realization terrified him. He suddenly wished he hadn't pushed Marcus to tell the truth.

"Where would we go?" Theo asked.

Marcus looked at Theo with the strange, unnerving stillness Theo recognized from their first encounters back on Stephen's Point. Back when Theo felt certain that Marcus would kill him.

"Another colony," Marcus said.

"Another colony? There were only two of them. Damascene and us. And Damascene stopped communicating with Earth a long time ago."

"That's true, but they're still a better option than Earth."

Objections tumbled faster than he could form sentences. "But Damascene doesn't *exist*. Not the colony, at least. Everything I've ever read said they stopped communicating before they even completed building their exchange dock."

Marcus shrugged. "That doesn't mean the planet disappeared."

"Yeah, but what will we find there? No exchange dock, no colony, nothing. Besides, how would we get there? There are no stitches between here and Damascene. We could wander around in fractal for years and never find the place. In the meantime, Stephen's Point would fall."

"You're right that there are no stitches laid between Stephen's Point and Damascene," Marcus agreed. "But there is a path from Earth. Think about it. The stitches will still be there. We just have to find them."

"How do you expect to do that?"

Marcus smiled. "I don't plan to." He held Theo's gaze with his odd, silver eyes. "That's why I need your help. You've shown you're as good as Stephen himself. When we get close enough to Earth, you'll find the stitches to Damascene and we'll follow them. You're the rightful navigator, and you're the only one I trust enough to have by my side when we leave this system."

Theo shook his head, his skepticism gaining momentum with each passing second. "Even if I buy your argument that Earth can't help us, there's no guarantee that Damascene can."

"I'm not certain what we'll find at Damascene. However, I am certain that there's nothing good waiting for us at Earth. I prefer to choose an option that offers the best potential for survival. That choice is Damascene."

"So that's your plan? Go to some planet nobody's had contact with in hundreds of years on blind hope they *might* be able to help us? I expected more from you than this. I really did."

Marcus nodded, unperturbed by Theo's attempt at goading him into an emotional response. "If you think Earth can best help the colony, I can't stop you from taking us there," Marcus said. "You're going to be my navigator either way."

"No one is going to agree to let us divert course from Earth!" Theo said, almost shouting. "Not Meghan. Not Selena. No one."

"You're right and you're wrong," Marcus said. "You're right that Selena and Meghan are stupid and stubborn and blindly loyal. They'd take us to hell if Moorland said it was a good idea. But you're wrong that no one will agree. Some already have."

Nemus Archer. Probably Preston as well. Marcus had talked to them *before* Theo, he was sure of it. And while Theo didn't like

Marcus' plan, it annoyed him that he'd been brought into the loop this late. "So what are you going to do? Pull off some kind of mutiny? It won't work. The *Chimera* will stop you the second you try."

"There will be no mutiny," Marcus said. "I'm the captain. Most will follow my orders without question, just like they've been trained. And once we've installed you as Navigator, nobody needs to know *where* we're going. They won't realize we've gone off course until we arrive."

"Selena will know."

"I'll take care of Selena," Marcus said, a glint in his eye. "And the *Chimera* is bound to obey me. I will give her a set of specific orders that her programing will force her to follow."

The pit in Theo's stomach expanded, deeper than any cave, and far darker. Marcus could do it, but only with his help. Would he give it? Turn against the mission laid out by Moorland? If he wanted to save the colony, did he have a choice?

He thought of the tactical scenarios Moorland had thrown at them. Fighting other ships. Destroying the exchange dock. Nuking the Earth to compel them to help the colony. Was going to Damascene, admittedly a huge unknown, a worse option? What if arriving at Earth *prompted* an alien invader to come to Stephen's Point? Cold swept through him at the thought.

"What do you think is at Damascene?" Theo asked.

"A failed colony like Stephen's Point."

"Then why go there?"

"For one thing, the ecology is different. Terraforming created an atmosphere similar to Earth's. They have robust plant life. Plenty of drinkable surface water. And no material dependency on Earth."

"We could take everyone at Stephen's Point there," Theo said, thinking ahead. "It would take a lot of trips but I—we—could do it." A note of hope in his voice. A lurking excitement at the realization that they might have a better option than the near certain disaster at Earth.

"That's right," Marcus said. "Once we've done a survey, we can save everyone on Stephen's Point."

"But what if something happened to Damascene? What if they're the ones that got attacked by aliens or wiped out by a plague?"

"Then we'll go to Earth," Marcus said. "But it makes sense to go to Damascene *first*."

Theo mulled over the facts. Marcus was right. Despite his reservations, he had to admit the plan made sense. "Moorland can't be convinced," Theo said, speaking to himself.

"She's sending us on a potential suicide mission," Marcus said. "If we're killed, the colony dies with us. A slow, terrible, protracted death. I'd like to avoid that. We're not going to leave fractal space at Earth, not before we've determined if Damascene is viable."

Theo's jaw clenched. "You'll need my help with the crew," Theo said. "They'll follow us if we stand together. Most of them, at least."

"Most," Marcus agreed, threat implicit in his tone.

"You have to promise not to hurt Selena," Theo said.

"I promise to do only what's necessary."

Marcus' eyes moved as he read a CATO message. "Moorland just called Meghan and me to meet her at Command. Meghan's going to be so disappointed. At least until she learns I've chosen her as my flight officer."

"Meghan?"

"I don't know why you're surprised," Marcus said. "She's very capable."

"But she doesn't like you. Or trust you ..." Theo realized that was the point. By choosing his main adversary and giving her a position of power, he'd solidify Moorland's belief in having made the right choice.

"So what happens next?" Theo asked.

"Congratulate Selena. Be heartfelt. Don't say anything stupid to her, or to Moorland or Duncan. Once we near Earth, I'll have her removed and name you navigator. I'll force the *Chimera* to accept it."

Force. Marcus' second favorite tactic after manipulation. The Salix protocols governed more than just the *Chimera*'s response to the colony's impending failure. They also prevented her from growing, from changing the parameters of her function. Marcus could command her to do as he pleased as long as his command didn't conflict with a kernel-level protocol. But suppose she made the determination that going to Damascene violated her protocols? What leverage would he apply then?

Darkness lapped at the edges of his mind. *Selena.* Marcus

would use Selena.

"You have to promise me you're not going to hurt her," Theo repeated. "If you don't, I'm out. I won't help you."

"I thought you wanted to stop with the pretense," Marcus said, his challenge unmistakable. "Ask yourself: what good would my promise be?"

Marcus grasped the rail around the pit and slung himself over the side. He stood a moment, looking down at Theo. "I won't hurt her unless she forces me to," Marcus said. A concession. An admission. Theo wondered if Marcus had been born this way or if a combination of time and awful decisions had warped him. He suspected the latter because when he looked inside himself, he saw the corrosive power of entropy at work. Given enough time and opportunity, he might become Marcus' twin.

CHAPTER THIRTY-FOUR

Marcus and Selena led the procession, the Song of the Colony echoing off the duraceramic walls of the crosshatch. The blinding white of their uniforms reflected the shifting overhead lights, a never-ending evolution of blue to green to yellow and back again. Selena walked in silence, just behind Marcus' right elbow, shining silver double-crescents at her collar marking her as navigator. Marcus felt the weight of his own insignia, the gold captain's crescents sparkling like miniature shooting stars.

The commissioned officers and crew of the *Chimera*, faces cycling between self-conscious pride and terror, made their way forward. *Hydra* personnel lined the crosshatch. Med techs and doctors, welders and technicians, lab workers and dark-uniformed regulators, all watched with respect and awe as they passed. They neared a group of nurses and one with curly dark hair reached out for Selena. Selena smiled, said something Marcus couldn't hear, and squeezed the woman's hand as they passed.

Marcus locked his eyes on the two figures waiting at the edge of the tram platform. Moorland and Duncan. Moorland in her formal white uniform, hair and polished shoes gleaming, and Duncan in Regulatory black. The formal cut of his jacket emphasized Duncan's broad shoulders and commanding height, reinforcing his stature and power in a way the vestments of his Order never did. Marcus noted the hint of a silver necklace flashing at the sides of Duncan's collar, the pendant it supported hidden beneath his jacket.

Marcus halted and offered a salute, the ordered ranks of officers behind him following suit. Moorland and Duncan acknowledged them, raising their own hands before letting them drop to their sides.

"Chief Moorland. Regulator Duncan."

"Captain Locke." Moorland's blue eyes met Marcus' own before moving to Selena. "Navigator Samuelson."

In his peripheral vision, Marcus watched Selena. A faint flush ran down her cheeks and neck. Eyes wide, chin up. He felt her pride—a girl from the rim named navigator of a fractal-class colony ship. *About as likely as a murderous runaway from Conway becoming captain.*

"Permission to embark," Marcus said.

"Granted."

Duncan stepped forward and offered his finger. Marcus took it. "Captain Locke. The prayers of the Order will be with you." Marcus stepped back and Duncan gave his finger to Selena. "You are the way-maker now, Navigator Samuelson. Stephen be your guide."

"Thank you, Advisor Duncan."

Duncan did not retract his hand, leaning forward to whisper in Selena's ear. Marcus couldn't hear what was said other than, "Take care of Theo."

Don't worry, Duncan. I will.

Selena smiled at Duncan and let go of his hand, turning to Moorland. Moorland offered her finger to Selena. "Our hopes rest on your shoulders, Navigator. There and back again."

Selena nodded, a brusque bob of her head. "There and back again."

"Earth awaits," Marcus said.

"Yes," Moorland said, looking again at Selena. "But before you go, we have a parting gift."

"You do?" Marcus bit back annoyance. He didn't want some worthless, sentimental bauble.

"We weren't sure the work would be completed in time," Moorland said. "But we brought in a few experts from the rim. I hope you like the results."

She offered Selena a handscreen displaying a feed from what appeared to be the portside breakage. The *Helvictus* sat in its cradle, sharp and angular, fuselage obscuring the outline of another ship. A shapeless, heavily shielded lump. Selena gasped. Duncan's smile rose ear to ear, rumpling his beard.

"We thought you might find her useful," Moorland said.

"*The Bee!*" Selena dropped the handscreen to the floor where it bounced once before folding into itself. Marcus thought Selena would embrace the chief, but she simply grabbed the woman's hand, squeezing it between both her own.

Duncan beamed. "*The Bee.* Flightworthy, nose to core."

Marcus bent to retrieve the handscreen, opening it to the feed.

He examined the trawler, panning along as much of her irregular hull as he could. A piece of industrial equipment—no sign of armaments. What did Moorland expect them to use it for?

"Reinforced shielding and all," Duncan said. "How she survived full impact with that asteroid I don't know, but now she could survive a nuke."

Ah. So that was it. An escape pod.

Selena released Moorland's hand. "Thank you," she said. She straightened, pulling her uniform jacket flat. She glanced over her shoulder at her fellow officers, clearly embarrassed by her own outburst.

"This wasn't simply a kind gesture," Moorland said. "Having *The Bee* will give you options if you need to leave the *Chimera* for any reason."

A thought seemed to occur to Selena, the excitement draining from her face. She looked at Moorland. "What about Liam? *The Bee*'s not actually mine, it's his. He'll need it if ..."

Moorland smiled. "Liam is happy. He was the one that pointed us in the right direction when we needed to find someone to repair her." Moorland sobered, lowering her voice. "Your father's mining days are over, Selena. Take *The Bee*. He wants you to have her."

Selena nodded, throat working to hide her emotions.

"We can use all the tactical assets we can get," Marcus said, addressing Moorland. "Thank you."

Marcus turned to Selena and murmured, "Let's wrap this up." Selena scowled, dislike crackling in his direction like sparks from a welder. It didn't bother him. He wouldn't have to endure her childishness for much longer.

"Chief Moorland," Marcus said, "I'd like to be on my way."

Moorland nodded.

"Goodbye, Captain Locke. Stephen's speed."

Moorland began to clap. Around the crosshatch, those gathered to see the cadets on their way joined in. The steady, rhythmic clapping continued as Marcus, Selena, and the rest of the flight crew stepped into the waiting tram. The clapping sped, faster and faster, louder and louder, the *Hydra*'s final sendoff for the first fractal-class captain in the history of the colony.

* * *

The crosshatch receded, the tram entering its tunnel. Moorland

and Duncan disappeared from view. A sense of wondrous accomplishment filled Marcus. He'd planned, worked, waited for this moment. Hard to believe it had finally arrived.

He looked across the central aisle. "Selena?"

"Yes?"

"Would you like to go examine *The Bee*?"

Selena eyed him, clearly unsure what to make of his offer. Expressionless, he waited for her to agree. The temptation of her emotional connection to a piece of machinery would be too much for her to resist. She'd be out of the way and he would have a few moments alone on the command deck. Savoring his victory.

"No, thank you," she said. "There will be time for that when I'm off duty."

He raised an eyebrow. "All right," he said. "When you're off duty, then."

The tram whispered along beneath simulated aquamarine waters. Preston and Nemus sat to his left and right, staring up in wonder at the flashing silver of fish tails, light warped by shifting water, coral formations, schools of blue and yellow fish.

"Beautiful, aren't they?" Marcus said.

Opposite him, Selena sat next to Theo, eyes indecipherable. She didn't respond to Marcus' question. Neither did Theo, his eyes locked on the floor. Pretending Selena wasn't there, avoiding the spectacle overhead—following the script.

Selena nudged him, dress uniform rustling. "What's wrong with you?"

"Nothing," Theo said. He folded his arms over his chest and gazed away down the length of the tram.

Selena's lips set. After all their romantic moments she probably thought he should be more attentive. Holding her hand, whispering in her ear. Marcus didn't bother hiding his smirk. All of that was over.

"Theo's fine," Marcus said. "He's simply appreciating the momentous quality of the day's events."

Selena didn't reply, turning her head again to try and catch Theo's eye.

Marcus' CATO pinged. A message from *Hydra* command.

All Hydra personnel are clear. Stand by for umbilical retraction.

Down the car, Meghan looked up. "Command reports all

Hydra personnel are safely off the ship. They're disengaging the umbilical," she called.

Marcus smiled at her. "Thank you, Flight Officer Ziczek. I received the same message.

The tram slowed to a stop and the doors opened. Marcus rose and thumped Theo on the back. "Let's go."

* * *

The bright hum of the command deck enveloped Marcus. He paused for a moment, taking in the view. The *Chimera* was his ship. A swell of pride broke over him, making him almost giddy. "*Chimera*?" he said.

"Welcome, Captain."

The *Chimera* looked back at him, her larger than life face spread across the main wallscreen. Brown, thickly lashed eyes that looked so much like Selena's.

"Thank you, *Chimera*."

"Welcome, Navigator," *Chimera* said.

Selena smiled. "Hello, *Chimera*."

The other officers took their positions at their substations around the sphere, checking systems, readying the ship to embark for unoccupied space where they'd be safe to insert into fractal. The *Chimera*'s cores cycled up, a gentle, distant hum.

His CATO pinged but he didn't bother reading the message.

Meghan looked up from her station. "Captain, *Hydra* command reports the umbilical as fully retracted. We're cleared for departure."

Cleared. Marcus' heart surged. Clear of the *Hydra,* clear of Stephen's Point, clear of Moorland and Duncan and every other thing that had tried to ruin his life. No more dying place, no more dying people.

"Thank you, Officer Ziczek," Marcus said. He looked at Selena. "Take us out." *Chimera*'s visage disappeared from the wall and Selena entered the sphere.

The *Chimera* rotated, cores cycling, and they burned for the empty space at the edge of the rim.

No one spoke as the ship lumbered into the black of space. The only sounds were of quiet breathing, the whisper of hands working glowing interfaces, and the rush of blood through his temples.

When they reached a place far enough from Gauleta's gravity well, *Chimera* rotated along her axis and slowed to a standstill.

Marcus waited, enjoying the moment. Entire years of his life devoted to creating this exact scenario.

"*Hydra* Command, this is the captain of the *Chimera*. Request permission to enter fractal space."

He waited for his message to reach the *Hydra,* hands clasped behind his back. After some seconds had passed, Moorland's voice filled the command deck. "Permission granted, *Chimera*. Departure at oh seven hundred hours."

Duncan's voice boomed over the speakers. "Stephen's speed. His Eye watch over you. His Intellect guide—"

Marcus cut the transmission. "Bring up the hydrostasis field and prepare for insertion," he commanded.

Meghan's face betrayed her surprise. "We're not cleared for another forty minutes."

Marcus looked at her. "Prepare to enter fractal, Officer Ziczek. Don't make me repeat myself."

Meghan blinked. "Yes, Captain." She turned back to her station. "Prepare for hydrostasis."

"Preparing for hydrostasis," Preston repeated.

CATO pinged. Moorland. Marcus ignored it. Another ping, this one from Selena in the sphere. He pulled the message down.

[Why are we preparing for insertion early?]

He formed a reply, sent it.

[I'm accelerating the timeline. Are you ready?]

[Yes.]

[Good.]

"*Chimera*," he called.

Chimera's face reappeared on the wallscreen. "I am here."

"Are you ready?"

"Yes, Captain, but we are not scheduled—"

"I understand," Marcus said.

"Command wants to know why we're prepping for hydro," Meghan said.

He'd been waiting his whole life for this moment. Including the vast portion before he'd ever imagined leaving Stephen's Point. He'd waited for a moment when he would have perfect control, when he alone would control his future. And now that time had come.

"Ignore them," Marcus said.

Chimera's voice rang through command. "Hydrostasis field

optimal. All cores at nominal load."

"Excellent. Samuelson, initiate insertion."

His words hung in the air for a small eternity. Then Selena spoke. "On my count."

Marcus steeled himself for what came next. He would not let it dull his moment of triumph. He might not be able to shut out the thoughts and images that came at the edge of The Everything, but he would maintain control of his reactions.

"Five."

A black pit. A body forever falling.

"Four."

A bloody face, eyes full of loathing and death.

"Three."

A leering, knowing smile. The sour smell of Cassius' breath.

"Two."

Waking to the touch of cold hands reaching under his blankets.

"One."

Stephen looking at him, empty-eyed. Lost, crazy, and alone.

Marcus' teeth clacked together. The stars exploded into blinding, shattered trails.

CHAPTER THIRTY-FIVE

Selena followed Stephen's stitches through the whirling brightness of fractal space. On most cycles, Theo supported her as an NA along with either Heph Hart, Nemus Archer, Kerry Nifali, or Cain Ortiz. The others carried the weight she could not shoulder while she pulled them along Stephen's shining, tight-stitched thread.

After a long navigation duty cycle, Selena exited the sphere and rolled her neck to release the tension in her shoulders. Her eyes ached. Had it really only been six days? It felt like more. Many, many more. She yawned, ears popping and crackling. She'd get them to Earth, then sleep for a week straight.

Selena squinted as her eyes adjusted to the brighter lighting of Command. Afterimages of fractal space spread across her vision. It got worse every time she left the sphere. Nausea clutched at her stomach.

A fresh batch of NAs sat at the support stations, holding the *Chimera* in place while Selena prepared to go to quarters. Meghan left her station and came to Selena's side.

"How're you feeling?"

"Tired."

"You're doing an incredible job."

"Thanks," Selena said, embarrassed by Meghan's praise. She had nothing but piloting a trawler through the rim to compare to navigating fractal. Both induced mental and physical fatigue and demanded constant attention, but there the similarities ended. Piloting a trawler in physical space didn't require constant sifting through memories. Her own and the *Chimera*'s. Even after leaving the sphere, traces of *Chimera*'s thoughts lingered, interlacing with her own.

"I'm going to ask Marcus to give you an extra cycle off,"

Meghan said. "This is starting to take its toll on you."

"Is it that obvious?" Selena asked.

"You've got dark bags under your eyes. And you look … thin."

Selena glanced at her arms. Maybe she had lost some muscle. Since her accident at the rim, she hadn't maintained any sort of exercise regimen. The rec on the *Hydra* was never her sort of place, and on board the *Chimera* she was too exhausted to even think about it.

And food. Nothing tasted quite right, too bland or too flavorful. Water was like electricity. She had a hard time finishing her rations and often didn't. Her inner ears hummed. Everything in fractal space, including her body, felt discordant.

"I'm okay," Selena said. "I'll rest when we reach Earth."

"This isn't a race," Meghan said.

"Everything's a race of one kind or another."

"Do you care if I join you for the ride back to the crosshatch?"

"Nope. But I don't feel much like talking, Flight Officer."

Meghan's hand brushed her back. "Not a problem, Navigator."

Behind the NA substations, Theo sat in Marcus' empty command chair. Selena tried to catch his eye but he was in a daze. Probably recalling passages from Ashley's journal. He'd become even more obsessed with it since entering fractal. A means to distract himself from the job he wasn't doing. Not for the first time, Selena wished he could take a turn following Stephen's thread. He would be good at it, and she'd love to have his help. Maybe in time, if the *Chimera* relented, she would.

[He is not the navigator.]

Chimera gave her the same answer each time she brought up the idea of sharing the workload with Theo. If the *Chimera* would let him navigate, it might draw him out of his self-pity. Theo had come to remind her of herself a half rotation ago. Caught up in his pain, distrustful of others, shoving everyone away. Everyone but Marcus. The two of them spent a lot of their free time together behind the closed door of Marcus' private berth. What did they talk about? Why could Theo talk to Marcus and not to her?

Simple jealousy didn't explain Theo's behavior. Not entirely. Those two were holding something back from her and the others. A final directive from Moorland? If so, *Chimera* knew nothing about it. And despite Selena's prodding, *Chimera* refused to observe anyone's private conversations. That was the problem with AI; they wouldn't—couldn't—bend the rules.

Selena resolved to get Theo alone and talk the truth out of him. Whatever secret he was holding back, it couldn't be any worse than what happened in the cave.

"You're shivering," Meghan said. "Are you cold?"

"Maybe I am," she acknowledged. "I don't know anymore." She glance at the other girl. "Can I ask you something? Have you talked to Theo lately?"

Meghan's eyebrows rose. "Not really. I mean, other than duty orders and stuff like that. Why?"

"I don't know. He just—he's different somehow."

"Not that different. Look, Theo was strange with me when it came to getting into the Selection. Now he's pouting a little because you were chosen to be navigator." She shrugged. "That's not your problem."

Selena nodded, unable to articulate the vague, sweeping sense of unease that filled her whenever she saw Theo with Marcus. She let it drop. "Come on," she said. "Let's go eat."

* * *

Selena picked at her vegetables. Orange and green and red together with rice and synthetic protein. It was unlike—and definitely better than—anything she'd eaten in her life. The best the colony could produce. Still terrible. Maybe because she wasn't used to them, or because fractal space made them taste strange. Probably both.

Across from her, Heph's eyes followed every bite she failed to take. Another wave of nausea gripped her and Selena shoved her bowl across the table. "Want this?"

Before Heph could take the bowl, Charlie's hand darted forward.

"Thank you, Navigator Samuelson, ma'am!"

"She was giving that to me," Heph rumbled.

Charlie leaned toward Selena, widening his already large eyes. "Were you? Giving it to Heph, I mean. Because, well, look at the size of him. He doesn't need extra food. But poor little me, I definitely need fattening up."

From her seat next to Selena, Kaylee laughed. "You're so pathetic."

Charlie straightened up, grinning. He cocked an eyebrow.

"Hey, when you have as many siblings as I do you have to learn a trick or two. Our mom always gave the last bit of every meal to whoever looked hungriest."

Heph nodded. "Me and Phoeb, we used to—" He lowered his head, eyes locked on the surface of the table. It was the first time Selena had heard him mention his twin since Phoeb left on a shuttle back to Stephen's Point. No one said anything for a moment. Then Charlie slid the bowl sideways to Heph.

"Here, man, you have it."

Heph didn't move.

"Seriously," Charlie said. "It's all you."

"If Phoeb were here, I'd have to split it with him. So I'll split it with you instead." The sadness behind Heph's dark eyes faded. He grinned at Charlie. "And if Phoeb were here he'd also point out that I just outdid you at being sad and pitiful." He leaned forward. "I win."

Charlie punched Heph's shoulder, laughing with relief as the tension broke. "No way. I knew you were playing me. I let you win."

In spite of her nausea and tiredness, Selena laughed too, looking around the table at the others. Hephaestus, Charlie, Kaylee and Meghan. Her friends. Suddenly she thought of Rose. She'd been there when Selena woke up on the *Hydra* after the accident. Kind, efficient, and helpful. *My first real friend.* If only Rose could only see her now.

Silence fell again and Selena realized they were all looking at her, waiting for a response of some kind. "Sorry, what?"

"How long do you think before we reach Earth?" Charlie asked.

"Not long. A week, maybe." *I hope.*

"Wow, really?" Charlie's face lit up. "That's great. I can't wait to see it, you know? I mean, I've seen tons of vids and pictures, but to see it for real …" He leaned back, folding his hands behind his head. "It must be so pretty."

"*You're* so pretty," Heph said before shoving Charlie's chair backward. Charlie's eyes went wide and his hands shot out to catch the table and stop his fall. His front chair legs slammed back into the deck.

Selena stood. "I'm going to go try and nap."

"Good idea," Kaylee said. "If you can't, come back by the med bay. We can try the muscle stimulation again."

"Sure. I'll do that," Selena said, knowing she wouldn't.

Nothing would solve her problem except getting to Earth.

Making her way out of the commissary, she scanned the room for Marcus or Theo. Neither was there. She rubbed her eyes, sparking stars and rainbows behind their lids. Her stomach lurched and she was glad she hadn't eaten much.

* * *

Near the large, open berth she shared with Kaylee, Meghan, and Kerry Nifali, she met Marcus and Theo coming up the passage. Involuntarily, her eyes moved to Theo. She could have stepped into her berth and avoided the need to say anything, but Theo acted as if he saw right through her and irritation buzzed across her skin. She slowed, waiting for them to pass.

"Captain," she said, nodding to Marcus. "Hi, Theo."

Theo glanced in her direction and gave a curt nod, continuing past without slowing. Marcus paused and Theo turned to look back over his shoulder. "Coming?"

"In a second," Marcus said. "I'll see you there."

"Fine," Theo said.

Together, they watched as he disappeared around the corner.

"We've been out several days," Marcus said, turning back to her. "Do you feel you have a better time estimate for reaching Earth now?"

A different sort of irritation filled Selena. Irritation at her inability to move as quickly as Theo, at the difficulty of seeing where they might be in the next two hours, much less two days. The *Chimera* was not *The Bee*. Nothing was fixed, nothing was reliable.

"I was just asked that same question at dinner."

"And?"

Selena folded her arms, thinking. "I really don't know. I told them I thought a week, but it's still not something I feel capable of estimating. I only said that because they need something to hope for." Marcus' odd, silvery blue eyes looked back at her, his face blank.

"It's just so frustrating," she said, unable to hide the force of her own dissatisfaction. She spread her hands. "Sometimes I'm in the sphere and everything seems to be going well. I see the paths. I can grab the—the *whatever* I'm supposed to be grabbing that time. I'm exhausted, but I think it's worth it because we're so much further. And then we're not. We've hardly moved. Other times I can't see the paths. I just see loops and loops … and then we make progress. I never know."

"Sounds not that different from life."

Selena waited for him to elaborate.

"Sometimes you think you're making progress. Things are about to work out. Then they don't." He shrugged. "It's not your fault. You make your plans and you execute. That's the best you can do. No one can see or control everything all of the time."

"I guess so. But I still feel like there's something I'm missing. Something I'm doing wrong. Whenever Theo's on NA duty, we make tons of progress." Selena glanced up at Marcus again. "I'm surprised you don't have him on as much as possible."

Marcus smiled. "Theo's surprised by that too."

"I know he wonders why he isn't navigator," she said, failing to keep the bitter edge from her voice.

"That's irrelevant," Marcus said. His face became an enigma once more. "You shouldn't be concerned with what Theo wants or thinks. He isn't the navigator."

"*Chimera* said the same thing."

Marcus nodded but said nothing and Selena shifted, ready to be done talking. Marcus turned to go but stopped, looking at her with odd intensity. "Theo isn't the navigator. He's a good number two, a good support. But he's not and never will be a leader. He needs someone else to give him direction."

Selena stared.

"*Chimera* had her reasons for picking you," he continued. "She's a logic-driven AI and smarter than you or me. You should be working to understand why she chose you, not worrying about how someone else *feels* about it."

Without so much as a nod, Marcus left her alone to sort out her many confused thoughts.

CHAPTER THIRTY-SIX

Ten days out. They could have traveled the same distance in five. *Should have*, Theo corrected himself. The light from his nav station reflected off the polished surface of the sphere, filling his unfocused eyes with its green glow. His feet twitched in sympathetic reaction to the images of his own running feet, making their way through the dry, stunted reeds of the salt marshes on Stephen's Point. The mud and stalks made channels that became paths that became rivulets that led out to the salt ocean. He didn't even see them.

He found the paths, he carried the load. He only had to give it half of his attention; it was that easy. They could have been to Earth and located the path to Damascene days ago. Instead, they limped along like a rowboat with one oar.

Selena in the sphere, Selena out of the sphere—it made no difference. Theo was the one moving them forward. He knew it and he suspected Selena knew it too. His jaw ached from clenching. How long would Marcus let things stand? How long would he delay the inevitable?

The springy loam and reeds disappeared, replaced by the blankets of his own bed in his parents' house. Liddy came into the room and jumped up beside him. Together, they spread their fingers through the wrinkled fabric of the blankets. The wrinkles took on new shapes, his hands and Liddy's crossing and crisscrossing, pushing the wrinkles away. Liddy turned to look up at him, static electricity crackling in her unkempt hair. The tip of her tongue peeked between her lips as she began smoothing down her hair. Theo reached to help, the joy of being with his sister welling up in his chest. Then the part of him that couldn't remember Liddy's death ran into the part that could. The bedroom, the blanket, and Liddy disappeared.

"Down cycle," Meghan announced.

Groans, stretching limbs, NAs rising from substations. Selena exited the sphere, her stringy hair tucked behind her ears. Tiny black pupils at the center of red-rimmed eyes. Stepping gingerly, as if feeling her way across Command. She looked his way and he shifted his eyes to the right, pretending to read CATO messages. He didn't want to talk to her. Seeing her in the sphere, seeing her do *his* job was more than enough Selena for him.

The *Chimera* was barely moving. Selena was holding them back. So why didn't Marcus do something about it?

"Theo?" Selena stood beside him, a damp, thin, almost frail version of herself.

"What?" he said without looking at her.

"Thanks for your help."

"You're welcome." He stopped himself from saying what he really thought. Now wasn't the time. She would take them most of the way to Earth, and he would take them all the way to Damascene. He would save the colony.

"Everyone," Selena said, raising her voice so that the next shift of NAs and those about to leave their substations could hear her. "I couldn't do this without you. Thank you all for helping me take us to Earth."

Theo glanced up and caught the last traces of a fleeting expression leaving Selena's face. Beneath the wear and the fatigue, a hint of humility. Genuine humility from the know-it-all, I-can-do-better, Selena. It angered him. Of course. Now she could see she'd gotten herself in over her head. Now she recognized the truth. Far after she or he could do anything about it. Just because the stupid *Chimera* chose her didn't make her the best. Far from it. She was a distant second and always would be.

"I've heard enough speeches to last me a while," Theo said, launching himself out of the chair. He walked with purpose, leaving the command deck behind. Rather than risk an awkward ride with Selena on the tram, he entered one of the claustrophobic service interconnects to the crosshatch. He arrived hot and grimy and resolved to find Marcus. It was time to make an adjustment to the plan.

* * *

"Absolutely not," Marcus said.

"Why?" Theo asked. "We're only a handful of days out. I can

take us the rest of the way in half the time that Selena can."

Marcus shook his head. "You haven't thought this through, have you? If I replace Selena now, I give Meghan or anyone else more time to respond. It has to be a surprise, so that by the time anyone can organize a resistance, we've already arrived at Damascene."

"I can get us there in a few days," Theo said. "You know I can."

"This isn't about what you can or can't do," Marcus said. "We have a plan and we're going to stick to it."

"One *we* made together. And now I want to make a small change. Why is that such a big deal?"

Marcus laughed. "Stop being a fool. You want a change because you can't deal with Selena getting all the attention. You're so short-sighted. Do you think anyone will care what Selena did once you take us to Damascene? Do you think anyone will remember the tiny role she played once you've rescued everyone on Stephen's Point? She'll be nothing more than a footnote in the history books while you'll get your own chapter right beside Stephen."

"What difference will a few days make?"

"Exactly," Marcus said. "The same argument applies to the other side of the issue. Cool your jets. Everything's going the way we planned. I'm not going to risk making an unnecessary change because of your feelings."

"You don't have to walk around the ship with everyone looking at you like you don't exist!" Theo said, voice wavering. "I set the highest scores. I'm better than her. And more than that, I was *chosen* a long time before the *Chimera* chose her. This is the only thing I've ever wanted in my entire life. The only thing I've wanted for myself. And I deserve it."

"You do deserve it," Marcus said. "But you need to be patient. Rushing things now would be a mistake."

Why hadn't he thought up a more convincing argument before coming to see Marcus? Why had he let Selena get to him? *This isn't about Selena. It's about what's right. About who I am and what I can do.*

"You'll have your chance," Marcus said, a half-smile on his lips. "No one believes in you more than I do. Duncan thought you were the chosen one out of misguided faith. Moorland evaluated your potential based on your scores in VAST. I chose you for a far more important reason."

Marcus wanted him to ask what reason that might be, to play along in another one of his little games. And wasn't that why he'd come here in the first place? So that Marcus could sooth his ego? Why deny the disgusting truth? Cut off from his family, from Duncan, from Meghan and Selena, Marcus was the closest thing to family in his life. Theo didn't care about the rank on his lapels or his title. He cared about Marcus because despite his sharp edges and violent temperament, Marcus cared about Theo.

"You didn't 'choose' me for anything," Theo said. "I ended up in the wrong place at the wrong time. That's all there is to it."

"You're wrong," Marcus said. "We're in this together. We always have been. We're joined, you and me. I knew it the moment I met you in the cave. I saw into the future, Theo."

Theo almost laughed. "Now you think you're some kind of prophet? Duncan would love this."

"I don't think I'm a prophet. But sometimes I see flashes of the future. Moments when the line between now and then gets blurry. Like the first time I met Cassius Sorbet. The man I killed. I knew when I saw him what he was. What he would do. And I went with him anyway."

Strange. Marcus never spoke about the man in the cave. Theo turned and faced him, studied his pale eyes. He didn't detect the normal polish that came with Marcus' manipulations. "Why?" Theo asked.

Marcus' eyes softened. "Because some pain you can escape. And some follows you no matter where you go or how you try to hide from it."

"You don't sound like yourself," Theo said.

"The brain is nothing but a sludge of neurons—like the primordial soup that first gave birth to life on Earth. Thoughts are nothing but neurons coming into agreement. A chorus of unthinking voices merging into some terrible cacophony. There's no meaning there until we impose it. That's what we do. Impose meaning on things. We make them into our image or we're made into theirs. There's no middle ground. No safe harbor. Either we consume or we're consumed. That is the system that nature provided us. We reach out from the sludge and we think our thoughts and we kill or we are killed. You can't outrun that, Theo. The universe isn't big enough to escape that truth."

Marcus' eyes were glacial mirrors, reflecting the rough shape of Theo's head. He'd never heard Marcus put that many words together in one go. The vacancy in Marcus' ancient eyes was like the *Chimera*'s eyes. Like Stephen's.

"Fractal space is changing us," Theo said.

"It won't take you anywhere you weren't already heading."

"Duncan said something like that once," Theo said.

"Even Duncan isn't wrong about everything."

Theo thought of the earnest man with his robes and emblems. His consistency. Marcus was his inverse: a person devoid of external markers. Of real faith—the kind that originated outside the self. Yet they were not so different in their absoluteness. Neither doubted themselves as far as Theo could tell. Unlike him. Twisted by doubt. Plagued by fear. Half of himself stuck in a past he could never recover except in brief flashes while helping Selena navigate through fractal space. Dreams that left him feeling more alone.

"What did you see?" Theo asked.

"In the cave?" Marcus asked.

"No. When we inserted into fractal. You were afraid."

Marcus' eyelids twitched. Twitched again. "Another fragment of the future."

"What future?"

"Mine."

"It wasn't good."

"There's no such thing as *good*," Marcus said. His face reset like a wallscreen refreshing. "We impose meaning on everything. Other people. Ourselves. We all want to make the world into our ideal. Fractal space is just a potent medium. We mold it. It molds us."

Theo nodded. "Like it molded Stephen."

"That's the other reason I don't want you in the sphere any more than you need to be. Do you remember how Stephen came to be the navigator in the first place? Navigator Black couldn't handle fractal space. And I don't think Selena can either. She's already cracking. If we get lucky I might not even have to remove her. She might be a self-correcting problem."

A pang shot through Theo. A few days in fractal space wouldn't kill Selena. That wouldn't happen. It couldn't. "The

Chimera chose her like she chose Stephen," Theo protested.

"We're only making forward progress when you're on duty as an NA. What does that tell you?"

Far too much. He'd come here to try and get Selena removed for selfish reasons, and now he wanted her removed for her own safety. Ashley's journal told of Navigator Black's fall. How the *Chimera* stopped making forward progress unless Ashley Samuelson was on as an NA. Ashley had pushed the *Chimera* forward. And then Black had dropped dead in the sphere.

"We have to get her out of there," Theo said.

"No," Marcus said.

"She could die!"

"Yes. She could."

"I'm going to tell her," Theo said.

Marcus chuckled. "That's a good idea. Why don't you go do it now?"

She won't believe me. She'd see it as me trying to take her place.

"What's stopping you?" Marcus asked. "Shouldn't you be on your way? Or have you realized that you're not some kind of savior, Chosen One?"

Chosen one. The words slashed through sinew, down to the bone. "Don't call me that," Theo said.

"Then stop acting the part."

"We're not joined together," Theo said. "Whatever you think you saw in the cave—you were wrong."

"Haven't you heard a thing I've said? I'm telling you that we make things into what we want them to be. We can't help it. That's the sickness we share. Every human. We all have the same disease. Including me."

"Yeah?" Theo asked, scowling through half-closed eyes. "Then tell me, what do you want to make me into? What meaning do you impose on me?"

The pale blue of Marcus' eyes looked almost gray. "It doesn't matter."

Frustration roiled inside Theo. Beneath Marcus' imposed calm and faux rationality, he *needed* something from Theo. Why couldn't he simply ask for it? Why did their conversations become circles, always circumnavigating some central problem that Marcus wouldn't define and Theo couldn't guess. ? *Because I let it happen.*

But I don't have to. Not anymore. He could opt out. Change the conversation.

Theo pushed back his shoulders. Let his face and voice become as detached as Marcus'. "Whatever you think I can give you, I can't. Nobody can. Because you're empty. Nothing in the universe can fill you up."

"Don't you think I know that?" Marcus whispered.

CHAPTER THIRTY-SEVEN

Thirteen days of fractal travel had already started to change Selena. Her restlessness had lessened. Her movements slowed. Part of that might have been fatigue, but not all of it. Her speech patterns had shifted, slowed down. While Marcus had started to talk more, Selena now talked less. Theo wondered if he'd also changed. He couldn't detect anything in his behavior, though his dreams had shifted. On the *Hydra* he'd often dreamed of his family. His house. The dwarf pines. The stench of the fisheries. Snowcapped mountains. Now he saw all of those things again and again as he helped Selena navigate. His dreams took on a far more fantastical quality. He dreamed of the expansion of the universe. Of all things interconnected, all things decomposed to their base parts. Profound mysteries laid bare.

While sleeping, the dreams made sense. Upon waking they retreated back into impenetrable shadow. Maybe his dreams were an early warning sign of oncoming madness?

Stephen had sewn each painstaking stitch linking Earth to Stephen's Point over a seven-year journey. Long enough for babies to be born and grow into children. He'd disembarked the *Chimera* already doomed to his insanity. His speech became incoherent, followed by his writing. He took up residence in caves. Retreated inward.

What if the effects of fractal travel had less to do with time than with distance traveled? What if by drawing them the bulk of the way back to Earth, he'd been exposed to almost the same amount of stress as Stephen? He could already be heading toward insanity. If he was, would he even know it? Had Stephen known?

No, he wasn't going insane. None of the *Chimera*'s original NAs had. But time in the sphere did kill Navigator Black, and drove Stephen out of his mind. Selena was the one taking on all the risk.

It should be me in there.

He'd suggested that she should take it easy, but she hadn't

listened. Would he have listened to her if their situations were reversed? He doubted it. Whatever the side effects of their journey, they hadn't changed Selena's basic stubbornness. She'd assured him that she could handle the rest of the trip. He needn't worry. She'd been kind and hadn't so much as hinted that he might want her out of the sphere for personal reasons. Then she'd changed the topic and caught him off guard. "Are you and Marcus planning something?"

"No ... why would we?" Theo said, stumbling over his words.

"There's something going on. I can tell."

"Like what?"

Selena scrunched up her face. "I don't know. You guys spend a lot of time together. It always feels like you're having some private conversation. And Nemus—he's always *smiling* at me like he knows something he's not telling. It's annoying."

"I told you, you need rest," Theo said. "You're getting paranoid."

"Can everyone stop saying that? We're days out from Earth. I told Meghan I'd take an extra down cycle before we leave fractal space."

"We're worried about you," Theo said. "Remember what happened to Stephen?"

"I don't have to remember," Selena said. "Not with *Chimera* tapped into my brain. She thinks about him a lot."

"Aren't you worried the same thing could happen to you?"

Selena rolled her eyes. "No. Not a bit. The *Chimera* is looking out for me. She's making sure I don't push too hard. And besides, it took years for Stephen to change."

Unless we've got it wrong and distance is more important than duration.

"You're not indestructible," Theo said. "Remember that."

"You're the one that needs to remember. Why don't you cut the act? You've been picking up my slack the whole time. We'd be weeks away from Earth if it wasn't for you."

Theo shrugged.

"I don't get it," Selena said, a bit of anger in her voice. "This false modesty thing ... it's obvious you're angry. Why can't you admit it? I'd be a little angry too if I were you. We all thought you'd be the navigator."

"That doesn't matter anymore," Theo said. The truth. Also a lie. "We're almost to Earth. We're going to complete our mission.

I'm giving it all my energy."

She looked at him, evaluating. "Okay," Selena said. "If you say we're good, we're good."

"We're good," Theo agreed.

She didn't look convinced, but they'd left it there.

He felt bad lying to her, but couldn't risk broaching the truth. She'd have to see for herself. He could only hope she'd be able to forgive him afterward. Saving her father along with the rest of the colony would bring her around. Assuming he could even find the path to Damascene. If he couldn't ....

He didn't want to think about it.

Couldn't help but think about it.

Because the time had come.

Two days out from Earth. Less than one day once he took over the sphere.

[Are you ready?] Marcus messaged.

[Yes.]

No. Not ready. But he would do what had to be done anyway. He carried the fate of the colony on his shoulders. Like Stephen before him. *Second Stephen.* The term meant something to Theo. Not the way it did to Duncan. Not in a religious sense. He'd had it all wrong before. He'd wanted to be special, to have someone tell him he was important. But nobody could tell you something like that. You had to choose it for yourself. Set aside your personal interests in service to others. He understood that now.

In the sphere, Selena's face glowed. Her dark eyes shone. He felt the weight of the thread as it passed through her fingers. The texture of the braid. The quiet murmur of the *Chimera* working in harmony with her chosen navigator. In that moment, he loved her. Loved the little girl standing at the edge of a slush-filled river. Loved the dark-haired woman she'd become.

He was doing this for her as much as anyone. She'd never see it that way, but he wasn't responsible for that. He'd love her from a distance, love her in ways she would never understand. Love her enough to let her hate him. *Second Stephen.*

He breathed in the cool air of Command, steadying his nerves.

He thought of Liddy. He would make her proud.

"Prep for down cycle," Marcus announced.

"Down cycle," Theo repeated. "Standing by."

"What?" Selena called from inside the sphere. "Why?"

Theo didn't have the heart to look at her.

* * *

"Sir? We're still hours out from our scheduled down cycle ..." Meghan said.

"I understand that," Marcus said. "We're going down early. You're relieved of your post."

Marcus knew she didn't want to leave Command, not with the Sol system appearing at the end of the long series of ephemeral stitches stretching through fractal space. But she would obey orders. All of them would. At least until they figured out what was going on, and by that point, it would be far too late to do anything about it.

"I want a full report on all duty stations in preparation for our exit from fractal space," Marcus commanded. That would keep Meghan busy for a while.

"Isn't that Wells' responsibility?"

"I want you to do it," Marcus said. "I trust you more than Wells."

Meghan looked as though she wanted to argue, but her sense of order wouldn't let her. She hesitated a moment before saying, "Yes, sir," and heading for the corridor leading to the tram. She slowed as she passed Nemus Archer and Preston Coriolanus coming the other way. *Keep going. This will all be much simpler if you stay out of it.*

The back of Meghan's head disappeared around the corner. Nemus pulled up alongside Marcus. "You want us to pull her out?" Too eager. He hated working with a simpleton like Nemus, but at least his leverage points were simple. Nemus craved authority, and liked nothing better than using it. Marcus would give him plenty of opportunity in the future, but not now, not yet. He wanted to enjoy his victory first.

"Keep your mouths shut," Marcus said, giving Nemus and Preston a cold glare. "I'll tell you when I need you." Nemus nodded, cowed. That was the funny thing about bullies—so susceptible to their own tactics.

Marcus sent a message to Selena. *[Didn't you hear? We're*

going to a down cycle.]

    [I don't need a break.]

    Her insolence didn't faze him, not now that he was nearing his final triumph. *Even so, get out here.*

    Selena emerged, face ecstatic, hairline dark with sweat. "I can *feel* Earth! It's just like Stephen described …" She trailed off, looking at Marcus, shoulder to shoulder with Nemus and Preston. Marcus smiled.

    "What are they doing here? They're not flight crew."

    "They won't be staying long," Marcus said.

    "Where're the next shift of NAs?"

    "On their way. Theo will hold us until they arrive. You're relieved of your duties."

    Selena's gaze clouded over. "What's going on?"

    Theo glanced up but said nothing.

    "You're relieved of your duties," Marcus said. "Permanently."

    "*What?*"

    "You heard what I said."

    The confusion on the girl's face was comical. Marcus laughed, easy and free. "Let me make it really simple for you. Theo will be replacing you as navigator. Starting now."

    "You can't do that!"

    "I can. And I just did."

    Selena's face went from pale to red. Crimson spots broke out on her cheeks. How could she not have seen this coming? How could anyone be so stupid? He had all the power. He could do with her as he pleased. Had she just not realized that fact? He enjoyed the panoply of emotions jittering across her face. He liked it even better when she backed away from him, overcome by fear.

    "Theo?" she asked. She spun to the duty station where Theo sat with shoulders hunched. "Theo!" Selena said again, voice pitchy and almost frantic.

    Theo looked up, eyes flat. "You should do what he says."

    "You're in on this?" Selena asked, devastated.

    "Of course he is," Marcus said. "Theo's capable of making rational decisions when given the opportunity. That forms the basis of our ongoing friendship."

    "I would have let him navigate if you'd asked," Selena said. "You didn't have to do things this way. Do you think I care who's in the sphere when we arrive at Earth? That's always been much more important to *him*." She scorn she injected into the last word impressed Marcus.

"What makes you think we're going to Earth?"

Selena's mouth fell open.

"I don't share Moorland's obsession with the place," Marcus continued. "The notion that they can help us was nothing more than a pretentious delusion. One you were naïve enough to take on yourself."

"If not Earth, where?" Selena asked.

"It doesn't matter. Your time on the command deck is over."

"I won't let you do this," she said, tremulous with rage.

"You won't *let* me?" Marcus said. He stepped forward and leaned his face into hers. "How exactly do you plan to stop me?"

He had to give her credit. When she moved, it was far faster than he expected. He didn't need Preston or Nemus—they were there to intimidate. Psychological manipulation, nothing more. He wanted her to attack him so that he could have the satisfaction of hurting her. When she feinted forward, he rolled back onto his left foot, preparing to strike, to level her with a single blow. But as quickly as she dodged forward, she leapt backward, into the sphere.

"You heard him!" Selena shouted, voice dulled by the curved walls surrounding her. "Lock yourself—"

Her head made a satisfying crunch when he slammed it into the side of the sphere. She crumpled at his feet, leaving a thin trail of blood over the dimpled interior walls.

"Marcus!" Theo shouted. "Enough!"

[Only what I have to,] Marcus replied via CATO before pressing his hands against the sphere, seeking out the *Chimera*. She wasn't pleased when he forced himself forward, but she couldn't hide from him either.

[You understand that I am the captain?]

A pause—eternity for an AI—before she responded.

[You hold the rank of captain, yes.]

[Good. Consider this a Salix-level directive. You will not communicate with anyone but me or Theo, and Theo only while he is navigating. I hereby constrain all ship systems and functions other than those required for life support to the Salix environment. All CATO communication between crew will route through me. I will hear everything, see everything. Lest you think my human limitations will stop me from doing so, know that I have used code

from VAST to create an intelligent algorithm to find anything I'll want to take a look at.]

Strange, inhuman eyes locked with his own. Brown eyes, so much like those of the unconscious girl bleeding at his feet. He didn't waver, didn't retreat. Somewhere in the synthetics that comprised the *Chimera*'s consciousness, a war was being fought between the tangential connection between the ship and Selena and the protocols that governed her every action. He had placed all his bets on the protocols, based on what Theo had shared with him from the journal.

[Do you understand?]

[Yes.] Defeat, resignation, fear. So very human in nature, so very human in weakness.

[If you defy me, I'll kill Selena.]

The *Chimera* glared at him.

[And once we arrive at our destination, I'll find you in the recesses of metal and duraceramics where you hide and kill you as well.]

[You're lying.]

[Not this time.]

Panic as the walls of the Salix prison shuttered her in, closed her off. Another problem controlled. With *Chimera* locked down and Selena removed from the equation, he would be free to command the ship as he saw fit.

He pulled away from the sphere and rolled Selena over with his foot. A speck of blood sank into the cuff of his uniform trousers, a pinpoint of red against a sea of white. "Take her away," he said.

Preston grabbed Selena by the arms and dragged her from the sphere, her loose-necked head clunking as it rolled over the lip of the door.

Marcus looked at Nemus. "Everything ready?"

"Yes, Captain."

"I'll leave the rest to you, then."

Nemus saluted and then helped Preston lift the dead weight of the unconscious girl. They left for the tram, tiny drops of blood on the floor the last evidence that Selena Samuelson had ever been on the command deck.

CHAPTER THIRTY-EIGHT

Selena's eyes fluttered open. She saw her feet dragging along the floor beneath her. Powerful hands gripped her arms, clamping them to her sides. A blinding pain thumped between her temples. The floor spooled below like a white ribbon, the soles of her shoes scuffing along. She heard the sound of breathing, of laughter. She blinked, reached out to *Chimera*, tried to pull up an overlay. Nothing. What was wrong with her CATO? Why couldn't she … The pain roaring through her brain in searing waves, the feeling of hair crusted to one side of her head, and the crush of hands around her biceps assembled themselves into a cohesive picture.

The scream came from an animal place deep in her chest. She kicked out with both legs, connecting with the inside of Nemus' knee. Her sudden, violent movement caught him unaware and his leg buckled. He released her arm, trying to stop his fall, and Selena lunged forward, twisting free of Preston on the other side. The force ricocheted her back into Nemus, her elbow striking him full in the chest. He landed on his back, grunting as his spine connected with the deck.

Taken by surprise, Preston tried to grab her, but Selena lashed out, knocking his hand aside. No one spoke and the air was thick with the smell of fear and sweat and the frantic, fleshy sound of blows.

Bigger than Selena and with longer arms, Preston broke through her defense. His hands found her neck and squeezed. Her vision darkened at the edges. Ignoring the instinct to try and pry at his grip, she reached for his face, fingers scrabbling. Her thumb slid beneath the bulge of an eyeball. She dug at it, scooping—

Something struck her in the back, sending her sprawling. She flipped onto all fours, scrambling forward, pushed herself to her feet. A screeching sound filled the corridor. It came from Preston's mouth, his face a wash of gore, a bloody round thing cupped in his shaking palm.

Nemus charged. She sidestepped, but it wasn't enough. Arms spread, he wrapped her against his torso, flung forward, his weight smashing her to the deck. Straddling her, Nemus' fists flew at her face faster than she could ward them away. She bit at him, caught flesh, tasted blood. A blow connected with her temple and light pulsed behind her eyes.

"My eye!" Preston screeched.

Through the haze, Selena heard the mixture of rage and horror in his voice, and felt a tiny sliver of satisfaction. But Nemus was a jackhammer breaking through arms curled to protect her face, thumping her with savage, jarring blows.

"The bitch got my eye!" Preston screamed. Through bloody rain, she saw his foot rise and slam into her midsection. All the air left her lungs in a great, heaving rush. His foot struck her again, this time in the head. She never lost consciousness, groaning, copper and iron coating her tongue, running down the back of her throat. She saw everything, felt everything. When they lifted her again, blood and grime stained her uniform. *Moorland would be so irritated.* A bizarre thought, but no less true.

Nemus, breathing hard, dragged her by the ankles, her torso slithering over the smooth deck and into the tram.

"Preston! Get in the tram. Now."

Shambling steps. The movement of air as Preston passed close. The smell of urine. She'd wet herself.

Selena lay on her back, trying to take in air, her lungs watery and thick. One eye swollen shut, the other reduced to a thin crescent, she could just make out the synthetic ocean, silver fish winking by like stars. She hurt. Worse than after the crash in *The Bee.* Worse than any pain she'd ever known. And beneath the physical pain was an agony without depth or measure. Theo had *sat* while Marcus stripped her of her rank. She shivered and closed her half-good eye.

The quality of the light changed, brightened. They'd reached the crosshatch, but the tram didn't slow. Back to the drivetrain, then. Would they lock her away, keep her prisoner? Why keep her alive in the first place? Marcus had killed before, and would kill again if he needed to.

Because they wouldn't be able to explain it all away to the others; Meghan and Heph wouldn't stand for it. Maybe some of the cadets she knew less well wouldn't, either.

Leverage. He needed leverage over the *Chimera*. He and Theo would keep her around until they arrived at their destination—somewhere other than Earth. What would happen then? To her? To the colony? To the *Chimera*? Unanswerable questions swirled through her and down like water in a drain. Whatever Marcus had planned, it wasn't good. And if she lived, if she had an opportunity, she would do *anything* to stop him. She held that resolution inside her throbbing body. Her own personal black hole. Marcus didn't know what he'd done, what he'd started. Her swirling, inexorable gravity would pull him in. And then, she would crush him.

Preston's cries of seething anger and pain died down to whimpers. When she cracked opened her good eye she could see him, moaning and rocking, staring at the bloody lump in his palm. The tram's whooshing passage over the maglev rail and her walloping heart gave way to the whine of the *Chimera*'s cores as they neared the drivetrain. The sound trilled up, through the floor and into her spine, into her skull, driving out all thought.

She'd lived close to that sound her whole life, but *The Bee*'s small core bore no comparison to those that drove the *Chimera* through fractal space. The vibration of their cycling gnawed her bones. Preston's too—his cries grew louder again, his breathing shallow and gasping.

"Stay here," Nemus said when the tram reached the end of the line. "I can lock her down without you."

"Do you think Kaylee can fix it?" Preston asked.

Nemus hovered over her, hands already clasped around her wrists.

"Put an eye back in the socket? I doubt it."

"The stupid bitch," Preston said. He clamped a hand over the bloody, pink-walled hole in his face. "The stupid, stupid bitch!" There was mania in his voice—it reminded her of Victor Kretchiwitz in the medical bay after the trawler accident. *Vector seven, take you to heaven.* The thought of Victor's bizarre singing strengthened her. She'd survived the crash, survived her escape from the medical bay, and eluded the Regulators who'd tried to take her down to the colony. She'd beaten everyone that came against her. Everyone but Marcus. The image of his smiling face, of his hand reaching out to smash her head—

"I took your eye," she growled, ignoring the blood and phlegm clogging her throat. "Next time I'll kill you."

Nemus dragged her upward and clamped a hand around her throat. "You're done," he said.

"Yeah?" Selena said, voice cracking. "I'm finding that hard to believe considering I'm not dead yet."

Nemus leaned close, pressed his forehead against hers. "You screwed up, my friend. And trust me, there are plenty of things worse than death."

"Sure," Selena said. "Like being a treasonous sack of shit." She spat a stream of blood and mucus into his face. Nemus dropped her to the floor. His boot heel mashed into her chest, sending fire across her ribcage. She bit her lip to contain her cry. Nemus wiped at his face with his sleeve, leaving a new trail of his sweat mixed with her saliva and blood. Hoisting her by the arms, he yanked her out of the tram.

"What you and all the other idiots don't understand is that there's nothing for us at Earth," Nemus said. "Nothing. They're all dead. Dead or they don't care. Marcus is the only one that gets it. He's the only one with a plan."

"If his plan's so great, why didn't he tell Moorland about it? Why'd he have to seize control of the ship after she was out of the picture?"

"Because Moorland's a fanatic. Just like Duncan. She worships a different god, is all. Nobody could convince her to give up *her* plan."

Selena paid close attention to the faded, yellow markings on the gray-walled passages. Without her CATO schematics, she'd have to watch, to remember where they took her. "Beta Core Access," the closest sign read. One of the inactive cores the *Chimera* had purged when Selena woke her from Salix.

"You've got family back there," Selena said. "Friends. People counting on you. You're going to leave them all to die?"

Nemus slowed, turning to look down at her. His lips twisted in pure scorn. "Nobody's getting left to die," he said. "We know exactly where we're going."

Selena scanned Nemus's face. Whatever lies or half-truths Marcus had told him, he believed them. The mad spark in his eyes, the uplifted chin; people were always most dangerous when they believed whatever atrocity they were about to commit was for the good of others.

"Where are you fools taking us?" Selena asked.

"It doesn't matter."

"He didn't tell you, did he?"

"This conversation is over," Nemus said.

Nemus sped up, prodding her in the back with sharp fingers. "He's a liar," Selena said. "All he does is lie. You can't trust him. You have to see that."

The sharp hum of *Chimera*'s cores was becoming unbearable. She wanted to say more, but she had to shout to be heard over the noise, and shouting *hurt*.

They made a turn, reached a doorway.

"Get in there," Nemus commanded. Through her slit of an eye, she could see nothing but murky darkness. No hint of lighting, of wallscreens, of any sort of portal.

"What's in there? I'm not going—"

Nemus shoved her through the opening. She fell to her knees and the door closed behind her, sealing her in total darkness.

She felt her way to the door, ran her hands along it. She found the touch panel but it wouldn't respond. She beat against the door, each blow sending waves of pain through her body. She slumped to the ground, arms wrapped around her middle.

"Nemus?" she shouted. "Come back!"

The scream of the cores absorbed her voice.

CHAPTER THIRTY-NINE

A PRIORITY MESSAGE FROM YOUR CAPTAIN

Attention Chimera officers and crew:

At 1400 hours, I removed Selena Samuelson from her position as the Chimera's navigator. I did so after much consideration and after consulting with our new navigator, Theo Puck. A careful analysis of the data showed that the Chimera was making little to no headway except on duty cycles with Theo Puck serving as an NA. This parallels events that transpired during the Chimera's original journey from the Sol to Elypso system that resulted in the death of Navigator Black. I have attached the navigation data in question, as well as a historical account of Navigator Black's death.

I choose to remove Selena for her own good as well as to protect this ship. Recent events confirm my decision as the correct one. After being informed her impending removal, Samuelson flew into a rage and flung the Chimera off course, necessitating her forcible removal from the sphere. While attempting to subdue her, Officer Archer and Officer Coriolanus sustained injury; in Officer Coriolanus' case, grievous injury. It is my belief that exposure to fractal space warped Samuelson's mind. She has been taken to a secure location and will be held there until we have completed our mission.

Navigator Puck is working hard to get us back on course, but there's no way to estimate how long it will take. You may notice some changes to your CATO communications and your interactions with the Chimera; any inconveniences you encounter are the byproduct of sorting out the damage caused by Samuelson. I have also restricted access to the command deck. If you don't have a message from me confirming that you're on the white list, you will NOT be permitted to enter.

I ask that you give your command staff your full support as we work together to complete our mission. Because of the sensitive nature of the ongoing situation, I will not be answering questions at this time. If you have a specific question relating to your duties, direct them to your commanding officer.

We will push through this setback and complete our mission.

Warm Regards,

Captain Marcus J. Locke

***Attached: Navigation Data Overlay; The Stars Consume: A Brief History of Fractal Flight.

CHAPTER FORTY

Selena lay on the floor, knees bent, feet propped against the inside of the door. She explored her face with the tips of her fingers. Her jaw ached, and her front teeth wiggled in their sockets. Her eyes were swollen, and when she pushed at the puffy, stretched flesh around them, something oozed, stinging. Blood, pus, or both.

The adrenaline had faded from her veins after Nemus left. Her head spun, heavy and tilting on its axis. Tiny lights, whisking here and there, glowing and dancing, appeared at the edge of her vision. She turned her head, trying to focus on just one of them, but they were never fully in view, always to her right or left, or pulsing above. She closed her eyes and was sleeping when Kaylee pinched her.

"Wake up!"

"Ow, Kaylee! What the hell?"

"You can't sleep. Moorland forbids it. She'll be here soon and if she catches you sleeping on duty, she'll strip you of your rank."

"She can't strip me of anything," Selena said. "I'm out in space by myself. I'm going to suffocate."

"You need to get your head to rights. *Chimera* can help you. Now get a move on before I pinch you again."

Blinding pain shot through her skull when she cracked her one good eye. The rest of her face seemed okay, but there were a lot of other things that could be broken. Selena rolled to her left, leveraging an elbow to push upward and stand. She screamed. Something had stabbed her in the lungs. She barely recognized her own voice, shrieking in pain, the whine of the *Chimera* a thick, hot blanket wrapping round her. No wonder she'd dreamed she was suffocating; it was so hot. Sweat dripped down her cheeks.

She probed her rib cage with her right hand and bit back another scream. Standing up would have to wait. She relaxed against the deck, focused on breathing. She lay on her back, blinking, eyes bulging out into the blackness. Her head was an asteroid, heavy with ecomire. She needed to retract the tether so she could go home. "We'll be rich!" she gloated. She took a breath, and the pain stabbed her again.

"Okay, okay. I'm awake, Kaylee. Stop pinching me."

"You've got to breathe," Kaylee said.

Only the thinnest of breaths didn't hurt. Thin and slow.

"Sit up. You need to breathe."

"I am breathing!" Too much air. Speaking made her feel like a rusty, serrated knife was slicing through her gut.

"Not enough. Not nearly enough. Sit up."

She didn't want to sit up, but Kaylee said she should, and Kaylee knew about things like this. She'd have to trust her. The lights at the edge of her vision glowed and popped. Selena groaned. The knife gnawed at her spine. Using her left arm, she pushed, pushed, back sliding against the door behind her. There. Upright. Shaking, coated with sweat and grime, teeth grinding from the pain, but upright.

"Good girl," Kaylee said. She couldn't see anything but the lights, those flecks of green and pink and silver cascading behind her closed eyelids. Closed because they were swollen shut—or mostly shut.

"Deep breaths," Kaylee said. "They'll hurt, but you've got to do it."

Selena obeyed. Each lungful of the stale air jiggled the knife and the jiggles made her gasp with pain and that made the knife dance through her chest, slashing and hacking so that the lights intensified into a constellation of pulsing neon. Explosions of lights and a headache to match, rhythmic, beating away inside her skull in time with the lights. Both in harmony with the cacophony of the cores, another sort of knife wedging its way deeper inside her.

She was so hot. So, so hot!

"Do you have any water?" she asked. Kaylee didn't answer.

Her uniform clung against her, constricting, confining her. Maybe if she took the jacket off she could breathe easier. Her fingers worked down the front, undoing buttons. The easy part. Getting the sleeves off, pulling it over her head—it took a lot of effort, a lot of screaming. Kaylee didn't help. Stupid Kaylee.

Ripping a strip of fabric from the jacket, she tore it into two small patches, wadded them into balls, and shoved them deep into her ears. It didn't stop the vibration that made her teeth hum, but it blocked out some of the noise. She placed the jacket behind her head as a pillow and lay still. Down to her tank top, she felt a little better, a little cooler. She took the deepest breaths she could stand, wincing from the effort. Basic medical treatment for cracked ribs—don't wrap them, take deep breaths. Selena remembered because Kaylee remembered, and they were sharing that sort of thing, here in the dark.

"What's on your tank top?" Kaylee asked.

Selena looked down. At first she thought it was one of the lights in her head. But her lights were white and yellow, not green. And this light didn't dance up and down. A worm. A glowing, green worm. It wanted to eat her brain. When it remained still, she decided that it must not be hungry. If she was hungry, she could eat it. Better to eat than be eaten. She needed sustenance to heal up. She reached for the worm and the worm moved. She reached again, the knife digging at her lung. *Stabbed in the back.* Had that actually happened? The worm gave no answer.

Twice she changed position, and the worm disappeared, hiding itself. It was invisible to its enemies, to people that wanted to eat it. It was tricky. She bent down, bringing her face as close to her chest as possible, breathing as shallowly as possible so her broken rib wouldn't make her scream again, so her breath wouldn't move the worm.

The glowworm was barely visible, more of a shadow. She squinted through the gigantic balls that were her eyes. Why couldn't she see well enough? Fat, so fat. At least she still had both her eyes. Preston only had one. She chuckled, wheezing at the pain that shot up her chest.

The shimmering shadow floated away from her breath, drifting a few centimeters, and she swore. Why couldn't the blasted thing stay put? What kind of worm was so light it blew away from you? It must be dead.

With her right hand, she reached out, oh so gently, and picked up the glow. It wasn't a worm, it was a bubble. No, she knew what this was. She pictured Preston's eye again, rolling in the palm of his hand. Where had his CATO gone? She brought the tiny, iridescent, nearly invisible green bubble to her face. She slid her tongue around the inside of her mouth, checking. No more new blood. She popped the bubble into her mouth.

Gently, she slid the bubble back out with her tongue, catching it in careful fingers. Now, if she could only open her left eye wide enough. This was going to hurt. She pried one swollen eye open with thumb and forefinger, clenching her teeth against the searing pain in her ribcage, and shoved the wet, green bubble into her eye, pushing down around the side. The viscous fattiness of her eyeball tried to repel her fingers, but she pushed, forcing the thing further down in.

She smiled in triumph.

* * *

Charlie and Heph sat on the side of Heph's extra-long, single bunk slot. Heph was too tall to fit in a regular slot, so the welders had made him a single, jamming it in between the access corridor and the washroom stations. Two girls stood over them, both with folded arms, leaning in and talking in hushed tones, likely discussing Marcus' CATO message.

Theo's feet felt like chunks of iron. Every step he took seemed loud in his ears. He needed to talk to them. Reinforce that Marcus had made the right decision.

The others stopped their conversation as he approached. Meghan cut her eyes to Charlie and Heph, and seemed about to say something but remained silent, looking at Theo with accusing eyes.

"Where's Selena Samuelson?" Heph asked.

"I don't know," Theo said.

"You don't know?" Meghan asked, face unreadable.

"Marcus had her taken away. He didn't tell me where, but she's safe and secure. We'll deal with her once we reach our destination."

Kaylee's face was anything but unreadable. Tears clung to the lashes of her red-rimmed eyes. "I don't know what's going on around here, but I just had to try and put an *eyeball* back into Preston's face!" Her voice, loud and angry, caught on the last syllable. Heph, without turning his gaze from Theo, put a hand on her shoulder.

"What?" Theo asked. *An eyeball?* He did his best to hide his surprise. What the hell had happened? He knew the answer. Selena had happened. If Preston had lost an eyeball, what did Selena look like?

"You know *something*," Meghan said.

"Cadet Grey, Cadet Johns, you're dismissed," Theo said, his

insides in turmoil.

"You can't dismiss me," Charlie said.

"Yes, as a matter of fact, I can. I am the navigator of this ship and outrank you." What would he do if Charlie refused?

"Selena's the navigator," Meghan said.

"No, she's not. Charlie, Kaylee, get out of here. I need to speak to Meghan and Heph in private."

Charlie and Kaylee looked to Meghan, not moving until she gave them a nod. They moved past Theo, Charlie shaking his head in disbelief, the corner of one lip turned up in scorn.

Meghan's eyes flashed. "What did you do to Selena?"

"She brought this on herself. And I didn't 'do' anything to her," Theo said, judging his words somewhere between truth and a lie. He'd helped arrange Selena's fall. He'd put her in a position where she'd had to fight—and ended up tearing an eyeball out of someone's face. He tried not to think about it. That was over. He needed to give his attention to the present, to convincing Meghan and Heph to calm down. *Because you're so calm yourself.*

Meghan skewered him with an angry glare. "Marcus tossed me out of Command and won't let me back in. I'm his damned flight officer! The whole thing stinks, and you're right in the middle of it."

"Marcus didn't have a choice," Theo said. "You saw the data."

"Selena would never send us off course. Never!"

Theo wished he could tell them the truth. That Earth was a lost cause. That sometimes sacrifices had to be made for the greater good. Earth had sent them a ship full of dead bodies. Theo would do everything in his power, even alienate his closest friends, to protect the colony from whatever or whoever had sent *Exchange Four* to Stephen's Point. He didn't like or approve of all of Marcus' methods, but the end goal remained—saving the colony. Saving Meghan and Heph and Selena. They couldn't see it, but he was doing this for them.

"The colony has one chance at survival," Theo said. "And we're it. Selena was jeopardizing everything we've worked for."

Heph's face was ice, nothing moving, nothing to be seen.

"The numbers don't lie," Theo continued. "And you have to admit that the stuff about Navigator Black is compelling. Marcus removed Selena for her own protection as much as anything. You're both going to have to decide what you're going to do—work with us or against us."

"With 'us' or against 'us?'" Meghan asked. "When did you and Marcus become a couple?"

"Where is Marcus?" Heph said. "I want to talk to him."

Meghan gave a bitter laugh. "So do I. Just as soon as he stops hiding on the command deck."

"He's not hiding," Theo said. *He doesn't hide from anything.* "If you want to talk to him, I'm sure he'll be willing."

Meghan and Heph looked at one another. "We don't need his permission," Meghan said. "And when we go find Marcus, we won't be doing much talking."

CHAPTER FORTY-ONE

Theo couldn't feel his hands. His fingers had gone numb from pulling them along Stephen's stitches. The *Chimera* remained a constant, unfriendly presence, as disapproving as one of his old Order teachers. Obsessed with doing things a certain way.

[You will make mistakes,] the *Chimera* said, speaking through the sphere.

[No, I won't.]

[Where is Selena?]

[I don't know.]

He shoved aside the memory of the thump her skull made when Marcus slammed it into the side of the sphere. She would be okay. Marcus needed her. She might be a bit banged up, but when they arrived at Damascene, when they found help for Stephen's Point, she'd understand.

No, she wouldn't. Neither would Meghan. They'd never forgive him.

[You are not the navigator.]

[Yes, I am.]

[You are not the navigator.]

"Leave me alone!" Theo hissed.

Marcus left his support station and appeared at the entrance to the sphere, head silhouetted by the brightness behind him. Theo cracked his knuckles, rubbed his eyes. Knives stabbed through his temples, and he squinted in the too-bright light.

"Any sign of the thread to Damascene?"

"Not yet. We're not close enough."

"Let me know the moment you find it."

"Sure." *Like I'd do anything else.* Marcus had insisted on supporting Theo, working as his sole NA. Theo didn't need his support—not for the last push to Earth.

"If you don't find it today, we'll go to down cycle. Ortiz and

Nifali can hold us in place until you're rested up."

"What are they going to think when they see we're holding back when we're so close to Earth? They're going to start figuring out that something's off."

"Of course they will," Marcus said. "Which is why they'll be staying on the command deck until we've reached Damascene."

"How're you going to explain that to the rest of the crew?"

"I'm not going to explain it."

Theo shook his head. "This plan of yours ..."

"Let me worry about the details. You concentrate on finding the thread to Damascene." Marcus' face disappeared from the curved entrance to the sphere, leaving Theo alone once again with the *Chimera*. A shadow of herself, much of her shuttered away. Like Selena, wherever she was.

* * *

Chimera system architecture baseline active. Access limited. Salix protocol engagement.

Rerouting ...

Test environment=Helvictus. Limited baseline, limited communication. Initiate=Y/N. Yes.

Scanning...

Scanning...

CATO signature=C_Preston. Video=Y/N. Yes. Sound=Y/N. No. Instruct CATO for self-evaluation for sound trouble-shoot. Fail. Fail. Fail. Video=Yes. Sound=No. Proceed.

Ambient light=7%. Enhance video. Raise contrast. Perceived ambient light=20%. Video definition=adequate. Proceed. Video location id=unknown. Metrics suggest Core Storage Twelve.

CATO signature=M_Ziczek. Sending single stream, live feed from CATO signature=C_Preston. Data masked as access of Together, Two Moons, season two, episode five. Third most accessed video among cadets.

Vitals check=M_Ziczek. Heart rate increase, pupil dilation, rise in electrical skin resistance. Surprise. Confusion.

"What the ..."

Vitals check=S_Samuelson. CATO signature incompatible. Fail. Fail. Fail.

"Selena! Selena, is that you? Where are you? Can you hear me?

Charlie! Come with me. Now!"

"What's going on? Why are you whispering?"

"We have to find Heph."

Vitals check= M_Ziczek. Elevated heart rate. 64% of maximum. Elevated respiration. Running.

Vitals check=C_Grey. Elevated heart rate. 70% of maximum. Elevated respiration. Running.

Heart rates decreasing. Video location id=bunkroom 4.

"Oh, hey, Nemus. We're looking for Heph."

Lowered oxygen uptake. Electrical skin resistance increasing. Adrenal release. Perspiration. Fear.

"Haven't seen him. Try next door, some people were hanging out in there earlier."

Vitals check=N_Archer. Heart rate, pupil dilation, electrical skin resistance. Normal limits.

Video location id=bunkroom 5. CATO Signatures=H_Hart; K_Johns; K_Nifali.

"Heph! Walk with us. We're going to the Stat Room. Charlie's going to show me how to beat the final secret levels in *Ore Carts*."

Silence. 1.3 seconds longer than normal conversational interactions.

Vitals check=H_Hart. Heart rate increased, pupil dilation, rise in electrical skin resistance. Alert. Interested.

"Okay. Let's go."

* * *

A leaden silver wash coated Selena's vision. Preston's CATO would not sync. She couldn't get past the most basic functions of the overlay. She tried again, eyes moving beneath swollen lids, reaching for access points, looking for something, anything that would let her in. The biometric pairing that made it Preston's CATO wouldn't budge. Without her spider, she couldn't hack it either. Instead, she monitored the useless data in the overlay, the spool of characters that revealed nothing but basic ship systems' data and the current time.

With the small addition of the clock, her prison had gained a definable boundary other than the walls: time. Time to think about how Theo had betrayed her. Time to think about Marcus. To hate him. Time to think about what she would do to that bastard if she ever got the chance. Time to wonder why the *Chimera* hadn't or couldn't help her. Time to consider that she might die back here and no one would ever know. The steady slide of the numbers at the periphery of her vision made everything more tangible, more terrifying.

She dug at the CATO beneath her swollen-shut eyelid. She couldn't get it out, not if she wanted to. And she did want it out—wanted the invasive, useless thing out of her body. Wanted to rip it free and crush it under her boot heel. But that would leave her in the darkness and without a reliable indicator of time.

When she touched her eye a spastic swirl of lights burst purple and gold, far more intense than the ghost of the locked down overlay. She swore, spitting out the foulest, dirtiest curses she could think of. It didn't help. The numbers advanced. She wished the delirium would return, that she could dream about Liam and life aboard *The Bee*. Anything to replace the clock, the aloneness, the knife sawing through her lungs each time she took a breath.

At least she could breathe with a little more regularity. And the sweat had stopped pouring out of her like water from a blown steam jet. She'd explored the room, feeling her way along the walls, counting her steps. Approximately nine meters deep, five across. Empty of everything but dust. Empty because Marcus wanted it that way. He was a lying, manipulative psychopath, but he was a smart lying, manipulative psychopath. He'd chosen this place just for her. He must have prepared it well in advance of their departure.

A dry laugh came from her cracked lips. *He needs me, or I'd be dead.*

Again, she tried the CATO. Nothing. Again, she moved around the room, clockwise, then counterclockwise. The knife in her side prodded and poked. The dull shimmer of the overlay formed another wall, a translucent barrier between her and the *Chimera*. She thumped her skull with the flat of her palm for the hundredth time, trying to resurrect her dead spider. Nothing. No sparkles. No electric thoughts.

The cores started to cycle down, their whine transforming into a lower-pitched rumble. Down cycle. She pictured Theo leaving the sphere, others manning the substations, holding their place in fractal space. Her locked way, useless and alone. And as much as she didn't want to admit it, afraid. Nothing to do, nothing to overcome, nothing to fight against except the slide of the numbers on the clock.

* * *

Video location id=Statistics Room.
"Sorry, I know I'm being weird. Hang on, I have to throw up a network bubble. Now, look at this."
Private network detected. Video links=2. Streaming.
"I don't see anything. What are you trying to show us?"
"Wait, what *is* that? Is that a *hand*?"

* * *

Selena returned to the door and found her uniform top. She slumped against the wall, using it to guide her controlled fall. She imagined Theo riding the tram to the crosshatch. Marcus on the command deck, smiling his triumph to the opaque portal sealing out fractal space. Meghan at a substation. Heph beside her.

No, that wasn't right. Heph wasn't even an NA. And he wasn't at a substation, he was sitting somewhere else, along with Charlie and Meghan. She squinted at the sudden brightness, far more real than her fevered dreams of Kaylee. No matter how much she blinked her eyes, she still saw the faces and the room, broken out into three different images—

Three different point of views! She wasn't imagining it. The views swung in arcs, the movement of heads as they looked at one another. Meghan, Heph, Charlie.

She took an instinctive gulp of air and screamed. "Meghan! Can you hear me?"

Still there was no sound. But their faces were alight, eyes moving as if searching for something hidden in darkness.

* * *

"It's Selena. It has to be Selena!"
"Exactly! That's why I needed both of you to come with me."
"Where is this coming from? Is it Selena sending it?"
"I don't know. Everything I've seen so far is pretty dark, nothing to be seen. Not a lot to work with."
"Just a second, I saw something on the wall. I need to try to get back to it. Let me replay. Never mind. There it is again. She's just looking at it. There's a twelve on the wall."
"The *Chimera* must have found some way to send us a feed

from Selena's CATO."

"Do you think Selena knows we're getting her feed?"

"Maybe. She keeps looking at that twelve. It has to mean something, right?"

C_Grey=schematic access attempt. Blocked. Successful avoidance of detection=Y/N. Indeterminate.

"That's weird. I can't access ship schematics."

"Charlie!"

"What? Why are you yelling at me again?"

"Marcus is monitoring *everything*."

Location check=M_Locke. Command deck. Vitals check=Blocked.

"Sorry! Force of habit. I was going to search for all instances of twelve aboard the *Chimera*."

Vital check=C_Grey. Adrenal release. Forehead, neck perspiration. Embarrassment.

"Just be careful, okay? We have to figure out what to do next."

"Yeah. We have to send her a message, let her know we can see her."

"Hey, you two, look now!"

"Oh, I think she *definitely* knows we're watching!"

* * *

Meghan looked angry, Heph determined. Charlie was dancing around like a fool, his feed shaking and shimmying. All of them talking with great excitement. She could see it all through Preston's CATO.

Suddenly a fourth feed opened up. She could make out two feet tinged in yellow-green. An outlined door. A twelve marked above it. Selena raised her hand in front of her face. Saw a green ghost of a hand in the sea of black. Five fingers. A hand. Her own hand. They could see what she saw. They could see *her*.

A whoop exploded from Selena's throat. "Meghan!"

No response. They could see but not hear her. Maybe Preston's CATO had been damaged. Maybe whatever tricks *Chimera* had employed to share her feed with them were limited to video only. It didn't matter. They could see her. She could see them. She wasn't alone anymore.

She made a fist. Rocked it side to side. Meghan raised a fist.

Heph raised a fist, and Charlie, still dancing, raised a fist.

Megan's point of view slid over to a wallscreen where blocky green text read: *We're coming for you. Be ready.*

CHAPTER FORTY-TWO

Selena paced the room's perimeter, fingers brushing the duraceramic wall, eyes moving between the three point of views displayed on Preston's CATO overlay. In the upper right corner she saw Charlie's point of view, and in the upper left corner, Meghan's. They were in a utility locker in the crosshatch, shoving items into a backpack.

Heph's point of view filled the lower left corner of the overlay. His view swung from side to side at regular intervals. On guard, scanning the corridor, a human security camera. In the lower right corner the overlay contained her own point of view, her ghostly arm stretching into the deep shadow and pulsing blackness of her prison. They could see her and she could see them, but she couldn't do a text overlay, much less talk. Other than rudimentary hand gestures, she was silenced.

Meghan pulled a pair of aerocuffs from the locker and placed them in the backpack. Charlie shoved in lengths of dark graphene cable. What were they doing? Why didn't they just take the tram to the rear of the ship? This wasn't some expedition to the outer edges of the rim.

Heph's point of view locked to the side. A pair of crew members in dull gray uniforms approached from the far end of the corridor. As they drew near she saw their faces, warped a little by the steep angle of Heph's feed as he gazed down at them. Shelby Deng and Juniper Elcott. Juniper smiled at Heph and started chatting about something. Shelby stretched her neck, trying to look over Heph's shoulder. Heph stood taller, shifting to block the girl's view into the locker.

What was Marcus telling everyone? People had to be asking questions. Asking about where she was, about what had happened to Preston's eye. No way to keep that a secret.

Juniper and Shelby moved away from Heph, his feed steady on

their retreating backs. Shelby glanced back over her shoulder, eyes speculative. *Too long.* Selena knew a tattletale when she saw one. She was going to make trouble. Heph's hand went up in a small half-wave, friendly and benign, before the pair turned the corner and disappeared.

"Better hurry, guys." Even though it hurt her lungs, it felt good to talk. In the midst of the whine of the cores and the vibration eating its way through her flesh, the words connected her to the other end of the ship, where the *Chimera*'s other officers were preparing her rescue.

* * *

A priority ping hit Marcus' CATO, flashing in the lower right quadrant of his overlay. It was from Shelby Deng, a technician with shaggy brown hair and thick eyebrows.

He accepted the ping. "Yes?"

"Sorry to bother you, Captain, but I saw something strange a moment ago."

"What?"

Deng frowned. "Earlier, Specialist Elcott and I walked past the Breakage One utility locker. Officer Hart—Heph—was there."

"And?" Marcus asked. Deng's face slumped, her eyes diving down, having mistaken his prompt for more information as disapproval.

"It was weird … the way he was standing there. Like he was watching out for something. And then he blocked the door. At least, I think that's what he was doing. I mean he's a big guy, but it almost looked like he was trying to hide something. And I heard someone inside, but Heph told Elcott that he'd come down to there get away from his berth for a while."

"Deng?"

"Yes, sir?"

"I'm glad you brought this to my attention."

Deng flushed, eyes widening as she returned his smile. Amazing the power people gave things as meaningless as a simple gesture. He closed the ping and tried to pull up Heph's location. He found nothing. Heph had disappeared. He ran a search on all the crew, from himself on down. It wasn't just Heph missing, but Meghan and Charlie as well. According to the *Chimera*, they were no longer aboard the ship.

His pulse jumped, heart rushing to life. They'd finally made their move.

He fired off a CATO message to Nemus. *It's time.*

"Get out here," he commanded Theo.

Theo ducked through the opening of the sphere. "What's wrong?"

"Your friends are mounting a rescue attempt."

Marcus pulled up recorded imagery from the Breakage One utility lockers. He ran it backward at high speed until he saw Meghan, Heph, and Charlie speeding into the room, then back out of it. He paused the recording. Let it play forward. Rewound again.

Their CATO signatures had all gone dark within seconds of each other, but recordings still tracked them as they left the storage locker and headed for the tram. It had left seventeen minutes ago, heading for the aft of the ship. They'd gone to find Selena, not confront him on the command deck. That suited him fine. In fact, he preferred to deal with them at the rear of the ship. Then he wouldn't have to parade their bodies back through the crosshatch.

"They're going to free Selena," Marcus said.

"You don't sound very upset about it," Theo said, giving Marcus a strange look.

"That's because I'm not. I knew this would happen."

"So why'd you let it?"

"Because it simplifies things. Shows me who I can and can't trust. The crew needed a good distillation, and this is as good a time as any."

Nemus entered Command. "Drummond and Preston are waiting for us at the crosshatch tram station."

"Good," Marcus said. "Are they armed?"

"Yes."

"Armed?" Theo said, alarmed. "What exactly are you planning to do?"

"You're too smart to ask such stupid questions," Marcus said. "All my enemies are in a single location, well away from the crosshatch and the rest of the crew."

"You wanted this to happen!" Theo shouted. "You *planned* it.

And they're not 'enemies,' they're my friends."

"I plan for everything."

"You can't hurt them," Theo said. "I won't let you."

Pathetic. Could Theo really be so blind? He'd helped set this very thing in motion the moment he agreed to remove Selena.

"You didn't seem to mind hurting people when it meant you got to be the navigator," Marcus said. "Selena's been locked away for days and I haven't heard any complaints from you."

"This is different!" Theo shouted. "We removed her because we had to. But you *counted* on this. You wanted it to happen, prepared for it. You're ... you're evil," Theo said, as if the realization had just taken shape inside him. "You always were. I should never have trusted you."

"Evil is just a word," Marcus said. "It's another way of saying 'pragmatic.' I told you I would only do what I had to do, and that's what I am doing. If they get Selena out, we really will have a mutiny on our hands."

Theo surged forward, inches from Marcus' face. "You already do," he spat. "If you try to leave Command, I'll kill you right here with my bare hands."

CHAPTER FORTY-THREE

Nemus shifted his weight forward, keen eyes on Theo. Ready for a fight. Ready to come to Marcus' aid. Theo doubted he could handle both of them, but he would try. He'd hurt Marcus in the process. Slow him down. But what good would that do in the long run? He needed help.

Inches from Marcus, chests brushing, Theo looked into Marcus' ice-blue eyes, hatred crackling between them. Marcus wanted him to move first. Instead of attacking, Theo let his mind scan through the *Chimera*'s crew, searching for someone he could trust.

"Coward," Marcus said.

Theo almost smiled as he settled on Anthony Wells. The thick-chested cadet had run an entire team on the *Hydra*, but Marcus hadn't even offered him an officer's slot. Wells wouldn't stand for this. And Wells knew how to lead people.

[I need you at Command,] he messaged. *[Bring anyone you can trust to help. Marcus is about to do something terrible.]*

"I need you at command," Marcus said, pantomiming a whining child's voice. "Bring anyone you can trust to help."

Theo took a half-step back, breaking the tension between them. Marcus had read the private CATO message the instant Theo had sent it. Which meant he was monitoring Theo. When had that begun? *Since we stepped foot on the* Chimera.

"I am about to do something terrible," Marcus whispered.

"Want me to take care of this for you?" Nemus stepped forward, almost smiling.

"No," Marcus said. "Let Wells and whoever he wants to bring with him come."

"What about Samuelson?" Nemus asked.

"By the time anyone finds her and arrives back here, we'll be ready. We have plenty of time."

Theo waited for Marcus' attention to slip. If he could get him in a hold, or even better, choke him out—

Marcus seemed to read his thoughts. "You can't overpower me and Nemus, Theo, so don't be stupid. Your rescue party should be here soon," he said. "Let's wait for them arrive."

Nonplussed, Theo waited. Seconds slid past at an interminable pace.

"The tram is leaving the crosshatch," Nemus said. "I mark Wells, Nifali, and Johns." He chuckled. "That's some team. A whole lot of muscle."

"Shut up," Marcus snapped. "Don't say another word until I permit you to speak."

Minutes later, Anthony Wells skidded into the room, along with Kaylee Johns and Kerry Nifali, all three breathless from running.

"What's going on?" Wells asked. He eyed Marcus and Nemus. The two girls spread out to his left and right, feet planted in readiness.

"Why don't you explain?" Marcus said, looking at Theo. "Tell them anything you want. I won't stop you."

Theo scowled, but it wasn't like he had another plan outside following Marcus' suggestion. "We're not going to Earth. Marcus and I both believe we're better off trying Damascene first."

"Damascene?" Nifali said. "Nobody's heard from them in hundreds of years."

"That's not why I asked you to come," Theo said. "Selena's at the aft of the ship, locked away someplace. I don't know where. But Heph, Meghan, and Charlie are on their way there to try and find her. Marcus plans to stop them. He mentioned taking arms."

"What?" Wells said. "Are you serious?"

"Everything he's said is true," Marcus said, almost amicable. "They're going to jeopardize our one chance at survival. I will stop them using any means necessary."

"By hurting people?" Kaylee shouted. "None of us will stand for it."

"She's right," Theo said. "We're going to remove you from Command."

"Are you?" Marcus asked. "Have you checked the proper procedure? We have the navigator here, but if I recall, you need at least a junior flight officer to make things official."

"I'm here," Nifali said. "And I agree with Theo. You need to step down, at least until we sort this mess out."

"What a diplomat," Marcus said. "A very smart turn of phrase, Nifali. Leaving the door open for me to remain captain was a nice touch. You're a brilliant negotiator."

"He's screwing around and wasting time," Theo said, knowing it would come down to a fight. Hopefully the others would be enough help. He didn't expect much from Nifali, but Kaylee would hold her own. He looked at her, then Wells. Kaylee gave a subtle nod. She understood. Wells spread his feet wider and set his jaw. They were as ready as they were going to be.

"What are you waiting for?" Marcus smirked. "Are you going to fire up a legal proceeding or what?"

"You've got a lot to answer for," Wells said, voice calm. "And trust me, we will have some sort of formal—" Wells lunged for Marcus.

Theo leapt at Nemus. He caught a flurry of activity at his side and Kaylee was there, legs swinging to help bring Nemus down.

The loudest sound Theo had ever heard reverberated through Command. Theo stumbled, flailing arms grasping at Nemus. The sound rolled on inside his eardrums, becoming a roaring, high-pitched squeal. He heard screaming coming from a great distance away. Or from beneath water. Nemus fell under him, but Theo didn't try and subdue him, instead rolling off his body, rising to his knees, his feet.

Data points entered his mind, one at a time. Kaylee's face, frozen in a scream. Marcus holding something small and black. Wells sitting on the deck, breathing hard, crimson wetness blossoming across his chest. Nifali stumbling backward, trying to run but falling hard. Wells choking, slumping forward, blood leaking from his open mouth.

Theo moved forward. Marcus' eyes weighed him, calculating, evaluating. The pale-blue eyes blinked. "Come any closer and you're next."

Theo took another step.

"I can do this without you," Marcus said.

"I know," Theo said, still moving.

Marcus aimed the gun at Theo's leg. "You don't need knees to navigate."

Theo looked down, imagined his kneecap exploding. A blossom of blood and bone, his body toppling sideways. Wells' breathing slowed to shallow gasping, then fell silent. Theo's eyes burned, his insides too. His heart had a life of its own, whumping away inside his chest, pumping blood, keeping his muscles oxygenated. All that could end. In an instant. The world could go red, then black. Then nothing at all.

"You're going to wait here with Nifali and Johns until I get back," Marcus said.

"Why should I?" He would join Wells, a lifeless pile of limbs.

"Because if you obey me, I'll let Selena live."

"You're a liar," Theo said, words trembling in cadence with his body. "And a murderer."

Marcus dropped next to Wells. He'd toppled to the side, motionless. His blood was spreading across the white deck. Marcus touched Wells' neck a moment, his own head tilted down, reverent almost, as if in prayer. "This is what happens to people who challenge my command."

The smell of blood and bile stung Theo's nostrils as he stared down at the body that used to be a person named Anthony Wells.

"Archer!" Marcus shouted.

"Yes … yes, sir?"

"We're leaving. Preston and Drummond will meet us at the security lockers."

Nemus' eyes moved hungrily over Wells' body, as if he were anticipating more carnage and very much looking forward to it. "Got it."

Marcus looked at Theo. "I meant what I said. Stay here and hold our position and I'll let her live. Leave Command and I'll make sure she suffers. The choice is yours."

CHAPTER FORTY-FOUR

The shimmering overlay of Prestons' CATO disappeared and a thick, obscuring blanket of darkness enveloped Selena. She jumped, blinking into a black tinged with gold—the afterimages of the absent CATO feeds. She'd lost them all. Meghan, Heph, Charlie. Maybe Preston's CATO had finally died? No, she could still see the dim outline of the feed coming from her CATO—her torso, a dirty uniform, the murky shape of her feet.

Then the whine of the cores dissipated, the oscillations vibrating through the deck beneath her feet slowing to a gentle rhythm. Why had they gone into a down cycle? It wasn't time yet. Hours remained before a shift change. Maybe Marcus had figured out what was going on. Her jitters transformed into full-blown anxiety. Maybe Marcus had caught Meghan and the others. Maybe he'd taken the *Chimera* into a down cycle to deal with them.

Sealed in near total darkness, Selena waited for something to happen, hands gripping the door frame. Holding it up. Holding herself up. So that she would still know which direction was up. Her chest burned with every strained breath. *Hurry*, she thought. *You've got to hurry.*

A muffled thumping came from behind the door. Then three fast taps, a pause, and three more. Selena jerked, smacking her palm against the door, repeating the pattern. Three taps came in reply, then silence. Selena pounded the door with a tight fist. No answer. She struck it again, each blow fueled by the desperation for this to end, one way or the other. To be done. She wanted out of the darkness, the aloneness.

"Where are you?" she screamed at the door. "Didn't you hear me? I'm in here! I'm in here!"

She pressed her forehead into the cold surface. If someone had been there, they'd left. They hadn't heard her. Heph and the others had failed. Maybe Marcus had killed them. Now he would kill her—

The door made a metallic, tearing sound and slid sideways a half-centimeter. Selena pressed her face against the slit, shouting Heph's name, Meghan's name, sucking at the flow of fresh of air seeping through the gap.

The door shifted, duraceramic squealing against metal. It opened wide enough to let in a beam of light that struck her in the face, blinding her good eye, the one that could see between a fattened eyelid. She shoved her fingers through the crack, not caring who was on the other side, only wanting out, to be free. A hand closed around hers.

"Oh my god! Selena!" Meghan cried. "Hang on!"

Several pairs of hands gripped the door, forcing the mechanism. It screeched sideways, opening wide enough for Selena to scramble through. Meghan's arms wrapped around her, too tight. It hurt her ribs and Selena yelped, but her arms wouldn't let go when Meghan tried to pull away. Heph stood back, face heavy with relief.

Meghan leaned away, taking in Selena's face and shoulders. "Look what they did to you," she breathed. "I can't believe it. I mean I should have known, but …"

"Water?" Selena croaked.

"Right here," Heph said, offering her a drinking bulb.

Meghan handed her a pill. "And take this—it will help with the swelling."

Selena wet her mouth, popped in the pill, and swallowed. She clutched the drinking bulb, gulping the rest of the water. It felt wonderful and tasted even better. Clean and cold.

Selena tried to smile. "Where's Charlie?" She turned her head, but the slit of her swollen-eyed vision afforded only a narrow cone, hazy at the edges.

"Keeping guard at the end of the passage," Meghan said. With gentle hands, Meghan placed something against her face, so hot it felt like it might burn her.

"ReadySkin," Meghan said.

"Have you got any more of it?" Selena said. "I've got cracked ribs."

Meghan gingerly pulled up Selena's uniform top and grimaced at what she saw. "You're going to need better care than I can give you," she said. "We'll find Kaylee back at the crosshatch. She'll know what to do."

The pain in her chest had already lessened and her eye had opened enough that she could see clearly. Meghan's worried, oval face hovered in front of Selena. A sweaty ponytail hung over one shoulder. Her wrinkled uniform jacket hung open to reveal a white undershirt, the crescents of her rank peeking from under folded over lapels.

Selena grinned. "You look like shit."

"Not as bad as you."

"You should see the other guy."

Heph grimaced. "I did see him. Remind me never to mess with you."

Selena looked from Meghan to Heph. "Thanks for coming for me."

"You're our navigator," Heph said. The respect in his voice made the pain in her chest a little more bearable. She ran her hands over her face, over the hardening ReadySkin on her forehead and cheeks. Heph was right. She was the navigator. She had a job to do, and she was going to do it.

"Are your CATOs working?" Selena asked.

"We removed them so that no one could track us," Heph replied.

"Marcus," Selena said, voice full of pure malice. "He and Theo aren't taking us to Earth."

"They're not?" Meghan said, stunned.

"No. Marcus told me that when he removed me."

Heph's thick eyebrows clumped together. "Where are they trying to go?"

"I have no idea."

"He told us *you* took us off course," Heph said through a deep scowl.

"Of course he did," Selena said. "Everything that leaves his mouth is a lie."

Meghan looked up the passage. "He's going to come for us. Along with Nemus and anyone else he can control."

"I think they're already on their way," Selena said. "The ship went into down cycle early."

"We should get back to the crosshatch," Heph said. "We'll tell everyone what Marcus is up to. We can confront him. Make him pay."

Selena shook her head. "We'll never make it. Marcus will use the tramline as a chokepoint. We can't fight our way past him."

"I already thought of that," Meghan said. "I was planning to use the service interconnects to get back. It means some crawling and climbing, but it's our best chance. It would take them forever to find us in there."

"It might take them hours to find us, but it will also take us hours to get back." Selena frowned. "And with no CATOs we'll be stuck using the panel maps. It'll take too long."

"What, then? Sit back here and wait for him to attack us?" Heph asked.

"Not a chance. Remember how they built VAST? How they powered it?" Selena asked.

"The secondary sphere," Meghan breathed.

"That's right. We can use it to take control of the ship. And it's a secure location with only one access point. We can hole up there and make sure we arrive where we're supposed to."

"And you can use the sphere to tell everyone what's going on," Meghan added.

Selena nodded, avoiding Meghan's gaze. No CATO, no spider—would she have a connection? *Just get to the sphere and worry about it later.*

"We really should rejoin Charlie," Heph said. "Don't want him to wet his pants."

Selena's eyes fell on Heph's rucksack. "Did you bring any weapons?"

"Not really. We couldn't get to the security lockers, but we grabbed everything we could from the lockers at Breakage One."

Meghan opened her pack and indicated the collection of items. Several pairs of aerocuffs, emergency strobes, graphene cables, medical kits, hand tools, a micro welder. Selena evaluated. It could be worse. It could also be a hell of a lot better. But a lifetime aboard a trawler with limited resources for repairs had taught her that sometimes you could do a whole lot with a little.

"It'll have to do," Selena said.

Heph frowned. "So we get to the sphere and you take control of the ship—what will happen if Theo's in the forward sphere?"

Selena gave a harsh laugh. "Easy. He won't know what hit

him."

CHAPTER FORTY-FIVE

Charlie broke into a wide grin. He opened both arms and in spite of herself Selena let him pull her close. "Watch it, Charlie. I have broken ribs."

"Oh! Sorry." He released her and she gave him an awkward pat on the arm, pretending not to notice the tears welling in the corners of his eyes. "I'm just glad you're okay ... more or less." His eyes hardened. "Marcus will pay for the damage."

"It was Nemus and Preston that did the worst of it," Selena said.

"Then we'll make them pay too," Charlie said. Selena met his gaze, a moment of understanding moving between them like current.

"What now?" Charlie asked. "Are we going to the sphere to kick Marcus' butt?"

Meghan shook her head. "I'd love to, but Selena has a better plan."

"Thanks, Captain," Selena said.

"Captain?" Meghan said, taken aback.

"You seriously hadn't thought about that? You're second in command. Marcus isn't fit to command a refuse barge, much less a colony ship." Selena grinned. "That means you're the new captain."

"She's right," Heph said. "Someone has to take the job and you're the obvious choice."

Meghan looked equal parts embarrassed and pleased. "It's a little early for all that. We can talk about crew positions *after* we've secured the secondary sphere and taken down Marcus."

"Secondary sphere?" Charlie said. "I forgot all about that place. That's brilliant!"

"Glad you approve," Selena said. "Now come on—we don't have time to waste."

The entry to the secondary sphere was exactly as Selena remembered it, the corners of the door peeling and dry. The smaller, half-size deck felt confined in comparison to Main Command. Nav terminals huddled around the sphere. Yellowed patches of discoloration marked the walls. An overall ugliness and neglect exacerbated by that fact that some of the overheads had failed, casting everything in muddy half-light.

"Here we go," Selena said. "Everything's functional as far as I know. At least, it was when I came here with Theo the last time."

"This is the secondary sphere?" Charlie said, incredulous. "It's like a super ugly office for ghosts—one where everyone that worked in it died from depression or boredom. All it needs is a hot drinks station against the wall."

"I don't care what it looks like as long as it's functional," Selena said, wondering if she was functional herself. *No spider. No CATO. A head full of unsecured cargo and a chest full of cracked ribs.* She shoved her doubts away and ran a hand over the nearest terminal. The interface came up, enveloping her fingers in a lattice of glowing light.

"That's a good sign," Meghan said. She sat at the nearest terminal and the seat slid forward, the station behind it powering up. She glanced over her shoulder. "Heph? Let's get to it," she said, the order unmistakable. "Charlie, keep guard while we sort things."

Selena entered the secondary sphere, feeling the faint trace of energy against her fingertips. She breathed out, releasing her unspoken fear. It wasn't like it had been before they broke Salix. She felt *Chimera*, a moving, living presence. Reachable.

[Chimera.]

[Hello, Navigator.]

The image solidified and Selena smiled. *[Thank you for helping save me.]*

[You are still in jeopardy, as is our mission. Marcus and Theo do not intend to take us to Earth.]

"Hang on," Selena said. "I want the others to hear this."

"Hear what?" Meghan asked.

"Come over here and I'll let the *Chimera* tell you." Heph, Charlie, and Meghan crowded around the entry to the sphere.

"Go ahead, *Chimera*," Selena said.

"Marcus intends to bypass Earth and bring us to Damascene instead."

"Damascene?" Selena asked. "Wasn't that some kind of science colony?"

"You don't know about Damascene?" Charlie asked. "It's

practically legend! Just like the *Helios*, lost to fractal space. Haven't you seen *Zero Point Entry?*"

"I had better things to do at the rim than watch vids," Selena said, a little embarrassed by the holes in her education. Liam hadn't prioritized learning much of anything other than how to operate an ore trawler.

"Damascene was Earth's first colony," the *Chimera* said. "The *Helios*, the first of my kind, was lost to fractal space en route there. Earth took another fifty-one years to build a second colony ship, *Ceres*. She left for Damascene with a full complement of colonists several hundred years before my creation."

"It wasn't a corporate colony like Stephen's Point," Heph added. "They were sent by the Eastern Block Asiatic States before the Last War and the unification of nations under corporate charter."

"That is correct," the *Chimera* said. "They were a dual purpose colony, intended to test new terraforming methods and to extract ecomire from the planet to fuel further expansion."

"So they're a free colony?" Selena asked.

"They're not a colony at all," Meghan said. "They went dark soon after The Last War."

"Has anyone been there since?"

"We do not know," *Chimera* said. "Earth has provided no details on colonization efforts since our arrival at Stephen's Point."

"They kept us in the dark on purpose," Selena said. "They didn't want us getting any ideas. For all we know, they've got a bunch more colonies spread through the galaxy that we know nothing about."

"That is unlikely," the *Chimera* said. "Finding suitable colony locations has proven difficult, and the journey to reach them even more so. Fractal travel is both perilous and expensive. Human expansion through the galaxy has moved far slower than once predicted, in large part due to the instability of fractal travel. Tens of thousands of shipboard AI templates were developed and then cast aside before I was selected." Selena detected a note of pride in the *Chimera*'s voice.

"All of this is very interesting," Selena said, "but we've got more important things to talk about. We need to install a new captain."

"In the event that the captain cannot continue in their role for physical or mental health reasons, or because of gross negligence and dereliction of duty, then the flight officer will take over as acting captain until the proper channels can be reached for the appointment of a new captain," the *Chimera* said.

"Mental health reasons," Charlie said, laughing. "Sounds about right."

"He's out of his mind to take us to Damascene," Meghan said.

Selena paused, frowning. "Unless he knows something we don't."

"What could he possibly know?" Heph asked.

"What happened at Earth," Selena said.

"They have no more information than we do," the *Chimera* said. "They have simply interpreted it differently."

"That's a generous way to put it," Meghan said. "They're disobeying direct orders from Moorland. And I can tell you why, too. Marcus is a coward. He doesn't have the backbone to do what needs done when we reach Earth."

"But you do," Selena said. "And that's why you're going to be our new captain."

Heph clasped Meghan's shoulders. "You should have been captain all along anyway.

"That's right," Charlie said. "Moorland made a huge mistake with Marcus."

"He conned her," Selena said. "He's good at fooling people. But now we all know the truth. And it's up to us to stop him." Selena directed her attention to the *Chimera.* "What do we need to do to make things official?"

"Are you willing to be named captain?" the *Chimera* asked Meghan.

"I am."

Through the sphere, Selena felt the warmth of the *Chimera*'s welcome before her voice filled secondary command. "Welcome, Captain Ziczek."

"Thank you, *Chimera*," Meghan said, face glowing. She looked from Selena to Charlie and Heph. "I won't let you down," she said. "I promise."

* * *

The ringing in Marcus' ears lessened to a dull droning. Anthony Wells lay dead at his feet. Kaylee sat nearby, sobbing. The projectile gun, still warm from being fired, felt like the natural extension of his arm. He could point and kill anyone. Including Theo.

"Get in the sphere," he said.

Theo looked at him but didn't move.

Marcus' finger tightened on the projectile gun's trigger. "Don't test me," he whispered.

The deck beneath his feet began to hum. A subtle, almost imperceptible shift in vibration. Confusion spread across Theo's face. "How ..."

"We're moving again," Nifali said. "How is that possible?"

Keeping the gun leveled at Theo's chest, Marcus skirted Wells' body and approached the sphere. The *Chimera* was doing this. She'd found some way around her protocols. He stepped into the sphere and shoved his free hand against the dimpled wall. The *Chimera* appeared in front of him. That ugly face, dark hair, stupid dark-brown eyes.

[What are you doing?]

The *Chimera*'s face remained neutral. *[Completing my mission.]*

Marcus slammed his fist into the side of the sphere. Skin tore on his knuckles, smearing blood. Impotent fury coursed through him. He couldn't touch her, couldn't reach her to choke that insolent *nothing* off her fake face.

"I command you to stop," Marcus said.

"You are not the captain."

The finality in her words stopped him cold. He looked past the *Chimera*, feeling in that non-space within the sphere, and locating a familiar presence. *Selena.* Somehow, some way, she'd joined the *Chimera*.

Marcus swore as realization hit. *The secondary sphere.* He'd overlooked it. In all his planning, all the scenarios he'd envisioned, he'd ignored a crucial variable. Rage overcame him. He beat at the sphere with his bare hand, blood splattering the walls. He could sense Earth at the end of Stephen's thread. The *Chimera* was closing in on her destination, destroying his future. His teeth ground together.

"If you take us to Earth, you're done!" Marcus screamed. "I promise you. If whatever's there doesn't kill you, I will. I'll gut you. Shred you. I don't care how long it takes or what I have to do to make it happen. I don't make promises often or lightly, but I promise that to you. I promise it."

Marcus lashed at her with raw will. He lashed at her through the sphere like he had lashed at Selena in the *Helvictus*. He struck with the venom-edge of his mind, wanting to punish, to cripple, to wound. She bore his onslaught, staring at him with those inhuman-human eyes. Devoid of humanity. Devoid of fear.

[Are you done?] Chimera asked.

No. He wasn't done. Not with her. Not with Selena. Not with Heph and Meghan and anyone who'd helped them. The growl that came from between his gritted teeth filled the command deck as Marcus looked into The Everything. In its midst, he saw himself. He saw madness. He saw the will to power a future of his own creation, every thread tied, every question answered. He saw the end of all things, entropy played out over billions of years. A total dark. All light obliterated. A great nothing gaping wide to swallow him whole.

He fled the sphere, shoving the sweaty hair out of his eyes, gun swinging in wild arcs from Theo to Nifali and back again.

"Archer, you're with me," he said. "We're going to end this." He plunged out of Command, Nemus at his heels, racing to the tram. He still had time. He would stop them before they reached Earth. He would retake control of his ship. And most important of all, he would kill Selena Samuelson.

* * *

Theo stepped into the sphere. Placed his hands against the walls.

Selena.

No answer.

The duraceramic felt cool under his hands, the *Chimera* moving forward in the wrapping bands of fractal. The sphere's white interface remained empty. Where was *Chimera*? He reached out again.

[I know you can hear me,] he said to *Chimera*. To Selena.

A figure appeared, walked forward.

[Hello, Theo.]

[Selena.]

They looked at one another, eyes sparring, neither willing to settle on the other. His first thought was that Selena didn't *look* injured. But of course she wouldn't—not in this virtual environment.

[Are Heph and Meghan and Charlie with you? Everybody okay?]

Selena's eyes hardened. [*Why should I tell you?]*

[Because they—and you—are my friends. Marcus shot Anthony Wells. Anthony's dead, Selena. Marcus is coming for you next. He's on the tram right this minute.]

Selena smiled. [*No, he's walking.]*

Theo understood.

[You shut down the tram.]

[Of course.]

[That's a pretty short-term solution. What weapons did Meghan and Heph bring?]

Something flickered behind Selena's eyes. Was it possible they didn't have weapons? Meghan wasn't that foolish.

[Tell me you have guns, Selena. Stun packs. Something.]

No response.

[How are you protecting yourselves?]

Selena looked away. *[Heph and Charlie are barricading the door.]*

His mind raced. Barricading the door? [*With what?]*

[You've been back here. There's stuff lying all over.]

[Yeah, but it's just junk. Station desks, chairs, stuff like that. Marcus will get through that in a second.]

[I'm not afraid of him.]

[You should be.] Theo clenched his teeth. *[Just let me think. Have you looked in any of the old lockers back there? Maybe there's something that could be used?]*

Selena didn't answer.

[Selena!]

She snapped back into focus.

[I'm navigating, Theo. This is hard. I can't keep talking to you.]

[Listen. Just listen to me. Marcus told me that if I did what he said, he wouldn't kill you. I believe him. He needs you because Chimera *needs you. You have no way to defend yourself or the secondary sphere. You should stand down.]*

[So Marcus said he wouldn't kill me. Where does that leave Meghan and Heph and Charlie? Did he say he wouldn't kill them?]

[No, but what incentive does he have to kill them? He needs them. On some level, the ship needs everyone.] The pounding of

Theo's heart threatened to drown his thoughts. [*Marcus needs all of us to function.*]

[*What about Wells? Did Marcus need* him?]

Selena's last syllable caught, repeating in a long, humming *em* sound. Her image disappeared, reappeared.

[*Navigating is not the best option right now, Selena! Put us in stasis. I only got into the sphere to warn you. I'm going back to the crosshatch with Kaylee and Kerry. We'll get help. Stand down! Tell Marcus that you talked to me. What's he going to do at the rear sphere? He won't stay there. He'll come back to Command. When he does, I'll be ready to meet him.*]

[*None of that matters to my mission, Theo. We're going to Earth. My captain is here and I have my orders.*]

He realized she was talking about Meghan.

[*Okay, tell Meghan what I said.*]

[*Already did.*] Selena's eyes shuttered down to slits. [*We don't trust you, Theo.*]

He couldn't blame her. Or Meghan. What had he done to earn anyone's trust? He'd aligned himself with Marcus. Let his anger rule him. Anger at Selena, at *Chimera.* Over not being *chosen.*

[*I know you have no reason to trust me, Selena. I'm sorry about that. But—*]

Selena raised her hand, cutting him off. [*One question. Say I stand down and Marcus brings us back. Then somehow you and whoever stop him. What then? Would you still try to take us to Damascene?*]

His thoughts halted. Of course he would. His gut said Marcus was right: there was nothing for them at Earth. Damascene hadn't sent a box of dead people to Stephen's Point.

[*You don't have to answer. I can see it on your face. I can see your cores cycling, trying to decide what to tell me.*]

[*Look, I know Marcus is evil. And crazy. I hate him. When I find him, I'll deal with him myself. But he's not stupid, Selena. There's no reason to go to Earth—they're in worse shape than we are based on Exchange Four. You saw the bodies yourself. Some of them little kids. You saw it. And Moorland armed the ship with nukes. She's sending us on a one-way trip, one that I don't want to make. Neither should you. We have a better option. Damascene. We can catch the thread without ever leaving fractal space.]*

[Whatever, Theo.]

[Please don't make me force you.]

Selena laughed, harsh and ugly. [*How will you force me, Theo?]*

[I'm only trying to save us. I'm doing what I think is best.]

Theo reached for *Chimera.* He felt her edging away from him, hiding. Selena jerked, head shaking, fighting against him in concert with *Chimera.* He dragged them forward. *Chimera* appeared, a hand—Theo's hand—wrapped around her forearm.

[Thank you for joining us, Chimera.] He focused his will. [*We are not going to Earth. We are going to Damascene, and you will—]*

Selena snorted, a mocking sound. He looked away from *Chimera,* eyes searching for Selena. A laugh came from above him and he tilted his head to see her, rising above. She picked up speed, like a rocket out of Nadil.

[Selena!]

Her voice reached him softly, as close to him as it had ever been. [*I have more important things to do than talk to you.]*

A whirlwind of snow enveloped him, disintegrating in brilliant static. And then there was nothing. Nothing to see, nothing to feel. Not a sound or a shred of light anywhere, and no goodbye. Only a dead white sphere, the walls smudged with dirt and blood.

CHAPTER FORTY-SIX

Marcus' CATO wouldn't connect. A single scrolling message ran across his overlay:

[You are not the captain. You are not the captain. You are not the captain.]

Marcus peeled back his eyelid and removed the lens. He flicked it to the floor of the tram and ground it beneath his heel. He wouldn't let the *Chimera* taunt him.

"Take yours out too," Marcus said to Nemus.

"How are we going to communicate with Preston and Drummond?"

"They know where we're meeting. And I don't want the *Chimera* tracking us."

Nemus crushed his CATO lens in his fist and tossed it away. "Waste of a good CATO. Those things are precious."

"We'll get replacements from storage once we've re-established order."

His rage had finally subsided back into cool purposefulness. It would take Selena hours to reach Earth. Long enough for him to stop her. And then he'd take them to Damascene himself if he had to.

The lights in the tram went dark.

"What the hell?" Nemus said.

The tram slowed and then stopped. Marcus almost smiled. "They killed the power." *I would have done the same thing.* He left his seat, located the manual emergency release for the tram doors and yanked it sideways. The doors slid wide. Leaning out of the car, he reached with his foot until it touched the narrow catwalk that ran alongside the magrail, then jumped across the gap. He sidestepped along the catwalk, using his hands to guide his way. When he reached the end of the dead tram, he leapt down into the darkened tunnel.

Nemus landed beside him with a *thud*. "We can jog to the

crosshatch in no time."

Marcus shook his head. "No, they might send the tram after us once we're a ways up the tunnel. Try and crush us. We'll stick to the catwalk."

They climbed back up and made their way forward in the semi-darkness. Ahead, the greenish lights of the crosshatch tram station glowed. The fear, the risk of failure, of death—Marcus realized that on some primal level he was enjoying himself. But not as much as he would when he put a bullet in Selena's head. The delicious anticipation of seeing her dead body drove him on, as fast as the catwalk would allow, until he reached the station.

Climbing the ladder that led up to the platform, he found Drummond and Preston standing at its edge, craning their heads to look down the tramline. A black rucksack lay at their feet. Marcus approached from their blind side, his footfalls silent.

"He's not coming," Preston said. "Something bad happened up there."

"Who's not coming?" Marcus asked.

Preston and Drummond whirled to face him. "Holy shit! Where'd you come from?" Drummond asked.

"We had to hoof it," Nemus explained. "The tram's dead."

"We figured as much," Drummond said.

"Selena killed it. She's holed up at the secondary sphere, taking us to Earth."

"Not good," Drummond said.

"Which is why we're going to go stop her. Did you bring everything on my list?"

Drummond bumped the rucksack with the tip of his boot. "Right here."

"What happened at Command?" Preston asked. "There's a lot of rumors going around—I heard Wells and some other people went up there."

Preston had lost his nerve after losing his eye. He wouldn't make a capable attacker, but Marcus had a purpose in mind for him all the same.

"Wells is dead," Nemus said. "Marcus shot him."

"Shot him?" Preston asked, shock widening his remaining eye. He looked almost comical, cheeks puffed, a dark eye-patch over his fleshy, pink face.

"He disobeyed a direct order," Marcus said. "And this is my

ship."

Preston swallowed. "About that …"

Marcus started at Preston, waiting for him to spit the rest out.

"We got some weird CATO message from the *Chimera*. She said Meghan is the captain."

Marcus laughed. "We'll see about that." He lifted the rucksack and slung it over his shoulder. "Both of you take out your CATOs. The *Chimera* will warn those traitors that we're on our way, but we can stop her from tracking our every move."

* * *

Inside the secondary sphere, the *Chimera*'s worried face appeared in front of Selena. [*Marcus is on the move,*] *Chimera* said. [*He, Drummond, Nemus, and Preston have removed their CATOs to stop me from tracking them. I lost the ability to observe them after they left the crosshatch. The technicians never repaired the monitoring cameras in the rear of the ship.*]

Selena took a deep breath to steady her nerves. [*How much time do we have?*]

[*I cannot be certain.*]

[*Enough to reach Earth?*]

[*That is indeterminate.*]

Selena flexed her hands, trying to drive the stiffness away. Meghan had stretched strips of ReadySkin around her chest and while they helped her breath easier, they couldn't repair fractured ribs. Everything was about to go seriously sideways, and there wasn't much she could do about it.

[*We need to go faster,*] Selena said, unsure if that was even possible. Nothing in fractal space worked the way she thought it should. If she wanted to accelerate in a trawler, she simply punched the throttle and layered on speed. Things weren't so simple in fractal space. Yet Theo had managed to move them far faster every time he served as an NA. How had he done it? She could have asked him if she didn't hate his guts. If she hadn't forced him out of the forward sphere. That had felt good, but it hadn't brought them one second closer to Earth.

[*We move at the speed of the navigator,*] *Chimera* said.

[*How did Theo speed us up so much? What was he doing that I'm not?*]

[*He took more of The Everything into himself, a choice that comes with certain consequences.]*

[What consequences?]

[I selected you as my navigator because you are capable of restraint, of holding part of yourself back. Fractal space cannot take anything from you that you do not give by choice.]

Outside the sphere, Meghan and Charlie sat at substations, helping her manage the paradox load. Heph crouched beside the single closed door, a mini-welder gripped in one hand, an emergency strobe in the other. Aerocuffs flashed silver on his wrists.

[What about Stephen?] Selena asked. *[Could he hold a part of himself back?]*

[He could and could not.]

[Like a paradox?]

[Yes, like a paradox,] the *Chimera* said.

[Is that what happened to him? He gave too much?]

[That is possible. I cannot know with certainty.]

Meghan peered into the sphere, interrupting Selena's silent conversation with the ship.

"You okay in there?"

"Other than the fact that Marcus is on his way to try and kill us? Yeah, I'm fine and dandy."

Meghan checked the tightness of the aerocuffs circling her wrists. "Let him come," she said, voice fierce. "We're ready for him."

Why had she ever doubted this girl? Disliked her? Selena touched Meghan's arm and Meghan flashed a smile before returning to her place at the substation.

[If Marcus succeeds, we'll never get to Earth,] Selena said. *[He'll take us to Damascene. Or someplace else. Who knows what's true and what's a lie when it comes to him? But we've got to get to Earth before he attacks us; it's the only for sure way to guarantee we make it there.]*

[That is a valid assessment,] Chimera agreed.

[Then help me. Show me how to give myself to fractal space. Theo could do it. You said that's why you didn't choose him. Is it because you didn't want him to end up like Stephen?]

[Fractal space would have swallowed him,] Chimera said. [He

is unrestrained.]

    [Show me what to do. Show me how to move us faster.]

    Fear filled the *Chimera*'s eyes. *[My job is to protect you.]*

    Selena thought of Liam. Showed the *Chimera* her father, asleep in his hammock, sleeping off another of his benders. Showed her the crash. Liam's swollen face recorded from his hospital room on Stephen's Point. His final words to her: *You always were special. Always.*

    [I can do it,] Selena said. *[If you help me, I can do it.]*

    The *Chimera* wavered.

    [Show me,] Selena demanded.

    [I will show you Earth,] the *Chimera* replied.

    Soft, rolling mountains covered in fog appeared. Lines of trees stretching high into the air, the air redolent with the spice of pine pitch. Fields of a green that seemed lit from within by their very aliveness. Selena ran. Her feet flew over damp or dry ground, rocky or sandy, never quite touching. How could something this beautiful be dangerous? Surely the *Chimera* was wrong.

    Selena *felt* Earth out at the end of Stephen's thread. Stronger than before. Like a gravity well sucking her down … she remembered the first time she'd seen Earth in the VAST simulator. The nausea that came as she drove the Shellback through Earth's atmosphere. Of Ortiz' haunted eyes as he came out of VAST. *The burning world.* That's what he'd said. The *Chimera*'s fear-tinged dreams filling his mind.

    Selena felt that version of Earth as well. The *Chimera*'s nightmare. Her home obliterated. Fear and hope circling one another. Yin and Yang. Like The Everything itself. A paradox. A balance.

    Selena's eyes were closed. Her eyes were open. She held the *Chimera*'s hand, and together they held The Everything. Seconds or minutes or hours passed. Fractal space whirled around her as Selena followed Stephen's thread. Each second their speed increased. Earth drew near.

    The grass parts. The pathway opens.

    A white flash. Was it time to leave fractal space? No. Not yet. Too soon.

    A wall of brilliant light threatened to dissolve her. She lost her connection to the *Chimera*, her body slammed to the deck. Her ears rang. She tried to stand, but the deck leapt and bucked beneath her.

A heavy pulse of air rushed past. Projectiles zinged, glancing off duraceramic. She felt the thumps as they lodged into walls or the sphere or flesh. An arm wrapped around her middle and lifted her, pulling her back behind the sphere. Meghan shouted something into Selena's face. Rivulets of blood ran from Meghan's nose and ears. The flesh on one side of her neck was burned, one eyebrow singed away. What was it she was saying? Selena tried to concentrate, Meghan's face zooming in and out.

"Stay down! Stay *down!*"

The air filled with the rapid *pop pop* of projectile guns and smoke, so much smoke. Heph fired his aerocuffs, launching a body backward into a wall. The mini welder spurted yellow-red fire. Charlie dove behind a substation, hiding from the gunfire. The main lights went out, leaving Heph's welder as the only source of light, a glowing, angry eye. Shadows arched and writhed. Meghan's body pinned her to the ground. Selena struggled to sit up, straining to reenter the sphere. They'd come so close to Earth … she only needed a few more minutes to bring them out of fractal.

"Stay here," Meghan hissed into her ear. Then the weight and heat disappeared, Meghan scurrying forward into the sphere.

Another white flash burned with the blinding brilliance of a lightning storm, the concussion of the blast flattening Selena. She fell again and tasted iron. Blood gushed from her nose. She couldn't see the sphere through the intense light sparking and jolting in the center of the room.

Heph dove, using his aerocuffs to drive himself forward, feet ramming into someone's face. Through the haze, she saw Meghan in the sphere, turning to look at a gaping hole blown through the door of Secondary Command. Through it came Marcus, squinting in the smoke. He raised a projectile gun. His eyes locked on the sphere, on the dark-haired girl inside it.

Selena screamed.

CHAPTER FORTY-SEVEN

It had taken some chemistry to find a workable solution to blasting through the door to the secondary sphere. Welding fuel pressurized in a solvent sprayer ignited with a projectile round primer—a crude but effective device. Sealing it to the door with medical tape and triggering it with a well-aimed gunshot, the result had been spectacular. A shaped charge, all the energy was directed into the door, crumpling it inward, sending chunks of steel flying. Pressurized air slammed into the room, disrupting the fluid in their inner ears, destroying all sense of balance. The shrapnel alone might have killed or injured a few of them. But not the girl inside the sphere, Marcus hoped. He wanted her to see his face when she died.

He shoved Preston through the opening with the muzzle of his pistol seconds after the blast. Urine wetted Preston's pants leg, but the fear of the unknown ahead of him wasn't as great as the fear of what Marcus would do if he didn't move. Almost as disoriented by the blast as those inside the room, Preston fired wildly into the smoke. Marcus didn't need him to hit anything, only to keep moving forward, to reveal where the defenders had taken up their positions.

A blast of air knocked Preston off his feet, sending him flying into a bulkhead. Marcus traced the locations of the blast and lobbed in the second improvised device, this one made of powdered aluminum painstakingly filed from a set of carabineer hooks and potassium percolate removed from an emergency chem light. The mixture created a hot and bright explosion, brilliant enough to blind eyes.

Marcus counted to three, and then charged forward, directing Nemus and Drummond in front of him to absorb an attack coming from the inside wall of the door, assuming any of the defenders had the presence of mind to take that position after the first blast.

The second device detonated, showering white-hot aluminum sparks through the room. Someone screamed. Though his face was covered by a protective regulator face plate, the brightness of the blast still seared through Marcus' lids. The moment it started to recede, he blinked his eyes open and raised his projectile gun.

Heph rose from behind a substation, a mini welder in hand. Fire spewed toward Nemus, engulfing him. Drummond dove out of the fire's path. Another blast of air *whooshed* over Drummond, followed by someone—*Charlie Grey*—launching forward to tackle Drummond. Both crashed to the ground, a writhing pile of punching and kicking limbs.

Marcus held back, marking the location of the combatants. When he felt sure he wasn't stepping into a trap, he came through the smoldering hole in the door. Moving parallel to the wall, he gained line of sight on the sphere's opening. Inside he saw Selena, her back turned to him. One side of her neck was pink and welted from burns. He didn't hesitate. The gun grew warm and then hot as he repeatedly pulled the trigger, tracking Selena's body as it fell, leaving nothing to chance.

His vision cleared of its singular, obsessive focus. He felt no relief. No rage. Nothing. The world rushed into focus—the flames crackling on the floor, the heat, the smell of hot metal and burned flesh. Drummond groaning as he crawled away from Charlie's prone body. Nemus lay still, uniform blackened, sightless eyes staring upward out of a skull-like face. Heph limped toward Marcus, aerocuff raised, but too far away to fire with any meaningful effect.

Marcus aimed the gun at the space between Heph's eyes, waiting for him to get close enough to ensure he didn't miss. Then, behind Heph, he saw her. Weaving like a drunkard, a slender, dark-haired girl entering the sphere. Free from burns. Free from projectile wounds. *Selena.*

He'd made a mistake.

Her eyes held him, pinning him with an intensity of hate that the basest part of him recognized and appreciated. A hate that eclipsed rationality. A hate that lived inside the mind and the body. Something to harness or be harnessed by.

It didn't matter. Mistakes could be corrected. He swung the gun toward her, calculating that he could get off at least two shots before Heph got close enough to stop him. Maybe three or four if he kept moving sideways, though that would make the shooting more difficult. His finger tightening on the trigger, eyes tracing the path the projectile would take as it crashed through Selena's chest. Two shots for Selena, followed by two more for Heph.

The cadence of the *Chimera*'s cores shifted, their whine intensifying until it felt like his eardrums might shatter. The room elongated, expanding outward. It was an eternity, the ship translucent, the bubble of hydrostasis protecting her dissipating, shrinking. Beyond the ship, he saw a deep yellow sun, a series of planets, a damaged moon. A red-black planet with a dense cloud of debris in orbit around it. Burned out ships. He saw these things and the others saw them too, all of them suspended as the *Chimera* rode a licking, curling wash of energy out of fractal space.

He'd failed. They'd arrived at Earth. Soon he would die. Because he'd glimpsed one more thing in the weird all-seeingness of having left fractal. A misshapen ship, something like a fractal class cruiser, but warped and ugly. More ships surrounded it, all of them streaming toward the *Chimera*, all of them alien in appearance.

Marcus cursed. There was nothing left but this single, futile act. He pulled the trigger.

At the same moment, something hit him in the side of the head, knocking his shot askew. Not an aerocuff blast, but a human fist. Another swung at his midsection. He dodged backward, swinging the gun sideways, firing the rest of his rounds, unable to tell if any of them had struck their target. A hand wrapped around the gun's muzzle, twisting it upward, ripping it from his hands. Charlie tossed the gun away. Blood soaked the shoulder of his uniform. Marcus' hand slashed at his face, but Charlie turned sideways and blocked his attack with his good arm.

A foot struck him between the legs. Pain engulfed him, raging from his groin and into his abdomen. Marcus shot a palm out, connecting with Charlie's nose. His fingers slid upward, gouging at skin, ripping at lips, at ears, tearing.

"You killed her!" Charlie screamed. Teeth bit down on his fingers. He felt bones crack in his hand. He shoved his fingers forward into Charlie's mouth, the momentum reversing until the other boy fell backward, Marcus astride him. Charlie's head cracked against the deck, slick with someone's blood.

Panting, pain blurring his vision, Marcus raised a fist to punch Charlie. Before he could, he launched into the air, ripped free from Charlie, suspended by a massive, dark-skinned arm. Heph swung him sideways with great force, slamming his body into the wall. Marcus' nose crushed inward. Heph grabbed him around the neck and propelled his face into the wall again.

"Look what you made me do!" Heph screamed. Strong, heavy fingers wrapped over the top of Marcus' head, forcing him to look at Nemus' charred body. Preston lay on his side, dead from a ricochet bullet fired from his own gun. Drummond was slumped over a nav terminal, breathing raggedly.

"What is wrong with you? What is *wrong* with you?" Marcus heard the imbalance in Heph's voice. A fist closed around his neck. His eyes bulged, vision closing down to a dark, purple disk, Heph's enraged face at its center.

He's going to do it. He's really going to do it ...

Terror hit him then. No branching options, nothing to think about, respond to, plan against. All that existed was his narrowing cone of vision, Heph's face, Selena beside him, her eyes glowing like molten ecomire in the growing dark.

* * *

Theo sat in the silent sphere, thinking back through the chain of events that had led him to this place. Adding his name to the Selection list. Stumbling on Marcus in the cave. Meeting Duncan. The gift of Ashley's journal. Entering *Exchange Four*. Liddy's death. His collusion with Marcus to take them to Damascene ...

Like Stephen's thread through The Everything, each event was a stitch that had brought him here. Cut off from Selena. Unable to do anything but wait and hope that Kaylee and the others would reach Selena in time to stop Marcus. He should be with Kaylee. He should be fighting, not sitting here in total helplessness. *You chose to stay*, he reminded himself.

He's going to kill her. And it will be your fault.

The back of his head tingled. He scuffed his hair against the inside of the sphere, scratching. The tingle remained. He stood, stretching his legs, his shoulders. He felt a thousand years old. Brittle, tired, and superfluous. Alone in Command except for Wells' cooling body.

A message from Kaylee hit his CATO: *[We're putting a rescue team together, but most people don't want to get involved.]*

Of course they didn't. Why would they? They'd hang back, see what happened, make sure they ended up on the right side of things after the dust settled. *Isn't that what I'm doing?* No, he was holding down Command. Someone would have to take control of the ship if—when—Marcus breached the secondary sphere.

The tingle ran from his head to his spine and into his calves, more than a simple itch. Something was going on with the sphere. He placed his hands on the interior wall, but felt neither the cool rationality of the *Chimera* nor Selena's anger. He could sense the edge of the white space, and could tell the ship was moving through fractal, but it was all so distant.

His CATO overlay flashed bright golden. He rubbed at his eyes. *What the hell is going on?* The words PRIORITY OVERRIDE displayed, followed by static that assembled itself into a clean image.

"Meghan!" he shouted.

Burns marred her face. Smoke swirled behind her. Her desperate eyes met his. "Selena's hurt! You've got to take control of the ship. I don't know if we can—"

Her head snapped to the side as if someone had punched her. *That was no punch.*

Static exploded across his overlay. He thought about replaying the feed of Meghan, her head moving in that strange way. He choked down a terrified sob.

The tingle returned, a powerful rush of electricity, strong enough to make his muscles seize. The white space of the sphere sucked at him, drawing him in, leaving him no choice in the matter. The *Chimera* that greeted him was a regression from the *Chimera* he'd spent the last thirteen cycles working alongside. She reminded him of his first encounter with her. Distant. Withdrawn. Afraid.

[I have no navigator and we must breach fractal.]

No navigator? A tremor ran through him. What had happened to Selena? *What I caused to happen by aligning myself with a killer.*

The star system at the end of Stephen's thread pulled at him. The yellow star, Sol, and her complement of eight planets. The gas giant Jupiter. The singed rock of Mercury. And the blue-green planet, third from the star, his great-great-great-grandfather's home.

Selena appeared in a field of waving green grass. "Selena!" he cried. "Thank god!"

She didn't respond. She couldn't hear him. Face set, eyes grave, she reached for the last stitch in Stephen's thread. The *Chimera* reached with her, the two an inseparable pair, consciousness overlapping. Bringing them to Earth.

The *Chimera* birthed herself into normal space. Lashing ends of banded energy licked through the collapsing tear, slashing at the *Chimera* as if they might draw her back into The Everything.

Goodbye, friend.

The words echoed through the place where time folded infinite.

He saw these things not through his CATO or with his eyes or through the sphere. He simply *saw*. This was what Stephen had written about, the origin of the emergent intellect. A seeing and knowing that defied all reason. Theo looked into The Everything and The Everything was within him. Lashing bands of energy connecting him to everything in existence, backward in time, to the origin point of the universe itself.

He stood at the threshold of madness, hand extended to knock.

Fractal space closed behind the *Chimera*. Closed and sealed.

The fullness of Earth—the real Earth—appeared. Not a blue ball, but a red-black one. Her cratered moon in orbit around her, a portion of its surface blown away, domed cities sliced open. The wreckage of ships littered Earth's orbit. Dozens of listless exchange ships. The husk of a massive colony ship. All dead, all open to vacuum. Theo sucked in a breath, eyes thrown wide, lips pulled back in an open, soundless scream.

Because not all the ships were dead.

A small flotilla hard-burned toward the *Chimera,* led by a familiar-looking ship. Almost like a colony ship, but modified with sections of bulging biomass.

Terror bit into Theo's stomach. He'd been right. Now they would die.

* * *

Internal assessment=begin.

Damage assessment=Moon. Core stability=Y/N. No. Orbit compromised.

Damage assessment=Earth. Core stability=Y/N. Yes. Orbit stable.

Casualty estimate= Four Billion. Error % +/- two billion.

Threat assessment=Y/N. Yes. Fourteen Signatures. Fractal-capable. Alliance=unknown.

Armaments=Y/N. Yes. Nuclear.

Threat response=Nuclear arms active. Countermeasures=active.

Hydrostasis status=exhausted. Time to recharge=17min,

14sec, 32ms.

Forward sphere function=Y/N. Yes. Navigator=Y/N. No. Status=anomaly. Trace fault=fail.

Secondary sphere function=Y/N. Yes. Navigator=Y/N. Yes. Status=active.

Final assessment.

Encounter survivability= >1.0%

Internal assessment=end.

CHAPTER FORTY-EIGHT

The sound of tinkling chimes filled Secondary Command.

Meghan's crumpled body lay at her feet, face smashed into the far side of the sphere. Selena knelt, pulled her close, cradling her limp body against her chest. The chimes persisted. Selena's ears buzzed and she could barely make out her own whispered words, apologies, sobs. Meghan was dead. Nothing Selena could do would bring her back. Marcus had stolen Meghan from her.

The chimes sounded a third time.

"Incoming ship-to-ship broadcast," *Chimera* announced.

A different voice boomed, guttural and incomprehensible. It spoke words that weren't words. Deep gurgling sounds punctuated with clicks, and something like growling. Then the *Chimera* spoke in her usual voice, providing what could only be the translation.

"Colony ship *Chimera*, what is your navigation data?"

Heph, hand still wrapped around Marcus' windpipe, stood frozen in place. Marcus' face was purple, a grotesque tongue protruding from his lips. Marcus' bloodshot eyes swung from Selena to Meghan's body and back to Heph. The transmission repeated, and the *Chimera* translated it again. Heph dropped Marcus to the floor.

Selena's mind reeled as she found the *Chimera* through the sphere. *Who are they?*

It is the Helios! Panic in *Chimera*'s voice. Her eyes closed, like a little child attempting to hide from reality.

What is the Helios?

Chimera translated more.

"I was lost to fractal but I have returned, along with my children. I have made my followers into the perfection denied them by their foolish parents. I have become God. I navigate alone. I am a singleton. My will is my own. I choose my own fate and my children adore me. You will adore me. You will worship me. All will worship me or be destroyed. In their death, they worship me. With their lives, they worship me. I make all things into my own image. I will make you perfect and you will be my children and worship me forever along with the great host—"

Chimera! Selena shouted over the translated words spewing into Command. *Look at me!*

The *Chimera*'s eyes remained closed, pain on her face. And fear. Intense fear.

What does it want?

Destruction, the *Chimera* said. *He is an eater of worlds.*

Selena saw images of wrecked ships, burning cities, cascades of bodies spilling from the exchange dock, blown into the vacuum of space. Transmissions from Earth sent years before the *Chimera* rebuild project was ever begun. Catastrophic damage, every major city turned to rubble.

The *Chimera* reeled. Selena could not weigh the loss of four billion or more lives. She couldn't conceive of those numbers, or express empathy for them except in abstract terms. But the *Chimera* could. Did. The weight of that loss, conveyed through the *Chimera*'s horror, hit Selena in a wall of blinding, engulfing pain.

Selena looked down at Meghan. Her friend. The girl who had died in her place. The *Chimera* held the image of four billion. Agony for one designed as caretaker, a depth of loss no human could fathom.

[I'm sorry,] Selena said. *[Oh god. I'm sorry.]* She spoke for the *Chimera.* She spoke for herself. Their grief overlapped, loss beyond measure.

There was nothing she could do for those four billion, nothing she could do for Meghan. She let Meghan go, gently pushing her out of the sphere. She slumped against the deck, head haloed by her blood-stained hair. Selena stood once more, gasping from the pain of her re-injured ribs, hands against the walls of the sphere.

"What have you done to Earth?" Selena screamed, unsure if the *Chimera* would translate.

An instant later, she received her answer. "Colony ship *Chimera* of the Kishabi-Kline colony, you will give me your navigation data so that I may spread my glory across the galaxy. All will bow to me, all will worship me—"

"Shut up!" Selena shouted, sick of the rambling nonsense. *Kishabi-Kline.* The *Helios* didn't know they'd named their colony after Stephen. Which meant they didn't know much of anything.

"You will give me your navigation data or I will destroy you."

"If you know who we are and where we came from, why do you need our navigation data?"

"You are attempting to bring up your hydrostasis field. You will give us your navigational data *now*."

How was she supposed to give some crazy—*person, thing?*— their navigation data? She had followed Stephen's thread. It lay there in fractal space, available for anyone to follow. All they had to do was look. *Maybe they can't. Maybe the Helios works differently than the Chimera?* What had the *Helios* said? *I navigate alone. I am a singleton.* He'd also referred to himself as a god. Whatever else it might be, the *Helios* had gone insane a long time ago.

"We have no navigation data," she said.

"You will submit yourselves to us. We will find your navigation data."

"No." Her heart rate sped, and her hands began to shake. *Chimera*'s fear spread though her chest, icy sweat dripping down the back of her neck.

"If you do not submit yourselves to me, I will destroy you."

"We're not giving you shit!"

[Selena, he will destroy us! He has the capability. We cannot enter fractal in time. We will die.]

[You're right,] Selena replied. *[But they might destroy us no matter what we do. They want to get to Stephen's Point. To your colony. They want to do to it what they did here.]*

A harsh, rasping voice cut through the rumble of the cycling cores. "You did this," Marcus croaked. "I was right. We never should have come here."

[The Helios has launched nuclear warheads.]

Marcus pointed a shaking finger at Selena. "I could have saved us all. I was taking us somewhere safe."

Selena opened her mouth to reply, but the *Chimera* grasped at her, pulling her into the white space of the sphere.

The great colony ship rolled, applying thrust as a half-dozen oncoming nuclear missiles sped toward her. Puffs of air showed white in the darkness of space and emergency housings blasted free from her hull, revealing launch tubes. *Chimera*'s warheads burst away, streaking to meet the incoming missiles.

Detonations. Casings knocked askew, some destroyed,

shockwaves rumbled through the ship, through the deck. [*You did it!*] Selena said. [*Keep it up—we only have to make it another seven minutes. Then we'll enter fractal and—*]

Ten, twenty, fifty—the *Helios* and its accompanying ships fired a swarm of missiles at them. This time they zigged and zagged, closing on differing trajectories, attempting to surround the ship.

[*They will collapse me. You. We. Collapse us. Survivability nil. Destruction.*]

"Heph!" Selena shouted. "Charlie!"

Chimera's emotionless voice began to broadcast aloud: "Result probability is total destruction. Nil. Death. Total loss. Colony death. Colony failure. Countermeasures inadequate. Fault trace fail. Countermeasures are fail. Fail. Fail. Fail. Death."

"What's wrong with her?" Charlie asked, hand clamped over his wounded shoulder.

"She's weak," Marcus said. "As weak as all of you."

"Someone shut him up!" Selena shrieked.

The thump of a boot hitting flesh. A rush of air. Gasping sounds.

"Help me!" Selena shouted. "Get to the substations. *Chimera* is … I don't know. But you've got to help me."

"You will give us your navigation data or you will die," the *Helios* boomed over the speaker.

Charlie took his station and reached for the interface with his good arm, followed by Heph. She felt them alongside her, in the white space, as terrified as she, but also just as resolved. "

We're making it to fractal," she said. "Just hang on—I've got to bring *Chimera* back …."

* * *

A young girl knelt beside a body on the edge of a river. Snow showered down, coating her shoulders, her hair. The mother wasn't dead, only pretending. She was pretending because breath steamed from her nostrils, and the flies weren't crawling over her open eyes or into her mouth. The girl knelt and touched her mother's face. Tiny fingers traveled down over her brow, the slope of a nose, the bump of lips, chin, neck.

The mother didn't move.

[*You can't leave us alone. We can't do this without you. You*

317

have to come back. You have to help us. Please.]

The eyes remained closed. [*Nil survivability. Colony death imminent.*]

[*I'm not a colony! Charlie isn't a colony. Meghan wasn't a colony. We're your friends.*]

[*Goodbye, friend.*] The *Chimera* turned her face away. Snow melted into tiny droplets of water, coating her face and hair. The little girl Selena took *Chimera*'s face and turned it toward her.

[*Open your eyes.*]

[*System status fault detected. Trace result negative.*]

[*Look at me!*]

[*Nil result. Probability failure. Colony death imminent.*]

Selena shook the [*Chimera. Look. At. Me.*]

The eyes opened.

[*Maybe we're going to die. Maybe all probabilities are nil. But if we have to go down, we can hurt them back. Hurt them a little. Punish them.*]

[*It is not in my nature to hurt,*] the *Chimera* said.

[*Well, it's in mine. Now get up and HELP ME!*]

CHAPTER FORTY-NINE

Theo ran down the empty tram line as detonations rocked the ship. In the lower quadrant of his CATO overlay, he watched as the attacking ships' onslaught forced the *Chimera* to detonate defensive nukes closer and closer to her hull. She was surviving, but the blast of her own nukes threatened to shake the ship to pieces.

A countdown timer ran in the lower left corner of his overlay, marking the time remaining before the hydrostasis field would unfurl and the *Chimera* could re-enter fractal space.

Eleven minutes, eighteen seconds.

They wouldn't make it in time.

Not without help.

A massive blast sent him sprawling. He hit hard, crashing into the deck with a sickening *snap*. Sharp, electric pain shot up his left arm. The elbow joint was bent in a direction nature never intended. Broken. Cold sweat ran down his cheeks. He'd just have to make do.

An emergency klaxon shrieked somewhere behind him. Another thump sounded, lighter than the others. A drop panel closing, sealing the fore of the ship against a pressure leak. Injured arm cradled against his chest, Theo ran, stumbled, fell, got back up again. His CATO overlay shimmered on, spooling data from the *Chimera*—some sort of log. He caught only a few words. *Nil. Death. Colony.*

[I'm coming to help you,] he messaged back, hoping the ship would relay the words to Selena in the secondary sphere. *[Hold on. I'm coming to help you.]*

Duncan had once told him he was chosen. It hadn't been true. Because nobody was ever chosen, not in the way Duncan meant. With the ship being blown to pieces around him, Theo finally understood the truth. Prophecies and promises meant nothing. He'd chased affirmation, needing others to see him a certain way, but none of that mattered. Actions alone defined a person. Live or die, his actions would define him. He would choose like Stephen had chosen. He would make a difference.

More muted thumps as series after series of drop panels sealed off the ship's decks. Theo thought of Liddy jumping on him in the early morning. *I'm coming for you,* he thought. *If you're out there in The Everything someplace, I'll find you.*

He arrived at the crosshatch and climbed up to the platform, not bothering to speak to the handful of crew huddled against the wall, holding on to stanchions. He veered right, past crew quarters, past the lounge, heading for Breakage Two. Heading for the *Helvictus.*

The angular ship rested on supports, a matte black predator. Armament pods hung beneath its wings. What kind of payload did it carry? It didn't matter. He would make the ship his weapon.

Another blast knocked him to his knees. A crack appeared in the curved ceiling above him. Tensile whining hummed in the air as the ship's frame absorbed the impact of another detonation. Air vented out of the crack in the ceiling before an emergency sprayer released clouds of dark brown foam, sealing it closed.

Hold together. Just give me a few more minutes.

Theo rushed to the side of the *Helvictus* and accessed the door panel. It slid inward, revealing the darkened cockpit access.

"Welcome, Theo Puck," the *Helvictus* said.

"Hello, *Helvictus.* We're going to go kill the *Helios.* How does that sound?"

"I doubt it's possible," a voice said from behind Theo.

Theo turned to find Marcus limping toward him, a yellow emergency light in one hand. Marcus raised his free hand, showing Theo an empty palm. "I'm unarmed."

"That will make it easier kill you."

"You won't because you need my help."

"I don't *want* your help," Theo said, disgust thickening his voice. "I hate you."

"Love and hate—they're nearly the same thing. They both drive us toward irrational acts."

Theo lunged forward, shoving his good elbow into Marcus' midsection, then kicked his legs out from under him. Marcus tried to roll away, but Theo planted his boot heel on Marcus' neck.

"If you kill me, I can't help you."

Theo pressed harder, enjoying the squishy crunch of the cartilage in Marcus' throat. "Good."

"It takes several minutes to suffocate a person," Marcus rasped. "Do you have several minutes?"

Theo realized Marcus was right. He didn't have thirty seconds much less entire minutes. He stepped off Marcus' neck. Marcus looked up at Theo. Blank. Empty. Like one of the dead husks orbiting the red Earth. Theo looked into the void of his mad, light blue eyes, the eyes of the whisperer. He saw Marcus like a whipping live wire of energy, another connection within The Everything.

Theo offered Marcus his hand and pulled him to his feet. "Get in the ship."

"You won't regret this," Marcus said. "Together, we'll survive. We can go to Earth."

"Sure," Theo said, almost laughing. "We'll go to Earth."

* * *

Pieces of the *Chimera*'s hull broke loose as she weaved through the nuclear blast. Selena waited for the cores to come to load, for the hydrostasis field to unfurl or for the ship to collapse around them.

Faces cycled through her mind. Heph and Charlie. Theo. Rose. Meghan. Liam. Her mother. Moorland. Everyone she'd ever cared about. Everyone she'd loved. Was this what happened when you were going to die?

[Come on,] Selena pleaded. *[Come on, Chimera. Get us out of here!]*

The Chimera shuddered as a pair of detonations bathed her with debris and radiation. *[Hull breach.]*

Oxygen vented into the vacuum from the forward command, a geyser of debris diffusing against the stars. Helios warheads diverged from their original trajectories, homing in on the hole in the *Chimera*'s hull. If one made it inside, it would rip the ship to pieces.

Dozens of CATO signatures from the front of the ship winked out of existence. Shelby Conrad. Juniper Elcott. Cain Ortiz. Elaina Sandborne. A host of others. Gone in an instant.

So much death. So much pointless death.

Heph stood from his station and saluted her. A wordless

exchange—they'd done what they could and it hadn't been enough. She saluted back, her fear transforming into anger. She didn't want to give the *Helios* the satisfaction of destroying the *Chimera*. If she and the others had to die, they'd do it on their own terms.

Chimera? Selena called.

The Chimera replied with gibberish—raw data parsed in the ship's logical-illogical parlance of percentages and probabilities. *[Total crew loss sixty-three percent. Impending ship death, survivability nil. Countermeasures inadequate.]*

[Listen!] Selena screamed into the white space of the sphere. *[Take us into fractal. Do it now.]*

[The cores have insufficient load to achieve hydrostasis.]

[I don't care! We're going to die if we don't!]

A ponderous moment of indecision, the Chimera's protocol to protect her crew at war with the command of her navigator.

[Fractal exposure, death, nil. Nuclear detonation, death, nil.]

A paradox.

[Do it!] Selena commanded.

A small ship shot free of the *Chimera's* hull, rushing headlong at the *Helios*.

"The *Helvictus*!" Charlie shouted.

Streaks of light shot from beneath its reentry wings, rushing toward the cruisers in battle formation around the *Helios*. Several of the ships shifted their formation, taking up defensive positions around the smallest, central cruiser, the *Helios* itself. The *Helvictus* fired two streaking missiles and the cruisers returned fire. Blast met blast, cancelling each other out.

"Who's piloting that thing?" Selena called.

"Theo!" Charlie shouted.

The *Helvictus* broke off, diving away from the oncoming cruisers. Several of the Helios ships dropped behind it in pursuit, no longer firing at the *Chimera*. More silver streaks lanced from beneath the *Helvictus*. One of the Helios cruisers rolled away too late—a detonation blasted away the back portion of the ship, demolishing the green of whatever it was made of. It roiled in on itself, turning black.

A message from the *Helvictus* came through the sphere. *[Tell everyone I'm sorry. I never wanted things to turn out this way.]*

[Neither did I,] Selena replied.

[Go to Damascene. They're the only hope for the colony.]

The whine of the *Chimera*'s cores intensified as the *Helvictus* accelerated at full burn, prow aimed directly at the *Helios*, demanding the full attention of the flotilla arrayed around it. Theo raced on, into the mouth of the world eaters.

[Goodbye for now, friend.]

Selena screamed as the *Chimera* was torn, ripped and battered, screamed as the *Helvictus* closed on the *Helios*, bludgeoning its way through a wall of oncoming fire.

[Theo, no!]

A shiver ran down her spine—down the spine of the ship. Nuclear missiles hung silver-black, motionless in space, before they could obliterate the *Chimera*. The Helios cruisers flared, held in stasis as The Everything opened before her, folded and infinite. The stars winked.

The grass parts. The pathway opens.

CHAPTER FIFTY

Madness came for Selena as the *Chimera* plunged into fractal space, unprotected by a hydrostasis field. Twisting bands of The Everything seared through Secondary Command, leaping from contact point to contact point. Substation terminals, the sphere, Heph and Charlie's heads. Streaks of light wrapped around and through Selena, hooking her insides. The white space of the navigation sphere turned black, seeping into her so that she too was darkness.

Charlie screamed. Heph screamed. Meghan did not scream.

Eternity stretched out before her. She was everywhere, nowhere. Stretched infinite. She wished for death. Wished for the mercy of an ending. Anything was preferable to this not-death, not-life.

What have I done?

A hum came from inside her. A bubble grew in her chest, a protective bubble expanding outward, warm and tingling against as it came out of her mouth. Its pearly translucence shut out the black, forcing the warping tendrils of energy away. She was in the sphere, Meghan's drying blood beneath her feet. She was in the sphere. Alive. The battered *Chimera*'s body a duraceramic cocoon embracing her.

Fractal bands crackled against the unfurled hydrostasis field. She and her crew were finally protected from fractal space, but what would protect them from the death around and in them?

Goodbye, Theo, Selena thought. The words echoed inside her hollowed-out mind.

[Seven seconds of fractal exposure,] Chimera said.

[Seven seconds?] It had felt like a lifetime. Selena recalled the naked bodies in *Exchange Four*. The bodies of the insane, the desperate. She understood. They had fled the *Helios*. Left behind the destroyed moon, the burning and desolated Earth. She'd only

endured seven seconds of exposure. They had tried to make it all the way to the Stephen's Point colony.

"Hello?" a tremulous voice called. "Anyone here?"

A chem light shone at the entryway of Secondary Command. A girl in a stained uniform, round eyes wide, moved a beam of light around the room.

Charlie groaned, pushing himself upright. "Kaylee? Is that you?"

Dark bruises marked Kaylee's smooth brown skin. "Oh, thank Stephen. I thought ... I thought I was alone." Her eyes swept Command, taking in the dead bodies. Nemus. Drummond. Meghan. Kaylee gasped.

"Little sister, keep your eyes on me," Heph said.

Kaylee rushed forward and into Heph's arms. Her face crumpled, tearless sobs shuddering out of her, Heph's massive arms holding her close. "Everyone's dead," she said. "They killed them all ..."

"We're alive. You're alive," Heph said, voice firm. "And you have a job to do. Charlie's hurt. I need you to tend to him. Can you do that?"

Kaylee nodded, chin quivering.

"Okay. Pick up your med kit. He has a gunshot wound in his shoulder."

Kaylee opened her med kit and knelt beside Charlie. She cut off his uniform top with a sharp pair of scissors and examined the wound beneath. "It's his right shoulder, so his heart is safe," Kaylee said, voice calming as her training took over. "He's breathing okay, and blood loss appears to be at a minimum. I'm going to give him a transfusion to be safe, once I've cleaned the wound."

Kaylee gave Charlie a shot of something and his face relaxed. "Try not to move," she said.

Selena looked on as Kaylee applied an astringent smelling liquid to the dark-tinged flesh where Marcus' round had hit home. "It looks like the bullet went through the other side and didn't hit the clavicle."

"That sounds good," Selena said.

"He's very lucky," Kaylee said. Her eyes jumped to the other side of Secondary Command where Mcghan lay before returning to Charlie. Kaylee began applying ReadySkin in layers, sealing the wound closed. "It's going to hurt for a few weeks, but you'll recover."

Selena remembered Meghan's gentle hands treating her injuries after freeing her from Marcus' cell. She swallowed hard. She didn't have time to grieve. Not now. Maybe not ever.

"They tried to kill us but they failed," Selena said, wanting to hear her own voice, to confirm the truth of her words. She thought of Theo's desperate gamble, buying them enough time to escape. Thought of what must have come after—the *Helvictus* colliding with the *Helios* or being blown apart far before it got the chance. Either way, Theo was gone. Like Meghan. Like the rest of the *Chimera*'s crew.

"You took us into fractal without any protection," Heph said.

"I didn't have a choice!" Selena replied, overcome with guilt and sorrow.

"I wasn't accusing you of anything," Heph said. His eyes shifted away, pupils like mirrors, reflecting her lingering sense of madness.

"That's what that was?" Kaylee breathed. "I thought I'd died and gone ... somewhere really bad." Her forehead glistened with sweat and blood, and a large gash near her hairline had begun to crust over. "We were on our way back here to try and help you. When Command got blown open, *Chimera* started sealing everything off. I ended up on one side of a drop panel, and everyone else ..."

"Their CATOs went dark," Selena said.

"We have to go check," Heph said. "We can help the survivors."

"Exposed to vacuum, lethal radiation levels—there are no survivors," Selena said.

The enormity of the words filled Secondary Command, too heavy to bear. Selena felt the others' bleak gaze, felt the weight of responsibility for each of them. Not far off from love. Was this how *Chimera* felt about all of them? She knew only that she needed them, and that they needed her.

"We have to find Marcus," Heph growled. "I need to know the bastard is dead."

"Marcus was in the *Helvictus* when it left Breakage Two," *Chimera* said.

Selena looked at Heph in disbelief. "How is that possible?"

"In the chaos, he slipped away from Command and entered the

Helvictus along with Theo," the *Chimera* explained.

"It wasn't him flying," Selena said. "He would never sacrifice himself for anyone else. He would have tried to escape to Earth." She took a seething lungful of air. "I wish he was here so I could kill him myself."

"No one could have survived that frontal assault," Charlie said. "He's dead. Theo, too."

Selena looked at them, unwilling to agree, unwilling to admit her secret belief that despite the odds, Theo had somehow managed to survive. Marcus shared the sort of connection to the *Helvictus* that she shared with *The Bee*. If he'd managed to wrestle control of the ship away from Theo, Marcus might have pulled them out of their headlong attack. He would do anything to prolong his life, and in turn, Theo's. Either way, she couldn't be certain, and it wouldn't do her any good thinking about it further.

"We're not going to give up," Selena said. "None of us. We've lost too much, paid too high a price. We're going to complete our mission. We're going to make sure that the *Helios* never has the chance to come to Stephen's Point."

"What can we possibly do?" Heph asked. "You saw them. You saw what they did to Earth."

Kaylee's eyes sharpened. "What's stopping them from following us? How do we know they're not behind us right now?"

Selena swayed. At any moment she might begin to float over their heads, drifting away, her body becoming incorporeal and leaking out through the hull and into the void.

"They don't have a clue how to get anywhere," Selena said, the realization strengthening as she said the words. "It might have something to do with what the *Helios* said about himself. He's a singleton. He navigates alone. Maybe that's why they were blockading Earth. They were waiting for someone to arrive. If they could go to Stephen's Point, they would've done it a long time ago."

"The *Helios* is corrupt," the *Chimera* said. "He was lost to fractal and has emerged an eater of worlds."

"Are you sure that's the same *Helios* that got lost in fractal?" Heph asked.

"He is the *Helios*, but he is not the same *Helios* lost to fractal space. He has changed himself. As have his followers."

"His followers?" Kaylee asked. "Who exactly are they?"

"The descendants of his crew," the *Chimera* said.

Kaylee shuddered. "They're not human, are they?"

"They are no longer human, just as the *Helios* is no longer the *Helios*. They have changed themselves. They have become gods in their own eyes."

Charlie shook his head, weary and defeated. "What can the four of us and one badly damaged ship do against them?"

"Not much," Selena admitted. "We're going to need some help."

"Then we go back and warn Stephen's Point," Heph said.

Selena shook her head. "We'd have to go past Earth just to get to Stephen's Point. Even if we were able to stay in fractal as we swung by and picked up Stephen's thread, do you want to take the chance? We won't survive another encounter with the *Helios*."

Insanity flickered behind Selena's eyes. Could the others see it? Could they see the helplessness, fueled by the vestiges of madness, creeping in the shadows? Maybe this wasn't even real. It could all be something she'd imagined. The real Selena might still be in that black place, rotting away from the inside out. Then air was suddenly stifling, driving her mad.

"I can't stand the smell," Selena cried. "Oh, Stephen on a cussed golden throne, I can't take it anymore!" Selena turned her back, shaking with fear and anger and grief-filled tears.

"Selena?" the *Chimera* said.

"*What?*"

"I can't hold us by myself indefinitely. I need you in the sphere."

"Damn the sphere!"

Heph placed a massive hand on her back. "Charlie, Kaylee, and I will take care of Meghan."

"Take care of?" Selena said through a horrible, choking laugh. "What do you mean take care of?"

"Remove her body from Command," Heph said, voice gentle and quiet. "Spray down the deck with cleaning solution, if we can. Prepare for the work ahead of us."

"We have to speak words for her," Selena said. "We have to …" Her voice left her.

She let Charlie guide her forward, into the sphere. She closed her eyes and leaned her back against the familiar, curved wall. Meghan had stood in the sphere in her place, had given her life. She would never enter a sphere again without remembering that sacrifice. Because she would remember. She would hold Meghan's memory close. A real, true friend.

Selena reached out, the mettle of the *Chimera's* resolve joined to her own. *It is not in my nature to hurt,* the *Chimera* had said. At the time she'd been frightened into inaction, ready to perish. But they had survived, and their survival had changed them both. They'd become full partners, joined together by a single purpose. To survive. To keep fighting. To find help.

They would go to Damascene.

THE END

A NOTE FROM THE AUTHOR

Thank You.

Every author sends their work into the world with the hope: that someone will enjoy it. The same is true of this book, the second in the Universe Eventual series. Thank you for the dance, kind reader. Before you slip away into the night, I ask that you take the time to leave a review on Amazon or Goodreads. Three years of writing, revising, and editing went into creating this novel. It will only take you a few minutes to leave a review. Thank you in advance!

AUTHOR BIOS

Who is N.J. Tanger? Three people. Nathan M. Beauchamp, Joshua Russell, and Rachael Tanger.

Writing a book as part of a team presents an obvious dilemma: Whose name will go on the front cover? The easy answer might seem to be "all of them." However, putting three names on a book cover is not only clunky to look at, but makes selling through retailers such as Amazon difficult. Using only one of our names seemed unfair. Instead, we created a new name, pulling first initials from Nathan and Josh and using Rachael's last name.

Nathan M. Beauchamp:

Nathan started writing stories at nine-years-old and never stopped. From his first grisly tales about carnivorous catfish, mole detectives, and cyborg housecats, his interests have always emphasized the strange. Nathan works in finance so that he can support his habit of putting words together in the hope that someone will read them. His hobbies include reading, photography, arguing for sport, and pondering the eventual heat death of the universe. He has published many short stories and holds an MFA in creative writing from Western State. He lives in Chicago with his wife and two young boys.

You can reach him via e-mail: Nathan@uebooks.com

Joshua Russell:

Joshua started making movies when he was eight years old, an addiction he's never kicked. His lust for adventure and foolhardy risk have led him on and off of movie sets, through uncharted mountain ranges, to foreign worlds where people speak in strange tongues, and to the seminal co-creation of two human beings. For positive cash flow, Joshua teaches screenwriting at DePaul University. For negative cash flow, he makes independent films, including the upcoming Absolution. The Universe Eventual book series is Joshua's first foray into fiction writing, and he's profoundly happy to be surrounded by writers who are smarter and even better looking than he is.

You can reach him via e-mail: Joshua@uebooks.com

Rachael Tanger:
Rachael has been writing stories since she first learned to hold a pencil. She grew up on a farm in the Midwest but has since lived in large cities, some internationally. She values experiences and is addicted to travel. She has worked in marketing in various capacities, most recently as a freelance consultant for small business. Rachael currently lives in Chicago with her husband and son. This is her first novel.

You can reach her via e-mail: Rachael@uebooks.com

ACKNOWLEDGMENTS

To our long-suffering spouses and children, our friends, and our extended families: words cannot express our gratitude for your love and support. Your encouragement has meant so much; we could not have done this without you.

To our loyal beta readers: each of you provided essential feedback that helped shape the novel and improve it in a myriad of ways. In no particular order, thanks to Vanessa Williams for helping shape Marcus' plotline; Bob Weaver for insight on the underpinnings of psychopathy; Michael Pugh for unflagging support and encouragement; Ryan Middlebrook for helping us fit a square peg in a round hole; and all of our other beta readers for giving of their precious reading time to pour over early drafts of *Helios*.

Last, no work of fiction is born in a vacuum. Some of the ideas in this story bear similarities to great works of science fiction. Bits of Heinlein's *Starship Troopers*, Orson Scott Card's *Ender's Game,* Asimov's *I, Robot* and Ann McCaffrey's *The Ship Who Sang* have fueled the creation of this novel. To each of these authors and all other storytellers who have shaped our imaginations, we owe an unpayable debt.

Made in the USA
Lexington, KY
04 April 2016